"MICHAEL CRICHTON MEETS THE
BROTHERS GRIMM IN A BATTLE
TO DECIDE HUMANKIND'S
EVOLUTIONARY FATE."
—*Kirkus Reviews*

"An exciting thriller for fans of Robin Cook
and Michael Crichton."
—*Library Journal*

"A stunning, very frightening thriller
of DNA research run amok."
—*Chicago Tribune*

"A thriller ... swift pace and attractive
characters. Skillful."
—*Washington Post Book World*

TOM HYMAN

JUPITER'S DAUGHTER

AN ONYX BOOK

ONYX
Published by the Penguin Group
Penguin Books USA Inc., 375 Hudson Street,
New York, New York 10014, U.S.A.
Penguin Books Ltd, 27 Wrights Lane,
London W8 5TZ, England
Penguin Books Australia Ltd, Ringwood,
Victoria, Australia
Penguin Books Canada Ltd, 10 Alcorn Avenue,
Toronto, Ontario, Canada M4V 3B2
Penguin Books (N.Z.) Ltd, 182–190 Wairau Road,
Auckland 10, New Zealand

Penguin Books Ltd, Registered Offices:
Harmondsworth, Middlesex, England

Published by Onyx, an imprint of Dutton Signet, a division of Penguin Books
USA Inc. Previously published in a Viking edition.

First Onyx Printing, September, 1995
10 9 8 7 6 5 4 3 2

 REGISTERED TRADEMARK—MARCA REGISTRADA

Printed in Canada

To Nona and Bill

My special thanks go to molecular biologist Jack Greiner, for his generous advice and help on all matters scientific, especially the dauntingly complex subject of genetics.

Contents

New Year's Day, 1999

It had snowed all night, and the acres of fields and woods around the big house were covered with a thick, perfect blanket of white. The sun's light, low in the southern sky, reflected off the snow with a blinding brightness, but there was no heat in it. The departed storm had left the air clear and bitterly cold.

Anne Stewart practiced the piano all day.

She played to dispel a slight hangover from the previous night's champagne, and a deep, inexplicable melancholy that accompanied it. She had started practice at nine o'clock in the morning. It was now past three in the afternoon, and she remained intent at the keyboard, striving to induce her fingers to reproduce the difficult chords demanded of Mozart's Sonata No. 5 in G Major.

The room she practiced in, located in the south wing of the forty-eight-room Stewart mansion on Long Island's North Shore, was large and sunny, with tall windows on three sides.

Anne Stewart was twenty-six years old and a woman of exceptional beauty and grace. Her husband, Dalton Stewart, was away on business in the Caribbean. In the two years and three months that they had been married, he had been away much of the time. Anne was left alone on the estate, with twelve full-time servants and little to do.

Despite her youth and the enviable circumstances of her surroundings, she considered her life to be at a virtual dead end. Her depressions, at first fleeting, had in recent months come to cloud the entire day, making sleep difficult and the rounds of social duties her marriage required next to unbearable. Lately she had begun to wonder if she might be slipping into madness.

Only her music still had the power to lift her spirits. She could still enter into it with her whole being, place herself into an almost trancelike state of bliss that momentarily dissolved the reality around her.

But the hours of practice were taking a physical toll. Her back ached, and her wrists and fingers were stiff and sore from the thousands of times they had pressed the keys. She dropped her hands down at her sides and gently flexed her wrists to relax the muscles.

She gazed absently across the room in the direction of the big glass door that separated the music room from a larger, rarely used sitting room, cluttered with ornate, overstuffed Victorian pieces that had been in the house since the day it was built, a hundred years ago.

A girl of three or four years of age was standing on the other side of the door, with one hand pressed against the glass. The late-afternoon winter sun, slanting through the big windows of the music room, reflected off the glass of the door and partially obscured the girl's features, but there was no mistaking her presence. She was smiling at Anne with an expression of the most intense delight. Her blond curls had a blue ribbon tied in them, and she was wearing a perfectly pressed white cotton summer dress with a blue satin ribbon around the waist.

Her smile was loving and completely familiar, with a hint of mischief in it, as if she were about to say something she knew Anne would think funny. Yet Anne was quite certain she had never seen her before. The girl's luminous eyes glowed with intelligence and pleasure. Anne supposed that she had been attracted by the sound of her piano playing.

The sudden, inexplicable presence of the child filled Anne with an almost giddy sensation of joy. It was as if someone she loved tremendously had just returned after a long absence. Anne laughed, then stood up and hurried to the door, to invite the girl in.

But the moment she turned the doorknob, the girl vanished.

Anne stood motionless, her hand gripping the knob. She was afraid to breathe.

After an uncertain passage of time, she stepped back

from the door. She began trembling violently. Her sense of elation evaporated into confusion. She moved slowly across the room, studying the glass in the door from different angles, but the image of the girl did not reappear.

She had imagined it.

It didn't seem possible. In her mind's eye she could still picture the child perfectly, could still feel that oddly familiar smile. If it was an hallucination, its effect was overwhelmingly real.

Anne closed her eyes and shook her head. What would account for such a powerful illusion? Was it just some peculiarity in the light, combined with her fatigued mental state? Perhaps she had stayed too long at the piano, she thought. It had put her in an impressionable mood. She knew that such things could happen. Minds played tricks sometimes.

She sat a few minutes longer, watching the now pale, watery sun sink behind the bare branches of the trees that lined the fields on the southwest side of the house. The daylight faded and the room grew gray and chilly. She closed the cover on the keyboard and left.

The image of the beautiful child lingered with her for weeks, magnifying her frustration and her unhappiness. She began to think of the incident as some kind of premonition, and the thought haunted her.

She knew she could never have any children with her husband. And yet she felt absolutely certain that the child she had seen—or imagined she had seen—was her own.

PART I

MILLENNIUM

Winter and Spring, 1999

1

The Road of the Mountain Guns curled up the steep hill behind the Caribbean city of Coronado in a series of four hairpin turns. At the top of the hill stood the ruins of an old Spanish fort, whose gun emplacements had once guarded the harbor below.

The ancient fort and the corroded, moss-covered remains of the great bronze cannons had not so long ago been tourist attractions; but a decade of neglect had undermined large stretches of the road's surface, and bandits were said to lurk in the heavy roadside undergrowth, ready to pounce on the unwary traveler. Few people used the road these days, and those who did climbed it only for the most compelling reasons.

A man named Joseph Cooper had just such a reason. And as he made his precarious way around the giant potholes and deep, boulder-strewn washouts, he kept that strong sense of purpose foremost in his mind.

Cooper's skin was the darkest ebony. Everything else about him was as white as the midday Caribbean sun: his hair, his beard, his tennis sneakers, and the bleached, baggy shorts and voluminous shirt that flapped about his skinny trunk like a flag around its pole on a windy day. His bosses in Washington called him Mr. Stare, for the habitual dreamy, far-off expression in his sad eyes.

Half an hour before dark he reached the walls of the old Spanish fort at the top and paused to wait for the cover of nightfall. He watched the sun touch the western rim of the Caribbean. The ocean darkened to a deep purple and lights began winking on in the city below. They sparkled against the carpet of land like diamonds on black velvet. For these few minutes of tropical twilight, Coronado hid its destitute circumstance beneath an enchanted glow.

Cooper climbed down from the fort parapet and hurried through the encroaching darkness. The road continued a short distance beyond the ruins to a cluster of one-story brick buildings spread out on a wide, grassy hilltop plateau. The place had once been the campus of the Antilles Medical School. Abandoned by its American owners fifteen years earlier, the school had sat empty until five years ago, when the American doctor took up residence there.

Everything of value had long since been stripped from the premises. What remained had been left to the birds, the insects, and a profusion of tropical plants and vines that grew over the brick and tile surfaces and crept through the broken windows like green mold spreading across old bread. The once tended lawns, flower gardens, and brick walkways had deteriorated into a jumble of vacant lots, choked with tall weeds, broken glass, and rubbish.

Lights burned in the building the doctor used for his laboratory. Cooper peeked in a window. The doctor was sitting at a bench on the far side of the room, pouring some liquid into a test tube.

For several minutes Cooper crouched by the window, watching. Then, from his shirt pocket, he removed an electronic eavesdropping device the size and shape of a tenpenny nail and wedged it deep into the soft, rotting wood at the bottom of the window's frame. He installed a second bug in another window, then pulled a miniature transmitter-receiver from another pocket and tested the bugs. The lab was so quiet Cooper could not tell for several minutes if they were working. Then the doctor dropped something. Cooper heard it perfectly.

He hid the transmitter-receiver under the eaves of the roof. It would relay the sounds of the lab directly to a satellite in high earth orbit, which in turn would relay them to a recording device in a small, locked room at the sprawling thousand-acre complex of the National Security Agency in Fort Meade, Maryland.

* * *

Dr. Harold Goth held the test tube up to the light and examined the contents.

The tube was warm—exactly blood temperature. A few ounces of a thin, cloudy broth swirled against the glass walls. The mysterious soup was a rich mix of nutrient chemicals and bacteria cells.

The cells, some billion of them, were multiplying rapidly, doubling in number every twenty-four hours.

The doctor picked up a rotor lying on the bench, locked the test tube into one of the four slots on the arm, then slipped the rotor into place on the shaft of a small centrifuge. He set the timer on the machine and turned it on. With a low, intense hum the apparatus began whirling the tube faster and faster, until the cloudy liquid was being rotated at five thousand revolutions per minute.

Dr. Goth permitted himself a quick little smile. Despite the strain and fatigue of the past several months, he still felt that familiar excitement he had for so long associated with the hands-on practice of scientific routine.

After thirty minutes the centrifuge shut itself off. Goth retrieved the rotor and removed the test tube from its slot. Its contents had undergone a visible transformation. Centrifugal force had driven the cells to the rounded bottom of the tube, where they formed a compacted, gray-yellow mass. Goth poured off the now clear nutrient liquid from the top, added a small amount of fresh nutrient, and attached the tube to a mechanical shaker. The shaker broke up the pellet of cells at the bottom and caused it to mix with the new nutrient. A cloudy broth formed once again, thicker than before.

Goth removed the tube from the shaker, set it in a holding frame, and pulled the stopper from the top. Using a thin, hollow plastic rod called a pipette, he added to the soup carefully measured amounts of two chemicals— ethylenediamine tetra-acetate, or EDTA, and sodium dodecyl sulphate, or SDS. The EDTA would weaken the membrane walls of the cells in the solution by removing their calcium and magnesium ions. The SDS would dissolve the molecules of fat from those same cell walls, causing them to collapse and spill the cells' innards into the broth.

He shut the test tube in an incubator present at 98.6 degrees Fahrenheit and glanced up at the clock on the far wall. Twenty minutes past nine. It would take forty-five minutes for the chemicals to do their work.

Dr. Goth removed his wire-rimmed spectacles and wiped them with the bottom edge of his lab jacket. He had worked so very hard these last few months—sixteen to eighteen hours a day, every day, with barely a break. The effort had taken its toll. His eyes ached persistently, and he had trouble focusing. Periods of faintness and exhaustion were becoming more frequent and more prolonged. Even now, as he slipped his glasses back over his ears, his hands shook from the effort. When he stood, his legs trembled beneath him.

He forced his tired muscles into motion and stepped outside the laboratory for some fresh air. The moon was just rising. It cast a broad path of silver light across the Caribbean waters below. A tropical breeze was blowing in from the west. He inhaled deeply.

The island was in many ways a beautiful place, blessed with an idyllic climate and topography. Yet Goth did not love it here. He loathed the corruption and incompetence of the local government. He detested the laziness and insolence of the native population. He despaired of their poverty and their ignorance. But most of all, he hated the isolation. He was far from everything that was important to him. He was here not by choice but by a perverse twist of fate. He dreamed of the day he would leave the island forever and resume his place among the great scientists of the age.

When forty-five minutes had passed, the doctor returned to the lab and removed the test tube from the incubator. The membrane walls of the billion cells that had turned the mixture cloudy were now dissolved. The liquid was clear again. It was also viscous—about the consistence of egg white—and sticky to the touch.

Goth poured in a small amount of ethanol and rocked the test tube gently back and forth in his hand to mix it with the liquid. The transparent solution began turning gray.

He returned the tube to the centrifuge and let it spin for

another half hour. When he removed it the second time, the changes were dramatic. The ethanol, heavier than the liquid, had settled to the bottom. On its way down it had killed all the protein in the cells and caused it to precipitate out of the mixture. The protein now formed a white, coagulated band just above the ethanol.

Using a pipette with a bent tip, Goth painstakingly removed, one drop at a time, the clear, sticky liquid remaining at the top of the test tube and deposited it in a separate tube. He then poured a small amount of pure alcohol into the tube with it. The alcohol floated on top of the liquid. He plunged a thin glass rod through the alcohol and into the mixture and then slowly withdrew it. As the rod broke the surface, it carried with it, suspended from its tip, a long glistening, gossamer filament.

Goth pushed his glasses up on his forehead and brought the rod up closer to his eyes. In the lab's flickering fluorescent light the filament glittered wetly, like a thread of translucent fiber. He held his breath, lest his exhaled air disturb it.

The minute filament was composed of hundreds of thousands of individual strands, each vanishingly thin—a few ten-billionths of a millimeter in diameter—and visible by themselves only under the powerful magnification of an electron microscope.

They were fragments of cloned human DNA.

The visible presence of the miracle substance could still, after all these years of intimacy, make the doctor tremble with pleasure.

DNA—deoxyribonucleic acid. Entwined in the form of a double helix within the nucleus of the human cell, it carried the genetic code of life, the instructions that defined the form and behavior of every living plant and creature on earth, from the single-celled protoplasm to Homo sapiens.

Dr. Goth had dedicated his career to the study of this code. He was closer than anyone had yet come to a complete understanding of the immensely complex series of functions and interrelationships that DNA had scripted for the many thousands of genes that determined the genetic destiny of every human being.

Goth could now alter the script for many of those genes, and by so doing, rewrite the basic instructions that governed human life itself. Such an extraordinarily wide-ranging capability, not thought to be within the reach of microbiologists for decades, had elevated Goth to a unique and lonely position.

He was experimenting in the forbidden zone of the biological sciences: the so-called germ line—the DNA of the human reproductive system.

His quest had been prolonged and difficult. The controversial nature of his work had made it impossible to continue to finance his research through the normal channels of government and academic grants. Indeed, most countries had passed explicit laws banning any kind of tampering with the human germ line; and even in those countries where it was not strictly illegal, it was widely regarded as unethical and dangerous. No major biologic or medical scientific research facility in the world—commercial, governmental, or academic—dared involve itself with the germ line.

In order to keep his project alive, Goth had exhausted his own personal wealth and resorted to increasingly desperate measures of austerity. His original staff of six assistants was now reduced to one, and needed supplies and equipment had to be done without. Harassment and spying by government authorities had forced him twice to move his clinic to a different country, costing him precious additional amounts of time and capital.

Despite everything, he had persevered. And he knew the goal he had struggled toward for so long was now, at last, tantalizingly near.

With the eavesdropping devices in place, Joseph Cooper moved quickly from the lab across the dark, weed-choked campus to a small brick outbuilding. The windows were boarded up with thick planks and reinforced with steel bars. The building's one door was triple-locked. He took out a penlight from his pocket and shined it on the locks. There were two pin tumblers and one Medeco high-security—well within his range of expertise.

From his back pocket Cooper extracted a small leather

pouch. It contained a set of eleven basic lock picks that he had fashioned himself from strips of flat, cold-rolled steel, one-fiftieth of an inch thick, and three varieties of tension tools made from thin strips of spring steel.

He attacked the top pin tumbler first. He inserted a tension tool into the keyhole and slid it along the bottom of the keyway as far as it would go. Next he selected a pick with a serrated top and bottom, called a rake, and slipped it into the keyway above the tension tool.

He applied a slight clockwise turning pressure to the tension tool and then, grasping the rake, yanked it back out of the keyhole with a quick, controlled motion, to bounce the tumbler pins back up past the plug's sheer point. The tension tool twisted the cylinder to the right, free of the pins that had held it in place, and the latchbolt slid back out of the strike box and inside the lock housing.

The second pin tumbler took longer. It appeared to be a newer lock, and the tumbler pins wouldn't "bounce." Using a narrow pick with a bent end, and keeping a slight but steady clockwise pressure with the tension tool, he patiently felt out and lifted each pin past the sheer line. When he had raised the last, the plug turned and unlocked.

Predictably, the Medeco gave him the most trouble. He had not had a lot of practice with this type, and its design required that he employ two picks simultaneously at different angles on each pin to raise it. Holding the penlight in his mouth and steadying his hands against the door with his little fingers, he struggled for ten minutes before the lock finally yielded to his finesse.

Cooper opened the door cautiously and played the light around. Inside was a long, windowless storeroom. Shelves of large glass jars lined both walls. The air was heavy with the stale odor of formaldehyde.

Cooper walked slowly along between the rows, flicking his narrow beam of light back and forth. The jars glowed a ghostly, transparent amber. Each one contained the remains of a human baby. Some were fetuses—physically grotesque ones, with missing body parts, gross skeletal abnormalities, enlarged or distorted features, excess numbers of limbs, and other defects not apparent to Cooper's untrained eye. But many of the jars held what appeared to be newborn infants. Some were white; most were black. They were intact and looked relatively normal. Stillborn, he guessed.

Each jar was labeled with cryptic information that he couldn't decipher. Only the dates were apparent to him. The contents of some jars were ten years old. The newest was dated from eighteen months earlier.

For the next hour Goth busied himself preparing the strands of DNA for sequencing. He removed tiny amounts of the DNA-rich liquid from the test tube with a micropipette and mixed them in several small glass vessels with a series of biochemicals called dideoxy compounds. He then placed the vessels into a series of wells at the top of a sequencing apparatus, a clear plastic slab containing a thin gel sandwiched between sheets of glass.

When he was satisfied that everything was in order, he turned on the sequencer's heating element to start the separation, a process that would take all night to complete. In the morning the gel, with its newly acquired coating of the DNA-rich broth from the vessels, would be hardened into a plasticlike sheet. Goth would remove the sheet, treat it with special chemicals to fix it, and then expose it to X-ray film. The film would make visible about four hundred base pairs along a segment of the DNA, whose sequence he could then read. He would need to repeat this process sixty times to get a readout of the entire strand of DNA that concerned him. It was an outdated, time-consuming, and laborious method, but in his reduced circumstances he had no other way to do it.

He checked the thermostat that regulated the temperature of the sequencer to make certain that it was operating properly. A faulty mercury switch in an earlier one had ruined several gels and cost him a week's work.

Goth cleaned up the work area, picked up a folder containing the day's notes, and extracted the RCD—the removable cartridge disk—from the computer. He locked the folder and the hard disk in a cheap vinyl attaché case, turned off the computer and the lights, and left the lab, carrying the case with him. There was nothing more he could do until the morning.

He knew he was very close now. These results would have to be tested and retested, confirmed and reconfirmed, before he could lay all lingering uncertainties to rest. But he was close.

He locked the lab door and retreated down the narrow corridor to the small pair of rooms in the back of the building that he had converted into living quarters.

He removed a small cotton blanket from an ancient floor safe that sat in one corner of his bedroom, opened the safe, and slid the attaché case in alongside stacks of his research notes and a backup copy of the RCD. He closed the door and spun the dial to lock it again.

He had been thinking a lot about his future these past few weeks. Fifteen years ago, he had stood on a stage in Stockholm in a rented tie and tails and received the Nobel Prize in biology. He was only forty-five—one of the youngest scientists ever to have received the prize. How his spirits had soared that day—how invincible he had felt.

Would he ever again be so rewarded for his achievements? He knew it was unlikely, at least in his own lifetime. And yet the research for which he had won that Nobel Prize paled in significance next to his present work.

It was only months after receiving the prize that he began his work on the germ line. No one had supported his effort. On the contrary, everyone had condemned it. His colleagues had warned him that it would be professional suicide. His friends had deserted him, and so had his wife of twelve years, herself a prominent geneticist.

But Goth was not dissuaded. His motivations were complicated, but one reason dominated all others: the simple glory of the quest. He saw a unique chance to make an extraordinary contribution to science and to the future of the human race.

Someday, he thought, his accomplishments would set him apart as a man of the ages, as a name to be spoken in the same breath as Mendel or Pasteur, or even Einstein.

He stepped to the window and pulled back the edge of

the shade. The medical school's deserted buildings looked like a ghost town in the moonlight. Behind them loomed the crumbled towers of the old Spanish fortress.

Goth folded back the sheet of the narrow cot that had been his bed for the last five years and slipped under it. He looked at the two novels on the small steamer trunk he used as a night table. Both were Sherlock Holmes pastiches. He had read them once and found them thin; nothing, unfortunately, compared with the master. But he had read Arthur Conan Doyle through so many times over the past decades that he knew all the Holmes stories by heart. It was a shame there were no more. They had been his only escape from reality.

He took in a deep breath and let it out in a long, ragged exhalation of exhaustion and despair. There were stark realities to be faced. He needed money desperately. He was half a million dollars in debt. He had long ago liquidated all his possessions. And no one he knew of—no individual, no institution—was willing to extend him any more credit. If he did not get some financing soon, he would have to close the lab and abandon his work. Eventually, somebody somewhere else would make the same discoveries he had made and reap his rewards—and his immortality.

His effort would be wasted.

And his dream would die.

Goth removed his glasses, folded them carefully, and placed them beside the books on the steamer trunk. He turned out the light and lay back against the pillow, his eyes wide, his brain far from sleep.

There was only one possible way he could think of to get the money he needed. The thought of it made him shudder with disgust. But he really had no choice. He would have to do it.

Cooper pulled a small point-and-shoot camera from his pants pocket, checked the film, adjusted the flash, and began firing away. He moved quickly along the rows of jars, crouching and shooting, until he had photographed everything in the storeroom. The 35 mm lens took in a wide field, but the camera was loaded with a special high-density black-and-white film whose negative could be enlarged tenfold with no loss of definition.

Cooper would normally use several rolls of film and photograph everything two or three times, just to cover himself against any possible failure. But a nameless menace seemed to lurk in the thick, foul air. After only one roll Cooper began to tremble and sweat.

He started to reload and then gave up. He jammed the camera back in his pocket and bolted out of the shed. He fumbled in haste to relock the door and then fled across the grounds of the medical school back toward the Road of the Mountain Guns.

The moon cast a dim, shadowy light on the road's rutted surface. Cooper descended as fast as he dared, trying to shake the images of those jars of human fetuses from his mind.

2

From what Dalton Stewart had seen so far, Dr. Harold Goth's research center was a huge disappointment. Stewart had expected to find a modern facility, with state-of-the-art technology and dozens of white-frocked technicians watching computer screens. Instead there was this rundown collection of rooms with broken floor tiles, dirty windows, and ancient equipment, housed inside a decaying single-story brick structure which had not seen a coat of paint, a repointed brick, or a roof repair in over a decade.

The center had once been a medical school, Stewart had learned—one of those offshore diploma mills that used to crank out second-rate American doctors before it lost its accreditation back in the mid-eighties.

The only other individual on the premises besides Goth appeared to be a short, perpetually frowning dark-haired female lab assistant who didn't look old enough to have finished high school.

Stewart followed the four other visitors into a cluttered, dimly lit laboratory. The research assistant was busy in a far corner, fiddling with something on a counter top.

Five folding metal chairs, their seats blistered with rust, had been arranged for the visitors in a semicircle facing a battered oak school desk. The desk was buried under a haphazard pile of computer printouts and dog-eared books and manuals of every size and description, their pages bristling with reference markers made from torn shreds of paper.

Stewart brushed off the seat of the chair nearest the door and sat down on it. There was no air conditioning, and the oppressive heat was made all the more stifling by the accumulated odors of chemicals, mildew, and human sweat. He pulled a white cotton handkerchief from his pocket and patted his brow.

Stewart was the principal owner of Stewart Biotech, a conglomerate of chemical and biological manufacturing and research facilities. He was forty-six years old, tall and trim. His dark, handsome face and self-confident smile had graced the covers of many magazines, from *Fortune* and *Forbes* to *Time* and *People*.

He was a modern American success story. From a small, debt-ridden Long Island drug supply house he had bought with some money borrowed from an uncle, he had built an empire. It was a tribute to his skill at self-promotion that his personal net worth was estimated variously to be anywhere between one billion and three billion dollars. In fact, he was worth considerably less than a billion. How much less depended on the day of the week and the month of the year, because his fortune was in a constant state of flux. Like many entrepreneurs, he was an active, high-stakes gambler whose plunges could win or lose him millions every week. Even the banks who backed his financial adventures never knew for certain how much money he had.

Whatever his actual wealth, he was widely admired as a businessman with drive and imagination. His energy and enterprise—and his flair for publicity—had won him an international reputation and many powerful friends. Wherever he went, he was accustomed to making his presence felt. He projected an enormously appealing image of strength, charm, and sophistication.

Despite all these outward manifestations of success, Stewart was not a particularly happy man. He had been married three times, and he had no children. Behind the dashing, worldly image lurked an apprehensive, hungry soul, pursued by childhood insecurities and cravings that no amount of success seemed able to still.

At this precise moment, Stewart felt especially unhappy. He was beginning to suspect that he had made a dumb mistake coming here.

But still, he was curious. Dr. Harold Goth was one of the world's greatest biologists. Or at least he had been.

The file put together by Stewart's research department in New York presented a picture of a brilliant scientist in decline. As a leading figure in the fields of molecular biology and genetics, Goth had held important positions at three of the most prestigious universities in the world. He had written two books on genetics that were regarded as classics. He was also responsible for developing several breakthrough laboratory procedures and held a patent on a special apparatus he had invented to speed up the process of gene splicing. In 1984 he had been awarded the Nobel Prize in biology.

But like many men of genius, Goth was a maverick—a man who preferred to pursue his own goals. He was single-minded, egotistical, and contemptuous of anyone who disagreed with him. Former colleagues who had once admired his work thought that in the last decade he had lost his way. Others thought him simply power-mad—a man who had let his ego and his greed for renown get in the way of his responsibilities as a scientist.

Stewart's file showed Goth's problems becoming serious in 1992. He had publicly condemned a new law passed that year by Congress banning genetic experimentation with the genes of the human reproductive system—the so-called germ line. His defiance cost him his university teaching post and all the funding for his research. He moved his laboratory to Switzerland and raised enough money there to continue his work. But two years later controversy caught up with him again, and Switzerland sent him packing.

So here he was, Stewart thought, a fugitive—cast up on an impoverished Caribbean island, flat broke and desperate for help.

Under the circumstances, Stewart reflected, it was a tribute to Goth's still-powerful reputation that he had been able to command the presence of the five individuals who now sat in the stale tropical heat of his grubby little lab, waiting to hear what he had on his mind. Like Stewart, the other visitors were all enormously successful international financiers and industrialists, and all were heavily invested in biotechnology, one of the more cutthroat areas of modern business competition.

Stewart glanced down the row of chairs. His four companions wore varying expressions of boredom and discomfort. It amused him to see them in such modest surroundings, stripped of their usual protective layers of advisors, assistants, and bodyguards. Goth had been adamant—he would allow no one inside his laboratory or his office except the five principals. To make the humiliation complete, he had hired two local department-store guards to search each of them for weapons and recording devices.

In the chair next to Stewart sat the Kuwaiti prince Bandar, clad in a floor-length white *dishdasha* and a white *kufiyya*, held on his head by a twisted length of black cord. He had a nervous habit of pushing back the edge of the cloth with his fingers, like a woman brushing back long tresses.

Bandar was easily the richest of the five. His worth was stupendous—in excess of $100 billion. But the prince's wealth, derived from the huge oil reserves under his country's desert, was an accident of birth and geography, not the results of risk, intelligence, or hard work. The prince was childish, vain, and self-indulgent. He knew or cared little about business affairs. He hired others to do his work for him.

Goth had been smart to invite the prince, Stewart reflected. Bandar controlled a fortune so vast that even his sybaritic excesses could not deplete it. Underwriting Goth's research would be as insignificant an expense to him as throwing loose change to a beggar. And the prince's requirements for what he got in return would probably not be demanding.

In the next chair over from Bandar was Harry Fairfield, the British pharmaceuticals tycoon. Redheaded and ruddy-faced, Fairfield was a cockney from the London docks who had started his business career at sixteen as a drug runner for an East End gang. He punched and kicked and shot his way to the top of the drug trade, and by the early 1970s he was making millions wholesaling heroin and cocaine. In the eighties, weary of the building pressures from both the police and his rivals, he elected to get out of crime before he was either sent to prison or killed.

He invested his profits in legitimate drug companies and eventually made himself respectable.

Despite his new image, Fairfield's business tactics remained something of a holdover from his drug-dealing days. If the normal strategies didn't work, he didn't hesitate to use muscle or threats to intimidate his competitors. Beneath a veneer of British working-class respectability, Fairfield was a shrewd and primitive brute, the English equivalent of a Mafia don. He was disliked and feared throughout the industry.

Next to Fairfield sat Yuichiro Yamamoto, a Japanese industrialist whose companies were involved in a broad range of high-tech ventures, from computers to cybernetics to space vehicles. Yamamoto was probably the most cultured and urbane of the group. A handsome, diminutive man in his early forties, he spoke fluent, accentless English, dressed elegantly, and displayed a connoisseur's taste in everything from food and wine to art and music. He had been educated in the United States and England, and unlike many of his Japanese counterparts, he understood the Western mentality—and knew how to take advantage of it. Yamamoto was married to a relative of the Japanese royal family and had many powerful friends in that country's top business, social, and governmental circles. It was expected that he might one day run for prime minister.

Genetic engineering was a subject of interest not only to Yamamoto, who owned a company that manufactured human insulin and other genetics-based drugs, but also to the Japanese government, who saw it as the next great technology frontier—one in which they were determined to grab the lead. Yamamoto's presence here, Stewart suspected, represented not only his own interests but his government's as well.

On the far end, her straight ash-blond hair falling so perfectly that it looked as if it had been ironed in place, sat the German baroness Gerta von Hauser.

The baroness was dressed, rather incongruously, in a white tennis outfit, complete with eyeshade, sneakers, and ankle socks. Stewart suspected that the baroness was the kind of person who left nothing to chance, so he sup-

posed the tennis togs were a tactic on her part to demonstrate that she didn't take this meeting very seriously. It
was just a diversion for her—something she was manag-
ing to squeeze in between matches on the groomed grass
courts at the National Palace, where she was staying as a
guest of the island's president, Antoine Despres. Stewart
was not fooled. The baroness would not have traveled all
the way to Coronado for a game of tennis, even with the
president of the country. She was here for business.

Gerta von Hauser was in her mid-forties but looked
younger. Vigorous exercise, careful diet, and the energetic
attentions of an army of stylists, masseuses, pill doctors,
and cosmetic surgeons had seemingly frozen her aging
process in place. There were a few furtive wrinkles
around her eyes and throat that betrayed her true age, but
few people ever got close enough to her to see them.

She had acquired the title of baroness eighteen years
earlier through a brief marriage to the Baron von
Holwegg, a doddering Junker aristocrat more than three
times her age. He slipped in the bathtub and killed himself two months after their marriage. One of his servants
claimed he was roaring drunk at the time; others swore
that the baroness had arranged it. In any case, she re-
verted to her maiden name, von Hauser, but kept her dead
husband's title. This violated both German law and custom, but no one ever challenged her on the matter.

Dalton Stewart gazed at her long, tanned, well-muscled
legs and wondered if the sexual aura she projected wasn't
also a façade. The woman was so totally immersed in her
business interests that he doubted she had time for anything else. Among her legendary triumphs was her
bargain-basement buy-up of major oil, chemical, and nuclear industries throughout Eastern Europe in the wake of
the communist collapse. In the space of less than a year
(and amid unsubstantiated rumors of bribes and blackmail) she had made Hauser Industrie, A.G., the dominant
economic force in Poland, Romania, Bulgaria, the Czech
Republic, Slovakia, and the Balkan states. In the years
since, the financial benefits of that conquest had been
enormous.

The baroness's formidable position in the international

business community had an interesting history. She had inherited a dark legacy.

Like the Krupps, the Hausers had been for many generations one of the most powerful families in Germany and Europe. Gerta's great-grandfather had manufactured the mustard gas Germany used in World War I; her grandfather had used slave labor in his factories to build the V-1 and V-2 rockets Hitler launched against Britain. Gerta's father, Wilhelm von Hauser, had been an officer in Hitler's Waffen-SS. He was convicted of war crimes in 1946. After serving one year of a forty-year sentence, he was released by the Allies to help rebuild postwar West Germany. He quickly reassumed control of the family's business interests, and by the mid-sixties he had built Hauser Industries into the largest privately held company in Europe.

Baroness Gerta had succeeded her father to the company's top post ten years ago. Her ascent had been highly improbable. The Hausers were conservative Prussians, with a very traditionalist view of a woman's role. But Gerta was an only child. Her father had been desperate for a male heir, but her mother had been unable to have any more children after her.

Despite Gerta's early and strong interest in the business, her father refused to take her seriously. She got his attention, finally, by using some of her inheritance money to buy controlling interest in one of Hauser's competitors—a company that Hauser had almost succeeded in putting out of business. Within five years Gerta had turned the other company around and forced her father to buy her out to prevent her from annihilating his own subdivision.

Part of that buyout involved giving his daughter a prominent role in the running of Hauser Industries.

Then Wilhelm von Hauser had a stroke that left him paralyzed from the neck down. His daughter quickly took charge, and he died shortly after. In the decade since, she had increased the company's profits enormously.

Her success was undeniable but not uncontroversial. Rumors abounded, for example, that she persistently evaded German laws to sell third-world dictators chemical and nuclear weapons technology. Despite public complaints from business rivals, and some charges brought by zealous prosecutors, she had never received more than a few small fines from the courts, for minor offenses like the illegal dumping of toxic waste.

Two years ago, the baroness had acquired a large German pharmaceuticals company and a biogenetics laboratory. This accounted for her presence here today. If Harold Goth had made some big breakthrough in genetic engineering, Gerta von Hauser obviously wanted to know about it.

Stewart found it hard to take his eyes off the woman. The baroness seemed to have it all—beauty, intelligence, wealth, social position, and enormous influence. Beyond that, there was her reputation as someone who made underlings cower in fear and business opponents run for cover. Could she really be so tough? Stewart wondered. He couldn't help wondering what a sexual encounter with her might be like. The exotic perfume she was wearing teased his nostrils. His wife, Anne, was much younger and more attractive, but the baroness exuded a peculiarly tantalizing sense of mystery and danger.

A screen door slammed behind them, snapping Stewart out of his reverie. Dr. Harold Goth strode rapidly into the room, looking neither to the right nor to the left. He stepped behind the desk and focused his attention on a stack of papers sitting there.

He looked the part of the dedicated scientist, Stewart reflected—even a caricature of one. He was a frail, stoop-shouldered man with the owlish, blinking manner of some nocturnal creature uncomfortable in the full light of day. His face was slack and pale. Blue veins pulsed visibly through the translucent skin on his forehead. Skinny, hairless white limbs protruded from his shirt and shorts. Sparse tufts of gray hair clung to his balding scalp like weeds trying to grow from a rock. The bridge of his eyeglasses had a small strip of dirty white tape wrapped around it.

The doctor was carrying what appeared to be a medical supplies catalogue in his hand. He placed the catalogue on the desk in front of him and looked at his visitors for the first time since entering the room. He dispensed with the formality of even a short welcoming statement.

"I'm a scientist, gentlemen," he declared abruptly, "not a salesman."

Dalton Stewart stole a glance at the baroness. Her lower lip was curled in an expression of mild amusement. He wondered if Goth had annoyed her with his catch-all "gentlemen" salutation.

The doctor turned and with a jerky sweep of an arm took in the room around him. "Don't let my modest surroundings color your judgment concerning the ultimate value of the work I've been doing here," he warned. "You know my reputation. You know the value of my contributions to the field of genetics. I consider the project I am engaged in here to be more than just important. I consider it to be urgent. Therefore I have not wasted my limited time or resources on trivialities like paint and furniture."

Stewart suppressed a grin.

"Fortunately," Goth continued, "most genetic research does not require either a great deal of high-tech equipment or space. Most of everything I need—centrifuges, incubators, autoclaves, chemicals, lab supplies, microscopes, computers, and so on—I have right here in these few rooms. Some of my equipment is admittedly hand-me-down, but it's adequate."

Stewart doubted it.

"Much of the work of microbiology today is done on a computer. The hardware I have here is not the best or the fastest available, but I've managed to get by with it. The software I use are either existing programs I have modified and improved, or ones of my own creation. As for data, much of that I've also developed myself. And what I don't have right here is within easy reach of my modem and fax machine. This puts all of the world's genetic databases at my disposal. Beyond that, I can access thousands of volumes from dozens of scientific libraries. The fact remains, however, that with newer, more sophisticated computer hardware, I could do a lot more and do it much faster. That new computer equipment would cost about forty thousand dollars."

Goth paused for a moment and stared out the window

to arrange his thoughts. Prince Bandar flicked the cloth of his *kufiyya* out of his face and yawned noisily. A fly alighted on Stewart's cheek; he brushed it away. The baroness crossed her legs and began pumping her foot back and forth impatiently. Fairfield, looking terminally bored, leaned back and stretched his arms over his head. Yamamoto sat motionless, watching the doctor with an alert, attentive gaze.

"I have reached a critical stage in my research," Goth said, turning back to his select little audience. "The primary work has been done. All the necessary breakthroughs have been made. What remains is the painstaking but absolutely necessary task of checking and testing and retesting all the data. This takes time. And it takes money—money that I regrettably do not have."

Goth leaned a hip against his desk and picked up the catalogue he had placed there earlier. He opened it to a page marked with a paper clip and held it up. "Consider this little instrument," he said, pointing to a full-page color advertisement for some piece of scientific equipment. "It's called a PCR—a polymerase chain reactor. It replicates trace quantities of DNA. Having one would save me many hours of tedious labor. There are no secondhand ones available. A new one costs ten thousand dollars."

Dr. Goth opened the catalogue to another page. It showed a pair of beige boxes, somewhat larger than the PCR. "This is an ALPS automatic DNA sequencer. Hooked up with the proper computer equipment and program, it can sequence large segments of DNA. It can do in a few minutes what it'd take me days to do with the old X-ray gel method. And it's far more reliable. It costs a hundred and twenty-five thousand dollars."

The doctor closed the catalogue and dropped it back on the desk. "There is other equipment I could use as well. Beyond the additional equipment I also need financial backing to carry my work from the experimental stage to the stage of practical application. This means expanding the facility here and hiring more staff. With the added help, I could complete this last stage of my project in about a year's time."

Stewart shifted in his chair. What the hell was this secret project? Was Goth just building the suspense, or was he actually reluctant to tell them?

"As you know," the doctor continued, "I have chosen to work in an area of genetics considered taboo in many societies. As a result, I've had to put up with obstacles beyond those required of my research. Lack of funds. Bureaucratic harassment. Professional ostracism. Ridicule and libel from the media. Even sabotage and death threats from religious crackpots and political extremists. Yet I've continued on in the face of all this because I know the value of my work far outweighs any dangers or inconveniences I might face personally."

The unsettling thought crossed Stewart's mind that Goth's secret might be some wildly impractical fantasy. Years of research without results often encouraged a certain type of scientist to start seeing breakthroughs where none existed, to start making rash claims about discoveries not supported by his work. Delusions of grandeur were an occupational hazard for aging scientists, and Goth seemed to be showing some of the symptoms.

"What I believe I have accomplished, gentlemen," Goth said, "is, on one level, quite simple to describe."

Stewart leaned forward in his chair. Silence gripped the room.

"I've developed a better human being," he said.

3

Anne Stewart walked down the brick path that led from the main house to the guest cottage. She wore a white dress and carried a picnic basket under her arm.

It was an unusually warm day for early March. The sky was crystalline, the air sweet with the smells of early spring. The lawns, free of snow since the first week in February, were already pale green with fresh growth, and the forsythia bushes were putting forth their first yellow buds.

The lawn sloped away from the main house, an Italianate stone mansion of forty-eight rooms, in a broad apron many acres in size. To the north it stretched a thousand yards to the edge of Long Island Sound, where it enclosed a shallow cove of sandy beach. A large boat house dominated one end of the cove. To the east, south, and west, the landscape was an artful blend of gardens, stone walls, hedgerows, ponds, and small groves of trees. Beyond the immediate grounds lay hundreds of acres of fields, and beyond the fields was a deep border of forest—a small wilderness that effectively hid the estate from view, except from the waters of the sound.

The property, built by an oil baron at the turn of the century, was landscaped to re-create, insofar as such a thing was possible, the mood he claimed to have experienced while strolling the grounds of Versailles: an overwhelming sense of tranquillity and permanence.

At Anne Stewart's side was Alexandra Tate, a neighbor who had, in the two and a half years since Anne's marriage to Dalton Stewart, become a close friend. She carried a portable ice chest with two bottles of white wine.

The euphoric glory of the day had so far failed to improve Anne's mood. The dispirited gloom that she had felt through most of the winter still clung to her. She counted heavily on Lexy Tate's company to cheer her up.

The two women reached the guest house, a small Tudor-style cottage with vine-covered brick-and-wood walls and leaded glass windows. They stepped onto the terrace and looked around. On one side was a small duck pond ringed with lacy green boughs of hemlocks; on the other, a grove of maples, their branches still bare of leaves.

"Gorgeous," Lexy declared, taking in the view with a broad, encompassing sweep of her arms. "Paradise. This is it, right here."

Anne deposited her picnic basket on a big wrought-iron table, pulled out a chair, and sat down heavily.

Lexy propped a foot up on the stone parapet that enclosed the terrace. "Do you know what that word really means, by the way?"

"What word?"

" 'Paradise'!"

Anne shrugged. "Besides heaven, it also means a park. It's from the Latin *paradisus*. And/or the Greek *paradeisos*."

Lexy's mouth fell open. "How did you know that?"

"You told me. About six months ago."

"Did I? Christ, I must be getting Alzheimer's. Did I also tell you who told me?"

"Maybe not." Anne Stewart extracted a paper napkin from the picnic basket and began wiping away a sticky yellow coat of tree pollen that had accumulated on the table's glass surface.

"It was a guy I dated one summer when I was sixteen. He was a freshman at Princeton, and I was *very* impressed with him. An intellectual. His father wanted him to go into investment banking, but he planned to devote his life to poetry and booze. One night we ended up on the local country-club golf course. We wandered around the fairways in the moonlight with a bottle of vodka while he laid this *paradisus* line on me. The gist was that since we were, in effect, already in heaven out here on the golf course, that anything we did would probably have the Lord's blessing. I thought it was a pretty good argument, so I went along with it." Lexy came over to the table and sat down across from Anne. "We fucked our brains out on the fourteenth green."

Anne nodded absently. She continued to scrub the tabletop, pressing down with such force that the table's wrought-iron legs began rattling noisily on the stone terrace.

"I thought it was a kind of funny story," Lexy said.

"I'm sorry. You did tell me," Anne replied.

Lexy sighed and watched Anne in silence. Finally, she leaned across the table and grabbed her friend's wrist, stopping her in mid-wipe. "Are you compulsive about dust, or do you just harbor a secret desire to be a cleaning lady?"

Anne flushed in embarrassment. She released her grip on the paper napkin. "Sorry."

Lexy screwed up her face in a scowl and flicked a wrist at the napkin, as if it were a bug to be shooed away. It fell to the terrace floor. "If you're really so concerned about the dirt, you should go right over to that phone and call the housekeeper. Tell her the table on the guest house terrace is *filthy beyond description,* and she had better send someone down to clean it, *immediately.*"

Anne slumped back in her chair. "Oh, for godsakes, Lexy, I could never do that."

"You could too do it," Lexy insisted.

"I can't boss people around. It's not in my nature."

"You don't have to boss anyone around. You just have to be firm. You're letting the staff here get away with murder."

"Is this another lesson from you in upper-class manners?"

"If you like."

"Honestly, if it were up to me, I'd fire them all. I hate servants. I hate to be waited on. The whole idea offends me."

"Why isn't it up to you?"

"What do you mean?"

"If you really want to fire them, then why can't you? Maybe that's exactly what you should do. Let a few heads roll. And I'd start with your housekeeper, Mrs. Corley—the Wicked Witch of the West Wing."

"I've already tried. Dalton won't let me. 'Mrs. Corley's been with the family for twenty years. Can't do without her.' "

"You can't let Dalton push you around, either. He has to let you run the household. And Mrs. Corley hasn't been with the family twenty years. It's more like four. Before that, I think, she was an assistant warden at some maximum-security correctional facility upstate."

Anne shook her head. "He won't talk about it. Mrs. Corley's supposed to be showing me the ropes."

"Well, all she's doing is contriving ways to make you look stupid."

"She's very good at that."

"Boy, you really are in a down mood. You need some wine, quick." Lexy pulled a bottle from the ice chest and fished around inside the picnic basket for a corkscrew. "You can't let a few problems in the ranks spoil your day."

Anne took out silverware, plates, glasses, and linen napkins from the basket and arranged two place settings on the table. "It's not just about the staff. It's everything. I'm depressed all the time lately. And I'm not the kind of person who gets depressed. At least I didn't used to be." She pulled a plate of sandwiches out of the basket, removed the transparent wrap covering them, and then slammed the basket lid closed. "I'm just not cut out for this life, Lexy."

Alexandra popped the cork on the wine bottle with an energetic tug and filled the glasses to the brim. "Don't be a defeatist. Once you get used to it, you'll love it. I promise. You'll get on top of things eventually."

"I don't think I can stand another week. Who lives like this anymore? In a forty-eight-room house bulging with servants? Nobody, except heads of state—and maybe a few dotty old society matrons."

"Dalton likes to impress people," Lexy replied.

"You don't think much of him, do you?"

Lexy changed the subject. She picked up a sandwich and eyed it critically. "Did you make this yourself?"

Anne looked puzzled. "Of course."

"I could tell." Lexy fingered the sandwich as if it were a small animal that might bite her. "The bread still has the crust on it."

"You don't like crust?"

"I love crust—on pizza and apple pie. You should've let Amelia prepare the lunch. She's the cook. You may think that you're being Little Miss Helpful by barging into the kitchen and making these all by yourself, but what you're really doing is invading her territory. Humiliating her. You're telling her that you can do a better job than she can, even at something as dumb as making sandwiches."

"Amelia's a terrific cook," Anne protested. "And she knows it. I didn't want her to have to fuss with our little lunch. . . . Now you're making me feel really terrible."

Lexy took a bite of the sandwich, then hoisted her glass. "Let's get drunk."

Anne shook her head. "I've got a committee meeting this afternoon. We're organizing a charity fund-raiser for some inner-city children. . . ."

"Fuck the fund-raiser. The committee ought to mind its own business, anyway. Enjoy life. Drink your wine."

Anne took a sip and made a face.

"What's the matter?"

"It tastes bitter. What is it?"

Lexy laughed. "It's a forty-five-dollar bottle of white Bordeaux. And it doesn't taste bitter. It tastes *dry*."

"I'll never get beyond beer and vodka tonics."

"At least you didn't say wine coolers."

"Do you really love this life, Lexy? You put it down all the time."

Alexandra Tate hunched her shoulders and turned her palms up in a comic exaggeration of a shrug. "I don't know anything else. I was born rich. I make fun of it just to keep some perspective. A lot of it is stupid, pretentious, hypocritical, and boring. But I like the privileges. I'm a spoiled brat at heart."

"Well, I wish there were more spoiled brats around like you. You're the only friend I have these days."

"Oh, come on, Annie. Stop feeling so sorry for yourself."

"Everyone treats me like a leper. Haven't you noticed? Dalton's family and friends included. Especially Dalton's mother. If it was possible to be snubbed to death, I'd have been done in months ago."

"Give it some time. And don't take it so seriously. And Dalton's mother is the last person in the world who should snub you. Before she married Dalton's father, she worked in a massage parlor. And she didn't give massages."

"That's not true."

"Yes, it is."

"But why does everyone *hate* me so? It's incredible. Do they really think I'm so inferior in breeding and background that they can't even tolerate my presence?"

"It doesn't have as much to do with social class as you think."

"What does it have to do with? I've tried very hard to be nice to people. I really have." Anne's voice broke. She felt on the verge of tears.

"Annie. Listen. To the people around here you're an outsider. You grew up somewhere else—you went to different schools and different parties. You had different friends. These people all grew up together. They've all had the same experiences. They share the same values. Pretty boring, but that's the way it is. It's tribal. Self-protective. You'd get the same treatment if you moved into Little Italy, or a Jewish neighborhood in the Bronx, or a dinky little hamlet in New England. Close-knit people are intolerant and suspicious of outsiders."

"It can't be that simple."

"You're right. The Stewarts are still considered parvenus by the Old Guard, for one thing. And of course all the women are terrified of you."

Anne gaped at her friend in genuine astonishment. "Terrified of me?"

"Sure. You're too good-looking. They're jealous. And they think you're after their husbands."

"That's completely ridiculous!"

"I know, I know, but don't play dumb. You're a threat,

whether you intend to be or not. Look at you—twenty-six years old, long strawberry-blond hair, peaches-and-cream complexion, soft sexy voice, big blue bedroom eyes, a gorgeous face with a cute dimpled chin, a smile that could melt the Antarctic ice pack, and a body that should be legally classified as a lethal weapon."

Anne laughed. " 'Bedroom eyes'?"

"You have star quality—that indefinable, mysterious whatever-the-hell-it-is that makes you irresistible to any man with even trace amounts of testosterone in his blood. Even Giorgio, my gay decorator friend, told me he's in love with you. You're a knockout."

"Stop it, you're embarrassing me. And you're more interesting and sexier than I am, anyway."

Lexy shook her head firmly. "No. I have fat ankles and no boobs. And I sweat easily. I have to be sexy and interesting as all hell just to stay in the chase. You're in a different class altogether. *I'm* jealous of you myself."

"But the bottom line is I'll never be accepted here."

Lexy waved the idea away with a lazy flick of her wrist. "Don't even think about it. Because you don't need to be 'accepted.' It doesn't mean anything."

"Dalton thinks it does."

Lexy refilled their glasses. "Well, if it all gets too unbearable, you can always walk away from it."

"How can I? Dalton expects me to live up to the role."

"Do you love him?"

Anne thought about it for a moment, then sighed. "God, I don't know anymore."

"Well, Dalton just threw you into all this without any warning or any help. It's going to take time. If you really don't want to put in the time, you should just take your piece of the Stewart pie right now and split."

"What are you talking about?"

"Divorce. And your share of the estate."

"I signed a prenuptial agreement."

"Yeah? What's in it?"

Anne hesitated; she wasn't sure it was a good idea to share the details, even with Lexy. "Basically it's a million dollars ... if there are no children. ..."

Lexy banged her wineglass down all over the glass surface. It hit with a sharp crack, spilling liquid all over the glass surface. "A million dollars? That's what you get? Are you joking?"

Anne felt a surge of guilt. "You think it's too much?"

Lexy rolled her eyes, stuck out her tongue, and clutched her stomach. She scraped her chair back across the terrace and pushed herself to her feet. She staggered around the terrace in an operatic exaggeration of someone taking violently ill, flinging her arms out and lurching drunkenly from side to side.

Anne laughed out loud. Lexy finished her performance by leaning over the edge of the terrace and pretending to throw up in the bushes. She returned to the table, wiped her mouth with her napkin and gulped down half a glass of wine. "Did you ask me if I thought it was too *much*?" she said. "Is that what you asked me?"

"That's what I asked you."

"Well, Jesus, Mary, and Joseph, Anne—Dalton's worth over a *billion*. He's one of the richest men in the country—in the world! A million dollars is an absolute criminal outrage. It's nothing for Dalton Stewart. Why did you ever agree to it?"

Anne flushed. "A million dollars is a fortune to me. And what right would I have to take Dalton's wealth? It's his. He earned it. I didn't."

"He didn't earn it, Pollyanna. Nobody ever *earns* a billion dollars. That's not humanly possible. He stole it. It's called high finance. Or investment banking. Or venture capitalism. But it's actually more like grand theft. Normally it wouldn't be legal, but at Dalton's level normal doesn't apply."

"That's very cynical."

"Realistic. Money—if you have enough of it—turns the normal workings of society on its head. People get bought, seduced, intimidated, and crushed. And laws get ignored. Or they get rewritten."

"You make business sound like organized crime."

"Right. The only difference is the businessmen use lawyers and paper instead of hit men and bullets. Most of them, anyway."

"That still doesn't make it okay for me to take it from him."

"Why not? Dalton Stewart took it from someone."

Anne Stewart crossed her arms. "Let's change the subject."

"Listen to me," Lexy continued. "If word ever gets out that Dalton got you to agree to a prenuptial with a pathetic million-dollar payoff, you'll be able to hear people laughing as far away as New Zealand. You were suckered. If I were you, I'd get a lawyer to take a look at that agreement right now, and see if he can't break it."

"No, damn it. I stand by what I said. I don't care where it came from, I don't want to take Dalton's money. I'd have a hard time accepting the million."

"At least show the agreement to a good divorce attorney. I know just the guy. I dated him a few times—"

"I'm not planning a divorce."

"Okay, okay. I was just—"

"Just shut up and pour me some more of that terrible-tasting wine I'm supposed to think is so great."

Lexy topped off Anne's glass.

"Why is everything always about money?"

"Nobody can think of anything more interesting."

"I can."

"What?"

Anne looked into her wineglass. "Kids. A happy family."

"Kids? Is that what you want?"

"Don't look so surprised. That's why I got married."

Lexy shrugged. "So have some. I think you've got space in the house for a nursery."

"Don't you want to have children someday?"

"No. I'm too selfish and spoiled. I like the fucking part okay, but it's all downhill after that. Nine months of fatness, morning sickness, maternity clothes, and labor pains, and then you segue right into spitting up, messy diapers, food on the floor, and temper tantrums. It's not an attractive scenario. I'm just not the mother type, I'm afraid. I've never met a three-year-old I genuinely liked. . . ."

Anne wasn't listening. She felt a sudden flood of anger. "I gave up a career—or at least the promise of a career—to marry Dalton and have children. But he lied to me. We can't have any."

"You never told me that."

Anne sank back against the chair. The wine had loosened her inhibitions, and she had to share her misery with somebody. "And he won't let me go back to work. He wants me to spend the rest of my life playing the piano and smiling and making small talk with his friends and business associates. I think he sees me as a business asset. Just another of his acquisitions. He needed something young and female and cute to run his household, carve out a prominent niche for him in society, and make his male friends jealous of him. Someone who'd stay home and not interfere too much in his life. That was supposed to be me. We really have nothing in common. Our lives barely even overlap anymore. He's away six months of the year. And when he's around, he pursues his own interests. He doesn't like anything I like—music or science. Or literature or the theater or the opera. He claimed he did, but he doesn't. He likes business. He sees it as a kind of modern version of the hunt. A blood sport. It occupies all his time. It's what gets him excited. The smell of money. He can never have enough. He lusts after it. You ought to hear him go on about it sometime. It's quite amazing."

Anne picked up the wineglass and stared into it. "He also likes other women. I've learned to ignore it. If I bring it up, he just denies it and says I'm too jealous and possessive. The affairs never seem to amount to much. It's just constant screwing around. Picking up women in London or Paris or Rome or Berlin or Philadelphia or wherever his business takes him. Having a good time here, there, and everywhere—rewarding himself for all his hard work."

"Christ, you never told me any of this."

"It's been building up."

"You think he still loves you? At all?"

"I don't know. He used to say he did. He doesn't anymore. And I don't ask him. So I don't really know what he feels anymore. All I know is that we've become a big disappointment to each other."

4

A prolonged silence greeted Goth's announcement.

The doctor stuck out his chin defiantly. "You're skeptical, of course," he muttered. He folded his arms across his bony chest and leaned against the cluttered bookcase behind his desk. "You five, of all people, with your experience in the marketing of applied genetic engineering, shouldn't be so incredulous. You all know that altering human genes has become a routine procedure, carried out every day in hospitals and clinics all over the world. Genetic engineering has come a long way since the eighties, when they first synthesized human insulin."

A fly landed on Goth's arm. He ignored it. "Many kinds of diseases, from high blood pressure to cancer, now yield themselves to gene therapy. And other, more benign abnormalities can be repaired as well. Genetically produced human growth hormone, for example, is not only employed to cure dwarfism, it's used cosmetically—to add inches to a normal person's height. Anything that can be traced to a defect in a gene, or a group of genes, can, in theory, be cured. And in genetics these days, theories are rapidly becoming realities."

Goth continued in this vein for some time, expanding upon the increasing role that recombinant DNA was playing in everyday life: how plants had been genetically engineered to better resist disease and drought and still produce more and better-tasting food; how cattle had been engineered to produce more beef on a diet of less grass; how most of the major hereditary diseases—Tay-Sachs, sickle-cell anemia, Huntington's chorea, cystic fibrosis, among others—could now be screened and the defective genes responsible for the anomaly repaired.

Stewart felt his mind begin to wander. He glanced across at the others. The prince had folded his arms and slumped back in his chair. Fairfield was cleaning his fingernails with a pocket knife. The baroness was still rocking her foot back and forth. Only Yamamoto seemed to be paying full attention. He sat rigid in his chair, hanging on Goth's every word.

The doctor began striding back and forth behind his desk, punctuating his remarks with hand gestures. "The one area where the miracles of genetic engineering have not been applied is to the human reproductive system," he said, his brittle voice suddenly strong with passion. "And the reasons are obvious. Modifying the genes of one human being changes only that individual. When he dies, the altered genes die with him. But if one alters the basic DNA sequences in a fertilized egg—a zygote containing both parents' chromosomes—then the changes become immortal. They will manifest themselves in that individual and all that individual's future offspring. And these changes will in turn be passed on down to the children of that person's children, and their children's children, for generations to come. And if the genetic alterations are effective ones—ones that contribute to survival—then those who inherited them will thrive and multiply."

Goth stopped pacing and turned to face his small audience. "This frightens many people. Change is always frightening. And changes in the human germ line bring into play one of the most powerful forces of nature—that of evolution itself."

The scientist gazed over the heads of his listeners. "I am the only researcher in the field of genetics working in this forbidden area," he said, biting out his words slowly. "My reasons for doing so are compelling ones, but I won't bore you with them. Suffice it to say, I am now able to engineer a series of genetic alterations in the human embryo that will produce some very marked improvements."

Goth picked up a sheet of paper from the desk, consulted it for a moment, and then put it back down.

"My procedure will essentially do three things," he said. "First, it will raise the intelligence quotient by a fac-

tor of one. This means that a child destined by its genes
to have an average IQ of one hundred will instead have
an IQ of two hundred. That's well into the highest range
of genius. Obviously such a change will make a profound
difference in any child's prospects in life."

The biologist had everyone's full attention now.

"Second, the child will enjoy an exceptionally high
level of health and physical fitness. Its muscle strength
will be increased by a factor of between point two and
point three. That doesn't sound like much, but it would
make a young girl as powerful, pound for pound, as a
fully developed male athlete. It would put the average
male into the championship weight-lifter class. Further,
there'll be no physical deformities, no inherited diseases.
No insanity. The immune system will have the highest resistance to all forms of pollution and disease. Health will
be superb. This individual should seldom, if ever, fall ill
throughout its entire life. And that life expectancy, given
our present diet and living conditions, will be one hundred and twenty years, conceivably more."

Yamamoto let out a small gasp of astonishment. The
baroness shook her head in disbelief. Stewart didn't know
what to think. He doubted that what Goth was saying was
possible.

"In the near future I expect to be able to bring many
new areas under control. All those inherited genetic fac-
tors specific to the parents, for example—patterns of
baldness, color blindness, height, weight, color of skin,
eyes, and hair—shape of facial features, breast size, metabolism rate, and so on. Eventually, in fact, it will be
possible to fine-tune the procedure so that parents will
be able to choose all of a child's attributes, from its physical appearance to its personality. I've already mastered
the knowledge and techniques required for all these mod-
ifications, but they're largely cosmetic. They can wait."

Goth paused. A pleased, triumphant grin lit his sallow
face. "One final thing my procedure will do," he said. "It
will enhance the child's five senses—increase the range
and acuity of its sight, hearing, smell, taste, and touch.
You can well imagine how this will heighten its aware-

ness and understanding of the world around it, and how much this will enrich its life."

The doctor came around from behind his desk and stood directly in front of his five seated visitors. "The technical biological details for how these things are accomplished are naturally quite complex," he said. "Only another geneticist could understand them fully. I must emphatically state, however, that what I am describing to you is not science fiction. All the techniques I've developed and refined to accomplish the enhancements I've just mentioned are either already being employed in some other form somewhere else, or can be quickly learned by any competent biotechnician. For that reason, I have taken great precautions to keep my work secret."

The doctor's voice took on a harder edge. "But my work is not yet complete. As I've already explained to you, I need a considerable amount of money to complete this project. I estimate ten million dollars just to clear my outstanding debts and finance a year's worth of additional research. More may be required beyond that. I can't predict precisely what the final cost may be. But I can predict one thing. There isn't a potential parent on the face of the earth who wouldn't do almost anything—pay almost anything—to get for their future offspring what I will soon be able to offer them."

Finished with his pitch, the doctor leaned against the edge of his desk and looked expectantly at his guests: "Questions?"

The baroness immediately challenged him. "What you say you'll soon have to offer is in fact illegal to sell."

Goth nodded. "Of course it is. In Germany. In England. Japan. The United States. In many countries. But not everywhere. Not here, for example. That's why my lab is here. It's an inconvenience, but not a serious one. As long as the research and the clinical procedures—gene alteration and implantation—are done here, there's no problem. It isn't against the laws of any country for its citizens to travel here to have such things done."

"What about your assistant?" the baroness asked. "How much does she know about your program?"

"Kirsten? She's been with me for two and a half years. She's well acquainted with it."

"Can you trust her?"

Goth looked pained. "Of course I can trust her," he snapped.

"How do you know?"

Goth considered the question impertinent. He ignored it and pointed his finger at Fairfield.

"What's the drill, then?" the Englishman demanded. "What do we get back for our lolly? A happy glow? Believe me, mate, I don't need any more charitable contributions for my tax returns. Inland Revenue's already got their fingers up my ass."

The doctor gritted his teeth at the Englishman's vulgarity. "Those who finance me will share in the profit when the procedure is marketed. And I have no doubt those profits will be immense."

"Do you expect us to form a consortium?" the baroness asked.

"What do you mean?"

"Do you expect us to invest in you as a group?"

Goth threw out his hands. "I suppose that's up to you. I invited the five of you hoping that at least one of you would agree to underwrite my project. If more than one wishes to be involved, that's fine. I must warn you, however, that if any of you contemplate sending down a fleet of lawyers to nitpick, then you can forget it. I've already drawn up a very simple contract form. It's only a few hundred words long. I'll give you each copies to study. I'm amenable to reasonable changes, but I'm not amenable to letting any of you try to tie me up with yards of red tape and hundreds of pages of legal mumbo-jumbo. The intent of that tactic is obvious—to take advantage of the other party."

"Lawyers are necessary to draw up the legal documents," the baroness replied coolly.

Her command of English was excellent, Stewart thought—and embellished with a charmingly Germanic lisp, particularly when she pronounced her *r*'s. Their eyes met briefly.

Goth folded his arms across his chest. "I insist this be done on my terms."

Yamamoto had the next question. "I can understand, Doctor, how you might have perfected your genetic techniques to enhance IQ, health, and longevity—and even physical strength. But your claim to be able to expand the ranges of the senses—how is that possible? I thought such capacities were very limited in the human genome. Where do you get your model for this?"

Goth nodded. "I'm not just repairing defective genes, or bringing ordinary ones up to the human optimum. In some cases I'm adding new ones."

"How can you do that?"

"I'd prefer not to say anything more on the subject."

Yamamoto shook his head in disbelief. He followed up with another question. "We all know that everyone's genome is different. Everyone is a special case. How can you have devised a single formula that will achieve the same results with two very different embryos?"

"An intelligent question," Goth admitted. "I have devised a software program—a very complex program that requires a very large operating environment. Once an embryo's genome has been deciphered, this program scans the genome's three billion base pairs and determines the genetic alterations necessary to achieve those results you just mentioned—superior intelligence, health, physical strength, and sharper senses. The program can cope with the widest variations. It won't convert them all to the same thing, but it can bring them up to within a narrow range. I might add that the active DNA in one human genome differs from another by only a minute fraction of one percent. Most of the DNA in our chromosomes is, as you probably know, silent. Long sequences may differ from individual to individual, but they don't do anything. They don't code for any proteins; they don't control or regulate anything. They're filler. Junk. Good only for purposes of genetic fingerprinting."

"Does this program of yours have a name?" Yamamoto asked.

A sheepish grin transformed the doctor's normally

stern face. "Yes. It's called Jupiter—after the Roman god."

"Does this . . . Jupiter program actually carry out the genetic alterations itself?" Yamamoto asked.

"No. It produces the blueprint—the final correct readout of base pairs. The actual reordering of the embryo's DNA structure has to be done the old-fashioned way—in the lab. But of course most of this procedure is now computer-driven also. Like space flight, it wouldn't be humanly possible otherwise."

Dalton Stewart spoke up. "What we've heard is quite fascinating, Doctor, but a big problem still remains—at least for me."

"And what is that?"

"So far you've shown us no evidence that Jupiter actually works. How do you know it does? Have you performed any trial runs? Do you have any test results of experiments done on real people? We can hardly accept your say-so on something as farfetched as what you've just outlined. We need to see convincing proof. Do you have any?"

There was an immediate buzz of agreement among the others. "Excellent point," Yamamoto murmured.

Goth didn't reply immediately. He removed his glasses and held them toward the window, squinting at the thick lenses. Then he wiped them slowly with the bottom edge of his lab coat.

"Well?" Stewart demanded.

Goth hooked his glasses back around his ears. "I see the point, of course," he admitted. "I confess I don't know much about financial matters. The intricacies of business are as much a mystery to me as I assume the world of microbiology is to all of you. But this much I know. Even the most cautious venture capitalist realizes that there is no such thing as a risk-free investment. If I could show you proof—ideally in the form of a real child demonstrating the abilities my genetic program will make possible—then I would hardly need your money to complete my research. I could set up my clinic tomorrow and start making it myself. I could even franchise the procedure—set up a string of clinics around the world. I could set up my own biogenetics company and sell stock in it. Let's face it, gentlemen. I could get rich overnight."

"Suppose one of us was willing to put up the money," Yamamoto said. "What share of the eventual profits would you offer?"

"Half," Goth replied. "Fifty percent, minus operating expenses, to be shared equally."

"Not enough," Baroness von Hauser interjected.

"Why not?" Goth shot back. He appeared stunned. Stewart smiled. Goth obviously thought his fifty-percent offer was more than magnanimous.

"You haven't thought it through," the baroness informed him. "When you finish your research, the money isn't just going to start rolling in. There'll be substantial development costs. Setting up clinics, for example. Hiring qualified doctors and training biotechnicians. Who's going to pay for all of that? Obviously it'll have to be your backers."

Goth frowned. "Well, what do *you* consider fair?"

The baroness scratched her bare knee as she thought about it. Stewart watched the lazy movement of her red-painted fingernails along the tanned surface of flesh and felt a warm tingling sensation in his groin.

"Ninety percent," she said.

Goth's face turned from its pasty white to a mottled purple. Stewart chuckled. The baroness was beginning to show a little of the steel under her luxurious exterior.

"I could never agree to anything like that," Goth protested, when he had found his tongue again. "That's not profit sharing—that's exploitation."

The baroness made no effort to defend her offer. She just shrugged and flicked her fingers in a gesture of dismissal.

The room grew very still. Stewart looked around. No one else had any questions. They all appeared ready to leave.

"I'm amenable to discuss percentages," Goth said, attempting to resuscitate the discussion. "I'm not interested in personal enrichment. I just want to get on with my work. You must understand that. My work is everything to me. Please think about what I've said. My discoveries are real. Jupiter is real. If any of you wish to pursue this further, you can find me in my lab."

With a tight-lipped grimace of defeat Goth picked up the catalogue he had shown them earlier and prepared to depart. "If I don't hear from any of you in a couple of days, I'll seek help elsewhere."

Harry Fairfield raised a hand. A mischievous grin lit his ruddy face. "I have another question, Doctor."

Goth glared at Fairfield with obvious distaste. "What is it?"

"Can this Jupiter program of yours do anything about cock size?"

Everyone laughed except Harold Goth. He jammed the catalogue under his arm and stormed out of the room, the veins in his forehead pulsing with fury.

5

Anne Stewart walked unsteadily across the mansion's dimly lit entrance hall to the enormous winding staircase. She grabbed the banister railing as if it were a lifeline, and hauled herself up the interminably long flight of stairs, consciously placing each foot as she went.

How she hated this house—so large and cold and intimidating. Nothing in it had anything to do with her. Not one piece of rare antique furniture, not one bit of hand-painted wallpaper or linen drapery. Not one painting or mirror or candlestick holder. Not even the piano. It had all been here when she arrived, and would probably all be here when she left. Most of the rooms never saw anyone for weeks at a time, save an occasional domestic with a vacuum cleaner and a dust rag. It didn't feel like home at all. It felt like an institution. It reminded her of one of those mansions that had once belonged to some long-dead famous person and were now open for public tours. All it lacked were the brass stands with velvet-covered ropes and a few signs admonishing visitors not to touch anything. How was she ever going to go on living here?

She reached the safe harbor of her bedroom at the end of the second-story hallway. Once inside, she locked the door behind her and collapsed onto the bed.

The damned committee meeting. She had missed it. She considered calling Mrs. Talley to apologize and make some lame excuse, but she didn't trust her tongue to get the words out.

Instead, she called down to the kitchen and mumbled something to Amelia, the cook, about not feeling well. She intended to retire early, without dinner.

As soon as she lay back against the pillow, the ceiling

over her head began revolving slowly. She closed her eyes, and the bed began to roll. She opened her eyes. The ceiling was still spinning. My God, she thought, five o'clock on a Monday afternoon and she was drunk. *Oh, Lexy, why did you do this to me?*

A tide of nausea surged toward her throat. Clutching the bedpost to steady herself, she swung her legs over the side of the bed and sat up. Praying that the floor wouldn't tilt beneath her, she got to her feet and lunged toward the bathroom, hands cupped over her mouth.

She reached the toilet on her knees, groped blindly for the sides, and retched noisily into it.

After a few minutes she felt marginally restored, but she was reluctant to move. The cold porcelain lip of the bowl felt good against her forehead. Without looking, she reached up and tripped the flush mechanism.

She wished that she were back home in Vermont.

Home. Something she had never really known. The closest she had ever come was a run-down three-room rental in a destitute mill town out in a depopulated wilderness called the Northeast Kingdom. And she never really wanted to go back there.

Georges and Marie-Claire Beauregard. French Catholic and poor. And both dead now. She had loved them, she supposed, even though they weren't her real parents.

She didn't know her real parents. The state's Department of Social Welfare had taken her from them when she was three years old. Barely more than children themselves, they had neglected Anne so completely that the welfare officials feared she might starve to death. Or so Mama Marie had told her when she was growing up.

Nothing about her natural parents remained in Anne's conscious memory. Even their names were absent. Anne's life did not really begin until the age of seven, when Georges and Marie-Claire rescued her from a series of foster homes. A childless middle-aged couple from the province of Quebec, they adopted her, and she became Anne Marie Beauregard.

They did the best they could, but Anne's life was bleak. Georges died when Anne was eleven, and Marie-Claire, fragile and superstitious even when Georges was alive, simply couldn't cope with his death. She stopped cooking, stopped cleaning, stopped getting dressed. She waited out the rest of her life in bed, in front of a TV set. Anne, not yet a teenager, was forced to take over the household herself. She did the shopping and the cleaning and the cooking. Georges had left no money. They lived on welfare and a minuscule retirement pension from Georges's years with the Canadian National Railways.

Anne rarely thought of those years—not because the memories were so painful but because there was so little worth remembering. They were a blur of fatigue and drudgery, a bleak gray existence in a world in which there was neither time nor money for dates or parties or even decent clothes.

Keeping house, taking care of Marie-Claire, and going to school consumed her days. She came to hate that small TV set at the foot of Mama Marie's bed. It stayed on around the clock, blotting out real life with an endless drone of soap operas, sitcoms, cop and detective dramas, quiz shows, talk shows, and commercials. It still disturbed Anne to be in a room with a TV set turned on.

She found her escape in books. If it had not been for the town library, inadequately stocked as it was, her life would have been impossibly grim.

In June 1989, five months before her seventeenth birthday, Anne graduated from high school. Anne had gone to the ceremonies by herself, feeling miserable and alone amidst her happy classmates and their families. When she got home, she found Marie-Claire propped against her pillows, her eyes staring vacantly at the TV screen. Nearly an hour passed before Anne realized she was dead.

Anne pulled down the toilet seat and struggled to her feet. She washed out her mouth at the big marble sink and brushed her teeth. She still felt drunk, but at least the nausea had subsided and the floor was holding steady.

Marie-Claire's death freed Anne. She took a job in a local health clinic, and when she had saved a little money, she enrolled at a nearby two-year community college. She did so well there that she was able to transfer to the University of Vermont on a scholarship. At the university she blossomed. She chose biology as her major, and she excelled at it, much to the surprise of the male-chauvinist head of the department. Even with the scholarship, she still had to work part-time as a receptionist at a medical center to support herself, but for the first time she began having a social life. Her astonishing good looks, hidden from the world during her high school years, were hidden no longer. Male students followed her around like a permanent band of courtiers, constantly vying with each other for her attention.

She lost her virginity to her piano teacher, a handsome, charming professor in the school's music department. He threatened to kill himself if she didn't consent to marry him. She agreed reluctantly, but was able to back out at the last minute when he confessed that he had been married twice before and had five children.

She graduated from the university with honors and went to work at a biological supply house in her hometown, Burlington, Vermont. After two years there she had made up her mind to go back to college for an advanced degree. She had decided to pursue a career in biology, probably as a teacher.

But that decision got canceled.

One day Dalton Stewart walked into her lab, flanked by his chauffeur-bodyguard and a couple of assistants. He was looking for the head of the accounting department. It seemed that he had just bought the company, and he wanted to see the firm's financial records.

He was tall and charming in a worldly way that impressed Anne enormously. He was also very rich—the ultimate eligible bachelor. *People* magazine had recently run a story on him, detailing his high-powered business and social life. He had dated many celebrities, and there were always rumors flying in the gossip columns about whom he might marry next.

On his way out of the building, he returned to the lab and handed Anne a note that sent her pulse hammering: "You're an extraordinarily beautiful woman. Will you have dinner with me tonight? I'm staying at the Ethan Allen Hotel. Please call me there."

Anne didn't call him. She had a date with her boyfriend, Matty, and she had no intention of breaking it, even for Dalton Stewart. The idea of going out with him terrified her, anyway. He was divorced, nearly twice her age, and impossibly glamorous. And she was put off by the implicit assumption in his note: that she'd come running just because he was who he was.

To her astonishment, he reappeared in the lab the next day and asked her to dinner again. She blushed and stuttered, but turned him down. This time she lied and told him she already had plans for the evening. He persisted, and finally got her to agree to see him the following Friday. He was supposed to be at a business conference in Barcelona, but he said he'd change his plans just to see her.

Her friends in the lab, meanwhile, were going quietly berserk. They couldn't believe that she had had the nerve to give him such a hard time. She should jump at the chance to go out with him, they insisted. Anne wasn't so sure. She couldn't understand why someone like Stewart should show any interest in her in the first place. They couldn't possibly have anything in common. The day before their Friday date, she called his office in New York and canceled.

Anne removed her dress and her underclothes and stepped into the shower. She turned the water on as cold as she could stand it, let it run for a few minutes, then mixed in the hot until the spray felt warm and soothing. She stood under it for a long time, until she was aware of nothing but the pleasant sensation of the water beating down on her shoulders and back.

Dalton Stewart had refused to give up. The more she resisted him, it seemed, the harder he tried. Finally, in the mistaken belief that the only way to discourage him was to go out with him and get it over with, she agreed to a date.

And some date it turned out to be.

Stewart suggested they start early and do a little sightseeing. At five P.M. his chauffeur drove them to the Burlington airport. They boarded his private jet and circled over Lake Champlain. Anne was delighted. She pointed out some of the landmarks of the city of Burlington below.

"Have you ever seen the Eiffel Tower?" Stewart asked.

Anne laughed. "In Paris? No. Someday, though."

"How about right now?"

"Right now? What?"

"Let's go see the Eiffel Tower."

The twin-engine Lear altered course to the east, climbed to thirty thousand feet, and flew to France. They talked through the evening and had dinner on the plane. After seven hours, just as dawn was breaking across Paris, Anne looked down and saw Sacré-Coeur, Notre-Dame, the Arc de Triomphe, and, of course, the Eiffel Tower. The magic of the moment moved her to tears.

Through some friend in the French foreign ministry Stewart arranged for customs at Orly Airport to admit Anne into the country without a passport, and they had breakfast at a lively café on the Left Bank. After that they spent the day shopping and touring the city in a limousine. He had rented a double suite for them at the Hôtel Meurice on the rue de Rivoli. Their windows looked out over the Tuileries and the Louvre.

Anne had dreamed for a long time of seeing Paris. Now there it was, right outside her window. She felt giddy, euphoric. In her entire life she had never been any further from Burlington, Vermont, than Boston, Massachusetts.

They had dinner at L'Hôtel with a famous French actress and her producer husband. Anne charmed them with her provincial Canadian French, and the producer offered her a part in his next movie. Everyone drank a lot of wine, and the mood was festive.

At one point Dalton leaned close and whispered in her ear. "Can I ask you an important question?"

Anne shook her head playfully. "No. Only silly questions are allowed today."

"Okay. A silly question then. Will you marry me?"

Anne felt her heart flip. "That *is* a silly question," she replied.

Later, at the Brasserie Lipp, they sat at a crowded table with more famous people—many of them acquaintances of Dalton's—and drank more wine. There was a well-known American TV journalist and his writer wife, and so many others who came and went during the evening that she lost track. During the quieter moments, Dalton continued to press his case for marriage, painting a stirring picture of what a wonderful life they would have together. She protested. They barely knew one another, after all.

On their way back to the Hôtel Meurice at three in the morning, Anne, sleep-starved and bleary with jet lag, said she'd at least have to have some time to think about it. In the elevator up to their suite she said yes, she probably would marry him. Dalton completed his whirlwind seduction that night in bed. Anne succumbed almost with relief.

The best surprise was how exciting the sex was. In retrospect, much of it had to do with the circumstances— the wine, the sense of dislocation, the removal from everything familiar—which let her surrender so completely to the sensual side of her nature. She had had sex with four other men—the music professor, Matty, one previous boyfriend, and another professor, who had forced himself on her in his office. None of them had given her pleasure like this. If she wasn't yet in love, she decided, it was certainly a great beginning.

A month later, Anne Marie Beauregard and Dalton Francis Stewart III were married at a small private ceremony on Long Island. Dalton apologized for insisting that everything be done so quickly, but there were so many demands on his time, he felt that if they didn't get married now, the opportunity might be lost forever.

After a short honeymoon in the Caribbean, Dalton parked Anne in his estate on Long Island and went on with his life as before. She rarely saw him anymore. The last time had been a week ago. He was just back from somewhere and on his way to somewhere else. They had dinner and spent the night at the family's brownstone on Fifth Avenue. The next morning he was gone.

The sex that night had been rushed and perfunctory. Dalton brought her some gifts and asked her if there was anything she needed. Otherwise, he was his usual distant, distracted self.

Thinking back on that incredible courtship, Anne now saw it in a new light. Dalton had approached their relationship as if it were a contest and she were the prize. Once he decided he wanted her, he had gone after her, pulling out all the stops. And her early resistance had only increased his determination. He wouldn't quit until he had subdued her.

She had consented, she realized with some mortification, just because it was so much a part of her nature to be agreeable. He had bulldozed her, and she had been too polite and intimidated to resist, or to insist on a larger say in matters. She hadn't negotiated with him. She had surrendered to him. And now that he had the prize, his interest in her had faded. Professions of love notwithstanding, he didn't seem to want a real relationship. He didn't seem to care who she was or what she wanted out of life.

She had tried to persuade Dalton to let her take a job in Manhattan—she had been offered a research position at the Rockefeller Institute that she very much wanted to take—but he had talked her out of it. He told her that her social status made any job, especially a career, out of the question. While he succeeded in the world of business, he expected her to succeed for them in the world of society. It wasn't enough to be rich, he insisted; one also had to know the right people, do the right things, be seen at the right places. It was up to her to see to these matters. That was to be her career.

She had tried, but she had little feeling for society and its demands, and no desire to rise in it. It was all painfully boring and phony.

And then there was the matter of children. She had told him before they were married how much she wanted children—how important a family was to her. He had agreed enthusiastically. It was important to him also.

But he had insisted from the very beginning that she use birth control. One night, after a particularly torrid bout of lovemaking, he asked her if she was remembering her pills.

"What if I said no?" she asked teasingly.

"I'd be upset," he replied.

"Why? I thought we were going to have children. Why wait? I'm ready now."

"No, you can't," Dalton replied, his voice suddenly tight.

"I can't? Why not?"

Dalton remained silent.

"You're frightening me, Dalton," she said. "Talk to me. Why can't I?"

Dalton sat up in bed. "I've got a problem," he whispered. "A bad gene. It can be inherited. It causes severe retardation."

Anne could scarcely believe his words. She felt as if he had punched her in the stomach. "Why didn't you tell me?" she demanded. "You owed it to me to tell me."

Dalton hid his face in his hands. "I know. I know. I wanted to. Believe me. But I was afraid you'd back out of the marriage. I didn't want to risk losing you. I'm sorry, Anne. Honest, I am sorry."

Anne felt cruelly deceived nevertheless. Life without children would be unthinkably empty. The following day Dalton made a lot of apologies and excuses and vaguely promised that if there was no other solution, they would adopt.

Anne stepped out of the shower and dried herself. She felt slightly better. She stood in front of the full-length mirror on the bathroom wall and studied herself in the bright light of the ceiling heat lamps.

Was she really beautiful? People always said she was, but she didn't quite believe it. She thought of herself as very average. Maybe that's all beauty was—being quintessentially average. At the moment she looked more bedraggled than beautiful.

She wrapped a towel around her waist and walked back into the bedroom. She shook her head. It hurt. She was still drunk.

She closed the drapes to shut out the late-afternoon light, then flung herself nude on top of the bed. The room felt hot, stuffy.

Her eyes wandered to the ornate molded plaster border that defined the edges of the bedroom ceiling. The corners were the fanciest—a delicate scrollwork of leaf clusters and other design elements she could not identify. Suddenly she spotted a small face, a chimera, hiding among the leaves. It appeared to be leering down at her. She squinted her eyes, but the face remained. Silly. An illusion caused by the room's dim light, she decided. If she opened the drapes or turned on a lamp, she knew, the face would disappear. She kept her eyes fastened on the small face until she began to feel dizzy again.

She rested a hand on her breast and brought her other hand up between her legs. She closed her eyes and squeezed her thighs against her fingers. Through the haze of the wine, she felt a warm rush of desire.

She squeezed her legs together harder and dug her fingers into her breast.

Tears welled from the corners of her eyes. Why did she have to spend her life feeling lonely and unloved?

6

Dalton Stewart came out of Goth's lab and walked straight to his rented Toyota Land Cruiser, parked just outside the building. Waiting for him were his chief executive assistant, Hank Ajemian, and his chauffeur-bodyguard, Gil Trabert. Ajemian opened the back door for his boss and then slid in beside him.

Stewart removed the gold fountain pen clipped to his shirt pocket and held it out. A miniature microphone and transmitter were concealed inside. Goth had refused to allow any recording devices inside his office, so Stewart had resorted to using a bug with a remote transmitter. "Did you get everything?" he asked.

Ajemian picked up the portable laser-disk recorder from the floor and set it on his lap. "Came through perfectly."

Trabert started the jeep and wheeled it slowly out of the weed-choked lot. Prince Bandar's jeep was already bouncing down the hill, trailing a cloud of dust. Yamamoto and Fairfield, who had come out behind Stewart, were just getting into their vehicles.

Stewart craned his neck around to look back toward the lab's entrance. He was wondering what had become of the baroness. He had hoped to speak to her, but she was nowhere in sight.

Stewart looked at his chief assistant, slumped forward in his wrinkled suit. Ajemian was short, overweight, and bald. He suffered from allergies that caused dark circles under his eyes and gave his Brooklyn accent an added overtone of nasal congestion. He presented a dramatic contrast to his tall, slim, well-manicured WASP boss.

"You heard it all," Stewart said. "What did you think?"

Ajemian closed his eyes and sniffled. Some plant pollen in the air was making his nose run and his eyes water. "Goth sounds a little off the wall to me," he ventured.

"You think so?"

"Well, you asked the key question," Ajemian answered, instinctively flattering his boss. "Where's the proof? He said he doesn't have any, so what the hell is he talking about?"

"You think he's a fraud?"

"I don't rule it out. More likely Goth is conning himself. He wants to believe he can do these things. Maybe he needs to believe it."

"You think we should forget it, then?"

Ajemian pulled a tissue from his pocket and blew his nose loudly. He hated it when his boss put him on the spot like this. "Well, what's he offering us? Basically nothing—beyond his word. And I don't think that's worth much. As you yourself said—"

"Stop quoting me, for godsakes. I know what I said."

Ajemian nodded.

"I want to think about it," Stewart decided.

Both men were clutching the edges of the seats in front of them to keep from being thrown around by the rough mountain road. Stewart appraised his chief assistant. He was wearing that hang-dog look he put on whenever Stewart was abrupt with him.

He paid Hank Ajemian a million dollars a year, along with stock options, a fat expense account, and a complete medical plan. And Ajemian was worth it. He didn't have much imagination, but he was quick and savvy, and an absolute wizard with a balance sheet. He could cut corners and bend rules with the best of them. He knew how to pull out all the stops to outwit a rival in a deal or to confound and defeat an army of regulatory investigators. He could put together—or take apart—a deal like no one else Stewart had ever known. When Ajemian was doing the numbers, the competition didn't stand a chance.

And Stewart trusted him. He was loyal. And it wasn't just his personality that made him that way. He owed Stewart a lot.

In 1988 Ajemian had been hit by both the SEC and the

United States Attorney General's office in a Wall Street securities fraud case that sent him to the federal penitentiary in Danbury, Connecticut, for three years. When he got out of prison, in 1992, no one would hire him. He had a wife and three children, and he was reduced to sending his kids to live with relatives while he and his wife, Carol, cleaned offices to stay alive.

That was how he met Dalton Stewart. He was polishing his office floor one night when Stewart walked in. Ajemian had seen some papers on Stewart's desk relating to plans to buy out a small pharmaceuticals company in upstate New York. He couldn't resist pointing out a few ways in which Stewart might improve his bargaining position. Stewart, once he got over the shock of being given advice by a nosy cleaning man, was impressed. Despite Ajemian's jail record, he put him on the payroll as an investment consultant. Stewart had reason to be sympathetic. His own father had once gone to prison for a crime similar to Ajemian's.

In the years since, Ajemian had become Stewart's only real confidant.

"Goth's a crackpot," Ajemian declared. "You read the file. He's an embarrassment in the scientific community."

"He won the Nobel Prize."

"He's still a crackpot."

"Hold on a minute," Stewart countered. "Don't confuse being controversial with being crazy. The guy's a genius. Nobody disputes that. And I find it hard to believe that a man with his brains—and ego—would spend ten years working a dry hole. He's on to something. And if he can do what he says he can do . . ." Stewart paused. He felt a sudden euphoric rush, akin to the sensation he experienced when he decided to go after a beautiful woman. "There's an opportunity to make some money here, Hank. A lot of money."

Ajemian rubbed his nose. "Goth may be years from being able to produce the kind of genetic package he was talking about in there."

"That's part of the risk of backing him. But he's not asking for much, either. Ten million. That's not big money. We lost twice that last year on that damned drug-store chain you talked me into buying."

"It was only twelve million," Ajemian protested. "And the numbers were there—"

Stewart waved a hand to cut him off. "Think of the possibilities. If the genetic program works even half as well as Goth says it will, the market for it is unlimited. We're talking about the one thing that matters to people more than anything else in their life—their children. Everybody naturally wants the best. And a kid who's a genius? Who never gets sick? Who'll probably live to be over a hundred? My God, they'll be kicking the doors down. Everybody will want this. Those who can afford it will *demand* to have it."

The jeep reached the bottom of the mountain road, and Trabert swung it onto the highway and headed back toward their hotel on the west end of the island.

"If it works," Ajemian said. He pulled out another tissue to wipe his nose.

Stewart warmed to his subject. "We could build the first clinic right here. Just buy up that medical school up on the hill. It's perfect. Give Goth whatever he needs and put him in charge. Then buy up one of the island's best hotels. Or build one. Or two. People who come to the clinic could make it a Caribbean vacation. And we'd sock it to them. Make the deal so expensive only the rich could afford it. Hell, we could set almost any price we wanted. Figure a package deal of about a hundred thousand dollars per couple, everything included—food, transportation, hotel, and all the time they need at the clinic. Probably a week, with some future trips during and after the pregnancy. We might charge more for those. When the first clinic is going full blast, we build a second one. And another hotel. And then a third. When the island can't hold any more, we find a second island. And right now the whole region's economy is a shambles. We could buy up beachfront property for nothing on half a dozen out-of-the-way islands. Then invite some of the big, prestigious chains—Hyatt, Sheraton—to build here. And while we're at it, we'll buy out one of the local feeder airlines and expand it. Maybe we could even develop our own international routes. . . ."

Ajemian tucked the used tissue into his pants pocket. "What about legal problems?"

"I don't think there are any. In fact, the legal situation could work to our benefit. If genetic research on the germ line is illegal everywhere else, then people'll have no choice except to come down here. We'd have the whole market to ourselves—indefinitely. Even if someone stole the program, he'd be hard put to find a place to set up the sophisticated clinics needed to administer it. Of course we'd have to protect ourselves—keep the local politicians here happy. That shouldn't be hard. We can make the economy on this island boom."

Ajemian still resisted the idea. "What about Goth himself? He could be a problem. I heard him asking for fifty percent in there."

"I've been thinking about that. Fifty percent is out of the question, of course. Even a thirty-percent share's too high. But suppose we just offer him carte blanche. Go to him and say, 'Look, here's the ten million. It's a grant. No strings attached. Just get to work. When you've got your formula in shape, then we'll sit down and work out a long-term arrangement.' Nobody can possibly offer him a better deal than that."

Ajemian sniffled. "No, but what's to keep him from taking his formula to the highest bidder—after *we've* paid him to develop it?"

"Let him think he can do just that. He's arrogant enough to think he deserves it. And naive enough about business to go for it. But by the time he's spent our ten million, we'll own him. He'll have to get our permission to go to the bathroom. For openers, we'll buy the medical school and make ourselves his landlord. And we'll make sure that we have a copy of that genetic program of his physically in our possession before he can do anything with it. Then he'll have to accept whatever we put on the table."

Ajemian saw that his boss was not going to be dissuaded. He shifted his ground to tactical considerations.

"What about the others at the meeting today? We could have competition."

"I wonder. You can count Harry Fairfield out, for one. He's aggressive, but he's no good at development. He's after the quick buck. His attitude gave him away. He didn't take Goth seriously. And he's also in trouble with the British government."

"Tax evasion. That's nothing to Fairfield."

"Not that. Rumors are going around that he's been selling bad drugs through a generic-brand subsidiary. Scotland Yard is going to whack him hard. He'll be too distracted to get involved with Goth's program. Prince Bandar is out, too. He was too lazy to bother to do his homework. He didn't ask a single question during Goth's presentation. I think he was half-asleep."

"Yamamoto?"

"Hard to tell. He has big government connections. I can see him trying to buy Goth out. And if that doesn't work—which it won't—he might try to steal the program. The Japs would rather develop something like this on their own."

Ajemian nodded in agreement. "And I guess the baroness is out."

Stewart stroked his chin. "I don't know. She may be the one to worry about."

"I thought she pretty much told Goth no during the meeting."

"The baroness is clever. I've got a hunch that's the way she wanted it to look. But what did she actually say? She told Goth she'd demand ninety percent, not fifty. So she's already negotiating with him. And she knows as much about genetic research as any of us."

"Then she's trouble. Beneath that glamorous exterior of hers there's one tough bitch, no matter what you read in the magazines."

"Hell, we'll beat her pants off," Stewart said. He grinned. "Figuratively speaking, of course."

Ajemian wasn't convinced. "It just feels wrong to me."

Dalton laughed. "What kind of argument is that?" He banged the top of the seat back in front of him. "Come on, let's go for it."

Ajemian just grunted.

"As soon as we get back to the hotel I want you to do the following," Stewart said. "Find out who owns the medical school, and buy the whole thing, cash. They ought to be eager to unload it, considering the shape it's in. Get a binder on the property. Fly in a couple of our lawyers if you have to. Set up a shell company as owner. Then set me up with a date to see President Despres, ASAP. We've got to get his balls in our pocket right away."

"Should I scout out some beachfront properties as well?"

"That can wait. Let's not tip our hand. But call New York and put R&D on notice that when I get back I want to see on my desk a complete profile of this island— voting lists, tax lists, real-estate ownership, phone numbers, arrest records, gossip, everything they can lay their hands on. Then I want three detailed biographies—Harold Goth, Yuichiro Yamamoto, and Baroness Gerta von Hauser. Everything there is to know about them—their work, personal habits, friends, enemies, sex life, financial status, health, eating habits—the works. I want them fast. Put the whole department on them full-time."

Ajemian scribbled some notes to himself, then looked up. "What about this afternoon? You're scheduled to fly to Puerto Rico to look at that new chemical plant."

"Cancel it. I'm going back to make Goth an offer. I've just thought of a way to find out if this Jupiter program of his is the real thing."

7

Dalton Stewart found Dr. Harold Goth in his laboratory, hunched over a computer terminal. On a stand nearby, an old dot-matrix printer was cranking out a continuous strip of fanfold paper that spilled to the floor in an erratic, untended pile. The pages were covered with charts and diagrams.

Stewart was surprised that Goth was so careless of his security; he had walked right into the building and the lab unannounced and unseen. He was now standing ten feet behind Goth, and the doctor, riveted to his computer screen, was still oblivious of his presence. Kirsten, his research assistant, sat on a stool in the far corner, peering into a microscope. She had not noticed his entrance, either. Stewart cleared his throat loudly.

Goth glanced over his shoulder. He greeted Stewart bluntly: "What do you want?"

"I want you to succeed, Doctor," Stewart said, inflecting the words with all the warmth he could muster.

Goth dismissed him with a short wave of his hand. "If you're here to make me an offer, you're too late."

Stewart's genial grin vanished. "Too late?"

"The Baroness von Hauser has already made a proposal."

Stewart felt his pulse quicken. "Surely you haven't accepted it—have you?"

Goth shrugged. "It's adequate."

"But you haven't heard my offer yet."

"I don't want to."

"Don't be hasty, Doctor. I have a plan I think you'll find far more attractive."

Goth was clearly eager to get rid of him. "I really don't need a lot of money," he snapped.

"I understand. But there are other considerations, aren't there?"

Goth's eyebrows narrowed in a suspicious squint. "What do you mean?"

"What are the baroness's terms?"

Goth hesitated for a moment. "She's accepted sixty percent," he said, finally.

Stewart nodded. Obviously the doctor thought he had driven a hell of a bargain, getting her down from her pretended insistence on ninety percent. "How much capital is she prepared to advance to you?"

"Exactly what I demanded. Ten million dollars."

"How will she pay it out?"

"Spread over two years."

"And you're happy with that?"

"I can live with it."

"No other conditions?"

"Some oversight," Goth muttered. He wasn't crazy about that part of the bargain.

Stewart rested his hands on the counter top behind him and leaned back, calculating how he might best deliver the baroness a figurative kick right in her smart, round ass.

"That could be trouble, couldn't it?" he said. "I could be wrong, but oversight's likely to mean Hauser lawyers and CPAs constantly hounding you to account for every dollar. It could even mean Hauser biologists sticking their noses in your laboratory work. I understand the baroness has a reputation for meddling. She likes to be personally involved in her projects. Ask anybody who's dealt with her. They'll tell you the same. It could slow you down."

Goth slid a thumb and forefinger up under his glasses and squeezed the bridge of his nose thoughtfully. Bull's-eye, Stewart thought.

"I have to be a realist," Goth replied. "I don't expect anything better."

"Why shouldn't you?"

Goth chewed his lip. His skepticism was warring with his curiosity. "What are you talking about?"

"A better offer. I'll advance you all the money you require. Forget ten million—I'll go to twenty. And you can have the money when and as you need it. And you won't have to account for a nickel of it to anybody. How you spend it will be entirely up to you."

"And what percentage of Jupiter would you expect?"

"At this stage, absolutely none. There'd be no conditions attached to the money—none whatsoever. Consider it a research grant. Period. When you're ready to market Jupiter, we'll discuss percentages then. If we can't come to terms, you'll be free to take the project elsewhere. If you fail to develop a workable program, then percentages won't matter anyway."

Goth stared at Stewart disbelievingly; he was not a man accustomed to good news. "What's the catch?"

"There isn't any. I said no strings—I mean it. I respect your work. And I believe you can do what you say you can do. If I can help you, then we'll all be winners. To try to tie you down to an agreement now is neither necessary nor advisable, in my view. Look at it this way: if things go better for you than you expect, you might end up feeling I took advantage of you when you weren't in a strong negotiating position. That's exactly what the baroness is doing now. I want any arrangement between us to be completely fair. I want to lay the groundwork for an enduring association."

"And what about your twenty million? You'll no doubt expect that money back—with interest."

"Not at all. It'll be a tax loss. I'll set up a foundation specifically for this project, so that I can declare the sums charitable contributions."

Goth removed his glasses and wiped them with the bottom of his lab jacket. Stewart saw that he was wavering.

"I'm a rich man, Dr. Goth," Stewart said, reaching to clinch his argument. "I don't need to be any richer. The twenty million dollars is, quite frankly, not a lot of money to me. And even if it were, I've reached the stage in my life and career where the social worth of a venture matters far more to me than its potential profits. I can understand why you might have doubts, but bear in mind that what I'm proposing doesn't even demand any trust on your part. I simply give you the money you need, and you do what you have to do. Nobody'll be looking over your shoulder. No lawyers, no accountants, no scientific committees. I have absolutely no need to take advantage of you. The tax break I'll get is alone worth the investment. I won't lose out, no matter what happens. It's a perfect arrangement for both of us. All you need to agree to on paper is that you won't seek funding elsewhere—or enter into any legal contracts with anybody before I've had a chance to negotiate with you first."

"I'll have to think it over," Goth said.

"Of course. How long do you need?"

"A couple of days."

Stewart shook his head emphatically. "I appreciate that you're a shrewd bargainer, Doctor," he said. "But I can't let you shop my offer around. That'd be unfair to me. I tell you what. I'll leave the offer on the table for one hour. That should give you adequate time to decide. Then it's take it or leave it, I'm afraid."

Goth paced the floor. He asked Stewart to repeat his terms again. Then he asked a lot of unimportant questions: how soon he could get the money, and what bank he would use, and who would know about their arrangement, and so on. Stewart knew at that point that Goth had already accepted his offer. He just didn't want to appear too eager.

The doctor obviously thought of himself as someone who could never be seduced into compromising his ideals. And like most loners, he insisted on calling all the shots and doing all the work himself, because no one else could be trusted to do it right. He thought that this made him invulnerable, when in fact it was his major weakness. He thought that because he was a genius in the field of genetics, that made him a genius in other areas as well. If Goth had known anything about business at all, Stewart reflected, he would have known that in a matter as important as this he needed expert legal advice. But Goth didn't think that.

"Okay," Goth said. "But if you try to impose conditions after the fact, the deal is off."

"Understood." Stewart held out his hand. Goth hesitated, then took it. He had a lousy handshake.

"Since I'm taking all the risks, I do have a few questions I want to ask you, Doctor."

Goth looked mildly alarmed. "What are they?"

"First, I thought you were a little evasive earlier today when I asked you if you had ever tested Jupiter on a human subject. I find it hard to believe that you never have. So let me ask the question again."

Instead of answering the question, Goth excused himself and walked to the far end of the lab, where his assistant was still perched on her stool. She had barely stirred the whole time he was there. Goth ordered her to go find something for him. She objected briefly, then left the room.

"Can I trust you to keep something completely confidential?" the doctor asked, walking back toward Stewart.

"Of course. Absolutely."

"Very well . . ." Goth paused. A look of intense discomfort—almost pain—creased his face. "Two years ago forty women from the island volunteered for an in vitro fertilization program. . . ."

Stewart felt his scalp tingle with dread. "And . . . ?"

"None of the fetuses survived," Goth said, looking off into the middle distance.

"What was the problem?"

Goth waved a hand. "It's futile to try to explain it to a layman. Suffice it to say there was an unexpected anomaly in an altered gene sequence on chromosome 4, causing it to suppress the manufacture of a certain critical protein. Normally such an event wouldn't cause problems; anomalies of this kind are common and usually harmless. But in this case we were exceptionally unlucky. Slight as it was, the mistake made all the fetuses nonviable. It was impossible to know this would happen until we conducted just such a trial. None of the women suffered any ill effects. And of course I have since solved the problem."

"And have you tested your solution?"

"As soon as I have the necessary funding, I will. That's my first priority."

Stewart thought for a moment. "There could be other problems, then, couldn't there?"

Goth straightened his bony chest and tilted his head back. He didn't like having his competence challenged. "There can always be problems, Mr. Stewart. The human genome is a dynamic entity, in constant flux. No one will ever be able to ensure perfect results in every instance. There will always be the unexpected."

"I was thinking in more immediate terms. How close do you think you are to having a workable program?"

"I have it now. But I can't rule out the possibility of more problems. That's exactly why I need additional time. I must test the program thoroughly. This is a highly experimental area—immensely complex. No one else in the entire field of genetics is doing what I'm doing. So I have no support for my effort, no one to cross-check my results, no one doing related research. It's terra incognita, and I'm out there alone. There's a great deal I must do before I can be sure I haven't overlooked anything."

"I understand," Stewart said. Indeed, he thought the doctor was being remarkably honest. "I'm curious," he said. "Why did you choose to do this in the first place?"

"What do you mean?"

"You could have remained inside the scientific establishment. Why didn't you? Is the privilege of tinkering with human evolution worth all the personal and professional sacrifices you've had to make?"

Goth appeared astonished by the question. "I don't see it in those terms. Whatever sacrifices I've had to make—and may still have to make—I do in the name of a greater necessity."

Stewart was mystified. "What necessity?"

Dr. Goth picked up a book from his desk, opened it to a page marked with a slip of paper, and held it out for Stewart to see. It contained a color illustration of a band of five prehistoric males. Their faces were painted and they were wearing animal skins. They stood at what looked like the edge of a forest clearing. Their expressions were watchful, tense. Each man clutched a stone-tipped spear.

"This is us," Goth said, tapping the illustration with a

forefinger. "Homo sapiens. This is the way we looked about fifty thousand years ago. These men in the picture aren't hunting. They're going into battle against another group of Homo sapiens. Maybe the other pose a threat to this tribe's territory. Or to their food supply. Or to their women. Whatever the reason, they're getting ready for a fight to the death."

Goth dropped the book back on the desk. "Homo sapiens is the most successful animal species ever to walk the earth," the doctor declared, his words energized by a sudden display of enthusiasm for his subject. "He was ruthless and resourceful. And uniquely gifted with a large brain that allowed him to adapt to almost any circumstance. And he did adapt. He multiplied and spread out. He subdued his environment; he eliminated every challenge to his superiority—until the only enemy left was himself. And despite centuries of ceaseless mutual human slaughter, his success is still astonishing and undeniable. He has subdued the entire planet Earth. He owns it."

Stewart raised a hand to slow the tide of words. Inviting Goth to let off some steam might help cement their relationship, but he didn't want to hear an anthropology lecture. "What's your point?"

"Simply this. We're those same primitive people today. We have the same brain, the same emotions, the same capabilities, the same shortcomings, the same tolerances. We haven't evolved at all. In fact, as a species, we're now in serious decline."

"And so . . ."

"Don't you see? We've become victims of our own success. We've transformed the world to suit our needs, developed a technology so powerful that there's almost nothing we can't do. But we haven't advanced to keep pace with our own creativity. In fact, we've gone backwards. The improvements in our diet and our medicine and our technologies have only degraded our gene pool. It's allowed the least fit among us to survive, multiply, and contribute further to the decline of the species. And meanwhile we go on ransacking the earth's resources and polluting the earth's soil, water, and air at an ever-increasing pace. And unless we change our habits, we're doomed. The aggressive, adventurous exploring and fighting instincts that got us here are no longer adequate to solve our problems. Normally the process of evolution would correct the situation, would allow our species to adapt to our new circumstances—raise our resistance to the pollutants in the air, to the increased amount of radiation bombarding our skin, to the increasingly crowded conditions of our lives. But evolution is a slow process. It takes many generations of natural selection for significant mutations to occur and succeed. But we can't wait for that. We don't have the time. In anthropological terms, Homo sapiens has changed the world overnight. Now we must change ourselves overnight just to survive in the world we've created. We have to take the process of evolution into our own hands. We have to step in and take control of our destiny as a species."

Stewart was impressed. Goth's little speech had breathtaking implications. And he might even be right. "So the bottom line is that either we rewrite our own genetic code or we're out of business?"

"That's essentially it, yes."

"And that's what your Jupiter program is designed to do? Rewrite the code? Guarantee our survival?"

"Precisely."

Stewart shook his head dubiously. "I'll have to confess, Doctor, from what you told us earlier today your genetic changes just don't sound that profound. Or is there something you didn't tell us?"

Goth removed his glasses and polished the lenses with the bottom edge of his lab jacket. Stewart had seen him do it four or five times. It had become a neurotic tic.

"I told you the program would increase intelligence substantially," Goth replied. "And that in itself—if it became widespread—would have a revolutionary impact. If people were smarter, they'd be less prone to settle their conflicts with violence. They'd be more able to understand and solve the complex problems that beset us today. They'd understand where the true long-term interests of mankind lay. Consider population control. They'd not only understand the necessity for it, they'd do something about it. Take war. They'd see the futility of it. Or the destruction of the environment—they wouldn't tolerate it. They wouldn't tolerate a lot of things—murder, rape, torture, poverty, hunger, bigotry, despotism. . . ."

"What about your formula's enhancement of the senses?" Stewart cut in. "What's the point of that?"

"It'll increase an individual's survival value. His perception of the world around him will be widened. And that perception will mean greater knowledge and understanding."

"That might be more of an encumbrance than an advantage. Won't it overload the human nervous system with a lot of unnecessary additional noise?"

Goth shrugged. "This program is only a beginning. A prototype. It'll be refined and improved over time. The important thing now is to get started, before it's too late."

Stewart sensed that Goth was still keeping a lot to himself, but there seemed no point in pressing him any further. Jupiter, at this stage, was still more theory than reality.

"It's an exciting adventure," Stewart said. "I feel privileged to be able to assist you in it." This was the kind of flattery that rolled from his tongue automatically when he was engaged in winning someone's trust. He heard himself say it and realized with a pleasant shock that this time he actually meant it: it really was going to be an exciting adventure. It really could have profound social value. And the financial profits from it were going to be truly staggering. "How long do you think it'll be before you can test Jupiter on human subjects again?"

"As soon as I can set up a clinic with the equipment and the personnel I need for the gene alterations and the in vitro fertilization program, I'll begin the tests. It'll take several months."

Stewart leaned closer and lowered his voice. "Would you be willing to test Jupiter right now?"

"I'm afraid I don't—"

"On my wife."

Goth's eyes narrowed.

"That surprises you?"

"Why would you expose your wife to the risk?"

"You said you believed the program was ready."

"Yes, but I can't guarantee it'll work perfectly."

"I'm not asking you to," Stewart replied. "Look, I have a very young wife. We both want children, but it happens there's a problem. I carry an inherited genetic trait for something called fragile X syndrome. I had an uncle and a brother who were affected. I don't want to pass it on to children of my own. So we'd need to find a male donor for the sperm—"

"Not at all," Goth interrupted. "I know the gene responsible for it. I can correct the defect."

"Are you sure?"

"Quite sure. It's a relatively simple gene splice, in fact."

"Will you do it then? For me? And for my wife? She's terribly anxious to have a child."

"I'd rather not, frankly."

"Why? If Jupiter is as good as you say it is, then why not prove it to me first?"

"I'd prefer to test it on some volunteers with less at stake in the outcome."

"I understand. But look—if you're willing to correct the fragile X problem, why not go all the way?"

Goth shook his head. He removed his glasses and fiddled nervously with them in his lap.

"Is there some ethical worry? What's the worst that can happen? A spontaneous abortion? Those happen all the time anyway."

"The worst that can happen is a child with some undesirable mental or physical characteristics. . . ."

"Couldn't you detect those before birth?"

Goth rubbed his chin, thinking. "I should be able to. Yes."

"So the risk is no greater than the risk any mother bears in pregnancy. And the potential benefits are far greater. Really, Doctor, your reluctance makes me wonder if you believe in your own program."

Goth stood up. "It'll work. I know it."

"Then prove it to me."

Goth sat back down again. He said nothing for a long time. Stewart waited. He became aware of the research assistant, who had returned to her stool. Stewart had a strong impression that she was unhappy in her work. Maybe she just didn't like Goth.

"Very well," Goth said. "I'll do it."

Stewart thanked him profusely. He was enormously pleased. What better, quicker way for him to evaluate the true worth of the Jupiter program?

"But I'll have to insist on several things," Goth added. "I insist on performing all the medical procedures myself. And if they're successful I'll have to see your wife on a regular basis. I'll need to monitor the pregnancy closely. And I'll also need to supervise the delivery itself. And all procedures, including the delivery, will have to take place on this island."

"I see no problem."

"And finally—and this is most important—I'll want to have access to the child on a frequent and regular basis to follow its progress. That's the only way I can measure the true effectiveness of the altered gene sequences."

"I'll agree to all that," Stewart replied. "In return, I'd like to make one small but important condition myself. My wife of course knows about the fragile X syndrome. She'll be thrilled to hear that you can correct it. But I'd rather we not tell her anything more than that. I don't want to risk either scaring her or raising her hopes too high. She knows quite a bit of biology herself, and I'd rather let her think that the whole procedure is only to solve the fragile X problem. After she's had the child, and we know the program works, we can tell her everything. But let's wait until then."

Goth agreed.

"How soon can we do it, then?"

"I'll need to prepare the lab for the gene-splicing work, the egg retrieval, the sperm enhancement, and the zygote intrafallopian transfer procedure. And I'll need to test both of you—get a genome printout, take sperm and egg samples, and so forth. At least three months."

"Let's do it in three weeks. Crash program. I'll get you all the equipment you need in a week. Just give me a list. And I'll get my wife down here immediately so you can begin your testing."

"If you can get me everything I need that fast . . ."

Stewart shook Goth's hand again. This time the doctor squeezed back. He was beginning to get enthusiastic about the idea himself.

Stewart left Goth's laboratory bursting with an excitement he hadn't felt in years. He had just negotiated the deal of a lifetime—of a hundred lifetimes. The path ahead would no doubt be strewn with obstacles and dangers. But with a reasonable amount of luck, not only would Jupiter deliver him an extraordinary child, it would eventually make him the richest human being on the planet.

8

Yuichiro Yamamoto teed up his ball on the first hole, a 415-yard par four, on the Bethesda Country Club golf course, outside Washington, D.C. He pulled a driver out of his bag and hit the ball deep and straight down the fairway, where it rolled to a half in the grass, perfectly positioned for an approach shot onto the green.

His partner, Haikido Mishima, grunted a couple of words of praise and knelt down to tee up his own ball. Mishima was the number-three man at the Japanese embassy in Washington. He had been the number-one man some years before at the embassy in Mexico City, so he retained possession of the title of ambassador, even though his official position now was that of consul for trade and technology. His real mission was coordinating the embassy's clandestine intelligence activities. He was several years older than Yamamoto, and not nearly as accomplished a golfer.

Yamamoto could walk off the eighteenth hole of this course under par on a good day. But today he knew he'd be lucky to make eighty. He had suffered a sleepless night, followed by two overbooked and delayed plane flights—one from Coronado to Nassau, the Bahamas, the other from there to Washington. Mishima, on the other hand, was out of shape and not well coordinated. He'd be lucky to get in under 110.

The ambassador hooked his tee shot to the right. It landed short and rolled into the rough, leaving him no approach to the green. He slipped his club back into the bag with a dispirited sigh and climbed into the golf cart.

"I don't know why I play this game," he said. "It just

makes me ill-tempered. I'd much rather sit in a garden and read poetry."

Yamamoto smiled politely. He was quite fond of the ambassador. He was a cultured, educated man, with enormous grace and good humor. He was also charmingly self-effacing, even by Japanese standards, although Yamamoto suspected that there was a hint of mockery behind that modesty. "I predict you'll give me a very close game today," he said.

"Nonsense," the diplomat replied. "You know better. I'll be in the woods most of the time, looking for that damned little pockmarked white ball. No matter. I expect you'll make my morning worthwhile."

Yamamoto wasn't so sure.

"And I want all the details," Mishima added. "Even the seemingly irrelevant ones. We have eighteen long holes ahead of us."

Yamamoto briefed Mishima on the meeting at Goth's laboratory. He described those present—Prince Bandar, Harry Fairfield, Baroness von Hauser, and Dalton Stewart—and recounted the essential points of Harold Goth's presentation.

By the time he had finished his briefing, they were riding the golf cart toward the fourth green. Yamamoto had parred the first, bogeyed the second, and birdied the third. The ambassador had triple-bogeyed all three.

"How do you evaluate Goth?" Mishima asked. "Does he know what he's doing?"

"I wish I could answer that question, Ambassador, but honestly I can't."

"Why not?"

"His past achievements speak for themselves. He's a Nobel laureate. His brilliance as a geneticist is unquestioned. . . ." Yamamoto stopped the cart by the edge of the green. His ball was sitting on the green, just twenty feet from the pin. The ambassador's was buried in a nearby sand trap.

"But . . . ?" Mishima prodded.

"But for a decade now he's been following an extremely risky course with his genetics work. That puts his judgment seriously in question."

Mishima grabbed his sand wedge and waded into the trap after his ball. Yamamoto stood on the edge of the grass, watching.

"Maybe the potential reward is worth the risk," the ambassador said, bending down for a closer look at his situation.

"Maybe."

Mishima stepped up to the ball, took its measure, gritted his teeth, and swung lustily. A dense shower of sand spurted out in front of him. The ball remained stationary. "But you have doubts," he gasped.

Yamamoto nodded. "All he has is an untested formula. A computer program, actually. He calls it Jupiter. It might do what he claims, it might not. We can't know until he tests it."

"And of course that's what he wants the money for."

"Precisely."

Mishima, breathing heavily from his exertions, stood over the ball again and gave it another energetic wallop with his wedge iron. This time the ball shot out of the trap on a low trajectory, soared across the green like a stray bullet, struck the pin with a loud *bonk,* bounced ten feet straight up in the air, and came to rest three feet past the hole.

Yamamoto shook his head in disbelief.

Mishima beamed in triumph. "You think any of the others will make Goth an offer?" he asked.

"Baroness von Hauser already has. And the American, Dalton Stewart—I think he's up to something."

"What about the other two? Prince Bandar and that Englishman, Fairfield?"

"It's doubtful they'll do anything."

"What's the status of our own research programs?"

"At a standstill, like everybody else's."

"Why is that?"

"As you well know, Ambassador, experimenting on the human germ line is illegal in most countries, including ours."

The diplomat appraised Yamamoto with a sidelong glance. "But we're doing it anyway, aren't we?"

Yamamoto studied the green's perfectly mowed carpet

of bent grass. "Purely theoretical stuff—computer models based on genome studies, projections from animal experiments, that kind of thing. There's no clinical experimental work being done with humans—"

Mishima cut him off sharply: "I know, I know. We've become a more enlightened society in the past sixty years."

"I personally think we should be doing clinical tests on humans. No real progress is possible otherwise."

The ambassador removed the flag from the hole for his partner. Yamamoto crouched down to view the terrain. It was a tricky lie. It started off level; then ten feet from the hole the green slanted sharply to the left. Yamamoto gripped his putter and concentrated.

"I'm not so sure," Mishima replied. "Once an ethical boundary is breached, it becomes that much easier to breach the next one, and then the next, until one finds oneself, inexplicably, committing just the sorts of atrocities we once committed in Northern China."

Yamamoto overhit his shot. The ball rolled six feet past the hole. He glanced suspiciously at Mishima, who was still holding the flag. If he didn't know the man better, he would have sworn that Mishima had timed his words to disrupt his swing.

Yamamoto diverted his irritation into a tough question: "Can we afford to let the *gaijin* get ahead of us on this?" He hadn't intended to be so confrontational, but he felt deeply that this was a matter of the utmost priority for Japan. Failure to act would in the long run expose his country to a terrible risk.

"No," Mishima agreed. His tone was firm, emphatic. "We cannot. Our people's survival depends on successful economic competition. The potential economic benefits of a successful genetics package like this are obviously enormous. And if genetic engineering is going to make possible a superior race of men, then we must be that race. There can be no argument against that. None."

"I completely agree."

"But all the same, we must proceed in this matter with a strong sense of moral responsibility."

Diplomatic double-talk, Yamamoto thought. What Mishima really meant was, "We'll do what we have to do, but this time let's not get caught at it." "I agree with that also," Yamamoto said.

"So that brings us back to Dr. Goth and his remarkable but untested program. What do you recommend?"

"That we wait," Yamamoto replied. He tapped his ball impatiently and watched it overshoot the cup by four inches. "Let one of the others finance Goth. Let them test Jupiter. If it doesn't work, we'll have risked nothing—and lost nothing."

"And if it does?"

Yamamoto shrugged. "We could always borrow a copy."

Mishima stood by his ball, scratching his chin thoughtfully. Yamamoto began to twitch restlessly, waiting for his partner to make his four-foot putt.

The ambassador eventually got his putter lined up against the ball and hit it. "Borrow a copy," he repeated. He laughed quite explosively. "Yes. We could always do that." He watched his ball advance feebly toward the hole. His diplomat's mind had already converted the proposed theft into something vaguely acceptable. "And once we have the software program, we can trust our own scientists with it far more than we could ever trust Goth."

Mishima's ball reached the lip, trembled there, as if its progress had been arrested by a single blade of grass, and then fell into the cup with a gentle rattle. Yamamoto cursed under his breath.

Mishima tossed his putter into his bag with an uncharacteristic flourish and hoisted himself into the golf cart. He marked his card with the tiny stub of a pencil he was using and chuckled contentedly. "I believe I outscored you on that hole. Did I?"

"You did indeed, Ambassador," Yamamoto answered, smiling between clenched jaws.

9

Dalton Stewart was met in the reception area by the minister of information, Pierre Etienne Toussaint, and ushered into the presidential palace's cavernous dining hall.

Their footsteps echoed like gunshots on the carpetless stone floor. President Despres appeared to have a passion for white, Stewart observed: white marble walls and floors, white marble pedestals with white marble busts of Roman emperors. A ridiculously long dining table was covered with a white damask tablecloth, and the chairs all had white cloth cushions. The only touches of color were two faded tapestries on the end walls, and four potted jungle plants that occupied the corners of the gigantic hall. The effect was oppressive. It made the vast, eerily quiet, air-conditioned interior feel like a mausoleum.

Toussaint directed Stewart to a seat four chairs down from the head of the table and then disappeared. Stewart stood behind his chair and waited. He could hear occasional footsteps echoing on distant marble, but none came through the large doorway.

After an interminable duration, he heard a sudden flurry of footfalls. They beat on the stone floors in a hurried staccato, like soldiers marching double-time. The sound grew steadily louder.

Four of Despres's palace guards burst abruptly into the dining hall and positioned themselves one on each side of the room, forefingers ostentatiously curled around the triggers of their automatic weapons.

A tense, expectant silence fell. All eyes were riveted on the open doorway. Dalton Stewart found himself holding his breath.

After another delay, His Most Supreme and Enlightened Excellency Antoine Auguste Despres, President for Life of the Republic of El Coronado, came into the room.

After the dramatically staged entrance, Antoine Despres himself was a distinct anticlimax. He was short—about five-three—and slightly built, with a mulatto's yellowish-brown skin. His eyes were greatly magnified by the thick lenses in his glasses, and his round, bald head appeared too big for his scrawny neck. His suit was white and presumably well cut, but his sunken-chested posture largely defeated the efforts of his tailors.

The minister of information pulled out the chair at the head of the table and Despres sat down on it. Toussaint then took a chair opposite Stewart and gestured urgently for the American to sit down. Stewart sat. He suddenly realized the president was now staring at him.

"We are honored to have you visit our island nation, Mr. Stewart," Despres said. His voice was high-pitched and had an unpleasant grating quality to it.

"Thank you, Your Excellency," the American replied, a little too loudly. His words bounced off the walls and reverberated through the room. He lowered his volume and told Despres how grateful he was for the opportunity to meet him in person.

A servant appeared, carrying an ice bucket with a bottle of white wine inside. The minister of information opened the bottle, tasted it, and nodded his approval. The wine steward filled the three glasses and moved silently to a corner of the room.

President Despres made a long toast, the import of which was his hope that his country and the United States could overcome their differences and restore the beautiful friendship they had once enjoyed.

Stewart reciprocated with a toast of his own, praising Despres's enlightened leadership, his humanitarianism, and his outstanding achievements in making El Coronado a true showcase of modern democracy in the Western Hemisphere.

Despres answered with another toast. The exchanges dragged on for some minutes, severely taxing the American's inventiveness and requiring a refill of wine. By the time Despres had had his fill of flattery, Stewart felt exhausted and slightly drunk.

When the appetizer appeared—a cold fish soup of some kind—the president launched into a long, rambling defense of his administration and the wonderful things it had done for the country. He was a great patriot, loved by his people, but misunderstood abroad. All the problems of El Coronado could be laid at the doorstep of his enemies, who were jealous of his popularity and his achievements.

The President talked almost nonstop for nearly an hour, ignoring his lunch entirely. With the arrival of dessert he finally wound down and Stewart began his pitch.

"I come to you, Your Excellency, in the hope of getting your blessing for a clinic and a research laboratory that my company, Stewart Biotech, would like to open here in the near future."

The president raised a languid eyebrow. "And why have you chosen our little island for this?"

"Because this facility will be run by Dr. Harold Goth, the American scientist whom you have so graciously allowed to use your medical school for his research. He assures me this island is the perfect place."

"Does he?" The president's tone was mildly ironic.

"He said that if it hadn't been for your understanding, for your generosity and support, the important breakthroughs he's been able to make in his research would most likely never have happened. Now our company wishes to underwrite Dr. Goth's research so that he may accelerate his efforts."

The American continued his pitch. While careful not to refer directly to the island's abysmal condition, Stewart painted a glowing picture of the economic vitality that the president, with his help, could bring to his country if His Excellency was willing to give him a free hand. Goth's laboratory and clinic would eventually be expanded, he said. A constellation of special clinics would then be built, and they would, beyond any doubt, soon attract a great number of the world's richest and most important people. And these people would demand luxury hotels, restaurants, and stores to cater to their needs. El Coronado would eventually become one of the world's most exclusive resorts, and the islanders' standard of living would become the envy of the Caribbean.

But before any of that could happen, he explained, much had to be done. If the promise of Goth's research held up, then a substantial capital investment had to be made in the country's infrastructure. The airport had to be enlarged and modernized, the roads widened and repaved. This would cost many millions of dollars, which, despite His Excellency's already heroic achievements in improving the economy, the island obviously could not afford on its own.

But he, Dalton Stewart, could solve this problem. He could make this dream happen. He could find the investors and get their commitments. And even better, he could help His Excellency improve relations with the United States government. He even believed it was possible that he could help get U.S. aid flowing once again to El Coronado.

But to do all this, the president had to appreciate that he would need his full support and backing. He needed promises that bureaucratic obstacles would not be placed in his way, that red tape and the usual graft and corruption would be kept to a minimum, and that he would be allowed eventually to bring in thousands of foreign personnel to plan and execute these ambitious projects.

Stewart was careful to play to the president's vanity and greed and to make clear that Despres's ultimate authority would never be questioned or threatened in any way.

If Despres was excited by the scenario, he hid it well. "And what is it, exactly, about these clinics that will bring all these wonderful changes to this little island of ours?"

Stewart had anticipated the question. Obviously Despres already knew something of Goth's work, and he was certain to find out more as time went on. So it was important to tell him the facts. The president had many more questions, and it took over an hour for the American to answer them all.

By the time Dalton Stewart left the palace, a fresh

breeze had begun fluttering the palms along the avenue, lifting the oppressive weight of heat that had blanketed the island for the last three days. Behind the breeze, purplish black thunderclouds towered high over the western horizon, promising an imminent cloudburst.

Stewart climbed into the Land Cruiser, pulled off his white jacket, and sank back against the seat cushion. Trabert, the chauffeur, put the jeep in gear and accelerated cautiously down the street, steering between the potholes.

Ajemian looked at him inquiringly.

Stewart grinned. "The little bastard can hardly wait for us to get started."

His assistant settled his black leather attaché case on his lap and snapped it open. "Well, we've got bad news on a different front. I just got a call from the real estate agent. Baroness von Hauser made an offer on the medical school property this morning."

The news jolted Stewart. "How the hell did she manage that?"

Ajemian mopped his face with a damp handkerchief. "She offered a million two," he said. "With a cash binder of a hundred thousand."

Stewart fought down his anger. It was his own fault, he decided. After beating out the baroness's offer to Goth, he had assumed that she would just retreat from the field. He had underestimated the woman. "Who owns the place, anyway?"

"A local bank. It was a foreclosure. Sort of. What really happened is that the government confiscated it and turned it over to the bank. The bank, as you might guess, is owned by President Despres."

Ajemian tucked the handkerchief back in his pocket and handed his boss a thick stack of overnight faxes from the New York office. To each item Ajemian had attached a sheet suggesting appropriate or alternative actions to be taken. He uncapped a pen and handed it across with the memos.

Stewart looked at the pile with distaste. He wanted to focus on the threat posed by the baroness. "Any urgent stuff here?"

"No. Routine."

Stewart worked swiftly through the pile, scribbling his decisions on Ajemian's sheets as he went.

"We could still make a higher offer," Ajemian suggested. "Nobody's signed any contracts yet."

Stewart thought for a minute. "No. Let's let it go. In fact, it may be a break. It'd take too damned long to rehabilitate that property anyway. You saw it. It's a dump. Most of the buildings are ready for the wrecking ball. Let the baroness have it. We'll just relocate Goth to a better spot."

Ajemian looked at his boss questioningly. "Where?"

"There's a small private hospital on the other end of the island," Stewart said. "What's it called . . . ?"

"St. Bonaventure?"

"That's it. Good location, not too big, relatively modern. Let's buy it and turn Goth loose in it. Make him head of it, if we have to."

"Will he go along?"

"Why shouldn't he? It'll be ideal for him—air-conditioned research labs, clinics, the works. Find out who owns the place and set up a meeting."

Dalton Stewart handed the pen and the stack of memos back to Ajemian, who promptly returned them to the attaché case and closed the lid.

The skies suddenly opened up. Sheets of tropical rain cascaded like a waterfall against the windows of the jeep. Thunder and lightning boomed and crackled over the island like an artillery bombardment.

Stewart was pleased with his solution. He was going to stick the baroness with a worthless piece of real estate, just when she thought she had found a way to trump his deal with Goth.

But she had thrown him a scare. And he knew he had not heard the last of her.

Joseph Cooper awoke to hear the faint beeping of his satellite telephone, lying on the night table by his hotel bed. He picked it up. "Hello?"

"Mr. Stare?"

"Speaking."

"Please call your father."

Cooper muttered a groggy "Thank you," but the voice had already vanished into the ether.

He dialed a memorized number located somewhere in Fairfax County, Virginia, and waited. The "call your father" business was a simple security precaution—a way for his control, a man he knew only by the name Roy, to make certain that it was Cooper on the other end of the line.

"Stare? You there?"

"Yes."

"Goth is moving."

"Oh?"

"St. Bonaventure Hospital. Do you know where it is?"

"Yes."

"Check it out, please."

"You want it bugged, too?"

"That would seem appropriate."

"Yeah. Okay. . . ."

10

The baroness loved decisive moments.

Her opponent at the other end of the tennis court was Hans Dieterbach, secretary of foreign economic aid and development in the German government.

Dieterbach had played her even, six games apiece, and they were now playing a tiebreaker for the set. The score stood at 8–7. The baroness was serving.

Despite the chilly spring day, Dieterbach, a muscular man in his late forties, was sweating profusely. He had expected to win without much effort and had been irritated to discover that it was all he could do just to stay in the game.

Crouched at the baseline, waiting for her to serve, the sturdy German official looked stricken. His normally florid features had turned ashen. His mouse-brown hair, dripping with sweat, lay slicked back against his skull, as if he had just emerged from the shower.

The baroness bounced the ball on the baseline with a delicate, taunting leisureliness, giving Dieterbach plenty of time to reflect on his situation. She looked across at her opponent and smiled to herself. The possibility of losing to a woman would be causing him great stress. She tossed the ball skyward, arched her back, and swept the racket back far behind her head, as if to deliver an overhead smash. Instead, she sliced, whipping the racket face across the ball in a furious glancing blow, imparting tremendous spin but very little forward motion. The ball came off her racket strings whirring like a gyroscope and began losing altitude before it had even reached the net.

Dieterbach, expecting a deep drive on first service, was momentarily paralyzed, thinking she had mishit the ball and that it was destined to fall short. By the time he realized what was going to happen, it was too late for him to save himself.

He lunged forward, his face a mask of acute desperation. The tennis ball, dropping almost vertically, struck Dieterbach's side of the court about a foot from the net. Its spin caused it to bounce hard and low to Dieterbach's right, on a course parallel with the net and well below the top. Even if he had been able to reach the ball in time, its trajectory made it virtually impossible to return.

The secretary made the maximum effort nevertheless. When he saw he wasn't going to get to the ball in time, he launched himself into a dive. His racket went flying, and his 220-pound bulk pitched headfirst into the net.

The baroness suppressed her amusement. She recovered his racket, which had fallen into her back court, and carried it around to the other side of the net. Her opponent was still lying facedown in the dirt. "Are you all right, Herr Dieterbach?"

The secretary braced himself on one knee, then stood up, tottering and off-balance. He brushed off his shirt and shorts and took his racket back from the baroness. "I slipped," he complained. "Your damned clay court. I'm used to the all-weather."

"I'm sorry my court isn't up to your standards," she teased, walking alongside him.

Dieterbach snorted. "You're not sorry at all."

The baroness nodded. "You're quite right, Herr Secretary. I'm not sorry at all." She glanced at her watch. "Time for lunch."

They strolled up the winding path from the tennis court toward the back entrance of the eighteenth-century castle that served as the baroness's country retreat. The huge stone edifice, Schloss Vogel, was located in the mountains of the Bayerischer Wald, eighty miles north of Munich. The baroness kept a town house in Munich, where her company's headquarters were located, but she spent much of her time here at the castle.

The baroness served the secretary sandwiches and wine in an enclosed glass terrace she had had constructed on one of the castle's higher ramparts. From this lofty height they could dine and view the surrounding mountains and valleys for many miles.

Dieterbach eyed the baroness appreciatively across the small table. He had made advances toward her in the past, and she had deflected them each time; but he hadn't yet given up hope.

"I have a favor to ask," she said, refilling his glass.

"I expected you would."

The baroness batted her eyes flirtatiously. "I do enjoy your company, too, Herr Dieterbach."

"Not as much as you could, Baroness."

"Don't be naughty. I have something serious to discuss."

"I'm listening."

"You know President Despres of El Coronado?"

"Yes. In our office he's referred to affectionately as 'that little black swine.' "

"He needs foreign aid."

"He needs a firing squad."

"Fifty million marks. That's all."

"Never. He's on the department's shit list. Right near the top, in fact."

"Take him off it, then."

"On what grounds?"

"I don't know. Recent evidence of reform. Whatever excuses you people traditionally make when you change your minds."

"You're a very cynical woman, Baroness."

"I'm a very practical, realistic woman."

"Why should we help him?"

The baroness explained about Goth's program. She didn't tell the secretary that Dalton Stewart had already beaten her out of it. She made it appear that the deal would be in the bag for her if Dieterbach could persuade his government to open the foreign-aid tap for Despres.

"Why not give him the money yourself? Fifty million? You can afford it."

"He's already extorting me to the hilt."

Dieterbach looked uncomfortable. "It won't look good. Despres is an international pariah."

"But you can do it, can't you? It's so little money."

The secretary rubbed his chin and thought about it. "I suppose I could hide it in a larger program—the Caribbean Development Fund. But I'll have to twist some arms even so."

The baroness smiled and patted Dieterbach's hand. "I knew I could count on you."

Dieterbach gave her a pleading look. "I don't have to be back in Berlin until tomorrow, and my wife's in England. . . ."

The baroness slapped his arm lightly. "No, no. I have a killing work load today. Look, when you've got this thing done for me, come back and we'll celebrate. How's that?"

Dieterbach persisted a few minutes longer, for his ego's sake, then gave up.

The baroness saw the secretary to the front portico, where his car was waiting.

"You're a most desirable woman," Dieterbach announced in a solemn tone.

"Thank you, Herr Secretary."

"But you're not at all what you pretend to be, are you?"

The baroness affected surprise. "What do I pretend to be?"

Dieterbach stared at her knowingly. "You have enviable public relations, I'll say that. The government should hire you to advise our diplomats. *Auf Wiedersehen.*"

The baroness went up to her study on the second floor. The arrogant bastard, she thought. Thinking he understood her. How little he really knew. His attitude tempted her to take him off her books altogether. As soon as he got the loan to Despres in the works, she'd review the situation. God, how much had she paid him in bribes these past three or four years? It must be over half a million marks. Still, Dieterbach did deliver. That was more than one could say about many government figures she'd dealt with over the years.

Karla Schmidt, her private secretary, came in. "Everything for this afternoon is on your desk, Baroness."

The baroness looked at the pile of correspondence and telephone slips. Several hours' work.

"Photographers are coming at two from that English magazine, Baroness. And Herr Hellmann from Deutschebank at three. Lotte Brandt about the new ad campaign at three-thirty. And a woman from Earthly Scents at four."

"What does she want?"

"A new perfume endorsement."

"Not another one?"

"You're enormously popular," Karla said.

"You think so?"

"You're a role model to women everywhere, Baroness."

"Do *you* think I'm a role model?"

Karla blushed. "Of course."

Karla had worked for her longer than any other secretary. She often wondered why the poor woman put up with her; she knew she was a slave driver.

By six o'clock the baroness had cleared the day's business. She summoned Karla back to her study.

"What about Stewart Biotech?" she asked. "Have you found out if it's a public company?"

"It's not, Baroness. The Stewart family owns eighty percent of the stock. The rest is in the hands of Stewart lawyers and Stewart's chief assistant, Henry Ajemian."

"That's a pity."

The baroness had for a while entertained the notion of trying a secret buyout of Stewart Biotech. She was still furious that Stewart had outmaneuvered her with Goth.

But she had hardly given up. The profit potential in Goth's program was simply enormous—far greater than anything she had ever invested in. Still, there was something bigger in Jupiter than money. If it worked, it would open up a new dimension in her life—something beyond the now well-worn satisfactions of international business and finance, or the invisible political power she was amassing. Jupiter represented an opportunity that was impossible to quantify. And it beckoned to her like some forbidden thrill, some ultimate kind of satisfaction beyond normal mortal experience. Jupiter was the chance to influence the human race in a way it had never been influenced before. It was the chance to play God.

But if she was going to get possession of it, she knew she'd have to scramble. She had underestimated this Dalton Stewart. He was smarter than she had thought.

The baroness sighed at her own Machiavellian scheming. How naturally the determination to dominate others came to her. She had spent a lifetime perfecting it.

She said good night to her secretary, spent a few minutes reviewing some papers, and then turned off the desk lamp. She leaned back in her big leather swivel chair and stared at the painting on the wall. It was the work of an obscure artist from the late medieval period and depicted the Virgin Mary holding the baby Jesus to her breast. Mother and child both wore halos. It was pretty standard stuff from the period, and not terribly well executed at that. But something about it spoke to the baroness. Perhaps it was the expression of suffering on the faces of mother and child. The painting reminded her of the trauma her birth had caused her own mother—the woman had nearly bled to death—and the disappointment she had caused her father, who had wanted a son.

She grew up wanting to be a boy; it was the central emotion of her childhood. She had prayed that she would wake one day and find that God had made a mistake and that she was a boy after all. Because boys were strong and girls were weak. If she had been born a boy, her father would not have taken everything from her— her childhood, her virginity, even her fertility. The shame of those years burned in her still. She had wanted so much to love him, but he had made her hate him instead.

No one defended her through those years—no one, not her mother, not the servants, not her governess. No one. Her father ruled. Everyone was terrified of him.

Outside the household it was the same. Wilhelm von Hauser was far too important a personage in the community for anyone to risk his displeasure. Even the family physician—a despicable little toad of a man—colluded against her. He treated her for venereal disease. How old was she then—ten? He arranged an illegal abortion when she was only thirteen. The doctor who performed it was a drunk. She found out when she was twenty-two that he had so scarred her uterus that she could never have any children.

Survival demanded strength, so Gerta became strong. She learned how to kill her emotions. And she learned how to be patient. And one day her prayers were answered.

When her father was sixty-six, he had a stroke that left him paralyzed and confined to a wheelchair. He remained alert and conscious, but he was unable to move or speak.

She was appointed his legal guardian. Since she would inherit his majority interest in Hauser Industries upon his death, she convened the board and had herself named the company's new CEO. There was little opposition. She had already proved herself in the business world, and no one doubted that she was capable of running the company at least as well as her father had.

Next, she fired all the top management—all the people who owed their positions to her father—and replaced them with new people, loyal to her.

When she had consolidated her position in the company, she turned her attention to her father. She devoted herself to showing him just what it meant, just what it felt like, to be at someone else's mercy—someone who had been taught cruelty from an early age. He learned a lot in those last days—about helplessness, about suffering. About pain.

She kept him alive for six more months; then she let him go. No man was ever happier to die.

Baroness von Hauser walked over to one of the study windows and opened it. A chill breeze ruffled the drapes. The thousand acres of field and forest that comprised the estate of Schloss Vogel lay invisible below her in the darkness of the new moon.

She was emotionally dead inside. She regretted the loss, but it was the only way she could ever have survived. She liked to think of her unwillingness to feel love or compassion as a rare kind of strength. Love meant vulnerability, after all; and to be vulnerable was to negate the very purpose of her life, which was to rise to a position of such power that she could never be made vulnerable to anything or anyone again. Ever.

11

What a terrible way to get pregnant, Anne thought. It was like a rape in slow motion.

Looking down, she saw her spread thighs and bare knees gleaming unnaturally white in the bright bath of light over the operating table. Her feet were hooked in the table's stirrups, and Dr. Harold Goth sat on a stool positioned between them, clad in surgical green gown and cap.

He was slowly inserting a long, flexible probe into her vagina. She could see his latex-gloved hands twisting it steadily forward, and she could feel its hard, unyielding foreignness as it penetrated deeper inside her. Beside him was a small video monitor that allowed him to follow the progress of the probe with ultrasound.

"Relax," Goth commanded. "Don't tense your muscles."

He sounded irritated. But of course that was the way he sounded most of the time. He had explained the entire procedure to her, but not voluntarily. She had had to drag the details out of him over a period of days. He seemed from the outset to have adopted the attitude that the matter was really none of her business.

She almost wished now that she didn't know what he was doing. It was only making her more anxious.

Anne Stewart had found it hard to like Dr. Harold Goth. He was a stiff, introverted man with little warmth or charm.

She had spent the better part of four days at Dr. Goth's unfinished clinic in the new wing of St. Bonaventure's Hospital, where he had subjected her to seemingly endless batteries of tests and injections.

During those long hours in the clinic, she had tried to engage Goth in conversation on topics like music and literature. He wasn't much interested. The only thing she found out was that he had a passion for Sherlock Holmes—a subject about which she knew nothing. Her attempts to impress him with her knowledge of biology had made him even more uncommunicative.

He did discuss the fragile X syndrome with her. He explained how he would extract the DNA from her fertilized egg, how he would isolate the gene on the X chromosome that carried the faulty DNA sequence, and finally how he would use restriction enzymes to surgically splice and replace the area of faulty sequence.

She tried to draw him out as well about the so-called Jupiter program—the collaborative venture in which he and her husband were so deeply involved. But the mere mention of the subject seemed to make him nervous. He would only mutter something about "extensive gene therapy," or that it was all "too technical for the layman to understand." He finally got her off the subject for good by telling her that his contract with Stewart Biotech did not allow him to discuss Jupiter with anyone.

"But I'm the wife of the man financing your work," she protested.

Goth just pushed his eyeglasses back up the bridge of his nose and glanced away. "Then let your husband tell you."

Today the doctor was collecting her eggs. ("Harvesting your oocytes" was the phrase he had used; it made her think of the eggs as ripe little pumpkins.) Over the last several days her ovaries had ben stimulated by injections of Pergonal to increase the egg production, and now Goth was performing what he called a "transvaginal aspiration." Using the ultrasound monitor as a guide, he directed the probe into the vagina, up through the cervix, uterus, and fallopian tube all the way to the left ovary, suspended in the body cavity just outside the horn-shaped open end of the fallopian tube. One by one he burst the follicles surrounding the ripe eggs with the probe's needle and gently vacuumed the eggs into the probe. The eggs traveled back through the probe and out along a length of thin tubing into a suction trap.

Even with the light anesthesia he had given her, the pain caused by the procedure was considerable. The nurse standing behind her mopped her brow with a cool, damp cloth. Anne tried to distract herself by focusing on the suction trap. It consisted of a small glass test tube with a two-holed stopper in the top. The tubing from the probe was pushed just inside one of the holes. A second piece of tubing ran out from the other opening to the suctioning device. When the suctioned eggs reached the trap, they simply settled to the bottom. She wished she could see the eggs, but they were much too small—a mere two-hundredths of an inch in diameter.

As uncomfortable as the harvesting of the eggs turned out to be, it was a pleasure compared with the harvesting of Dalton's sperm the day before.

She and Dalton had had sex the night before in their hotel suite, and Dalton had made a big fuss about having to use a condom. He had had a difficult time getting it on, and an even more difficult time removing it. The whole business had been messy, time-consuming, and exasperating. It had put her on edge and made him angry. And of course it had ruined the sex.

Dalton stored the sperm-filled condom overnight in a glass jar in the hotel suite's refrigerator and presented it to Goth the next morning at the hospital. The doctor gazed incredulously at the rubber prophylactic lying at the bottom of the jar. He told Dalton that he had done exactly the wrong thing. He needed *fresh* sperm, and preferably after a day's *abstinence*. How many times had he told him that? But it was too late now. The procedure had to be done within the next few hours, no matter what. He directed Dalton to go immediately into the bathroom and masturbate into a plastic container.

Dalton was appalled by the idea. He was damned if he would do anything of the kind, he said, with everyone in the place standing around waiting for him. Goth insisted. Dalton still refused.

Anne finally saved the situation by forcing a compromise. If she and Dalton could have the use of one of the hospital rooms for half an hour, she would help him collect the sperm.

An empty room with a hospital bed was quickly found, and Anne and Dalton went inside and closed the door. Neither was in the mood for civil conversation, let alone sex. But it was a crisis, and something had to be done.

Since Dalton was unwilling to masturbate on demand, Anne did it for him. After a prolonged, sweaty effort, she succeeded in getting a quantity of her husband's semen into a plastic container.

The episode led to a bitter argument later.

"That was the single most embarrassing damned thing I've ever been through," he told her. "I hope the hell you appreciate it."

Anne was stunned. "*Appreciate* it? Do you have any idea of what Goth's putting *me* through? Don't you think I feel just as degraded by the experience as you? How selfish can you be?"

"You're the one who insisted on a child."

Anne swelled with fury. For the first time she actually felt a powerful dislike for her husband. "You bastard," she shot back. "You're the one who lied to me about the embarrassing condition of your genes."

She had never called anyone a bastard before, let alone belittled a physical shortcoming. She had wounded him deeply, and she knew it.

They eventually apologized to each other, but the damage had been done. The incident created a permanent distance between them, and it frightened her, especially when they had just made such an effort to reconcile their differences and commit themselves to having this child.

Anne looked down at the doctor again, bent to his task with his characteristic nervous intensity. The paper mask over his nose and mouth were causing his eyeglasses to cloud up. He removed them, wiped them hastily on his sleeve, and hooked the temples back over his ears.

She felt his hand pressing on her lower stomach. "You'll feel a little pain," he warned her. She closed her eyes and bit her lip.

In two days, she would have to come back for a second procedure—the reinsertion of her fertilized eggs into her fallopian tubes. Goth had explained to her what would happen in the meantime. Tonight, her eggs would be mixed with Dalton's washed sperm in a specially prepared medium and left to fertilize in a petri dish. The newly fertilized eggs would be allowed to divide three times. Then they would be frozen with nitrogen gas. Samples of their DNA would be removed from the cells; the flawed segment of DNA on Stewart's X chromosome that produced the fragile X syndrome would be cut out and the altered DNA spliced in its place. The fertilized eggs, or zygotes, containing their new pieces of DNA, would then be thawed out and allowed to continue dividing.

In a procedure called ZIFT (zygote intrafallopian transfer) Goth would make a tiny incision in Anne's stomach and insert a laparoscopic syringe loaded with the altered zygotes through her stomach wall to the open end of her left fallopian tube. There the eggs would be squirted into the tube and allowed to drift down through it toward the uterus. In about two days the eggs would begin arriving in the uterus. With any luck at least one of the zygotes would adhere to the wall of the uterus and start growing. Of course it would be much easier to squirt the eggs directly into the uterus through the cervix, Goth told her; that was the normal in vitro fertilization method. But impregnation rates were low. The ZIFT procedure more closely approximated nature and avoided irritating the uterus. Impregnation rates were much higher. That was especially important, he said, given the great amount of time and expense involved in retrieving, fertilizing, and genetically altering the eggs.

The sedative Goth had given her finally began to take effect. She was becoming light-headed, almost giddy. She could still feel a slight cramping pain from the probe as he worked it deeper into her lower abdomen, but now she felt insulated from it, almost as if it were happening outside her body.

Her mind drifted. She wondered about Goth. Why was he in El Coronado? A scientist of his stature should be associated with some prominent research center, not a small Catholic hospital on a remote Caribbean island.

She thought about Dalton. It was typical of him, refusing to disclose any details about Goth and the Jupiter project. He had never liked her inquiring into his business affairs. When they were first married it had hardly mattered. But as it became clear that Dalton's whole world revolved around his business, for him not to share anything about it with her was in effect to cut her off from everything that really interested him. And she was particularly annoyed in this case. She did, after all, have a degree in biology from the University of Vermont. She was far better able to understand what Goth was about than most people were, including her husband.

His refusal to involve her in matters of his company's business, or even take her into his confidence, left them with nothing to talk about, nothing to get excited about, nothing to share. And it left Anne frustrated. She would have been so happy to have taken a lab job at Stewart Biotech—any job. But Dalton still wouldn't hear of it

What kind of father would Dalton be? she wondered.

Anne opened her eyes and blinked in the bright light. She felt extremely groggy. Had she been unconscious? Dr. Goth was standing up and pulling off his latex gloves.

What a terrible way to get pregnant, she thought again. And what a terrible time to get pregnant—just when her marriage was beginning to feel as fragile as her husband's X chromosome.

Dalton Stewart followed Goth's research assistant, Kirsten, into the hospital cafeteria. He poured himself a diet cola and watched her carry her tray to a seat by a window against the far wall. It was the middle of the afternoon, and the place was almost deserted. He walked over to her table.

"May I sit down?"

She peered up over her glasses with a suspicious frown.

"I'd like to talk to you," he said.

"Okay."

"What's your last name, by the way?"

"Amster."

"German?"

"Danish." She took a bite from her sandwich.

"How long have you worked for Goth?"

"Two and a half years." She obviously wasn't eager for conversation.

"You enjoy it?"

"No. What do you want?"

Stewart laughed in embarrassment. " 'Don't feed me any bullshit,' is that it?"

She nodded.

"I want to offer you a lab job with Stewart Biotech in New York. Are you interested?"

Kirsten took another bite of her food. "Should I be?"

"I'll triple your present salary. And give you a cash living allowance. New York is an expensive city."

"What's the catch?"

"That you don't tell Goth why you're leaving or where you're going?"

"That's all?"

"No. I need a little favor."

"Let me guess. You want a copy of the Jupiter program."

Stewart looked at her. She met his gaze head on. "That's it," he admitted.

"Okay. For ten thousand dollars."

"The job in New York is what I'm offering."

"I don't want the job," she said. "I want the money."

Greed was everywhere, he thought. "Well, maybe I'll just go and ask Goth for a copy."

She wasn't bluffed. "He won't give you one."

"Are you able to make a copy—without him knowing?"

"Absolutely."

"You ever make one for anyone else?"

"No. The earlier versions were no good, anyway."

"How soon can you do it?"

"Tomorrow or the day after."

"Okay. Forty-eight hours. I'll meet you right here."

"With ten grand?"

"With ten grand. If you leave the island immediately."

"Then I want twenty."

Stewart took a deep breath. "Fifteen. Take it or leave it."

Kirsten shrugged. "I'll take it. Plus plane fare to Miami."

"I'll bring you the damned ticket myself."

Summer and Fall, 1999

12

Dr. Paul Elder came around the side of his desk: "Please have a seat, Mrs. Stewart."

"Thank you."

Anne held out her hand and the doctor took it briefly. His appearance startled her. He was the sixth pediatrician she had interviewed, and he hardly fit her image of a doctor. He was unusually tall. She noticed that he had to duck under the door lintel when he came in. His hands were big, and his head was broad, with prominent cheekbones and a mane of glossy black hair. His gaze was intense. It would have been intimidating in the extreme if it were not for his relaxed manner and big, easy grin.

His chin and upper lip had shaving cuts on them (a tiny piece of toilet paper still adhered to one of the cuts), and his gray, pin-striped suit pants were wrinkled. He seemed disheveled in the absentminded way of someone who never thought about his appearance—or about himself. If Anne had met him outside his office, she would have guessed he was a man of the outdoors—a bush pilot—not a doctor.

He wedged himself into his chair and folded his hands in his lap. Anne suppressed a giggle. He looked so comically outsized for everything in the room, including his desk and chair.

His eyes dropped briefly to her stomach, then came back up to meet hers. "Four months? Give or take a week?"

Anne laughed. "Oh, you're exactly right. How can you tell? Everyone says I'm hardly showing anything at all."

He chuckled. "It's not really your tummy size I'm going by. It's more your face—your complexion, and a few other clues I'm not sure I can articulate easily. All I know is that you look like a woman four months pregnant. And you look—well, to use a very unmedical term—terrific."

Anne felt herself blush slightly.

Dr. Elder cleared his throat and became more business-like. "So I suppose you're checking me out?"

Anne patted her stomach. "I want the best doctor for her."

Elder locked his hands together across his chest and began twiddling his thumbs thoughtfully. "I'm wondering why you had an amnio."

"I beg your pardon?"

The doctor grinned apologetically. "I'm sorry. You seem to know you're having a girl, so I assumed you'd had amniocentesis. I was just wondering why."

"I wanted to make sure everything was okay."

"*Is* everything okay?"

"Yes. She's doing very well."

Dr. Elder was interrupted by his nurse-receptionist. She told him that a Mrs. Somebody was on the phone about her daughter—something about a drug problem. He excused himself to take the call.

It was the first of a series of telephone interruptions. Between them, Dr. Elder filled Anne in on his medical education and his experience. He had been a doctor for fourteen years but a pediatrician for only eight. He had started out as a research specialist but ended up feeling he wasn't doing anybody much good, so he retrained himself for pediatrics. He had never regretted the decision. "I love kids," he said simply.

Anne looked around the office. There were photos of children and drawings by children plastered on every available surface. "Are any of these yours?" she asked, nodding toward the walls.

"Nope. They're all patients." He grinned proudly. He pointed out some of the photographs and told her about the children in them. "A lot of these kids are from one-parent homes," he said. "And their mothers can't afford good medical care. Who can, these days? I sort of get to be a part-time father to some of them—mostly in the form of advice. For a lot of these kids, their biggest health problem is a bad home. I try to do what I can on that front, but needless to say, I can't do very much. It's frustrating."

He took another phone call. Two things were becoming clear: Dr. Elder was dispensing a lot of health care free, and he was overburdened with patients. The big waiting room outside was jammed with noisy children and their mothers. It looked and sounded more like an out-of-control day-care center.

Anne studied Elder. Not married, she thought. No time for a social life. No wonder he looks so unkempt. He takes care of everybody, but he doesn't have anyone to take care of him. She felt like getting up and tucking in his shirt for him and running a brush through his hair.

"I'm sorry," he said when he hung up.

"I feel I'm taking up too much of your time."

Elder laughed. "No, no. Today's a slow day. I just hope you don't mind a lot of interruptions. It drives some people crazy, I know."

He had no sooner said this than a piercing scream from the waiting room caused him to jump up and run out. He was gone for about fifteen minutes. She could hear him talking earnestly to someone on the other side of the wall.

Anne decided that she wanted him as her pediatrician. She already knew before she came in that he was widely respected. Now she knew that he was also kind, intelligent, caring, and unselfish. He was certainly a light-year's improvement on the doctor she had had growing up in Burlington, Vermont.

Elder's only drawback seemed to be that he was already so overworked. It would be a struggle just to get his attention. She had an almost irresistible impulse to run right out into the waiting room and offer him her help.

The doctor ducked back through the door and squeezed back behind his desk. His expression was grim. "That was Jason. Father's an alcoholic. He beats the poor kid—and his mother as well. They don't have a dime, and the social services people aren't very responsive. I've reported the case four times now, and nothing's been done. I'm trying to get someone to at least monitor the situation, until we can get a court order against the father."

"How horrible!" Anne was pleased, though, that the doctor was so open with her.

"I'm rambling on. Sorry. Do you have any other questions you want to ask me?"

Anne shook her head. "I want you to be my baby's doctor. If you can possibly find time for another patient."

Elder laughed. "I only work twelve hours a day. And I take every other Sunday off. Usually. So you see, I'll have plenty of time. Do you live nearby?"

"No. Lattingtown."

"Oh. Where is that?"

"Long Island."

Elder's eyes narrowed. "You really want to come all the way into Manhattan for a pediatrician?"

"Yes. I want the best."

Elder shook his head. "I'm not the best. There're a lot of good pediatricians around."

Anne decided it was time to explain why it was so important that her baby have the best doctor she could find. She told him about Dr. Goth's in vitro fertilization. "My husband's family has a history of something called fragile X syndrome. I assume you know what it is—a genetic abnormality on the X chromosome. It causes mental retardation. Dr. Goth said he could repair that defect. That's why we went to the trouble of having the procedure. Otherwise, we couldn't have had any children. Naturally, we're very concerned about the baby. . . ."

During the course of her explanation, Elder's friendly, interested manner evaporated. He was regarding her now with a disapproving frown. "Dr. Goth?" he repeated. "Harold Goth?"

"You know him?"

"I know who he is. Where was this procedure performed?"

Anne felt uncomfortable. His sudden hard tone of voice had put her on the defensive. "In the Caribbean. El Coronado."

Elder shook his head, incredulous. "El Coronado? Never heard of the place."

"Doctor Goth has a clinic there—at a hospital. . . ."

"Whose idea was this?"

"Idea? My husband's. Dr. Goth is working on something for one of my husband's companies. . . ."

"Who's your husband?"

"Dalton Stewart."

"Of Stewart Biotech?"

"Yes."

Elder slumped back in his chair and ran his hands along the armrests.

Anne was startled by his abrupt change of mood. "Is something wrong?"

"What did Goth do to you?" he asked.

"Just what I told you. He repaired the gene causing the fragile X."

"Is that all he did?"

"What do you mean?"

"He didn't tamper with anything else?"

Anne stared at Elder. Why had he turned on her like this? "No," she said, in a small voice.

"Are you sure?"

"Why would he? I don't understand."

Dr. Elder avoided her eyes. He stood up, indicating that the interview was over. "You and your husband can afford any pediatrician you want," he said. "A whole staff of them, if you feel like it. You don't need me."

Anne was stunned. "But I want you."

Elder opened the door to his office, inviting her to leave. "Sorry. I'm much too busy. Good day, Mrs. Stewart."

A minute later Anne found herself standing outside on West Seventy-ninth Street. She was trembling with hurt and anger. She couldn't remember a more devastating rejection in her life.

She thought they had been getting on so well. She had never met a doctor she had related to so immediately, so completely. Why had he become so suspicious of her all of a sudden? As if she were hiding something from him?

How dare he throw her out like that? She was strongly tempted to march back into his office and demand an explanation.

She felt betrayed. It was as if her trust had been violated. Some part of her recognized that her reactions were

ridiculously out of proportion to whatever offense he had
committed, but she simply couldn't help it. She wanted
the best for her daughter.

She groped in her purse for a tissue and couldn't find
one. Tears started rolling down her cheeks.

"Goddamnit," she said. Several passersby glanced in
her direction.

"Goddamnit," she repeated in a louder voice. "Goddamnit!"

13

Dalton Stewart came into Anne's bedroom. The curtains were still drawn, shutting out most of the morning's light and the sound of the strong, gusty wind that had begun rattling the windows and blowing the leaves off the trees. Anne was lying on her side, eyes closed. He bent down and kissed her lightly on the cheek.

She opened her eyes and squinted at the bedside clock. "You're dressed already? It's only seven."

"Gil's taking me to the airport."

"Where are you off to this time?"

"Miami. Then back down to El Coronado. How are you feeling?"

Anne laughed. "For godsakes, Dalton, I'm feeling fine. I'm getting up in a few minutes."

Dalton frowned disapprovingly. "Why don't you rest for another day?"

"I've been resting for two days. The doctor said I could get up as soon as I felt like it. Well, I feel like it."

"For my sake, then. Humor me."

Anne put her hand to her mouth and yawned. "Dalton, I'm not going to stay in bed just to humor you."

Dalton jammed his hands into his pants pockets and began pacing the room. "Damn it, Anne, why take any chances? You know how much this baby means to me."

Two days before, Anne had tripped on the attic stairs and taken a bad fall. She had sustained a few bruises, but that was all. And her gynecologist had assured her that the fetus hadn't been harmed.

Anne rolled over on her back, her eyes following Dalton as he opened one of the drapes to let the light in. "Well, guess what, Dalton. She means a lot to me, too."

"I know. I'm sorry."

"I promise I won't go up into the attic again, okay?"

"You ought to stay off stairs, period. The house has an elevator. Use it from now on."

"The elevator happens to be broken. And more dangerous than the stairs, anyway. The gardener got trapped in it last October, remember? It was three hours before anyone found him."

"I'll speak to Franklin. We'll get it fixed immediately. And I want you to have someone with you from now on. All the time."

"Like who?"

"I've asked Mrs. Corley to hire a professional nurse."

Anne threw off the covers and sat up. "Dalton, that's crazy. I'm not sick, I'm pregnant. I don't need a nurse."

Dalton came across the room and sat down on the bed beside her. "I don't want to have to worry about you all the time. If you won't have a nurse, then at least a bodyguard."

"It was an accident, Dalton. For godsakes! If someone were trying to hurt me, or the baby, they'd think of something a little more ingenious than putting a rod from an old barbell set on the top attic stair. The chances of me going up there were practically nil."

"But the fact is you did go up there."

"Why are you sniping at me like this, Dalton?"

"Because I'm depending on you to take care of the baby."

Anne started to reply, then changed her mind. She stormed into the bathroom and slammed the door behind her.

Dalton paced over to the window. Anne's defiant attitude was something new. And it both galled and depressed him. He pulled the curtains back further and stared out over the grounds. It had begun to rain. The wind spattered the drops against the glass, partially obscuring the view.

He had somehow expected that Anne would always be grateful to him for having plucked her from poverty and obscurity and introduced her to a world of security and privilege that most women would envy. But she was not grateful.

He supposed he had made a mistake in marrying her. At the time she had seemed perfect. She was young, beautiful, intelligent, vivacious—just the kind of wife a man in his position needed. A woman who could turn heads wherever they went.

But now all he saw were her shortcomings. And ingratitude was the least of them. She did nothing for him socially. Not having been brought up in a world of class and privilege, she was at a loss as how to function in it.

The situation had to change. Either Anne would have to take up their cause on the social front, or he would have to consider divorcing her. Christ, he'd been through two divorces already. He didn't know if he could stand another one. But he saw now that what he really needed was a woman of established social prominence, a woman with the right family and breeding, with the instinct and the desire to enhance his own image.

He knew he was being selfish. And he did still have strong feelings for Anne. She remained a most desirable woman. But he had to be hardheaded about these matters. It was his future, after all.

He would have to face the matter later—after the baby was born. Until then, Anne's welfare had to remain uppermost in his mind.

Anne emerged from the bathroom completely nude. This was unusual for her; she was naturally a modest person. She was still angry at him, so she was pretending he wasn't there. Her six months of pregnancy didn't show very much at all. She had gained a few pounds, especially around the middle, but otherwise her body looked as shapely and voluptuous as ever. He felt a sudden strong urge to make love to her. It was the only way he could think of to try to bridge the widening gulf between them. Was she trying to communicate the same desire to him? He didn't know, and he was afraid to ask. She was never very receptive after an argument, anyway, he told himself, and he absolutely couldn't risk doing anything that might threaten the pregnancy.

He tried to smooth things over. "I'm sorry, Anne. I

shouldn't be blaming anyone for anything. You know how I am. If I don't feel in control I don't feel comfortable. So I worry about you. And the baby. That fall of yours scared the hell out of me. I couldn't help thinking that you might have lost her. And I couldn't help thinking how devastating that would be. She'll likely be the only child the two of us can ever have."

Anne snapped her bra together. The apology seemed to soften her somewhat. "But I can't just stay in bed for the next two and a half months. We live in the real world—or at least a very privileged version of it. We can't command that nothing bad happen. We can't foresee or forestall everything. I might just have a miscarriage."

"Don't even mention the word."

Anne looked at him speculatively. "Well, if we are unlucky and something bad does happen, we can always get Dr. Goth to work his little magic again, can't we?"

"What do you mean, 'magic'?"

"What do *you* think I mean?"

Dalton averted his eyes. For one terrifying instant he thought she knew that Goth had used the Jupiter program on her. Could she have possibly found out? No. Goth would never tell her. And no one else knew.

He had wrestled with himself many times about whether he should let her in on the truth. Because it was really quite a remarkable, exciting thing that Goth was doing. But why risk scaring her? If the baby turned out to be as extraordinary as he expected, then let Anne be overjoyed at the results. If the fetus miscarried, or turned out less than perfect, then it was obviously better that she didn't know and blame the failure on Goth—and on him.

And it was really too late to tell her now, anyway. He had to focus on one single, crucial matter—making sure that nothing happened to Anne for the next ten weeks.

"Why don't you come down to El Coronado with me?" he suggested.

Anne paused midway in buttoning her blouse. "Why?"

"Then I won't worry so much about you. Goth can monitor you on a regular basis. In fact, you ought to stay the whole time. I'll rent out the whole top floor of the hotel."

"I don't want to spend two and a half months on that island. I'll go crazy. There's absolutely nothing to do."

"You're not supposed to be doing anything."

"Yes I am. I'm just starting on a plan to redecorate this house, for one thing."

"That can wait."

"Dalton, I don't like the island very much. And it's hardly a good place to be pregnant. I'm much better off here. The food and water supply are much more dependable, and so is the sanitation and the health care."

"You'll be staying in a luxury hotel, Anne, not a shantytown."

Anne shook her head. "The baby's safer if I stay here."

"On one condition, then. You accept a better security arrangement."

"Like what?"

"A twenty-four-hour personal guard service. And a nurse. Nobody has to be at your bedside. A nurse in the house, on call—that's all. And an armed bodyguard."

"No bodyguard."

"That's essential."

"My God, Dalton, we already have a million-dollar security system around this place! It's like a fortress. Who's the bodyguard supposed to protect me against? The household help?"

"Okay. Just in the house, on call. And to accompany you on trips."

Anne sat down heavily on the bed. Her anger had turned to dejection. Dalton sat beside her and put his arm around her. "It's only for a short time, Anne."

Anne stared across the room for a few seconds, then nodded. "Okay," she whispered.

Dalton tried to kiss her, but she turned her head away.

"What's the matter?"

"I'm not feeling very friendly, Dalton. I'm sorry. Just leave me by myself for a while. We can talk later."

"I won't be here later."

"Call me from Coronado, then."

Dalton stood up and headed for the door, burning with frustration. He realized that the fate of his child—and the enormous investment that was riding on that child—

depended more on her now than on him. And that, of course, made him dependent on her as well.

It was an intolerable state of affairs, but there wasn't anything he could do about it.

14

Karla ushered the visitor into the baroness's exercise room, a spacious, plush-carpeted area on the top floor of her Munich office building.

The baroness was working on her rowing machine. She was dressed in black tights under white cotton shorts and a loose tank top. Her blond hair was pinned up. She was rowing quite fast. A slight sheen of perspiration glowed on her neck and arms.

The visitor stood awkwardly on the carpet, not sure what to do. The baroness kept on rowing. She eyed him critically. His name was Otto Mossler. He was young and muscular—a jut-jawed, blond-haired Aryan type with sharp blue eyes and a surly demeanor. He was wearing a brown suit that fit him badly.

Mossler managed a small German trucking company, TransEurope Express, for his father. The baroness had employed him occasionally. TransEurope's trucks had illegally carted thousands of tons of highly toxic wastes from the baroness's laboratories and manufacturing plants to secret disposal sites in Eastern Europe.

Mossler was also one of the leaders of Neues Deutschland, the New Germany party, a right-wing, neo-Nazi movement that had gained steadily in popularity over the past decade. Once a refuge for the lunatic fringe, in 1999 the ND boasted a membership of two million and had been polling a respectable ten to fifteen percent in recent elections.

Mossler hesitated, made a curt bow, then stepped a little further into the room.

The baroness pointed to a weight bench. "Please sit

down, Herr Mossler. Your posturing is making me nervous."

Mossler sat on the bench.

"We've had a good relationship with your trucking company," the baroness said, still rowing energetically. "I expect soon to have need of some manpower to perform some discreet services for me. I wonder if you might be able to provide it?"

Mossler looked confused. "Discreet services?"

"Dirty work," the baroness replied bluntly. "Things that I cannot risk having traced back to me."

Mossler grinned. His eyes followed the motions of the baroness's breasts beneath the tank top. "Of course, Baroness. I can provide you with any service you like—dirty or otherwise."

"I'm glad to hear it. I'll need several men to travel to an island in the Caribbean. There's something in a medical laboratory there that I must have. They'll have to break in, find it, and bring it back to me."

Mossler's eyes widened in surprise.

"Does that sound too difficult?" the baroness challenged.

Mossler stuck out his chest. "Of course not."

"Good. Find the men. They must be completely trustworthy. I'll have a detailed plan for you in a few weeks."

Mossler nodded.

The baroness quickly changed the subject. "How are things at Neues Deutschland these days?" she asked.

"We'll one day be the most powerful political organization in Germany," Mossler boasted. "We have the right message. The people are beginning to listen to us."

The baroness got up off the rowing machine and dried her neck and arms with a towel. "But you still must need a lot of money to realize these ambitions."

Mossler said nothing.

"In return for these discreet services, I'm prepared to make a sizable donation."

"Thank you, Baroness. It will be greatly appreciated."

The baroness walked over close to Mossler, still sitting on the bench. "And it will be kept secret."

He looked up at her. "Of course."

"No one must know I've even met you. Do you follow me?"

Mossler shrugged. He looked unhappy. "If you insist."

"I do insist. If it ever gets out that we've had any dealings, that's the end. No more money. Is that clear?"

"Quite clear, Baroness."

"Good. I'm glad we understand one another." The baroness reached down and squeezed Mossler's bicep. He flinched in surprise. "You must be quite strong," she said.

Mossler flushed and grinned.

"Can you box?"

"Box? Sure. Karate too."

The baroness squared off in front of him. "Stand up. Let's see what you can do."

Mossler's jaw fell. "What? Against you?"

The baroness smiled invitingly. "Why not?"

Mossler got to his feet. "I might hurt you, that's why."

"Really?" she taunted. "Go ahead and try."

"I'd rather wrestle you," Mossler said, leering at her.

"Very well. Try to pin me down."

"This some trick?"

"Herr Mossler, I'm beginning to think you're a coward."

Mossler scowled. He pulled off his jacket. "I'll try not to hurt you." He hunched his shoulders and lumbered toward her, angling for a hold. The baroness avoided him easily.

Mossler pressed his attack, feinting and lunging to grab her waist or legs. She sidestepped him and slammed the edge of her palm against his ear. He fell sideways onto one knee, scrambled to his feet, and lunged again. His face was red, furious.

They circled each other. Mossler spun around and momentarily caught her neck with his arm. But she ducked under and rammed a fist into his solar plexus.

He gasped and staggered backward. The baroness whirled, brought a leg up and around, and smashed her instep against the back of his neck with enough force to send him sprawling. His foot caught the edge of the rowing machine and he crashed nose-first into the carpet. He took his time getting up.

The baroness buzzed her secretary. "Karla, please come up and show Mr. Mossler out. I'm going to take a shower."

Joseph Cooper got another midnight call from Roy. "We're getting a lot of interference on the bugs," Roy said. "Something electronic in the hospital."

"I'll replace them."

"Never mind. We need something else. Listen carefully."

"Go ahead."

"Goth uses a removable computer hard disk with an important program on it. When it's not in the computer, he keeps it locked up somewhere. It's a black plastic cartridge, six inches wide, two inches high, four inches deep. I want you to get it, copy it, and put it back. And under no circumstances must Goth find out. Can you do that?"

"It won't be easy. He hardly ever leaves the lab."

"New Year's Eve," Roy said.

"What about it?"

"He won't be there then. And hospital security'll be lax."

"What's on this disk?"

"That's none of your business."

"No. I guess not."

"When you have the disk, call me immediately."

That afternoon the baroness drove to her country estate, Schloss Vogel, and had dinner with two guests, Katrina Zymonywicz and Aldous Sikorsky.

She had found them in Warsaw two years earlier. They had been attached to a theatrical company that had gone out of business and were reduced to doing street performances to stay alive. Aldous was twenty-four then; Katrina, twenty-one.

The baroness was immediately taken by them. Blond, and slight of frame, they both looked like teenagers. They possessed a wonderfully innocent, androgynous quality that spoke to her.

They were street-smart and intelligent, but hedonists at heart. When the baroness was reasonably sure of their inclinations, she made them a proposal: Come back to Germany and live with her. She would guarantee them a luxurious, protected life, free of responsibility. In exchange, they were to provide the baroness with sex. They were to be hers exclusively—to be available to her whenever she wanted them. And everything she did with them was to be kept secret.

They turned her down.

She kept after them, and eventually persuaded them to come to Germany as her guests and give it a try.

The baroness, who fired servants and employees on a regular basis, hadn't expected the ménage to work out for very long, but so far it had. She knew that one day they would probably leave just as suddenly as they had decided to stay. In the meantime, she'd extract what pleasure from them she could.

Although the two were now permanent guests at Schloss Vogel, she rarely saw them except when she was in the mood for their services. And she preferred it this way. She was interested in them solely as a means of satisfying her carnal fantasies.

Sometimes she enjoyed directing them in various sexual acts with each other, or playing games of bondage and discipline. But usually all she wanted from them was simply a massage and a tongue bath, and they had become skilled at obliging her.

After dinner the three retreated to the baroness's bedroom on the third floor and removed their clothes.

Ecstasy took the baroness longer than usual to reach this particular night, because her head was filled with thoughts of Jupiter.

She had done all she could do about the situation. Now there was nothing left but to wait for the right moment. She was sure that moment would come, but the waiting frustrated her enormously. She was constantly second-guessing herself, wondering if she had overlooked anything, wondering if there might have been a better strategy. Stewart should play into her hands eventually, but in the meantime events were not completely under her control, and that always made her nervous. The longer the wait, the greater the chance of the unforeseen.

And the longer she had to wait, the more she lusted after Jupiter. It was meant to be hers.

She closed her eyes and willed her body to relax. Aldous and Katrina applied their tongues, lips, and hands to her flesh. They started at a very languid pace and gradually, imperceptibly increased the intensity, exploring every inch of her until she was shuddering with pleasure.

Finally, her nerve endings screaming for release, she cried out, tensed convulsively, and exploded in a long crescendo of rapturous spasms.

When her orgasm had subsided, Katrina and Aldous turned their attentions to each other.

The baroness lay back and watched them. Later, when she was ready, they would start in on her all over again. She would sleep well tonight.

December 1999

15

Dalton Stewart signed the last of a stack of real-estate contracts and leaned back against the limousine's plush seat cushions. Hank Ajemian took the pile and neatly stacked it inside his briefcase. They were on their way to pick up Anne at the island's airport.

She was now eight months into her pregnancy and doing splendidly. Her suite at the hospital was ready. Stewart had supervised the details of the renovation himself. It was a small luxury apartment within the confines of the hospital, with every amenity and every protection, from an elaborate electronics alarm system to a round-the-clock staff of nurses and bodyguards.

Stewart had had two limousines flown down from New York. One of them, complete with two shifts of drivers on twenty-four-hour standby, was exclusively for Anne. The moment she went into labor, she could be whisked the ten blocks from the hotel to the hospital in a matter of minutes.

The second limo was a stretch Mercedes SEL-660 and had cost him half a million dollars by the time the customizers at the body shop were through with it. It was armor-plated, with bullet-proof glass, puncture-proof tires, and a 450-horsepower truck engine. Its top speed was 140 mph. It got seven miles to the gallon. Stewart intended to give it to President Despres as a special gift at the opening ceremony for Goth's new hospital wing next week.

"How much land do we own?" Stewart asked.

"I get eight thousand five hundred and forty-five acres," Ajemian said. "That includes over a mile of beachfront. The best beachfront."

Stewart felt a surge of optimism. Despite the headaches involved in trying to operate in a country that barely qualified as a third-world dictatorship, his efforts were beginning to show results. "Not bad. I'm surprised Despres hasn't interfered more."

Ajemian scratched his jowls with the back end of one of his cheap ballpoint pens. He always carried a pocketful of them, along with his wads of Kleenex. Stewart had given him two gold-plated Mont Blancs, but Ajemian never used them. "One reason is that we bought a thousand acres from him," Ajemian said. "At a grossly inflated price. Another is that any time he wants he can just take it all back from us."

"He wouldn't dare. He's still counting on me to get the U.S. foreign aid taps flowing for him again. We'll just have to keep dangling that in front of him for a couple of years."

"Well, I strongly recommend we stop buying for the time being. The word is out, and prices are starting to shoot up."

Stewart watched out the window as the countryside flew past them. "Property's still a steal. And once we start developing, vacant land values—especially the oceanfront—will go way up. We'll be able to make back our investment just by selling off a few hundred acres. I tell you what. Let's buy another five thousand. Put together some big contiguous parcels on the other end of the island. After we finish on this end, we can build a new clinic out there and develop a second cluster."

Ajemian uncapped a ballpoint and started scratching numbers out on a pad. "We're running up debt too fast," he said. "The banks are going to cut us off. They think we're crazy doing this anyway. Our exposure is ridiculous."

"Have the banks ever been right about anything?"

Ajemian pulled a tissue from his pocket and wiped his nose. "I know. But we're really stretched thin, Dalton. We had massive debt going into this affair. And our earnings are way down. The banks just aren't buying our projections anymore. We should be belt-tightening, not throwing money around."

Stewart groaned impatiently. He sometimes found Ajemian's obsessive caution maddening. This was one of those times. "We've been through this all before. There will never be another opportunity like this, Hank. Not in our lifetime."

Ajemian squirmed uncomfortably in his seat. "I understand. Sure. But we can cash in on it without laying out any more capital now. There won't be any money coming in on this for at least a year. And that's only if nothing goes wrong. And something always goes wrong. We're skirting bankruptcy now. I mean it."

Stewart was tempted to tell Ajemian the truth about Anne's pregnancy. It might make him feel better about the amount of risk involved. But he decided against it. It had to remain his secret. "All right. Forget the five thousand acres."

They discussed other business matters. Ajemian read aloud from a pile of faxes sent down from New York earlier. Stewart dictated a reply for each, leaving it to his assistant to flesh them out.

Stewart gazed out the side window of the limousine as he listened to Ajemian read the faxes in his high-speed monotone.

Coronado's midday traffic was limited almost entirely to trucks, buses, and bicycles, but progress was slow and exasperating. The Avenida des los Mártires de la Revolución del Ocho de Noviembre, or Avenida Ocho for short, was in a sad condition, now more dirt than macadam. Added to the choking dust from the neglected pavement were the eye-stinging belches of diesel exhaust from the trucks and buses, the cacophony of beeping horns, jingling bicycle bells, and shouts of ragged children darting among the vehicles, hawking everything from cigarettes to sex.

The buildings along the boulevard had been built in the nineteenth century by the French, who governed the island for over a hundred years. The French left in 1967, and the country's entire infrastructure looked as if it hadn't seen a day's maintenance since. The stone and plaster façades of the once proud town houses were chipped and dirty, and the windows were missing shutters. Balcony railings were frequently collapsed or broken; chimney pots sagged at crazy angles; and many of the roofs had been repaired so many times over the years with such a wide assortment of different-colored materials that they looked like patchwork quilts. The sidewalks were thick with beggars and gangs of unemployed males with nothing to do. Street brawls, public drunkenness, and petty crimes were commonplace, even in broad daylight. Only the enormous posters and murals of President Despres looked fresh and new. His bulging, bespectacled eyes and self-satisfied grin were everywhere, gazing down on his poverty-stricken subjects like some giant cat watching mice in a cage.

Stewart imagined the new city that would eventually sweep much of this poverty and misery away. He saw high-rise hotels and office buildings, bustling streets full of markets and theaters and restaurants, all catering to the explosion of tourism that he was sure would soon transform this benighted backwater into a Caribbean paradise.

Things were rapidly falling into place. Goth's clinic was now up and running. In another month Jupiter's first pilot test program would begin. If all went well with that stage, then several teams of publicists and advertising specialists Stewart had already hired would begin the work of developing a selective campaign to market the program. The campaign would be very upscale. Details would be put out in the most discreet fashion possible, through a carefully screened list of prominent doctors who might be willing to refer their richest patients.

The doctors should be more than willing, Stewart guessed, since he planned to offer a finder's fee of $25,000 for each referral. Such a generous sum would be possible because he planned to charge the first couples $500,000 per treatment—payable in advance. The rich wouldn't quibble with the price. Indeed, their ability to afford such an expensive medical service would in itself be a status symbol. And having a genetically superior child would be, among other obvious advantages, the very ultimate status symbol. Stewart anticipated a sizable waiting list within months.

At its present size and staff level, Goth's clinic would

be able to handle comfortably a dozen couples a week. That would generate grosses in the neighborhood of $25 million a month. Within the first year Stewart planned to expand the clinic to handle as many as forty-eight couples a week. That would quadruple income to around $100 million a month. The procedure was a relatively expensive one, since each treatment required extensive DNA analysis and genetic surgery; but at those rates the profit margins would still be enormous. Start-up and development costs would be earned out in the first two or three weeks of operation. After that, salaries and operating expenses would consume less than two or three percent of the gross take each month. Bribes, commissions, finder's fees, and local "taxes" to Despres would eat up another three to four percent. That left a net profit per month in the range of $90 million.

There would be no U.S. taxes. The money would be channeled into a foundation that Ajemian had established for the purpose called the Coronado Genetic Research Institute. The institute would keep its money in bank accounts already set up for it in Panama, the Bahamas, Switzerland, and Liechtenstein.

After a few years, when the carriage trade began to thin out, Stewart would build a series of satellite clinics around the island and set lower prices so that the world's vast middle-class market could be tapped. Fees could then be lowered to something like fifty thousand dollars per treatment.

The details of the broader marketing program would all be carefully worked out at the appropriate time. But one thing was certain: if the formula worked as Goth claimed, it would generate more money than any single product or service ever offered to anybody anywhere. There were many millions of potential customers. Stewart estimated the program could gross as much as a trillion dollars in its first decade. It was an absurdly astronomical sum, but he and Ajemian had brainstormed it several times. He estimated that in those ten years he could plausibly increase his own personal worth to two hundred billion dollars.

Two hundred billion dollars.

It would be the financial killing to end all financial

killings—one of the greatest transfers of wealth in history. In one decade it would make him the richest person on earth—arguably the richest individual who had ever lived. Since no one had ever accumulated that much wealth, there was nothing to compare it to, no way to measure its potential. But it would be breathtaking. The prospect made him giddy.

A permanent financial arrangement still remained to be hammered out with Goth, but Stewart saw no special difficulties in that area. Goth was as happy these days as a six-year-old on Christmas morning. Stewart Biotech had come to his rescue, and Stewart was counting on the likelihood that Goth would not want to see that relationship terminated. Once Goth had the women in the pilot program pregnant, Stewart would close a deal with him. He would offer him a fat yearly salary and expense account, plus a two-percent share of net profits from Jupiter. This would very quickly make the doctor very rich.

If Goth was greedy and held out for more, Stewart would be generous and up the doctor's percentages a fraction, but he wasn't about to make any major concessions. He wouldn't have to. He had the doctor in a legal and moral armlock. The new foundation owned the hospital and everything in Goth's labs. And all relevant government officials—including President Despres himself—were now on the foundation's payroll. If Stewart chose, he could kick the doctor off the premises—shut him out completely—and there wouldn't be a thing Goth could do about it.

The one potential threat—Baroness von Hauser—seemed to have vanished without a trace. That bothered him. The baroness had a reputation for persistence.

The next few weeks would be an extremely anxious time. He had overextended himself perilously, as Ajemian continually reminded him. If Jupiter was a failure, he'd be in trouble.

Everything now depended on that child growing inside Anne's womb.

16

Anne Stewart propped another pillow under her neck and sank back against the sofa, trying to find a more relaxed position. She rested her hands on her swollen belly and took a deep breath. The pregnancy had gone so fast and so smoothly, she found it hard to believe that the baby would soon be due. Despite the tensions with Dalton, she had never known a more serene period in her life.

Lexy Tate spread some beluga caviar on a triangle of toast and offered it to her. The hotel had sent up a table loaded with a variety of treats and delicacies, and Lexy was determined to take advantage of it.

Anne shook her head. "No thanks. I'll never develop a taste for that stuff."

"Pity," Lexy replied. She made a wolfish grin and stuffed the wedge greedily into her own mouth.

Anne felt a twinge of guilt. On her invitation, Lexy had come to El Coronado two weeks ago, moving into a suite on the same floor of the hotel as the Stewarts. She had planned to fly home to New York yesterday; but since the birth was now so close, Anne had begged her to stay on until the baby was born.

"The biggest New Year's Eve in a thousand years and he goes to a party without you," Lexy said. "I think it's pretty shabby."

"You know how he is about me taking chances. He still hasn't gotten over the attic stairs incident."

"That's no excuse. You're completely ambulatory. There's no reason he couldn't have taken you. My mother, for godsakes—she played golf right up until her water broke. She insisted on finishing the round before she'd let them take her to the hospital. I was born in the golf cart on the way back to the clubhouse."

Anne laughed. "You were not. You were born in Doctors' Hospital on Manhattan's Upper East Side. And your mother was in labor for twenty-three hours."

"Who told you that?"

"Your mother."

"She's a terrible liar."

"Why didn't *you* go with Dalton?" Anne demanded. "He did ask you."

Lexy piled caviar on another piece of toast. "He was straining to be polite."

"I hate for you not to be out celebrating because of me."

Lexy shrugged. "I really don't mind. I've been to enough parties—New Year's and otherwise—to last me until the *next* millennium. I've seen it all. And felt it all too. I was once goosed at a dinner party by the President of the United States—did I ever tell you that? I've also been groped under the table by a Belgian ambassador, and been barfed on by a senator from a state I won't name. Jesus, that guy was a jerk! And I once danced cheek-to-cheek with a president of Italy, who whispered obscene suggestions in my ear. At least I think they were obscene; my Italian isn't that great. Oh, and I once let an English MP have his way with me in a third-floor bedroom of my parents' house. That was a drunken New Year's Eve a very long time ago."

"Which Italian president was it?"

Lexy stuck out her tongue. She grabbed the TV remote, punched the On button, and began flicking impatiently through the channels.

All stations were focused on the impending Big Event. One channel was covering street parties in the capitals of Europe, where the early morning hours of January 1, 2000, had already arrived; another was interviewing the leader of a group of end-of-the-worlders standing vigil on a snow-swept mountaintop in Northern California; a third was running a documentary reviewing events of the past hundred years. On a fourth station a moderator was asking a panel of distinguished academics to predict what the next thousand years might have in store.

The panelists' predictions were not upbeat. The consensus was that Homo sapiens was in for some hard years. Man had so plundered and fouled the planet during the century now ending that the only real hope for the future seemed to lie in a quick and substantial reduction in the human population. The betting of the panel was that the early decades of the next century would witness a kind of apocalypse in slow motion, in which crime, disease, war, starvation, and environmental catastrophes would proliferate to such a degree that the human species, like an insect that had exceeded the carrying capacity of its habitat, might experience a massive dieback. Estimates of the size of the decline varied among the panel members from twenty to sixty percent of the earth's present population.

"That's a lot of funerals," Lexy said. "I should tell my broker to get me into mortuary stock."

Anne didn't laugh. There was so little good news these days. It was depressing to be reminded of the state of the world into which her daughter was about to be born.

The litany of horrors was lengthy. The TV panelists unburdened themselves like prosecution witnesses testifying to the criminal depredations of the human race. The evidence of guilt they presented was overwhelming.

"God, what a bummer," Lexy mumbled. She flicked through the channels again, and left the set tuned to the station broadcasting the European parties. "Might as well get drunk—what do you say?"

Anne rubbed her stomach. "Not supposed to."

"One little drink won't hurt. Especially at this late date. Come on. The hotel's left us a whole case of Dom Pérignon. A whole case! How many chances are you going to get to celebrate the beginning of a new millennium?"

Lexy went to the refrigerator in the suite's small kitchen and returned with a bottle and two champagne glasses. She popped the cork expertly and tipped the fizzing liquid into the glasses.

"Here's to that baby of yours, Genevieve Alexandra

Stewart," Lexy said, holding up her glass. "May she be as sweet and beautiful as her mother, and as big a smartass as me." Lexy drained her glass and refilled it. "How did you settle on the name Genevieve, by the way?"

"She was the patron saint of Paris. And I've always loved the sound of the name. I'm not sure why, but it makes me think of beauty and strength. I knew that if I had a girl she'd have to be a Genevieve."

Anne took a tentative sip of champagne and then suddenly stopped, as if she had heard something. A look of absolute astonishment transformed her features. She put her glass down, sat up, and leaned forward. "Oh my God," she whispered.

Lexy jumped up. "What? What's the matter?"

"My water just broke!"

At 10:45 P.M. Heinz Hoffmann wheeled the rented van into the hospital parking lot and parked it next to the new wing that housed Dr. Harold Goth's laboratory.

Hoffmann and his two partners, Dolf Greiner and Ernst Feldmann, had been in Coronado for three days, casing the hospital and working out a plan of attack.

Greiner, sitting on the passenger side, rolled down his window. It was a cloudless night, with no moon. The breeze off the ocean was damp and a little chilly. Light blazed from the windows of Goth's wing.

Feldmann, sitting in the middle, bent his head forward to peer out the windshield. "The stupid pig is still working in there," he said. "On New Year's Eve."

Hoffmann looked at his watch. "We'll just have to wait."

"What if he doesn't leave?"

"He's got to leave sometime."

Dalton Stewart pushed his way through the crowd toward one of the bars. Hundreds of guests in formal evening dress milled about, shrieking and laughing and bumping into one another.

The decibel level, building steadily since the early evening, was inching into the red zone. The orchestra, set up on a low stage at the far end of the palace's gigantic ballroom, was playing something, but Stewart couldn't hear a note. The thirty-foot-high ceilings and marble walls echoed and amplified every noise into a smothering, cacophonous din. He wished he had brought ear plugs.

Famous faces seemed to beam at Stewart from every direction—ambassadors, American congressmen and senators, movie stars, European royalty, jet-setters. Stewart was amazed that President Despres could command such a glittering attendance.

After a long wait amid a forest of outstretched arms and beseeching voices, Stewart rescued a scotch and soda from an overworked bartender at one of the dozens of bars scattered about the rooms of the main floor. Coddling the drink close to his chest, he maneuvered back through the crush of bodies, nodding and grinning absently as he went. He pushed open one of the French doors at the far end of the ballroom and stepped outside onto a large stone terrace.

From this side of the palace, the view was breathtaking. Across an immense sweep of lawn, the Caribbean sparkled darkly under the stars. A warm, soft breeze rustled the neat rows of palms that formed a border between the lawn and beach.

In less than one hour a new millennium would begin. It had been talked about so much in the past weeks and months, and examined so exhaustively by the media, that Stewart was heartily sick of the whole subject. Technically, the third millennium didn't begin until the following year, 2001; but nobody was paying much attention to that inconvenient little detail. The human race was celebrating the event tonight. It was certain to be the biggest drunken binge in human history.

Religious fanatics were predicting much bigger things, of course. Many believed that at midnight the heavens would be rent asunder and the entire earth engulfed in the fires of Armageddon. Stewart thought the idea of the world coming to a fiery end precisely at midnight quite laughable. But he felt a sense of foreboding nevertheless. It was a vague, unfocused anxiety—a fear, not of Armageddon, but of some undefined lesser catastrophe. He supposed it was related to Anne's pregnancy and the impending birth of their baby girl, Genevieve. So much was riding on that event.

But the worry seemed both more diffuse and more profound. It wasn't just the baby that brought on this peculiar sense of dread. It was the future. He feared that events might somehow overwhelm him, and cost him that energetic, driving, comfortable sense of certainty and self-confidence that had powered his success in life.

His mind kept slipping back to another New Year's many years ago, when he was sixteen. Why the men who came for his father had picked the last day of the year had something to do with the statute of limitations. At least that's the way his uncle Frank explained it to him much later.

His life had been so protected up to that day that he hadn't known what real misfortune was. It only made the anger, shame, and grief all the more intense.

The men were U.S. marshals. They handcuffed his father in front of him and his mother and took him away. His father returned home that same evening, after his lawyer had posted bail for him, but the event had already altered the family's fate irretrievably.

There was a big New Year's party that night, and Dalton had the prettiest date—Charlotte Kinsolving, the fifteen-year-old daughter of the town's richest family. Charlotte had promised to give him something "special" that night. He had no doubt what that something was going to be. News of his father's arrest had already spread, however, and Charlotte was not allowed to go out with him that night—or any night after that. Dalton stole a bottle of scotch from the liquor cabinet, jumped into his new Corvette—a present from Mom and Dad for his sixteenth birthday—and drove around aimlessly all night long, getting drunk and contemplating suicide.

The months that followed were an ugly blur. His father was fired from the stock brokerage house where he had worked for twenty years. Under pressure, he made a deal with the prosecutors. He pled guilty to three counts of stock fraud and one count of insider trading. In return for giving evidence and later testifying against several other brokers, he was fined five million dollars and sentenced to five years in a federal penitentiary. Many former clients of the firm sued him as well, and the Stewart family, once rich and respected, was suddenly bankrupt and disgraced.

Along with his beautiful, rich girlfriend, Dalton lost his cherished Corvette, his male friends, and everything else that meant anything to him. The family could no longer afford the country club where for years Dalton had swum, played tennis, and partied. The Stewart cook was let go, and so was the maid. Most humiliating of all, Dalton was forced to quit the posh private boarding school he had been attending for two years and enroll in the local public high school.

The family was socially ostracized. During the good times, they had made the serious social error of letting their wealth go to their heads. When the bad times struck, there was no sympathy from anybody, absolutely none. Even the people Dalton had assumed were old family friends refused to stick by them. And those who had not been friends relished the Stewarts' fall from wealth and privilege with gleeful satisfaction. Shopkeepers and other service people, whom the Stewarts had long treated with condescension, saw the chance to get even and took advantage of it. Their credit was cut off, and wherever they went they were treated as pariahs. The family's fall from grace was so shatteringly complete that Dalton never fully recovered from it.

The family house and all the furnishings were sold to satisfy lawsuits. His mother obtained a divorce, and Dalton was sent to live with his uncle. So deep was Dalton's sense of betrayal that he never once visited his father during his years in prison; and he saw him only once after he was released. His father committed suicide three years later. He was fifty years old.

Dalton's mother, still attractive at forty, married the lawyer she had hired for her divorce and moved with him to the state of Washington, where his family owned land. Dalton and his younger sister went with them. Dalton's stepfather helped put him through college and business school, but they didn't get along very well, and as soon as Dalton was able, he moved out.

New Year's Eve, 1969. It was burned into his soul. All these years later he could still not think back on that time without a feeling of sick terror in the bottom of his stomach. No matter that he was a hundred times richer than his father had ever been.

At the beginning of each year he projected that if he could increase his wealth by another ten or more million dollars in the next twelve months, he would at last put the fear of repeating his father's disastrous collapse behind him forever. But the fear persisted anyway, driving him to enrich himself further—driving him to take the kind of legal and financial risks that kept his empire vulnerable to exactly the kind of fate that had ruined his father. Dalton Stewart saw the irony, of course. The harder he strove to escape the trauma of his past, the closer it seemed to loom.

A sudden amplification of voices and music from inside snapped him out of his reverie. He turned to see one of the French doors open and a woman step through and walk toward him in the dim light. She was wearing a floor-length white gown that clung suggestively to her lithe frame. Her ash-blond hair was swept back in a regal style.

He had seen her in the hall earlier in the evening and had been quite puzzled by her presence. He had not yet spoken to her.

"So there you are, Herr Stewart," the baroness called. "I have been looking all over for you."

"What is he doing in there?" Feldmann demanded, his eyes nervously scanning the windows of Goth's lab. "It's New Year's. Why doesn't he go home?"

Greiner turned to Hoffmann, the driver. "How long's the plane going to wait?"

"Until two."

"Shit," Feldmann moaned. "We'll never make it. It's eleven-thirty now. Traffic is already horrible. It'll take us over an hour just to get to the fucking landing strip."

"We can always leave tomorrow," Hoffmann said.

"After we blow up his lab?"

Hoffmann thought about it. "Okay, then. Let's go now."

"He's still in there!" Feldmann moaned.

"We have pistols and masks. We'll just hold him up, get the disk from him, then get the hell out."

"What about my explosives?" Greiner demanded.

"How fast can you set them?"

"I need at least ten minutes."

"Okay. We'll take Goth with us, then. Dump him at the airport."

17

Lexy went immediately into action. A driver was posted on duty around the clock for Anne, but no one at the desk could locate him. Finally, with the help of a bellboy, Lexy got Anne down to the lobby and settled into a chair.

Then, with the bellboy and one of the night clerks, she spent fifteen minutes frantically scouring the hotel in search of the driver. The night clerk finally located him at one of the hotel bars. He was hopelessly drunk.

He insisted he could drive, but Lexy disagreed. She was so furious at him that she cuffed him on the side of the head and knocked him right off his bar stool, much to the amusement of the other patrons.

Lexy bellowed at the night clerk to telephone Dalton Stewart at the National Palace. She then ran downstairs to the hotel garage, located the Stewart limousine, jumped behind the wheel, and gunned it around to the hotel's front entrance.

The night clerk and a bellboy helped Anne out from the lobby and into the back of the limo. The night clerk said he couldn't get through to anyone at the National Palace.

"Keep trying," Lexy ordered.

The hospital was only ten blocks from the hotel, but the situation outside was chaotic. A multiple-car accident two blocks away had snarled traffic through the whole center of the city, and drunken pedestrians were spilling onto the streets in growing numbers.

Lexy sat in the driver's seat of the enormous vehicle, glancing nervously back and forth from the scene out in the street to Anne, lying across the limo's backseat cushions. "Are you okay, Annie?"

"I'm okay," Anne reassured her.

"No labor yet?"

"Just beginning. Don't worry. I'm sure we've got plenty of time."

Lexy looked out the windshield and shook her head. "Jesus and Mary. We'll need it."

Hundreds of stalled motorists were leaning on their horns. An ambulance and two Seguridad police jeeps, their sirens blaring and lights flashing, were trying to work their way through, with no success. People were everywhere—running, dancing, singing, screaming. On top of the deafening chorus of automobile horns and sirens, thousands of radios had been turned up to full volume all across the city. The crackle of the static sounded like flames from a burning building, and the music hammered the eardrums. Occasional bursts of gunfire and the hollow *thock* of bottles smashing against the pavement punctuated the wild cacophony. It was part celebration and part riot.

Five minutes passed ... ten minutes ... twenty. No movement. Lexy tried to back up, but the limo was blocked from behind by a long line of vehicles. In her frustration, she began pounding on the car horn like everybody else.

Anne tried to calm her, but Lexy was gripped with a determination too powerful to be denied. She opened the car door. "Be right back!" she yelled. She ran down the line of idling vehicles until she found a motorcycle. She gave the motorcyclist's shirt a hard tug. He jerked his head around in surprise.

"Want to make a fast hundred bucks?" she yelled.

"What?"

She jabbed her finger back in the direction of the Mercedes. "Back there! Pregnant woman!" She pointed up the street ahead. "Hospital! Emergency!"

After a few more minutes of desperate hand gestures and pleading, Lexy got her message across. The man turned his motorcycle around and walked it between the cars back to the Mercedes. They helped Anne out of the backseat and got her positioned astride the bike.

"How's it feel?" Lexy hollered.

Anne shook her head: very uncomfortable. The motorcycle's owner suggested she try sitting with both legs on one side. They helped her maneuver one leg around. That was better. The driver climbed on in front of her.

"Hold on to him for dear life!" Lexy yelled. "I'll run! Catch up to you at the hospital!"

"What about the limo?"

"The hell with it!"

Anne clutched the driver's shoulders from behind. He kicked the machine into gear and they started off, weaving unsteadily through the narrow spaces between the lines of stalled vehicles. Lexy trotted along in front of them, praying to herself that this was all going to work out somehow.

Between the gridlock of cars and the crush of pedestrians out on the street, the motorcycle did little better than a fast crawl. They covered the ten blocks to the hospital in about fifteen minutes. Lexy, her adrenaline pumping furiously, kept getting ahead of them and then backtracking to urge them on.

Lexy ran into the hospital first, commandeered an orderly and a wheelchair, and dashed back outside just as Anne and the motorcycle were pulling up to the front entrance.

They transferred Anne into the chair and the orderly wheeled her inside. Lexy turned to look for the Good Samaritan with the motorcycle. He was already coasting down the drive, revving the throttle on the handlebars.

"Hey!" she yelled. "Come back here! I owe you a hundred bucks!"

He waved a hand, kicked the machine into gear, and wheeled off into the din of people and traffic.

Lexy jogged back into the hospital. Anne was sitting in the wheelchair just inside the lobby entrance.

"Where'd the orderly go?" Lexy demanded.

"He wants to take me up to the maternity ward. I told him to call Dr. Goth first."

"Fuck Dr. Goth—we're getting you to maternity right away!" Lexy wheeled Anne off in the direction of the elevator bank.

From his chair in the hospital's main waiting room, Joseph Cooper had a narrow view of the shallow foyer and the locked door at the end of it that led into Goth's new wing. He had been sitting there, on and off, for five hours, waiting for Goth to leave.

Suddenly the door opened and Goth came hurrying out. *Thank God. Finally.*

Cooper waited until Goth was in the lobby; then he stood up and walked quickly to the door. He punched in a five-digit number in the electronic keypad on the door frame and pushed the door open. He had learned the combination by videotaping Goth and his assistants punching in the numbers over a period of several days.

The lights were on. Goth was coming back. Shit. He'd have to hurry.

Cooper trotted down the corridor to the laboratory and began looking around. He knew that Goth kept a copy—maybe the only copy—of the program in an attaché case that he always carried with him when he arrived and departed each day.

He spotted the case sitting next to a computer on a counter top. He opened it. No cartridge disk inside. He looked at the computer. It was on. The screen was filled with data.

He saw the RCD plugged into its bay in the front of the computer. He turned the machine off and was about to extract the disk when he heard voices. He ducked into a small lavatory off the lab and shut the door.

Before Lexy and Anne reached the elevator bank Goth appeared, a sticklike figure in a lab jacket with a fringe of gray hair trotting toward them, waving his arms wildly over his head. "Over here!" he yelled.

He took over the wheelchair from Lexy and wheeled Anne down the hall at a fast trot. Lexy ran behind him. Hospital staffers stood watching the frantic procession with bemused stares.

Goth led them into the locked wing of the hospital that housed his lab and clinic.

"This isn't the maternity ward," Lexy objected, as they raced down the clinic's deserted corridor.

"We have a special room for her," Goth explained. "Right in here."

Halfway down the corridor Goth stopped, opened a door, flicked on a light, and wheeled Anne inside. The room was large and decorated like a bedroom.

"Get her comfortable," Goth directed. "I'll summon the obstetrician." He darted across the hall and into his laboratory office.

Lexy helped Anne get undressed and into the bed. "What's happening? Any labor yet?"

Anne took a deep breath and uttered a low groan. "Getting some pain now."

"Jesus, we just made it. Do your breathing exercises."

Anne started exhaling short puffs of air.

Lexy squeezed her hand. "Christ, how can you be so calm? I'm twice as nervous as you are."

Anne managed a wan smile. "We have to try Dalton again. The number's in my bag."

Lexy fished through Anne's purse and dug out an address book. "Where'd you list it? Despres? Dictator? Despot? What?"

"National Palace."

"Of course." Lexy found the number, grabbed the bedside phone, and dialed. "It's ringing, but nobody's answering." She glanced up at the wall clock: 11:30. "Everybody there'll be drunk." She redialed but still got no answer. "I'll try again in a few minutes. Maybe the clerk at the hotel already got him and he's on his way."

Anne's labor pains became more frequent and intense. "I can feel her moving, Lexy!"

Lexy gritted her teeth in anguish. "Oh my God. Hold her in there, Annie. The cavalry is on the way."

Goth reappeared with a nurse—a thin, elderly black woman. She introduced herself as Katherine and immediately took charge, taking Anne's blood pressure and taping a fetal heart monitor onto her belly.

"Where's an obstetrician?" Lexy demanded.

Goth looked pained. "They're trying to find him."

"Him? There's only one?"

"One on duty tonight, yes. The switchboard is paging him. If necessary, I can do the delivery."

Lexy scowled at him. "Sure, and so can a cab driver, if he has to. What do you know about it?"

Goth straightened up, offended. "I've delivered dozens of infants. There's absolutely nothing to worry about."

Katherine mopped Anne's brow with a damp cloth. "How's the pain, honey?" she asked.

"Getting up there," Anne whispered. She was breathing rapidly.

The nurse gave Anne a shot of painkiller, then positioned herself between her thighs and examined her. "Fully dilated," she declared in an authoritative voice.

Goth nodded nervously and wiped his glasses.

"What's that mean?" Lexy demanded.

Goth pressed Anne's belly with his hands. "Baby's on the way. She's in a good position. Half an hour. Maybe less."

"Start pushing, honey," the nurse said.

Katherine and Lexy held Anne's hands and helped her time her pushes. Goth scurried frantically between the room and the adjacent lab to make sure he had in place everything he needed for the birth. Despite his assurances that he knew what he was doing, his obvious anxiety frightened Lexy. She watched him place a call to the hospital switchboard and once again demand the whereabouts of the obstetrician. Told they had yet to locate him, Goth cursed and slammed down the phone.

Anne, meanwhile, was too preoccupied with her labor to pay much attention to what was going on around her.

Lexy tried another call to the National Palace, and this time someone answered.

"I need to find Mr. Dalton Stewart!" she shouted. "It's an emergency. His wife's having her baby! He's there, at the party. Please find him at once!"

The voice at the other end answered in French and then hung up. Lexy dialed the number again. The same voice answered.

"Il faut que je trouve Monsieur Dalton Stewart, immédiatement!" she stammered loudly, in halting high-school French. *"Je sais qu'il est là. Voulez-vous le trouver pour moi, s'il vous plaît? C'est très urgent."*

The voice muttered something incomprehensible and put the phone down. Lexy waited for several minutes, watching with mounting panic as Anne began writhing and groaning again.

"Push, honey!" Katherine cried. "She's coming down. Push! Push! That's it!"

Goth kept checking the fetal monitor and talking to himself. Lexy had never seen a doctor so nervous. It suddenly crossed her mind that he might be worrying that Anne was going to need an operation. Clearly he wasn't going to be able to handle that. Judging from the nurse's confident coaching, Anne seemed to be doing fine. But Lexy had never seen anyone give birth before, so she really didn't know what to think.

Goth discovered he needed something. He ordered the nurse to rush over to the maternity ward and fetch whatever it was.

Katherine hesitated. She glanced at her wristwatch. "Spasms are only fifteen seconds apart."

"Then hurry up!" Goth shouted.

Lexy hung up the phone and came over beside Anne. "Go ahead," she said. "I'll take over."

Katherine hurried out the door and down the corridor.

Lexy dried Anne's brow with a towel. Anne had her eyes closed tight. She was clenching her jaw.

"You okay, Annie?"

"It hurts like hell," she gasped.

Goth slipped on a pair of latex gloves and probed Anne's vagina with his fingers.

Lexy watched his face. Strange, she thought: here he was about to deliver her baby, and he never seemed to look at or talk to Anne directly. He acted almost embarrassed to be there.

Goth nodded to reassure himself. "Crown's engaged," he said. "Just right. Shouldn't be long now."

A sharp series of spasms made Anne wail with pain. Lexy held Anne's hand and coached her to push. Anne cried louder.

The cry seemed to echo down the corridor. Lexy looked at Anne. Her eyes were shut and she was panting. Another cry came from the same direction. It sounded like the nurse, Katherine.

Goth stepped over to the doorway to look out. No sooner had he stuck his head through than he pulled it back inside. He stood inside the doorway for a few moments, as if debating with himself what to do.

Lexy glanced over. "What is it?"

Goth didn't reply. He seemed frozen in place, unable to move or think.

Lexy heard voices in the hallway. "What is it?" she repeated.

Goth pushed the door shut. He fumbled with the knob for a few seconds, searching in vain for a way to lock it. "There's trouble," he said. He reached for the light switch. The room went dark. "Call the police. Hurry." His voice was quaking.

"Police? What's wrong?"

"Just call them!" he commanded. "And for godsakes protect the baby!"

The doctor hesitated by the door for a few seconds more, then opened it and vanished down the corridor.

18

The baroness was wearing high heels, and she caught her step slightly on the terrace stone as she walked toward Stewart. She appeared a little drunk. Some of the champagne in her glass spilled. He could smell her perfume: subtle, yet potent—like violets with a trace of something faintly pungent underneath.

"How is your darling little wife?" she asked, leaning close to him.

"Not so little these days."

"Of course. She's having a baby soon, *ja*?"

"About a week."

"You must be very excited about it."

Stewart nodded.

The baroness fastened her eyes on him. When she talked, especially when she wanted to command someone's attention, she tended to stare. The tactic invariably unnerved people. Stewart stared back. Except for the Seguridad men who paced the perimeters of the lawns beyond, they were alone on the terrace, standing barely two feet apart.

The baroness smiled suggestively. "We have a lot in common, the two of us. Don't you think so?"

"I've never really thought of it."

"Haven't you?"

"No. Should I have?"

"I think I have been in your thoughts from time to time, Herr Stewart. May I call you Dalton?"

Stewart felt his face grow warm.

The baroness laughed. "I'm making you uncomfortable. I apologize." She perched on the wide terrace parapet and patted the space beside her. Obediently, Stewart sat down.

"I'm surprised to see you here," he said.

"Are you?"

"There must be some wonderful parties in Europe tonight."

"But the Caribbean is so lovely in the winter. Look at tonight. So beautiful. So mild. Quite romantic, don't you think?"

"I guess it is. Yes."

"Oh, and I must congratulate you."

"On what?"

"Why, what do you think? Winning Dr. Goth and his Jupiter program."

"That's generous of you."

"I'm not accustomed to being outmaneuvered. I confess you outsmarted me."

Stewart tasted his scotch. Her compliments seemed out of character.

The baroness became thoughtful. She pressed the edge of her champagne glass against her cheek. "But you've made some mistakes, *ja*?"

"Have I?"

"You failed to tie up Herr Dr. Goth with a contract, for one thing."

"That wasn't a mistake. It was part of the plan. After all, he turned your offer down and accepted mine."

"But you had no offer. You just gave him money. What kind of arrangement is that?"

He laughed. "A pretty good one, as it turns out."

"But you're taking too much risk."

"Not at all. As soon as Goth demonstrates that Jupiter works, we'll negotiate a contract. And we'll get much better terms, because Goth knows I've already contributed to his success. He's indebted to me." Stewart wanted to brag about how he had also persuaded Goth to put his program to the test by trying it out on Anne, but he thought better of it.

They gazed across the terrace at the party inside. The French doors had been opened to let in cooler air, and the noise inside was at a temporary lull, as if the crowd was catching its collective breath before the last mad dash to midnight.

"I could have made trouble for you, you know," the baroness said.

"Oh?"

She ran a fingernail teasingly along the back of Stewart's hand. "President Antoine Despres and I are very close friends."

"I'm not sure that's something to boast about."

The baroness laughed. "What I mean, of course, is that I have influence with him."

"I see."

"Certainly enough to keep him from causing you trouble."

"He's been no trouble at all."

"But eventually he might be."

"That's occurred to me."

"You should take me on as your partner. There could be great virtues in our working together."

Was she serious? He couldn't tell. "Do you think so?"

"Of course. We'd complement each other perfectly. And with my help you could get rid of Despres. I know a much less greedy individual who'd be very much in our debt if we helped him with a coup."

Stewart glanced around anxiously at the guards patrolling the lawn. The baroness was talking in a fairly loud voice.

"And let's face it, Dalton—you need more money and more trained personnel to put into this project. And I have both. Things would move much faster. Together we'd be able to command a world market for Jupiter."

"I'll certainly think about it," he replied. But he certainly didn't intend to do anything about it. Taking on the baroness as a business partner would be like inviting in the Mafia.

"There should be enough money for both of us, don't you think?"

"I don't know. I'm pretty greedy."

The baroness laughed. "So am I, *Liebchen*."

"How much profile do *you* think there'd be?" he asked.

He was curious to know how seriously she had thought through the possibilities.

"I estimate five hundred million dollars in five years. In ten years, thirty billion. Perhaps even fifty billion."

It was Stewart's turn to laugh.

"Why is that so funny?"

"Your estimates are modest, Baroness."

"Are they?"

"I expect to make that much in the first two or three years. In ten years, I'll gross a trillion."

The baroness's flirtatious manner evaporated. "What did you say? A trillion?"

"Yes."

"Dollars?"

"Dollars."

She rotated the stem of her champagne glass thoughtfully between her thumb and forefinger. "How much is a trillion?" she asked. "A thousand billions?"

"That's right."

The baroness looked out across the dark Caribbean sea. She took a deep breath. Stewart watched appreciatively as her breasts heaved under the thin material of her gown.

"No one's ever made so much money, have they?" she said.

"No one's ever had anything to sell like Jupiter."

"You don't worry that it's unproven?"

"No. I don't worry about it," he replied. Of course he worried about it constantly. But soon he'd know.

She regarded him intently. "That's the risk you take, isn't it?" she said. "If you want to be first, I mean."

Stewart sipped his scotch. The ice in it had melted, and it tasted watery. "That's the risk."

The baroness had recovered her cozy manner. She squeezed his hand suggestively. It set his pulse racing. "You see how much we think alike?" she said. "We both enjoy taking risks. That's when we feel most alive, *ja*?"

He nodded. *Ja.*

She moved her hand to his thigh. "I feel very alive right now," she whispered.

* * *

Anne raised her head from the pillows. "What's happening? Why are the lights off?"

"Some people out in the hall," Lexy whispered. She tried to keep the fear out of her voice. "Probably a New Year's party. The doctor's talking to them."

They could hear Goth shouting in the corridor. Someone answered him. Lexy couldn't catch the words. Then Goth's voice grew quiet.

Lexy groped in the dark for the telephone. She tried to dial the operator, but her hands were trembling so hard she kept hitting the wrong button. The hospital switchboard answered on the seventh ring.

"Get the police," Lexy said in a harsh whisper. "We're in the new wing. Someone's breaking in!"

The operator made her repeat the request three times, then laughed at her. "They'll all be drunk tonight, baby!"

Lexy raised her voice. "Goddamnit, call them! Quick!"

She put the phone down and tiptoed to the door. A sheet of paper taped over the small window stopped about an inch short of the bottom. Lexy bent down and peered out. She could see a short stretch of corridor. Directly across it was the open door into Goth's laboratory. The doctor was in there. Three other men were with him. One held Goth's arms pinned behind his back; another was poking a pistol against his chest. The third male was pulling what looked like blocks of clay from an overnight bag and sticking something into them. He prepared about a dozen blocks in this manner, then began attaching them to various surfaces around the room—to the underside of a counter holding a lot of expensive-looking computer equipment, beneath a sink, under a large wall of shelves stocked with boxes, books, and lab equipment. Plastic explosives?

Lexy groped her way back to the telephone and tried the switchboard again. The phone was dead.

She looked down at Anne. The thin rectangle of light shining though the door's small window fell across her face. Her eyes were closed. She was resting between spasms. In another minute she would be thrashing and groaning again. The baby could some out with the next big push. *Jesus, Mary, and Joseph, what a nightmare.*

Lexy rushed to the window. She could still see Goth and the two men guarding him. They were arguing. The third man suddenly appeared in the corridor. He opened the door to the room next to the lab and looked in. Then he went to the next door down and Lexy lost sight of him.

Lexy felt around for something to block the door. She found a metal chair and wedged it under the doorknob. Then she slid two other chairs and a large chest of drawers behind the chair. The tile floor had recently been waxed. A good hard shove from the other side of the door would likely push everything right back across the floor.

Anne started to moan. She clutched Lexy's hand and writhed on the bed, pulling her knees up to try to ease the pain.

Lexy tried to quiet her. She wiped Anne's brow with a damp cloth. *Where the hell are the police? Why don't they get here? Oh God, why don't they get here?* "Hold on, Annie. It's going to be okay." She wished she could believe it.

The doorknob rattled. Voices in the corridor grew louder. Lexy could see the silhouettes of two heads through the glass. They began pushing hard against the door. The chairs and the chest squeaked backward along the tile floor, and a vertical wedge of light from the hallway appeared along the edge of the door frame.

The wedge widened. Someone squeezed partway in, then braced himself against the doorjamb and shoved the furniture back several feet. He groped for the light switch. The overhead fluorescents blinked on.

It was the man with the gun—the one who had been questioning Goth. He walked into the room, then hesitated, confused by the sight of Anne and Lexy. He said something to them in German.

Anne opened her eyes and groaned.

The man stepped over. Lexy bent protectively over Anne. "Get out of here!" Lexy cried. "I've called the police!"

He pressed the pistol against the side of Lexy's head. "Who are you?" he demanded.

Lexy began trembling violently. "Get the hell out!"

A loud pounding at the far end of the corridor interrupted them. Someone yelled *"Polizei!"* several times.

The man took one last look at Anne and Lexy and then ran out into the corridor. Frantic shouts greeted him. Through the open doorway Lexy saw him drop to his stomach and train his pistol down the corridor and open fire. Magnified by the long cement-block corridor walls, the shots sounded like exploding grenades. They were answered by a deafening burst of automatic weapons fire.

The walls vibrated from the racket. Cement dust choked the air. The man on the floor tried to stand up. Blood ran from his mouth and ears. More gunfire. He jerked backward, as if caught by a sudden gust of wind, then leaned forward, his arms flung out in front of his chest in a vain effort to ward off the fusillade of bullets tearing through him. He sank down face-first onto the floor.

Lexy lunged against the door to close it. A ricocheting bullet struck her near the shoulder, spun her around, and knocked her down. Her left arm felt numb. She crawled to the door and managed to get it shut, then struggled over to Anne's bed.

Wild shouting in the halls. Something exploded. The blast blew the door in on a cloud of stinking gray powder. More shouting, and the frantic pounding of boots on the tile floor.

Through the ringing in her head Lexy heard Anne screaming. She sounded faraway. She tried to pull herself onto the bed to protect her. She lacked the strength.

She felt dizzy. The room was growing dark. She tried to raise her head up but couldn't. She blacked out, came to for an instant, then blacked out again.

When she surfaced a second time, the dust in the room had settled somewhat. Her blouse was wet with blood. Anne's screams had faded to a continuous moaning.

A man was coming toward her. She tried to yell for help, but all she could manage was a hoarse shriek. There was no one to help them anyway. She tried again to pull herself onto the bed.

God, please help us. Somebody please help us.

* * *

The noise from inside was growing louder. Several of the French doors were open, and partygoers were spilling out onto the terrace. The atmosphere of civilized restraint from earlier in the evening had completely vanished, washed away by the free-flowing alcohol. Guests were yelling or singing in loud voices. Others were dancing lewdly, embracing, rubbing against one another. Many were too drunk to stand.

Stewart could see a young male lying prone on the floor just inside one of the French doors. Apparently he had passed out, but there was a small pool of blood by his mouth. People were stepping over him as they walked through the doorway.

Stewart felt the baroness's hand traveling along the inside of his thigh.

"We should do something to celebrate," she said.

"Kissing is traditional," he replied. He slipped an arm around her shoulder and kissed her. The moist, warm softness of her lips, the mixture of champagne and perfume aroused him powerfully.

She pushed him away gently. "Kissing hardly seems enough to welcome in a whole new millennium," she cooed.

Waves of cheering and applause thundered out from the main ballroom. The countdown of the last minute of the old year had started.

A sudden shock of cold wetness in the crotch made Stewart jump. He looked down. The baroness had spilled champagne on his pants.

She giggled. "I'm really very sorry." She rubbed her hand against the wet area. His penis became instantly rigid. She pulled his hand up under her dress. "Take my underpants down," she instructed. "Hurry."

He reached up along her thighs with both hands and pulled her panties down over her knees. She braced herself against his shoulder and stepped out of them. They were white silk, with a broad trimming of lace, and they reeked of that same intoxicating perfume. She lifted her gown up to her waist, leaned back against the stone parapet, and opened her legs. He moved between them and they kissed again, this time with an angry passion.

The baroness clutched Stewart's head between her hands and pushed him down. He knelt awkwardly on one knee. She entwined her fingers in his hair and pressed his face into her belly.

A church bell in town began to chime midnight. Seconds later, another church bell began. And then a frenzied roar came from inside the palace and grew in volume until the terrace began to shake.

Dalton Stewart, his ears squeezed firmly between the baroness's thighs, could hear nothing except the wild beating of his heart.

The man coming through the door was black. Lexy had not seen him with the other men around Goth. "Please tell me you're the police," she groaned.

"What are you doing here?" he demanded.

Lexy bent over Anne. "She's trying to have a baby."

"You have to get her out of here. Right now. Come on."

Cooper got behind Anne's bed and began pushing her toward the door. On its big castors the bed rolled easily. Lexy followed, cradling her wounded arm. The hallway was choked with dust, but deserted. A shot rang out from somewhere in the building. Lexy crouched forward and ran.

A short distance down the corridor Cooper steered the bed around a corner toward an emergency exit. He yanked the door open, but the bed was too wide to fit through.

Lexy stumbled. She felt on the verge of passing out. She watched the black man lift Anne up out of the bed. It looked as if both of them were about to fall over. Another burst of gunfire rattled through the corridors. What in God's name were they shooting at? she wondered. Were they mad? She moved to Anne's other side. Anne managed to stand, but she was bending far forward to relieve her pain. Slowly, they maneuvered her through the door.

It was completely dark outside. They were somewhere around the back of the hospital. Lexy felt soft grass underneath. They walked Anne a short distance further and then lay her down on a sheet on top of the grass. Cooper positioned her on her back and propped her knees up. Between sobs, Anne panted noisily for air.

Lexy wanted to do something to comfort her, but she felt too weak to move. She knelt down beside her and held her hand.

"You know what to do?" Cooper asked.

Lexy shook her head. "No, goddamnit! Go get us help!"

The ground suddenly heaved beneath them as if from an earthquake. A row of windows in the hospital wing blew out in a bright flash, then subsided into curling billows of black smoke.

Cooper jerked his head around and swore under his breath. Without another word he scrambled to his feet and headed back toward the exit door they had just come through. Another explosion blew out more windows.

Anne arched her back and screamed.

Harold Goth struggled to his feet. A thick, stinking pall of smoke hung in the air.

He thought about putting a water-soaked cloth over his mouth and nose, but knew he didn't have time. He dropped to his hands and knees. There was less smoke near the floor, but he was already choking from the acrid fumes.

He crawled toward his computer on the workbench along the far wall. When he got there, he reached up for the program cartridge and tried to pull it out. The plastic was scorching hot. He snatched his hand back and forced his face up closer to the computer. He rubbed his eyes. The machine's plastic housing had been destroyed by the explosion. The cartridge disk was fused to the computer's frame.

The smoke was beginning to suffocate him, and it was getting intensely hot. Goth lay close to the floor, coughed, sucked in a rasping breath, and then struggled to his feet and dashed toward the filing cabinet in the closet next to the lab's lavatory. The cabinet contained the only backup copy of the Jupiter program.

He reached the cabinet, grabbed the handle of the top

drawer, and tugged. It was locked. He jerked hard on the drawer, but it refused to budge. The key was in his attaché case.

Goth dropped back to the floor and began searching for the case. He was certain he had left it by his desk, but he didn't see it there. He crawled along in front of the workbench, looking around the floor. It was nowhere in sight. He began to panic.

Then he saw it, wedged in a shelf under the bench. He pulled it out.

A hand reached swiftly around from behind him and grabbed the attaché case by the handle. Goth wrapped both arms around it and held on. The two men struggled for a few seconds. Then Cooper punched Goth once hard in the face and yanked the case free. He disappeared with it through the smoke.

Goth rose from the floor, choking and coughing, and staggered back toward the file cabinet. He pulled at the cabinet drawer in one last desperate effort to open it. The whole cabinet fell forward and pitched over on its side. Goth sank to his knees, his hand still clutching the top drawer pull. His eyes were watering so fiercely he couldn't see. His nostrils and his mouth were stinging with pain. He couldn't catch his breath.

Another charge exploded. This one had been set under a shelf full of chemicals just behind Goth's back. The blast shattered the jars and sent liquid chemicals spurting in every direction.

In an instant Goth was bathed in burning liquid. He slid face down against the floor, his hand still clutching the file cabinet handle.

Cooper rushed out the emergency exit, ran over to a lighted window near where the wing joined the main part of the hospital, and yanked open the attaché case.

There were papers in it, and a key, but no cartridge disk. He threw the case onto the grass and kicked it. He looked at the wing. There was no going back. The whole place was ablaze. Lexy crawled over between Anne's legs. She reached toward Anne's belly and in the dark felt a hard, round, slippery object. Oh God, she thought. Where's Goth? "Push, Anne," she whispered. "Push."

Anne cried out again—a long, anguished moan, directed skyward. Lexy felt the baby come squirming out into her hands. *Dr. Goth, where the hell are you?*

There was a tremendous wave of noise. It was deep and all-encompassing, like the noise of a crowd at a college football rally—the honking of horns and the deep-throated cheering of a hundred thousand voices.

Midnight.

Overhead the black sky blossomed with fireworks. Bright flowers of blue, red, silver, and green exploded with concussive booms and rippling crackles, lighting the patch of lawn around them as brightly as day.

The baby cried lustily.

Lexy held the infant against her. She saw the umbilical cord. It was wrapped around the baby's leg. She pulled it free, then glanced toward the hospital wing. It was engulfed in flame. Goth was never coming. She held the baby close to her, took a deep breath, put the cord in her mouth, closed her eyes, and bit down hard.

Once she had severed the cord, Lexy tried to tie it off, but it was so slippery and her left arm was so weak she couldn't hold it. She pulled off her blouse and used it to get a better grip. Finally she managed to knot the cord tightly against the baby's stomach. She wrapped the blouse carefully around the infant and held it close. Anne was sobbing convulsively from pain and exhaustion.

Lexy bent over her, cradling the child. "You did it, Annie!" she cried, suddenly overcome with tears herself.

In the flashes of the fireworks thundering overhead Lexy raised the tiny, blood-flecked creature up toward the heavens in a gesture of gratitude and celebration, then placed her in Anne's arms.

PART II

VALLEY OF THE LOST GENES

Winter and Spring, 2001

19

Anne Stewart patted the space beside her on the piano bench. "Come, darling, sit here with me."

The little girl toddled over to the piano, and Anne reached down and lifted her onto the seat. Genny settled her hands into her lap and gazed up at her mother with an expectant smile.

Genevieve Alexandra Stewart seemed the perfect child. She was bright, attentive, well-behaved, and as beautiful as Anne could possibly have expected. Her curly blond locks, button nose, luminous slate-blue eyes, and dimpled chin instantly beguiled everyone who met her.

For a twelve-month-old, her manner was extraordinary. She moved with the grace, strength, and sense of balance of a much older child. And she had a way of looking at someone that was completely captivating. Her intense eyes would focus on a person's face with an inquiring gaze that seemed to penetrate right through to some inner place with which the child could communicate. Some people found this unnerving. Lexy Tate, for one: she had already taken to calling Genny "Little Devil's Eyes"—a nickname that Anne did not find amusing.

During the first months of her life, Genny had cried a great deal. Mrs. Callahan, her nanny, thought the reason for the little girl's irritability was an abnormal sensitivity to touch. Anne sometimes wondered if it had something to do with the traumatic circumstances of her birth.

Now Genny rarely cried at all.

But she did exhibit some odd moods. Anne would sometimes walk in on her to find the child staring with rapt concentration at some object or other. Often she seemed to be looking at nothing but empty space. Watching Genny during one of these periods of intense, trancelike fixations, noticing how she sometimes tilted her head to one side or crinkled her nose, Anne had the extraordinary impression that Genny was imagining something—seeing, hearing, or even smelling something—that wasn't there. Anne had reported these peculiar states to Genny's pediatrician, but the doctor had dismissed them as being of no consequence.

Anne ran a hand over Genny's curls. "What would you like to hear, darling?"

"Star," Genny exclaimed in a bright voice.

Anne played through the melody of "Twinkle, Twinkle, Little Star" with her right hand. Genny listened with a solemn expression.

After a few repetitions Anne stopped. She brushed a vagrant wisp of hair away from Genny's forehead. "Would you like to hear a song about another star?"

Genny nodded her head emphatically.

Anne quickly searched out the melody for "When You Wish Upon a Star," added the appropriate chords, and then played the song, singing the words in a soft voice.

Genny's eyes followed her mother's fingers with rapt attention as they moved over the keys. Her face beamed with pleasure.

Anne was especially pleased with Genny's response to the piano, because there had been a period, only a few months back, when she feared that something might be wrong with Genny's hearing. The little girl seemed to wince at the slightest sound, and she still did not tolerate loud noises well.

"Do you like that song?"

Genny nodded.

"It's from a story called *Pinocchio*. It's about a little puppet, made out of wood, who wants more than anything in the world to become a real boy."

"Pin-*noke*-ee-o," the girl repeated, pronouncing the word perfectly.

Genny was undeniably precocious. By eight months she had begun to walk, and by ten months she had said her first word. Anne remembered the moment vividly, because the first word was three syllables long. It happened one afternoon in early November. Anne walked into her room to wake Genny from a nap. The child was already standing in her crib, waiting, her little hands impatiently clutching the rail. She giggled and then said something. It sounded like "Toronto." Anne thought she had imagined it, but Genny repeated the word, uttering the sound with an unmistakable clarity. Anne lifted her into her arms, shrieking with astonishment and delight. There was no mistaking it. Her little baby had actually said the word "Toronto." It was both funny and miraculous.

Anne remembered that Dalton had come into the nursery the day before. He had held Genny in his arms and talked to Anne about going to Toronto on a business trip. But of all the words to pick, thought Anne. Genny repeated "Toronto" a few more times that day and then promptly forgot it.

But "Toronto" had opened the gates. In the days that followed, new words poured forth from the little girl at the rate of three or four a day. Now, at twelve months—an age when most children had barely uttered more than a "Mama" or "Dada"—Genny's active vocabulary was well over a hundred words, and she was beginning to put them together into two- and three-word sentences.

Anne was still surprised—even a little frightened—by the strength of her own feelings for her child. Of course she had expected to love her without reserve, but she had never been able to imagine the depth and the intensity of the emotions this infant would stir within her. She understood now the truth of all those old clichés about mother love. She knew, without a second's doubt, that nothing else would ever mean as much to her in her life as this unique and precious, vulnerable creature, so full of needs and wants and demands. Nothing else in the world could possibly ever evoke such an all-consuming protective passion.

Anne embraced the demands of motherhood with enthusiasm and joy. But just as she knew that Genny would enrich her own life immensely, so she also understood that she would never be able to separate herself emotionally from her daughter's fate. Whatever happened to

Genny would, in effect, happen to Anne as well. She supposed this was what all parents felt, to a greater or lesser degree; but it came to her as a shock to discover that with the happiness there would forever be an undercurrent of anxiety, because she knew as sure as she drew breath that if anything bad should ever befall this child—if she should ever lose her—the pain would be more than she could bear.

Genny's arrival had worked an even more profound transformation on Anne's husband.

Immediately after Genny's birth Dalton fell into a severe depression. The cause was clear: Goth's death and the loss of the greatest financial opportunity of Dalton's life. After a couple of months, his gloom began to lift. He turned his attention to his new daughter and soon became an even more anxious parent than Anne. He seemed obsessed with the fear that Genny might not be developing properly. Although the child had been subjected to a heavy battery of tests during the first weeks after her birth, Dalton wanted more tests done—especially after she began exhibiting her trancelike moods. Over Anne's objections, he took Genny several times to special clinics in New York and Boston for further testing. Although absolutely nothing negative turned up, his anxieties remained. For a long time he clung to the conviction that Genny should be doing better, even though every book and every expert consulted suggested that her development was at the very least superior, if not extraordinary.

Then, for reasons Anne could only guess at, his worries about Genny vanished. He became the epitome of the proud and doting daddy.

One night after they had returned from a dinner party, he came out of Genny's room with tears in his eyes.

Anne looked at him in alarm. "Is Genny okay?"

He nodded.

"What's the matter?"

"I just . . . realized something."

"What?"

"How much I love that child."

Anne laughed. "Does it really surprise you?"

Dalton seemed to be struggling with his emotions.

"Yes. I've never had these feelings. I've just never loved anything—anybody—unconditionally."

"Does that bother you?"

"No. But I guess I've always been afraid of the idea. It takes ... I'm just not used to it, I guess."

They went into their bedroom and began to undress.

Dalton quickly recovered himself and laughed. "Too much to drink," he said. "Makes me maudlin."

"Maybe you ought to drink too much more often," Anne replied.

Suddenly Dalton dropped onto the bed. He looked stricken, as if overcome by some terrible realization. Anne sat beside him and put an arm around him. "Christ, what an ass I've been," he whispered, his voice choking.

"About what?"

He buried his face in his hands. "About you, about Genny. About everything."

Anne hugged him.

"I've been such a goddamned selfish fool all my life, Anne. And somehow I've never even noticed. I'm really sorry. . . ."

They both cried. He put his arms around Anne and they held each other for a long time.

From that night on, Dalton Stewart began making a genuine effort to be a good father and a loving husband. He agreed with Anne that it was essential that their child grow up in a happy and secure home, and he promised to do everything possible to repair the damages in their marriage. Their relationship became stronger than it had ever been.

Dalton neglected his work to spend hours every day playing with Genny, or just watching her. Everything the infant did—every move, sound, or facial expression—got his complete attention. He read all the books on child development and urged Anne to do the same. He was eager to know precisely what to expect at each stage of development. All their discussions centered around the baby and how she was doing. Every cough, burp, sneeze, or cry would send Dalton scurrying to consult a book or to call the pediatrician. The doctor, who had an office nearby in Great Neck, was Dalton's choice, not Anne's. She had wanted Paul Elder, the pediatrician she had visited in Manhattan before Genny was born. But since he had rebuffed her so rudely, she had accepted Dalton's choice without complaint.

They hired a nurse-governess also: Mrs. Denise Callahan. She was a middle-aged woman with impeccable credentials—she had been a nanny for one of the Rockefeller families for fourteen years. She was a stiff, rather formal person, and Anne didn't relate to her terribly well, but she had many virtues: she was steady, efficient, hardworking, knowledgeable, and completely reliable. And she was good with Genny. She didn't especially fuss over her, but neither did she ever show impatience or anger.

Although now Dalton was once more heavily immersed in his business activities, he still checked in on Genny's progress several times daily. If he was away on a trip, he always called at the end of the day for a full report.

Every time Anne thought of the changes that Genny had wrought on her mother and father in one short year, she felt moved to tears. Not only had the child brought great happiness into their lives; she had actually made them better human beings.

"Would you like to play, too? Here, give me your hand."

Anne took Genny's tiny hand in hers and brought it up to the keyboard. She held the girl's middle and forefinger together and gently pressed them on the G below middle C. Genny squealed with pleasure as the note sounded. Then up an octave they went, to the next G, then back to F, then E, C-sharp, D, A; D, B, A, G, F-sharp, G, C, and so on, until they had completed the song's melodic refrain.

Anne guided Genny's fingers through the melody a second time. With her free left hand she added some chords. Genny giggled with barely suppressed excitement all through the exercise.

Anne hugged her hard. Yesterday—the first day of the new year, 2001—had been Genny's first birthday. Anne had arranged a small party for her, attended only by Dal-

ton, Hank Ajemian and his wife, Carol, Lexy Tate, and
the house staff. Anne had tried to find a child Genny's
age somewhere nearby, but that part of Long Island's
North Shore was not a neighborhood of young families.

Lexy had stayed overnight, and she and Anne had both
gotten a little drunk, reminiscing about that fateful New
Year's Eve on Coronado. Lexy's gunshot wound was now
a small round scar about the size of a quarter, high on the
outside of her left arm, just below the shoulder. She was
very proud of it. She wore short sleeves as much as possible, just to show it off, and would regale anyone willing
to listen with an extremely detailed account of how she
had received it.

Anne picked Genny up from the piano bench and carried her back into the nursery. Mrs. Callahan was there,
putting clean sheets on the crib. Anne put Genny down.
The little girl scampered across to the enormous pile of
stuffed animals arranged on the window seat and began
pulling them down onto the floor and hugging them.

"Dalton and I are having an early dinner tonight, Mrs.
Callahan. He's leaving for Washington early tomorrow.
I'll be back to nurse her at eight."

Mrs. Callahan's expression became stern. "Very well,
Mrs. Stewart."

Anne smiled to herself. Mrs. Callahan didn't believe in
breast feeding after six months, and she had made her position in the matter quite clear. Anne had listened to her
advice politely and then ignored it. But now, with a year
gone by, she knew it was time that she come to some sort
of decision. Her head told her to begin weaning Genny,
but she was still reluctant to give it up. Well, perhaps another month, and then she'd decide.

Dinner with Dalton was a strained affair. The two of
them sat at one end of the enormous table in the mansion's forbiddingly ornate dining room and talked aimless
trivialities. Dalton seemed tense and preoccupied.

"Is something wrong?" Anne asked.

Dalton shrugged, then nodded. "Some business problems. Things are a bit difficult right now."

"You can't elaborate?"

"What's the point? You wouldn't understand."

"You promised me you weren't going to do this anymore, remember?"

"Do what?"

"Shut me out of your world. Maybe I *would* understand."

"I don't mean you *can't* understand. I just mean it's all rather complicated and boring to anyone on the outside."

Anne lifted her wineglass and looked at it. "So I'm still someone on the outside?"

"You know what I mean."

"I know that I've learned more from Hank Ajemian about the whole industry of biological engineering in the few times he's been here to dinner than I've learned from you in three years."

Dalton chuckled. "Ajemian likes to talk. Besides, he's got a thing for you. He likes to impress you."

Anne didn't reply.

Dalton sighed. "Stewart Biotech is in trouble. If we don't get some cooperation from the banks in the next few weeks, we'll have to go into Chapter 11."

"What's that?"

"We'll have to get protection from our creditors until we can reorganize."

"Bankruptcy?"

"Does that shock you?"

"Well, yes. Shouldn't it? I haven't had a clue from you that things were so bad."

Dalton stared at the big silver candelabra in the center of the table.

"Although from what I've heard, businesses do it all the time," Anne continued. "And go right on as if nothing had happened."

"It's serious, just the same. The banks would take control. And we could eventually lose the company."

"Why have things deteriorated so? Didn't you tell me that last year the company had the best year in its history?"

"It did. But it's complicated. We got overextended, and the economy turned sour, all in the same year. And we lost a lot of money in Coronado."

"How?"

"How do you think? We made a big investment in Goth. When the wing of that damned hospital burned down, everything went with it—Harold Goth, his research, his papers, his files, his computer disks—everything we had counted on to make back our investment. And we didn't have a dime's worth of insurance. Nobody would cover us."

"What was it that he had discovered? Why was it all such a big secret?"

Stewart looked faintly embarrassed. "We were afraid of competition. Goth had developed a gene therapy that could have been enormously profitable. At least that's what we thought at the time. Now, we'll probably never know."

Anne sensed her husband was avoiding something. "What exactly was this program of his supposed to do, anyway? You never really explained it to me."

"I'm not sure I understand it myself."

"I find that hard to believe."

"It had to do with a complicated series of genetic alterations to the germ line. Goth had developed a genetic formula of sorts that he believed could produce a child with superior attributes—health, intelligence, and so forth."

"Did he ever test his formula?"

Dalton looked directly at his wife. "Not that I know of."

"Why did you take such a risk on something untested?"

Her husband laughed nervously. "Good question. I was naive. And greedy. All I could think of was the profit it could turn. Maybe it was best that it all came to such a quick end. I doubt the formula would ever have worked."

After a silence, Dalton folded his napkin and dropped it on the table. "In any case, the whole venture cost us a lot of money." He pushed his chair back. "I'm going back into town tonight. Meet with Ajemian. There's supposed to be a snowstorm tomorrow, and we absolutely have to sit down and review our strategy before we see the bankers tomorrow. Ajemian thinks we can arrange for some short-term financing that'll at least give us a little breathing room—maybe four or five months. After that, who knows. Let's go in and see Genny."

On their way to the nursery they passed the music room. A light was on inside, and someone was hitting keys on the piano.

They looked in. Mrs. Callahan was standing by the door, hands on her hips. She turned and greeted Anne and Dalton. "I'm sorry," she said, "but she just ran in here. I was just about to take her back into the nursery."

Mrs. Callahan started toward the piano, but Dalton held her arm. "Wait a minute," he whispered.

Genny was standing between the piano bench and the keyboard, reaching up to the keys with her right hand and hitting them in a very deliberate pattern—G, G, F, E, C-sharp, D, A; D, B, A, G, F-sharp, G, C. . . .

Dalton glanced at Anne. "Did you teach her that?"

Anne shook her head. "No. . . . I played it for her, this afternoon. I did guide her fingers over the keys a couple of times. But that was all."

The three adults listened while Genny's tiny hand picked out the melody of "When You Wish Upon a Star." At the end of the song's refrain, she hesitated, then moved to her left to reach the keys further down the keyboard. She struck those in what appeared to be a random pattern.

Anne clapped a hand to her mouth. Dalton and Mrs. Callahan looked at her.

"Amazing," she whispered. "She's playing the same chords I used—one note at a time. Listen . . . those three notes were a C chord. Now an A7 . . . D minor . . . D minor 7 . . . G7. . . ."

Mrs. Callahan nodded. "Well, she's inherited your musical talent, Mrs. Stewart, that's for sure, the little thing."

Dalton Stewart opened his mouth to speak, but no words came out. His face had turned quite pale. He stared across the room at his daughter as if he had never seen her before.

20

Ambassador Haikido Mishima stopped and stared up directly over his head, shielding his eyes from the bright glare of the skylights. "I really don't feel entirely secure, walking under those things," he said.

"Those things" were several large airplanes suspended from the ceiling of the National Air and Space Museum, on Washington's Independence Avenue.

Yuichiro Yamamoto followed his gaze. "I don't think they'll fall on us," he said. "American technology isn't *that* bad."

Mishima chuckled. "I'm just a superstitious old man. Here, let's go this way. That looks interesting over there."

The two men strolled across the floor to the World War II aviation exhibit. Yamamoto had been to the Air and Space Museum many times, and he never tired of the place. Mishima, on the other hand, was not much interested. The ambassador's tastes tended more toward symphony orchestras and art galleries than science.

"Is Goth's program completely dead?" Mishima asked.

"Nothing survived," Yamamoto answered.

"What about that lab assistant of his? The one who promised to sell us a copy?"

"Kirsten Amster. She's disappeared."

"What happened to her, do you think?"

Yamamoto shrugged. "People disappear on that island all the time. Despres's security police. They're the lowest kinds of brutes. And I understand she was careless about going out after dark."

"We have no evidence, though."

"No."

"An unlikely coincidence, then, don't you think?"

"It's also possible that the baroness killed her."

"You shouldn't joke about such things."

"I'm not joking, Excellency," Yamamoto replied, annoyed. "She was suspicious of Amster."

"But why would she care? Stewart had already beaten her out of the Jupiter program."

"But she hadn't given up. It was probably her thugs who set fire to the laboratory and killed Goth. She may have been trying to steal the Jupiter formula. Amster may have died in the fire with Goth."

"But her body was not found."

"No."

"Surely the baroness is not so ruthless."

"I mention it only as a possibility."

"Do you think the baroness ever obtained a copy of the Jupiter program?"

"No. It's been over a year now, and our sources in Hauser Industries haven't heard anything of it. And there's no activity in any of their labs to support the idea."

"Do you think Dalton Stewart has Jupiter?"

"It would only have been prudent for him to protect his investment by making sure that at least one copy of the program was locked in a secure place. That's just my speculation, of course. No proof. And in fact, there's nothing unusual going on at Stewart Biotech, either."

"What about the Stewart daughter?" Mishima asked.

"She's normal, as far as we can tell. No signs of anything unusual. And we've read all the lab reports."

Mishima nodded approvingly. "What does that indicate, in your view?"

"Not much. Except perhaps that Goth's formula is at least not dangerous."

"But there could be hidden damage, couldn't there?"

"Yes. Of course."

"And she is only a little over a year old. Perhaps too early to tell anything, positive or negative."

"Perhaps."

"That may explain why Stewart hasn't yet done anything with the program. He's waiting to see if Jupiter works."

"That could be true also."

"It's really a great shame," the ambassador said, glancing around him with an anxious frown, "that we didn't get the Jupiter program from Amster sooner."

Yamamoto cringed inwardly. He knew the ambassador was going to criticize him for not moving faster. He had spent hours mulling over his failure, trying to anticipate the questions and be ready with the right answers. Now that the moment was at hand, he felt nervous and defensive. The ambassador was a far more skillful and dangerous interrogator than his self-deprecating manners would imply. Still, Yamamoto knew he was on solid ground. He had nothing to be ashamed of. "She wanted a lot of money," he reminded Mishima. "And your office was slow to give me the necessary approval. By the time it came, it was too late."

Mishima focused his gaze squarely on his companion. "Ah, but you never gave us any indication that the matter might be so urgent," he said, his voice soft as a whisper.

Yamamoto forced himself to meet Mishima's eyes head-on. "I had no reason to think it was."

Mishima nodded. It was a maddening habit of his, Yamamoto thought—always nodding, whether he agreed with what you were saying or not.

"In any case, it's too late now," Mishima declared. "We mustn't indulge ourselves in recriminations."

My sentiments exactly, Yamamoto thought.

They walked past an exhibit of the *Enola Gay,* the American bomber that had dropped the atomic bomb on Hiroshima. Yamamoto knew that Mishima had lost relatives there. Not that that mattered very much to Yamamoto. His own grandfather had died at Iwo Jima. He had lost two uncles at Okinawa. And a great-aunt had died in an air raid over Tokyo. Every family lost members. He resented the special status accorded those who had died at Hiroshima, or Nagasaki. War was war and dead was dead.

The two Japanese found themselves back in the museum's main hall. It was crowded and noisy.

"Jupiter is too important to drop," Mishima said.

Yamamoto waited.

The ambassador leaned toward his companion's ear. "There remains one further possibility open to us. We must try to get DNA samples from the Stewart child and her parents. If we can do that, then I think there is a way we can proceed. It will be difficult and tedious, but in the long run it might be the best approach. In any case, we must be wise enough to pursue it. Listen very carefully. This is what I want you to do. . . ."

Cooper sat in a soundproof room in the basement of a building on the huge NSA campus at Fort Meade. In the ten years that he had worked for Roy, he had been at Fort Meade only once before. He hadn't liked it then, and he didn't like it now.

Roy came in with two other men Cooper had never seen before. One was tall, the other short. Both wore crew cuts, gray suits, and that amusing manner of complacent self-importance that bureaucrats high up in the spy business seemed to favor. Roy introduced the tall one as Harry, the short one as Jack.

They each shook Cooper's hand and sat down across the small conference table from him. Cooper sensed that he made them uneasy. His bone-white hair and ebony skin tended to remind white people of cannibals. He ought to get a bone put through his nose, he thought, and really scare them.

"We're still very goddamned disappointed in what happened at Coronado, Mr. Cooper," Harry said.

"We've been through this a hundred times in the last twelve months. The place was blowing up around me."

"We now know who's responsible for that," Roy said.

"Who?" Cooper asked.

No one answered him.

"This nigger doesn't need to know. That it?"

They laughed, embarrassed.

"We've reviewed the tapes from your surveillance bugs," Jack said. "We think that the Jupiter program may have survived."

"Yeah? You know where it is?"

"We're getting close," Harry said. "We want you to relocate in New York City. We've arranged everything. Even got you a job."

"Oh?"

"At the Hilton hotel."

"As what? A bellboy?"

Jack shook his head. "You'll be in the kitchen." He grinned. His teeth were bad. "Have to keep you out of sight, you know."

Cooper bowed his head, doffing an imaginary straw hat in Jack's direction. He felt like saying "Yassuh" as well, but he knew that would be carrying insubordination too far.

"This is important, Cooper," Harry said, his voice suddenly stern. "Jupiter could be the biggest thing since they discovered the atomic bomb—"

"Bigger," Jack cut in.

"—and if it's that big, then there's only one nation on earth big enough to own it—the United States of America."

Amen to that, thought Cooper.

21

On his morning drive into Manhattan, Dalton Stewart tried to think things through. He let his head fall back against the plush black leather upholstery and closed his eyes. Inside the perfect cocoon of his limousine it was hard to focus on the reality facing him, because it was so out of place with the material luxury of his surroundings. But he knew it was there, lurking somewhere in the dark, waiting to destroy him.

He had never faced such a crisis before. His entire multibillion-dollar empire was now in a financial shambles. He had succeeded in maintaining an optimistic front in public and before his employees; but the word was out, and the situation was deteriorating hourly. Wall Street was awash with rumors, greatly compounding Biotech's already crippling money problems. The company's stock was in a free fall. It had lost eighteen points on the New York Exchange yesterday—ten percent of its value—and he expected worse today.

In the current climate he knew the banks would not give him another extension to keep Biotech afloat. In the five months since he had negotiated the last extension, the situation had not improved. In fact it had gotten measurably worse. He had lost the psychological edge in his dealings with them. They simply no longer believed in him.

He wondered why he was begging them so hard, anyway. Even if the consortium of banks agreed to a complete rescheduling of his debt, it was clear they would do it only on their own terms. They'd demand a seat on the board and complete financial oversight. They'd be looking over his shoulder at every business decision. He doubted he could tolerate it.

Chapter 11 bankruptcy would be even worse. It might offer him some breathing room—hold off his creditors and give him a chance to reorganize the company. But at bottom it was too extreme a remedy. He would lose financial and operating control. He would no longer be free to call the shots. His every move would need the approval of outsiders—a bunch of bankers, CPAs, and lawyers whose interests would not be his interests.

Stewart opened his eyes and stared out the window. A cold spring drizzle made the dirty streets and ugly houses beneath the expressway look even more desolate than usual. The ghost of his father was never very far from his mind—especially when he thought of Anne and Genny. They were his only consolation in the rising tide of financial misery around him. For the first time in his life, he understood the joys of being a husband and father. And now he was being forced to visit this calamity on them.

They would survive, just as he had survived his father's downfall. But the family's social position, buttressed entirely by money, would collapse along with his business. All the old-line families on whom he had expended so much effort to ingratiate himself would freeze him and his family out completely. He could already imagine their smug condescension at the news of his ruin. God, Anne was right, he thought. They were never worth the trouble in the first place.

He had to do something.

When the going gets tough, the tough get going. His father used to quote that old saw to him all the time, and it used to make him snicker in derision. But this time the memory brought tears to his eyes. All these years he had missed the truth hidden beneath the disgrace. His father, in his desperation to preserve the privileges and position of his demanding, selfish family—and to preserve what he assumed was the reason for their love and respect—had risked everything, absolutely everything, in one terrible, misguided gamble. He broke the law, he got caught, and he suffered the consequences. Suffered them with no small degree of stoicism, Stewart recalled.

And all these years he had despised his father. Because he had ruined the good times, because he had made Dalton ashamed of him. Dalton had seen only the failure. He had never considered the tragic bravery.

Now had come his turn to stare ruin in the face—and be brave enough to risk everything for it.

Hank Ajemian was waiting for him in his office when he arrived. His assistant looked more depressed than Stewart had ever seen him. He was sitting hunched forward on the sofa by the windows. The normal dark circles under his eyes now looked purple and puffy. His white shirt collar was wilted and grayish, and his suit was badly in need of pressing.

"What's the situation?" Stewart asked.

"We need twenty-four million by the end of the business day tomorrow."

"I know that. What about the bankers' meeting tomorrow?"

Ajemian sniffled. "All they're going to do is give us an ultimatum—no more extensions, no rescheduling, no new deals, no exceptions, no nothing."

"They've said all that before."

"This time they mean it. And we don't have anything left to offer them to make them change their minds, anyway."

"You've got to buy us some more time at that meeting, Hank—even if it's only twenty-four hours."

"You're not coming?"

"No."

"What do you expect me to tell them?"

"That I'm raising the money. Get us an extension until Wednesday. Tell them we'll have it for them by then. Absolutely without fail."

A long pause. Ajemian looked at his boss incredulously. "Will we?"

"I don't know. I've got an idea. If it doesn't work, then I really don't give a shit what the bankers do. I'll give them the keys and take a walk."

Ajemian started to protest, then sensed there was no point. "Okay," he said. "I'll stall them. They can't say no to twenty-four hours. When will I know whether or not you've got the money?"

Dalton considered for a moment. "Tomorrow afternoon," he replied. "Two o'clock."

"You're not going to tell me what you're doing?"

Stewart didn't like shutting his assistant out on such an important matter, but he didn't want to have to listen to arguments against his plan; he might be persuaded by them. "Not yet. No."

Ajemian stared at his boss for a few moments, as if trying to divine his intentions. "Okay," he said.

By seven-thirty the following morning Stewart was through French customs at Charles de Gaulle Airport. He went to a telephone, pulled a slip of paper from his pocket, and dialed a Paris number. He prayed. If Kirsten Amster wasn't there, he wasn't sure what he'd do. The number rang eight times. He hung up, then dialed again. Ten rings.

He dialed directory assistance. He made the operator repeat her information three times, to make sure he had understood the French. There was no mistaking the message: the city of Paris had no listing for a Kirsten Amster.

Stewart found a taxi and handed the driver a slip of paper with Amster's address written on it.

Rue Montgallet was a short and narrow street that connected avenue Daumesnil with the rue de Reuilly several blocks east of the Gare de Lyon. It was in an old working-class neighborhood of the city, and entirely unfamiliar to the cab driver, who managed two wrong turns before finally zeroing in on it.

Stewart pulled up his collar and walked down the block to number 15. It was a cold day. The same clammy drizzle he had left behind in New York seemed to have followed him to Paris.

The front door of number 15 was ajar. He pushed it in and peered around the small brown-painted vestibule. He brushed his wet hair out of his eyes and looked for the buzzer for apartment 3. He found it, third from the end, over its mailbox. Garibaldi, the nameplate said.

He checked the names over the other boxes: Abadji,

Jusson, Cameon, Bagoy, Sapon. No Amster. He stepped back outside to check the building number. It was 15.

A squat, muscular man in a corduroy coat and woolen hat came through the lobby's inner door, carrying a broom. The pungent odor of sardines wafted out behind him into the vestibule.

"Excuse me. Do you speak English?"

The man shook his head.

"Vous êtes le concierge?"

He nodded.

Kirsten Amster, it turned out, no longer lived at that address. Getting her new address took twenty minutes of hard bargaining and cost Stewart two hundred francs, but he walked away with a strip of brown paper torn from a shopping bag with the words "Apt. 6, 32 boulevard Raspail" scrawled on it in leaky blue ballpoint.

Stewart ducked into the Métro station at the end of the block and rode across the city to the rue du Bac, a short block from where the boulevard Raspail branched off from the boulevard Saint-Germain. The neighborhood was Left Bank chic, and many rungs up the economic ladder from the rue Montgallet. Stewart was seized by the sudden fear that Amster had sold the Jupiter program to someone else. That would certainly explain her move to a better part of town.

Stewart found number 32 a block and a half up. It was a large, immaculately maintained four-story apartment building. The name under the bell for apartment 6, on the top floor, was Steiner, not Amster. Stewart pressed it anyway. No answer. He looked at his watch: 8:30 A.M. He pressed the buzzer again and held it. Eventually a sleepy, blurred female voice boomed over the lobby's static-filled intercom: *"Qui est-ce?"*

"Kirsten Amster? *Est-elle là?*"

"No." The accent sounded American.

"Does she live here?" Stewart asked.

"Who are you?"

"Dalton Stewart. . . . I need to find her."

"Why?"

"An urgent business matter."

"She's not here anymore."

"Do you know where she is?"

There was a long pause. Dalton repeated the question. Still no answer. "Please," he said, looking pleadingly at the shiny metal intercom grille. "If you know her address ..."

"Try 9 rue Blondel."

"Where is that, exactly ... ?"

"Off the rue Saint-Denis."

"Thank you. Do you have a phone number ... ?"

There was no answer. The woman had shut off the intercom.

The rue Blondel was in the heart of the red light district. At this hour of the morning, with a cold, misty rain falling, the only prostitutes out were the hardy and the desperate, hunched against the elements in dark vestibules and doorways, calling out in stage whispers to the males passing by.

The entrance to number 9 was barricaded by a fat fortyish woman in a cheap cloth wrap. She was leaning against the door frame, smoking a cigarette.

Dalton cleared his throat. "I'm looking for Kirsten Amster. Does she live here?"

The woman glanced across the street, then shrugged. Stewart followed her gaze. Two men were watching him from a doorway. He extracted a hundred-franc note from his wallet and held it out toward her. "Kirsten Amster?" he repeated.

The woman snatched the bill smoothly out his hands and swept it into a pocket somewhere. She nodded quickly in the direction of the stairs at the end of the narrow, shabby hallway behind her. *"Deuxième étage. Au fond."*

Stewart moved up the stairs slowly, giving his eyes time to adjust to the dim light. The place stank of rotting food and urine. He paused at the second landing and then remembered that *deux-ième étage* meant the third floor in France, not the second. He climbed another flight. At the back end of the hallway there was a single scarred brown door with several locks on it. He knocked.

After a few minutes of persistent pounding, he heard a voice growl something in French from the other side.

"I'm looking for Kirsten Amster," he said.

"What do you want?"

"I need to talk to her. We had a business arrangement."

"Who are you?"

"Dalton Stewart."

A long silence.

"Please. I must talk with her."

He heard the snap of a lock and the rattle of a chain. The door opened an inch. Stewart saw a dark eye peering at him. The safety chain was lifted out of its catch, and the door opened wider. A puffy, bald, bearded, middle-aged figure in a gray undershirt looked him over.

Stewart glanced over his shoulder. The dim corridor behind him felt vaguely threatening. "May I come in?"

"You alone?"

"Yes."

The man let him into a small studio apartment—a galley kitchen and minuscule bath attached to a narrow, airless room with one window, shut tight and covered by ratty red velvet drapes. The walls were painted red, the ceiling light blue. Both colors were peeling.

A mattress lay on the floor in one corner. There was little else in the room—a table, a chest of drawers, a couple of beat-up chairs, an improvised bookshelf of stacked wooden crates. There appeared to be no closet. Clothes hung from hooks on the wall. The stale smell of cigarette smoke and human funk was strong.

Despite the desperate tawdriness of the place, it was surprisingly neat. The floor looked clean, and a stained quilt was tucked neatly over the mattress. There was a single lamp on the floor beside the mattress, and a stack of books on the quilt. A pile of pillows propped against the wall indicated that the man had been reading.

"My name is Joe Slater," he said. He sat at the table and gestured toward the other chair. Stewart walked over and sat down. Slater waved a hand around, inviting his guest to take in the surroundings. "Not exactly avenue Foch, is it?" he joked.

"Are there some people watching you?" Stewart asked.

Slater laughed. "You mean those guys across the street?"

"Who are they?"

"Fucked if I know. I don't pay any attention to them." Slater looked toward the kitchen. "I got a couple of beers in the fridge. Alsatian, not too bad. . . ."

"No thanks."

"A man never thinks his life'll come to this," Slater said. "Christ knows I didn't. I would have thought this romantic as all hell when I was in my twenties. But now . . . now it's just pathetic. I'm pathetic. I'll be fifty-three next birthday. I really didn't expect to live this long, you know that? I guess that's part of my problem. I've outlived myself. Hey, but you didn't come here to listen to my problems."

"I'm looking for Kirsten Amster."

"Yeah, you told me."

"Does she live here?"

"Not anymore."

"Where *does* she live?"

Slater's eyes narrowed. "She doesn't live anywhere. She's dead."

The news jolted Stewart powerfully. When he had recovered, he asked what had happened to her.

"She drowned. In the Seine. Last October."

"An accident?"

"That's what the police say. I think she was killed."

"Why?"

"That fucking genetic computer program."

"I paid her for it over a year ago. She cheated me. She sold me a disk with only half the program on it."

"You're not the only one. Everybody was after her for it."

"Everybody? Who?"

"I don't know who they were. It was none of my business. I told her to get rid of the fucking thing. But no. She kept dangling it out there, like bait, and upping the ante. She said she was going to make a killing with it. Well, she did that all right."

"Did she sell it to anybody?"

"No."

"You sure?"

"Positive."

"What happened to it? Do you know?"

Slater took a sip of his beer and said nothing.

"Do you have it?"

Slater looked Stewart over. "Yeah, I have it. Or I should say I know where it is."

"I'll pay you for it."

Slater gazed at him with his sad, rheumy eyes. After a pause, he shook his head in resignation.

"Ten thousand dollars," Stewart said. "Five in cash today. The rest as soon as I can verify that it's genuine."

Slater still didn't respond.

"I've already invested a small fortune in that program," Stewart added. "And I've already paid for it once. It's really my property."

Slater rubbed his face and sighed. "I won't argue with you, Stewart. But if I were you, I'd forget about it. Leave the goddamned thing alone. It's cursed. Look what happened to Goth. Look what happened to Kirsten."

"Will you take the offer?"

"What are you going to do with it?"

"Develop it, of course."

"Of course. And make more billions, right?"

Stewart didn't bother to reply.

"What do you need more money for?" Slater demanded. "What the hell do you do with it all? Does it make you feel good? Secure? Superior? What does it do for you?"

"It's a measure of success," Stewart answered. And failure as well, he thought.

"Is it?"

"Most people'd say so."

"Sort of a way to keep score, eh? The guy with the most marbles wins."

"Something like that."

Slater yawned. "You know what? It sounds pretty fucking boring."

Stewart felt the need to justify himself. "Not for me it isn't. There's plenty of risk. Uncertainty. You'd be surprised."

"Probably. You're taking a big risk here, I'll tell you that."

"Why?"

"I told you. The program's cursed. This guy Goth was playing God. He was fucking around with the fundamental mystery of life on earth. He was creating his own specs for building a human being. Stealing God's own thunder. Or trying to. How blasphemous can you get? But it so happens I need the money. . . ."

"Where is it?" Stewart demanded.

"Where it belongs. In Hell."

"Hell?"

Slater laughed. "Yeah. The Paris version."

22

Leonora, the Stewarts' upstairs maid, came into Anne's bedroom and began dusting the furniture. She paused at the dressing table, picked up one of Anne's hair brushes, and examined it, looking for loose strands of hair in the bristles. There were none. Two other brushes on the table were similarly clean.

She went to Anne's bed, picked up a pillow, and carried it over to a window. She found several strands of Anne's hair on the pillowcase. She removed them carefully, then fished in her apron for the small letter envelope. She folded the strands inside, licked the flap, and sealed it shut.

After cleaning the bathroom and making Anne's bed, Leonora went into the bedroom across the hall from Anne's, where her husband, Dalton Stewart, usually slept. She located more strands of hair on the pillowcases on his bed and sealed them in a second envelope.

She made his bed, cleaned the bathroom, dusted the furniture, and then moved down the hall to the room where the Stewarts' daughter slept. She examined the crib mattress and the bumper for loose hairs, but could find none. She located a few strands on the changing table nearby, but it was impossible to be certain whose head they had fallen from—the child's, her mother's, or her nanny's.

Leonora finished cleaning the front rooms and moved to the north wing. Mrs. Callahan was in the nursery, reading a magazine. Whenever Leonora saw her, she seemed to have her nose stuck in a magazine. Except when Mrs. Stewart was around, of course; then she was all bustle and business.

The Stewarts' daughter was sitting in the middle of the floor, stacking alphabet blocks. Mrs. Callahan looked up, saw Leonora, and turned back to her magazine. As for the child, she was concentrating so intently on her blocks that she seemed not to notice the maid's entrance at all.

She was a beautiful Anglo child, Leonora thought, with the same angelic disposition as her mother; but there was something disturbing about her. The girl had a peculiar way of looking at you. She acted as if she were seeing something on you—as if you had a big spider crawling on your head, or something. It was a little bit spooky.

Leonora sometimes wondered if the child might be possessed. Her aunt Carolina, in El Salvador, had seen such cases. Still, there was nothing evil about the girl that the maid could see. It was just that funny look she had, as if she were seeing things that weren't there.

The maid dawdled, stretching out her cleaning chores, hoping Mrs. Callahan might leave the room for a moment. She knew the woman suffered from a bladder problem.

Leonora turned on the vacuum cleaner and worked it back and forth on the carpet. Genny waved her little arms, afraid the vacuum was going to knock over her blocks. The maid moved the machine around them with great care.

Finally Mrs. Callahan stood up. "Watch her for me, Leonora. I'm going to the bathroom."

"Yes, ma'am."

The moment the nanny disappeared through the doorway, Leonora turned off the vacuum and knelt behind Genny. From her apron she extracted a small pair of fingernail scissors and quickly snipped off a strand of Genny's blond locks. The girl felt the back of her head with her hand and quickly looked around.

"*Buenos días, niña,*" Leonora said. "*Qué tal?*"

"*Buenos días,*" Genny replied, imitating the maid's accent perfectly. "Why did you cut my hair?"

"Just a little piece," Leonora said, tucking the hair into a third envelope and sealing it. "For my collection. I collect hair from all my friends."

Genny regarded the maid with those laserlike gray-blue

eyes. "I think that's silly," she declared, in a very adult voice. She turned back to her blocks.

Mrs. Callahan returned and Leonora quickly finished her cleaning. As she was leaving, the alphabet blocks Genny was playing with suddenly caught her attention. The maid had been studying English very diligently, and she was proud of her reading ability. Genny had arranged some of the blocks in a long line. The side facing Leonora showed all capital letters: WHATEVERYWOM-ANSHOULDKNOW. At first they appeared to be randomly arranged, but on closer inspection, Leonora thought that they spelled out something. She puzzled over them a few moments longer. Then the individual English words jumped out at her: "What every woman should know."

"Madre de Dios," she whispered. She hurried from the nursery, feeling short of breath.

Later, riding into town with Mrs. Corley, the housekeeper, Leonora realized that what the girl must have done was copy the letters from the cover of one of Mrs. Callahan's magazines. She couldn't remember seeing any magazine on the floor anywhere near the child, however. And she had vacuumed every inch of it. How could that little *niña* be so smart? The child must be a very special gift from God, she thought. Or the Devil.

In town, Leonora met the man in the greeting card aisle at the big CVS drugstore, as arranged. He dressed very well and had excellent manners. That seemed to be true of most of the Asians she had seen since coming to the United States.

She gave him the three envelopes. She had marked them clearly, but he ripped them all open right there in the aisle and looked inside each one. Finally he nodded and smiled and told her that she had done an excellent job.

She had met him the week before. He worked for a big shampoo manufacturer. His company was doing a big study on rich women's hair. It was all part of a major project to develop a new shampoo. *Muy importante,* very hush-hush. She had to promise never to tell anyone of her secret little mission on the company's behalf.

He handed her an envelope from his inside suit pocket and, with a small bow, turned and left the store. The envelope contained five twenty-dollar bills.

The man's story was a bit farfetched, but Leonora hardly cared. If he wanted a few strands of someone's hair, what could be the harm? Especially if he was willing to pay her a hundred dollars for them.

Leonora slipped the bills into her purse. And speaking of hair, she thought, she ought to take a look at those elegant new electric razors for women she had noticed at the front counter.

23

Dalton Stewart and Joe Slater emerged together from Slater's studio apartment on the rue Blondel. The fat woman was still by the doorway, smoking a cigarette.

Stewart noticed a couple of prostitutes huddled in the shadows of a narrow alleyway across the street. Behind them, Stewart glimpsed the same two men he had seen earlier. They were sitting on chairs tilted back against the alley wall. As soon as they saw Slater and Stewart they stood up.

"Are they going to follow us?" Stewart asked.

"Afraid so."

"Who are they?"

Slater pulled up the collar of his coat against the damp. "I told you—I don't know."

"You know what they want?"

"What do you think?"

Stewart watched the men out of the corner of his eye. They had come out of the alley and were walking single file along the narrow sidewalk on the other side of the street. Their presence unnerved him. "How do they know you have it?"

"They don't," Slater said. "Right after Kirsten was killed some people approached me and offered me money. I told them I didn't know anything about my computer program. After that, these guys appeared. I've tried a hundred times to shake the bastards. I even moved twice. But somehow they always find me again. They've ransacked my apartment five times. They're waiting for me to lead them to Jupiter. I know it."

"What are we going to do?"

"Lose them."

They took the Métro to Denfert-Rochereau, changing cars several times en route. From there they walked a few blocks down the boulevard Saint-Jacques, turned right onto the rue Dareau, then left onto the rue Broussais, and finally left again onto the rue Cabanis, which ran along the grounds of the Centre Hospitalier Sainte-Anne.

Slater stopped in front of a small shop window. "Let's wait here. See if they're still around."

Five minutes passed.

"No sign of them," Stewart said, getting impatient.

"Don't be hasty. They're clever bastards. Follow me."

Slater retraced their route all the way back to Denfert, his eyes probing every doorway, alley, and storefront for any sign of a tail. Satisfied at last that they had lost them, he led Stewart along an even more circuitous route back to the rue Cabanis.

"This way." Slater climbed over the low stone wall that bordered the hospital's small park. Stewart followed, feeling increasingly foolhardy.

Slater led him a short distance through some heavy bushes until they came to a low shed used to store equipment for ground maintenance. Slater yanked open the shed's door and ducked inside. He took a shovel leaning against the back wall and scraped several inches of dirt from the floor until he had unearthed an old iron manhole cover. He pried the cover up with the blade of the shovel and slid it aside.

Stewart peered down into blackness. "Where the hell does it go?"

"To the catacombs," Slater replied. "Kirsten's idea. She had a job here at the hospital lab. Some co-workers showed her the entrance. They used to go down here sometimes, just for the evil thrill of it. Used to party down there, she told me." Slater pulled a pair of small flashlights from his pocket and handed one to Stewart. "You'll need this."

Slater lowered himself into the opening, feeling for the top rungs of the iron ladder attached to the stone-lined walls of the well. He turned on his flashlight and began a cautious descent.

Stewart took a deep breath to steady himself, then followed.

A hundred rungs down, ten stories under the city of Paris, Slater stepped off the ladder onto a dirt floor and shined the flashlight around. Stewart, his arms and legs trembling from the exertion, reached the floor right behind him.

They were standing at the edge of a network of underground passages that honeycombed the earth underneath the "three mounts" of south Paris—Montsouris, Montrouge, and Montparnasse. The huge warren of tunnels dated back to the Roman era. Sections of it were open to tourists during the summer months. But now, in early spring, the catacombs were locked, cold, and dark.

Slater led the way, stepping carefully, swinging his flashlight back and forth ahead of him to scare off the numerous rats that inhabited the dank underworld. He frequently caught their eyes in the light, and their dark brown backsides as they scurried into the protective dark.

"Christ, they're as big as cats," Stewart said.

"The French Resistance used the catacombs to hide out from the Germans," Slater replied. "The krauts were afraid to come down here. I'm not too crazy about it myself. It's goddamn spooky."

Stewart agreed. It was all he could do to fight off the impulse to turn and flee back up to the surface.

After nearly a mile's walk through damp-walled, narrow tunnels, they arrived at the section known as the Ossuary. Here, in countless rows along the cave walls, were arranged the bones of hundreds of thousands of skeletons removed from the cemeteries of Paris at the end of the eighteenth century. The long galleries of neatly stacked human skulls and tibias branched out in every direction to form a uniquely macabre spectacle—a veritable subterranean world of the dead.

Stewart followed the beam of his flashlight, staring open-mouthed at the morbid panorama that surrounded them. It was so utterly ghoulish, he thought—like a scene from Dante's *Inferno,* or the literal Hell of a medieval morality play. Stewart shivered involuntarily.

They arrived at a small, steep-vaulted chamber off the

main galleries, where the bones were arranged in a low semicircular wall to form a kind of altar. Slater shined the flashlight through the eye sockets of a skull sitting at the top of a neatly stacked pile. He patted the skull. "Probably a beautiful woman, once upon a time. Or maybe a whore with the pox. Or a thief who beat his wife. Hell, maybe it was Marie Antoinette. We'll never know."

The stale, humid air seemed to swallow up Slater's words even as he spoke them. Stewart shuddered again. "Hurry the hell up. This place is getting to me."

Slater lifted the skull from the top of the pile, set it aside, and reached in among the bones to retrieve a metal strongbox. He twirled the tiny combination lock and the lid popped open. Inside, swathed in several layers of bubble wrap, was a single black plastic RCD computer cartridge. Slater closed the box and handed it to Stewart. "You take it. I don't even want to touch it. As I said before, the fucking thing's cursed."

Stewart tucked the box under his arm. He felt immense relief. "This is the only copy?"

Slater laughed. "You want to look around for others?"

Stewart shook his head. "Let's get out of here."

They started back. A little way along the tunnel, something fell to the ground behind them. It made a soft plop as it hit the damp dirt underfoot. Stewart whirled around, pointing the flashlight down the pitch-black passageway. Nothing. His pulse was racing.

"Just a bone," Slater said. "Knocked over by a rat."

They increased their pace. The humid underground atmosphere caused Stewart to break out into a sweat.

They came to a place where the tunnel divided into two separate passageways. Slater stopped. "Did you hear something?"

"No."

"Listen. . . . A soft drumming sound."

Slater directed his flashlight down one branch of the tunnel, then the other. In the second passage the beam of light picked out a crowd of rats, galloping toward them.

Slater froze. Stewart immediately turned and fled.

Fifty yards down the tunnel he was soaked with sweat and his heart was pounding. The floor of the passage was uneven, and Stewart, in his panic, stumbled and fell. The rats shot right on past him, hugging the edges of the tunnel on each side of him.

Stewart scrambled back to his feet. The strongbox with the cassette in it had slipped from his grasp. He found it in the dirt and picked it up.

He brushed off his pants and jacket and stood, catching his breath. He was shaking. Stupid, he thought, letting a few rats throw such a scare into him.

He shined the light down the passageway. No sign of Slater. Which way had he come? He looked down the other way. The long dark tunnel looked the same in both directions. He called out to Slater.

No answer.

Stewart knelt and tried to find his footprints on the floor, so he could determine the direction in which he had come. The dirt was packed so hard it was impossible to make out anything.

He stood up and called Slater's name again. Still no answer. He called out a third time. The walls seemed to muffle his voice, soaking up the sound before it had traveled any distance at all.

Finally he thought he heard something faint far down the tunnel. A yell? A scream? Slater. It was certainly Slater. He took off at a trot back down the tunnel toward the sound. He came back to the place where the tunnel divided.

He heard Slater's voice again. It was coming from the tunnel on the left. He started to call, then checked himself. Slater was talking to someone. He sounded agitated.

Stewart advanced cautiously along the tunnel, listening. Slater's voice was getting closer, but numerous alcoves branched off both sides of the tunnel, and Stewart couldn't locate the exact direction of the sound.

Then the main passage curved sharply to the right. Stewart stopped and turned off his flashlight. He could see faint light reflected off the tunnel wall ahead of him. He approached on tiptoe and looked around.

He saw Slater. He was on his knees, squinting into the bright glare of a flashlight, and struggling to stand. Two men were standing over him. The quick blur of a boot flashed through the beam of light and hit Slater's stomach. Then an arm with a club descended against Slater's skull. Slater grunted and slumped face-forward into the dirt.

The men watched him for a few seconds, then began swinging their clubs methodically against his skull, taking their time in the wavering light of their flashlights to land their blows on target.

Stewart dared not move or breathe.

Finally, mercifully, they stopped. One felt Slater's neck for a pulse, then said something in German. They ransacked his pockets, then ripped his clothes off and looked through them frantically. Unable to find what they were looking for, they got to their feet. One of the men kicked Slater in the side of the head. They exchanged a few words and then started off in Stewart's direction.

Stewart ducked into one of the alcoves. They passed by him without seeing him and vanished up the passageway.

When he was sure they were some distance away, Stewart edged back to the corner and turned on his flashlight.

Slater lay motionless on his back.

Three rats had already found him. They were creeping around him, tentatively sniffing, touching. One climbed onto his stomach and walked across it, scratching and sniffing.

Stewart shook his head. He felt on the verge of throwing up. He turned and retreated back the way he had come.

They had to know he was down here, he realized. They would likely wait for him at the top of the long ladder in the tool shed in the garden of Sainte-Anne.

He would have to find another way out.

For over an hour Stewart roamed the dark labyrinth of underground passages. He began hyperventilating. He shook and trembled and his clothes were drenched in cold sweat. He talked out loud to himself to fend off the building waves of terror. The additional fear of a possible heart attack forced him to stop and catch his breath.

When his pulse had slowed, he set off again, moving at as fast a pace as he dared. His heart thumped, loud and fast and heavy, like the footfalls of someone running for his life.

He kept imagining he could hear real footfalls, pounding in the dirt behind him. A hundred times he shined the flashlight behind him to make sure no one was there.

The flashlight eventually began to dim. The thought of losing the light altogether sent a fresh shock of panic through him. He started turning it off and on at intervals to preserve the batteries.

Just as the flashlight failed completely, Stewart stumbled onto a large, sturdy circular stairway. He felt his way up the dozens of steps in the pitch-dark.

At the top he found himself in a small building on the place Denfert-Rochereau. Sun was shining in the windows. There were signs and a ticket booth. It was the tourist entrance to the catacombs. No sign of anyone watching.

Thank God, thank God.

The outside door was locked. He opened a window and climbed out.

After a change of clothes at his hotel, Stewart checked out of his suite and took a taxi to Orly Airport. In an hour he was on a plane to Munich.

24

On the ride in from the Munich airport Dalton Stewart popped a couple of ibuprofen caplets into his mouth. Earlier, after the terrifying episode in the catacombs, he had swallowed a Halcion tablet to calm his nerves, but it hadn't worked. He could feel the pill's chemicals thrumming through him; but instead of boosting him into a kind of aggressive alertness, they had kicked his sleep-starved system over the edge. He felt raw, punctured—as if his strength and courage were leaking out of him. A look of ragged desperation was not the look to bring to a meeting with Gerta von Hauser. Especially this meeting.

The baroness greeted him in her office with a kiss and then stepped back and looked him over. She seemed pleased to see him again.

They had parted on ambiguous terms. Their affair, if it could be called that, had ended the same night that it had begun—in the frenzy of the New Year's celebration at President Despres's palace in Coronado. Stewart had had no communication with her since, but he had thought about her frequently over the past year and a half.

"You look rather haggard, Herr Stewart," the baroness said, in her overrounded English accent. She offered him a seat beside her on a long leather sofa.

Stewart sank into the cushions. His eyelids felt heavy. "Too many plane flights," he complained. "It's the damned recycled air. I think the pilots must get a kickback from the airline on every canister of unused oxygen they save."

The baroness murmured something in agreement.

She looked better than he had remembered her. She was wearing a hand-tailored charcoal-gray business suit. It was subdued but flawlessly cut, draping her lithe figure perfectly and presenting a striking foil for her magnificent blond hair, which she now wore long.

He mustered the energy to throw out a few compliments. The baroness gave him a quick, impatient smile. She asked about Anne and their child but didn't appear much interested in Stewart's answer. She wasn't one to waste time on small talk, anyway. She moved directly to the point: "Naturally I am curious to know why you have come to see me."

Stewart reached down for his attaché case, clicked open its brass snaps, and pulled out a black plastic RCD. He held it up in front of her. "You know what this is?"

Her eyes focused on the object, then back on him. "I expect you're going to tell me." She smiled.

Stewart placed the RCD on the low marble table in front of the sofa. "It's Goth's Jupiter program."

The baroness seemed slightly startled. "Where did you get it?"

"I had the foresight to acquire a copy before Goth's death." He was oversimplifying considerably, but he had no intention of telling her about Slater and the catacombs.

The baroness picked up the cartridge and turned it over in her hand several times, as if she were examining a small sculpture for flaws. "Why have you not done anything with it?"

"I didn't think it worked. Now I know that it does."

The baroness looked mystified. "And you want me to help you develop it?"

"Exactly."

"Why do you come to me? Why don't you test it yourself?"

A wave of faintness forced Stewart to close his eyes for a few seconds. He bent his head down and pretended to study something on the floor until the sensation had passed. "I need backing," he said.

"It can't be very expensive to set up a trial. . . ."

Stewart's mouth was dry. He licked his lips and tried to suppress the humiliation he felt. "No. You don't understand. I'm in financial trouble. Biotech is facing bankruptcy." His voice stumbled on the word "bankruptcy."

The baroness settled back against the sofa and crossed

her arms. A visible thrill of satisfaction lit her face. "And you hope to save yourself with this?" She nodded in the direction of the black plastic cartridge on the table in front of them.

"I'm willing to offer you a large percentage. In return for enough cash to get the banks off my back."

"How much cash is that?"

"Twenty-four million."

"You can't raise even that much?"

"If I could I wouldn't be here."

"I see." The baroness seemed suddenly offended. She moved from the sofa to her desk, as if to distance herself from Stewart's request. "You expect me to give you twenty-four million for only a share of the program's profits?"

"Baroness, the twenty-four million is a loan. You'll be paid back in full. I'll even leave the terms to you."

"What equity are you offering me?"

"Fifty percent of Jupiter."

The baroness shook her head. "That's not equity. That's—what's the American expression?—a pig in a poke."

"I'll put up the necessary shares of Biotech as collateral as well. God knows I'm not trying to cheat you. The banks have gotten cold feet. I'll have to file a Chapter 11 and try to reorganize."

"How soon do you need this money?"

"Immediately. Today."

The baroness swung her chair away from the desk and gazed thoughtfully out the window. Stewart had laid out his position naked and unadorned. He knew his desperation was showing, but he was too exhausted to try to paint a less stark picture of his situation. She would likely see through any obfuscations anyway.

The baroness swiveled her chair back to face the desk. She brushed some imaginary dust from the desk's polished surface. "I cannot do it, Herr Stewart. And certainly not on such short notice."

Stewart listened for even a trace of indecision in her tone, but he heard none.

"Even if you have the real Jupiter, I have no faith in

it," she continued. "Not anymore. It hasn't been tested. It may be worthless. As for your Biotech stock, that can't be worth much, either, if your financial situation is so bad."

Stewart held up a hand in protest. "The company's basically sound. That's the irony of the situation. We overextended and we had some bad luck. Goth's death to begin with, of course. And then some damaging lawsuits, coupled with a major business recession. But these are all surmountable problems. All we need is a little time. But the damned banks are running scared. They're in bigger trouble than Biotech, and they're looking for assets to shore up their own shaky finances."

"You've made some bad business decisions," she countered. "Don't blame the banks."

Stewart drew a breath to rebut her, then let it out in a long, tired exhalation.

"Would you like something to drink?" she asked, suddenly solicitous.

"Yes. Black coffee."

The baroness called an assistant on the intercom and gave the order. They looked at each other. The baroness shrugged. "I'm really sorry, Dalton, but you're not making me a realistic offer. I'm surprised that you even came to me for help."

He didn't reply. He still had his hole card, and he was thinking how best to play it.

The coffee arrived. The baroness fussed impatiently with the ruffles of her blouse as he drank it. She had given her decision, and now she wanted him to leave.

Stewart picked up the RCD and held it out in front of him. "Baroness, we once fought each other for this. Because we were both smart enough to know how much it could be worth. Now here it is. And I'm offering to cut you in on it—not just because I need your help but because there's enough profit here for both of us. It could make us the two richest individuals on the face of the planet."

"I'm sorry that I can't help you."

Stewart opened his attaché case again. He put the cartridge back inside and pulled out a videotape. "Do you have a VCR?"

"Dalton, I'm a very busy woman. . . ."

"It'll only take a few minutes. It'll be worth your time, I promise."

The baroness opened a panel in the wall near a wet bar to reveal a large TV and VCR. He handed her the tape. She inserted it in the machine and waited.

"What is it, for heaven's sakes?" she demanded.

"Watch. You'll see."

A little girl appeared, wearing a pink dress. She looked at the camera and smiled.

"Our daughter, Genny," Stewart explained.

The tape showed Genny progressing in age through a series of standard home video scenes—breast feeding, playing with her dolls and stuffed animals, eating at her high chair, taking her first steps, running around the house, playing with her mother and father, playing with her nanny.

"This was put together from several hours of videotapes done over the course of Genny's first year," Stewart explained. "There she is down at the guest cottage last summer. She was walking at six months."

The next scene showed Genny talking. Her mother's voice off-camera was asking her to introduce her stuffed animals. She held up each one in turn and recited its name.

The baroness crossed her arms impatiently. "What is the point of this?"

"This last scene was taped a few months ago," Stewart said, ignoring her. "Genny's fourteen months old here."

The camcorder zoomed slowly in on Genny, standing in front of a grand piano, rubbing her hands energetically along the bench seat. Suddenly she turned to face the keyboard and began playing the melody to "When You Wish Upon a Star." She played it once through, perfectly, then stopped, turned, and smiled at the camera.

The tape ended. The baroness reached forward, stopped the VCR, ejected the videotape, and handed it back to Stewart without a word. She walked to her desk and then turned around to face him.

Stewart followed her across the room. "Do you need an explanation?"

She shook her head. "You do amaze me, Dalton. *Mein Gott* . . ." There was genuine admiration in her tone. "I can see its advantages instantly. It let you be the first to know whether or not Jupiter worked. Quite inspired, really."

Dalton returned the videotape to his attaché case. His exhausted body felt a feeble but encouraging trickle of hope.

"But your wife was not afraid?"

"No."

"She was quite brave."

"Not exactly. I didn't tell her."

"How was that possible?"

Stewart explained that Anne thought Goth was making a single repair to one known genetic defect. "No one knew. It was between Goth and myself."

"And your wife still doesn't know?"

"I think it's better not to tell her. At least not yet."

"No one else knows?"

"You're the first."

The baroness kept shaking her head in disbelief. "You have had the girl tested?"

"I have her medical records with me. She's completely healthy. No problems at all. No abnormalities, nothing. She's a superior child in every way."

The baroness pulled a stack of letters from her In box, sat down, and began signing them. "Perhaps it's only a coincidence. There are such things as child prodigies, you know."

"You don't believe that."

The baroness shrugged.

"Fifty-fifty share," Stewart said. "Plus fifty million in stock, on whatever terms you want. All you have to do is put up twenty-four million cash, now."

"I'll think about it."

"I don't have time."

The baroness tossed the stack of signed letters into her Out box. "Give me two hours, then. I'll talk to my lawyers."

"Of course."

"I can't promise anything."

"I understand."

"It's three now. Come back at five-thirty. I'll have an answer then."

"Five-thirty," Stewart repeated. He picked up his attaché case and left.

The two and a half hours passed with excruciating slowness. Stewart walked the streets of Munich, ate a bratwurst and drank a glass of beer in a café, then walked the streets some more.

He knew he was taking a tremendous risk. He was practically putting his future in her hands. But he believed that he could control her. There was not a shred of evidence to suggest that she could be manipulated by him or by anybody—quite the contrary—but his ego wouldn't permit him to think otherwise.

When he returned to her office, the baroness was no longer alone. A narrow-headed man in his forties, with slicked-back hair, a high collar, a toothbrush mustache, and a sour expression, was sitting beside the baroness's desk. Stewart was immediately encouraged. This looked like her money man.

The baroness introduced him. His name was Richard Spengler—a company lawyer. Stewart shook his cold, damp hand and sat back down on the sofa.

"I wish to make a counteroffer," the baroness said in a brisk voice.

"I'm listening."

"I will loan you the twenty-four million dollars on the following conditions," she began, dropping her gaze to a sheet of paper on the desk in front of her. "One, an equal share with you of all profits from the Jupiter program. Two, a fifty-one-percent interest in Stewart Biotech. The twenty-four million dollars will be paid back either out of your profits on Jupiter or directly from gross, pretax earnings of Stewart Biotech, whichever becomes available first. For my part, I'll agree to undertake all initial expenses for developing the program—finding a suitable test site, outfitting and staffing a clinic, arranging for trials, and so on. When you've recovered your financial position, we'll share all future costs equally. There remain a lot of details to settle, of course, but those are the principal points. If you accept those, we can conclude an agreement."

Stewart's jaw tightened. "Fifty-one percent? You expect me to give you controlling interest in Stewart Biotech? For a twenty-four-million-dollar loan?" He said this in a very loud voice.

The baroness exchanged glances with Herr Spengler. He pursed his lips primly and nodded.

"The only way I can protect a loan that large is to have control over the company using it," she replied.

"Even the banks aren't that greedy."

The baroness folded her arms.

"The answer is no," Stewart said. "You'll have to accept much less. I offered the stock as security. As collateral. That's all. Until the loan is paid back."

"That's not good enough. I want stock."

"If you want stock, you can't expect a cash repayment of the loan as well. That's absurd."

"That's my offer, Dalton."

He thought the baroness was just staking out a tough bargaining position, but she wasn't. She meant her original offer to stand. That was it. Period. Take it or leave it. Stewart argued heatedly with her for half an hour, but she refused to budge.

He left her office, finally, telling her that he needed some time alone to think. He felt sick, confused, and angry. The woman was unbelievable. She knew she was his last hope, short of bankruptcy, and she intended to extract the maximum from him—strip him of everything she possibly could.

He went outside and walked the streets again. It had begun to rain hard. He pulled his coat collar up around his neck. He was shivering violently, and his joints and his muscles ached. His knees felt so weak and rubbery he feared that he might fall down. He retreated into a bar, ordered a drink, and downed another Halcion.

She had calculated her offer with a brutal precision, he thought. No matter how much he hated it, it still came out as the best alternative. It boiled down to a choice of giving control to her or to the banks. And the banks wouldn't lend him the money he needed to develop the Jupiter program. And that was what mattered. If he could just get the baroness to back off from her demand of controlling interest, he decided, he'd accept her offer. Then Jupiter would get developed, and it was Jupiter, after all, not Stewart Biotech, that held the key to a vastly richer future.

And he was pretty sure she'd accept less than controlling interest in Biotech. She was too smart—and too greedy—to hold out for the impossible.

And there was another reason. He had heard the men in the catacombs—the same men who had been watching Slater's apartment—speak German. It was close to certain they had been sent there by the baroness. Despite her tough bargaining stance, she still wanted Jupiter as much as he did.

He called the baroness from his hotel. "Forty percent of all common stock," he said. "And two seats on the board. Take it or leave it."

"Fifty percent and four seats on the board. That's the best offer I can possibly ever give you, Dalton."

"Sure. Forty-five percent and three seats. And that *is* the best you're ever going to get from me."

There was a long silence on the other end of the line. Stewart waited, holding his breath.

"Very well."

"Good. Draw up the papers. I'll initial a draft tonight. Tomorrow I'll send Hank Ajemian over to hammer out the details. I'll need you to transfer twenty-four million dollars to my bank in New York by noon tomorrow. I'll give you the account number tonight."

"I'm pleased," the baroness admitted, when they had settled their deal. Suddenly her voice was warm, sensuous. "It'll be a great adventure, I think."

Stewart didn't reply.

"Oh, there is one other condition," she added.

"What's that?"

"Your daughter, Genny. I'd like to meet her very much. If she's the living proof that Jupiter really works, I must see her myself, don't you agree?"

"Of course," Stewart said. "Why not?"

He hung up the phone and collapsed heavily onto the bed. He pulled the comforter up over himself and fell asleep, fully dressed.

Winter and Spring, 2002

25

A last hurried survey of the situation downstairs assured Anne that everything was in order. Amelia, the cook, was working furiously on the menu; the servers were properly dressed and instructed; the wines were chilled, the bar was set out, the hors d'oeuvres made; the newly decorated dining room was spotlessly clean, the silver was polished, the places set, the candles and the flowers arranged.

Anne rushed upstairs to change. Guests would be arriving in fifteen minutes. Dalton was already pacing the downstairs halls impatiently, drink in hand.

Her husband had so many times in the past reminded her that her performance as a hostess reflected on him that she was invariably in a state of nervous apprehension whenever they were entertaining.

But tonight she was more anxious than normal. This dinner was no ordinary affair. It was for Stewart's business partner, the Baroness Gerta von Hauser. Every time Anne thought of the word "baroness" she felt her throat constrict. God knew what the woman was accustomed to, but it had to be pretty grand. She was not only a baroness, she was the head of a huge European business conglomerate.

Dalton had gone out of his way to reassure her. The baroness, he said, was really very likable and easygoing—not at all the demanding autocrat some had made her out to be. But beneath her husband's assurances Anne detected his own nervousness. The woman had recently saved Stewart Biotech from bankruptcy with a big cash loan. Dalton obviously wanted this dinner to make the best possible impression on her.

Lexy had helped Anne choose the wine and the menu. Anne had suggested they should try some German dish, in honor of the baroness, but Lexy had vetoed the idea. "Germans are not gourmets. They eat cabbage, potatoes, and a variety of vile sausages. The menu has to be French."

In consultation with Amelia they settled on quenelles of pheasant with morel sauce for the main course. It was a daunting choice, given the long preparation time required, and the difficulty of finding both fresh pheasant and fresh morel mushrooms in the same season. But Amelia was enthusiastic. For the wine, Lexy chose a great Rhône, Beaucastel's Châteauneuf de Pape 1989. For dessert they agreed on something Amelia had found in an old French dessert cookbook—a rich, complicated winter holiday cake made with hazelnuts, Swiss bittersweet chocolate, and Dutch cocoa, called Gâteau Castel Vallérien aux Noisettes.

"If the baroness has any taste, Amelia will astonish her," Lexy said. "If she doesn't, at least the rest of us will all know we've had a great dinner."

Lexy had also helped Anne pick out a new evening gown for the occasion, and Anne wished she'd hurry up and get here.

Anne slipped into the gown and fussed with it in front of her dressing room mirror. It was black, with long sleeves. It was also cut very low back and front, and decidedly clingy. She had never worn anything so daring before. She would never have chosen it herself, but Lexy had insisted. It was a matter of association, Lexy had explained. The baroness naturally expected to be in glamorous company.

Anne picked out a long string of pearls and wound them twice around her neck. She decided they called too much attention to her bosom. She tried half a dozen other necklaces. None of them looked right. Where the hell was Lexy anyway?

The guest list was small—only a dozen—but Dalton had made sure it was high-caliber: none of your boring local WASP gentry, jet-set riffraff, or Wall Street types this time around. Besides Lexy and a male friend, Carlton

Fisher, who was curator of antiquities for the Metropolitan Museum of Art, there would be Henry Klein, secretary of state in the last Republican administration, and his wife, Claudette, an imposing social figure who sat on the boards of half a dozen cultural and philanthropic organizations; Charles VanDamme, the president of International Airlines, and his new wife, the famous actress Sylvia Sanders. And of course, Hank and Carol Ajemian. Since the Baroness was coming alone, the table was balanced by inviting an extra single male—the Broadway producer and director Freddy Abbot.

Lexy finally breezed into the room, a full glass of white wine gripped precariously between thumb and forefinger. "Wow! That gown!" she exclaimed. "Fantastic."

"I'm scared to death. What am I going to say to these people? A secretary of state? A German baroness?"

Lexy handed Anne her wineglass. "Have a taste. Settle your nerves."

Anne took two deep gulps.

"Hey, take it easy. You don't want to pass out before the soup course."

Lexy picked out a small gold necklace from the jewelry case on the dresser and put it around Anne's neck. "Black and gold. You'll look like a goddess. Now, two things: One, don't worry. Two, don't try too hard to be amusing. Just be yourself. The men aren't going to hear a word you say, anyway. Just smile and ask a lot of intimate questions. Everybody loves intimate questions."

"I'm depending on you to keep things lively."

"It won't be necessary. Tonight's crowd is strictly A-list. They're all super-articulate egomaniacs. You'll have to shout to make yourself heard over the din. It'll be the best dinner party you ever had." Lexy handed Anne a set of her gold earrings. "Here, put these on. That's all you need."

Anne stood in front of the mirror and adjusted the earrings. "I have great news," she said. "Dalton finally said okay. I'm going to have a real job!"

"You're joking."

Anne squeezed Lexy's hand in glee. "Biotech has a

small research facility half an hour away from here. I'll have my own lab and two assistants! Isn't that great?"

Lexy laughed. "Sounds like nepotism to me."

"Some friend you are."

"I'm happy for you, of course. What'll you be doing?"

"Tell you more later," Anne promised. "Go ahead down. I've got to go check on Genny."

Her daughter was in the nursery, eating dinner with Mrs. Callahan and watching a videotape.

"Mommy, you look so pretty!"

Mrs. Callahan murmured her agreement, although Anne thought she seemed a trifle shocked by the gown. Anne gave Genny a quick hug. "The baroness wants to meet you," she said. "I'll come up and get you in about half an hour. Then you let Mrs. Callahan put you right into bed, okay?"

"What's a baroness, Mommy?"

"It's a special name given only to very special ladies. And I want you to be very nice to her."

"Does she have any name besides baroness?"

"Yes, but you can call her baroness."

"Miss or Mrs. Baroness?"

Anne and Mrs. Callahan laughed. "Just baroness," Anne said.

Anne arrived on the ground floor just in time to greet Carol and Hank Ajemian. She gave each of them a hug and hurried them into the library, where Dalton was already engaged in a lively conversation with Carlton Fisher and Freddy Abbot.

Henry and Claudette Klein arrived minutes later, with Charles VanDamme and Sylvia Sanders right behind them.

Lexy's predictions were exactly right. The guests crowded into the library and within minutes all were talking at once. The mood was relaxed and jovial, almost boisterous—as if they were all old friends who hadn't seen each other in ages. Anne was showered with compliments and was soon beaming.

Dalton came over. "Everything okay?"

Anne squeezed his hand. "Yes. But where's the baroness?"

Dalton glanced at his watch. "Good question."

"She hasn't called."

"It's begun to snow outside," Dalton said. "Maybe that slowed them down."

Another half-hour passed ... still no baroness. The cook was getting anxious, and the guests were beginning to expect dinner. Anne went upstairs and told Mrs. Callahan to put Genny to bed.

Ten minutes later the baroness arrived, chauffeur and bodyguard in tow. Dalton did the introductions in the library.

Anne found the woman intimidating. She looked both regal and gorgeous, like a movie star. Her gown was subdued, but it complemented her figure and complexion perfectly. Her makeup was artfully invisible, and every strand of her blond hair rested exactly in place. She acted as if she dressed this way every evening of her life.

The baroness seemed preoccupied. She greeted everyone in the most perfunctory manner and then stood aloof from the others, as if she preferred not to talk with anyone.

The festive mood evaporated. The guests began looking about awkwardly and staring into their drinks. The baroness hardly seemed the shy type, Anne thought. What was her problem?

Lexy came over. "Don't worry. A temporary lull. A little culture shock. Things'll improve as soon as we get into dinner."

Dalton came by. "Remember, the baroness wants to meet Genny."

"It's awfully late. Is it that important?"

"Absolutely."

"All right. I'll bring her down. But just for a few minutes. We've got to start dinner. Amelia is about to start screaming and throwing things."

Anne raced upstairs. Genny was in bed but still awake. "Would you like to come downstairs to meet everybody?"

The little girl jumped up, immediately excited.

"Just for five minutes. Then right back to bed."

"Okay. Do I have to get dressed?"

"No. We'll put on your bathrobe."

Genny clutched her stuffed animal. "Can I take Rabbit?"

"Okay."

Anne guided Genny around the room and introduced her. She was mildly astonished at how the child poured on the charm. Someone asked her how old she was, and there was a widespread expression of disbelief when they learned she was just past two years of age.

Anne introduced her to the baroness last. Genny did a little curtsy and said "Good evening, Baroness," in a very formal tone. Everyone laughed.

The baroness smiled—the first time she had smiled since her arrival. She came up close to Genny and bent down to take her hand. Genny backed away. Her cheerfulness vanished, replaced by an expression of wild-eyed fear.

The baroness stepped forward again, murmuring some endearment in German. Genny backed away again. Panic lit her eyes. She pressed her lips together as if she were about to burst into tears. Anne put a hand on her shoulder and pushed her gently toward the baroness.

Genny exploded in a rage. She twisted away from her mother and uttered a high-pitched scream that froze everyone in place. Anne caught her, but Genny punched her hard on the arms, twisted free again, and ran from the room, wailing loudly.

Anne was dumbstruck. The child had never done anything like this, ever. She caught up with her on the stairs and followed her into her bedroom.

Dalton quickly escorted the guests into dinner.

Anne picked Genny up in her arms and rocked her gently. She soon calmed down.

"What's the matter, darling?"

Genny buried her face in her mother's shoulder.

"Did something scare you?"

"Baroness."

"She scared you?"

"Yes."

"But why?"

"She's bad. I hate her."

Anne held her daughter in her arms for a few minutes,

then tucked her back in bed. She fell asleep almost instantly.

Anne returned downstairs, wondering how she was going to explain Genny's embarrassing behavior. She could hear the baroness's voice as she approached the dining room. The shock of the incident with Genny seemed to have jolted the woman out of her unsocial mood. She was laughing at a story Dalton was telling her.

Anne was relieved to see that everyone else at the table was chatting amiably. Lexy and Henry Klein were joking about some movie they had seen recently. Claudette Klein and Charles VanDamme were engaged in a discussion about the new politics of Eastern Europe. Freddy Abbot and Sylvia Sanders were telling each other show business anecdotes. Carlton Fisher and Carol Ajemian were talking about primitive art.

Anne sat down next to Hank Ajemian.

"Is Genny all right?" he asked.

"She's fine," she replied in a low voice. "But I'm so embarrassed. She never behaves like that."

"What set her off? Do you know?"

Anne hesitated, then spoke in a whisper only Ajemian could hear. "She doesn't like the baroness."

Ajemian stole a glance across the table and curled up his lip in a sly smile. "She has good judgment," he whispered back. "Neither do I."

The quenelles of pheasant were perfectly prepared and elegantly served.

Anne and Hank Ajemian talked about Goth and Coronado. "My own gut instinct," Ajemian said, "is that Jupiter's a fraud. I could be wrong. But that's my feeling. They're going to set up a test program. So we'll find out who's right."

"Why would Goth have tried to perpetrate a fraud?"

Ajemian cut into his pheasant with his fork. "I don't know. But Dalton and I spent hours hunting through the hospital, through Goth's apartment, and through that old medical school up on the hill, looking for records. We couldn't find anything."

"Couldn't everything have been destroyed in the fire?"

"Maybe. But there ought to have been at least some

traces of his work around somewhere. All we found were
a couple of boxes of old bones, some fetuses pickled in
jars, and some old scientific journals. But no research. No
computer printouts, nothing."

After dessert the party moved into the library for coffee. Anne immediately went over to the baroness. The
woman smiled and complimented Anne on the dinner. As
she spoke, her eyes appraised Anne with a keen, feral
hardness. "You look quite lovely, Frau Stewart."

Anne blushed. "Thank you. Please call me Anne."

Her eyes explored the exposed swell of Anne's bosom.
"Your husband never told me how beautiful you were."

Anne didn't know how to reply. The tone in the woman's voice had an insinuating, almost flirtatious quality to
it. If she had been a man, Anne would have assumed she
was making a pass.

"I'm very sorry about our daughter," Anne said. "I
don't know what got into her. She's usually so well-
behaved."

"It's quite all right," the baroness purred. "Perhaps I
shall have another opportunity. Your husband has told me
so much about her, you know. Naturally I wanted to see
this extraordinary child for myself."

"Fathers like to brag," Anne replied, forcing a smile.
"But it's true that Genny is quite precocious. . . ."

"I am so relieved to hear that."

The remark confused Anne. "You are?"

"Of course. And you should be congratulated. Such a
very brave woman."

"Brave?"

The baroness laughed. "Don't be so modest, Frau
Stewart. To be willing to volunteer for such a procedure
demanded great courage. You must have had to overcome
many fears. Many things could have gone wrong, *ja*?"

"The procedure is actually pretty commonplace these
days," Anne replied, still puzzled.

The baroness ignored her reply. "When I think of you
and your daughter I think of Mary and the Virgin Birth,"
she said, arching an eyebrow. "And born exactly at the
beginning of the third millennium. Extraordinary. Almost
like the Second Coming. Really quite extraordinary."

Anne wrinkled her brow in complete bafflement. "I'm sorry—I don't think I know what you're talking about."

The baroness took a sip from her demitasse and placed it on a side table. "My dear," she said. Her tone was patronizing. "I'm talking about Goth's procedure, of course. The Jupiter program. I know you've kept it a big secret, but of course your husband had to tell me about it to get my financial backing. It was a very clever idea. Inspired."

Anne felt her pulse racing, but she still didn't quite get it. "What was?"

The baroness waved a hand impatiently. "Using you as the program's guinea pig, of course."

Anne blinked. She tried to say something but couldn't. She suddenly felt faint. She managed a barely audible "Excuse me," then turned and started out of the library. Everything became a blur—the faces of the guests, the sounds, the rooms, the furniture. She found herself running upstairs.

Genny's door was open, and a night light burning. Anne pressed herself against the side of the crib and looked down at her sleeping daughter.

She felt a wave of terror, then rage. After a few minutes the narcotic of psychological shock took hold and submerged her thoughts and emotions in a kind of twilight numbness.

She pulled Genny from the crib and cradled her in her arms. "My God, my God, what have they done to you?"

The little girl woke and stirred uncomfortably for a few moments, then drifted back to sleep in her mother's arms.

Lexy appeared in the bedroom doorway. "I saw you dash out," she said. "Are you all right?"

Anne squeezed Genny against her. "No. We're leaving."

"Say that again?"

"Genny and I are leaving."

Lexy threw up her arms in confusion. "When?"

"Now."

"Why? What's the matter? Where are you going?"

"I can't explain. Can we stay with you?"

"With me? In the city? Sure, I guess so, but—"

"I want to leave right now. Get your car."

"Jesus, Annie, hold on a minute—"

"Now. Get your car. We're leaving right now. Right now!"

26

It was two days before Anne could bring herself to speak to her husband, even over the telephone.

Dalton Stewart begged, pleaded, cajoled, threatened. He pointed out again and again that she was being unfair. His gamble with her pregnancy had paid off, after all—paid off magnificently. Genny was a beautiful, superior child. "Goth was a genius," he argued. "He was going to do some genetic repairs anyway, to fix the fragile X syndrome. It was perfectly logical of him to ask if I might not want to try the whole package. There was hardly any risk. He swore the program would work. You might have miscarried, that's all."

"*He* asked *you*?"

Dalton hesitated a moment. "Look, Anne. It seemed like a hell of a good idea to me. It *was* a good idea. And there was never any real threat to the baby."

"Are you trying to convince *me* of that, or yourself?"

"It's the truth!"

Anne once would have been eager to believe Dalton. She had dreaded arguments and confrontations ever since she was a little girl. She associated them with loss and abandonment. A strong disagreement with anybody always seemed to put the world in abrupt danger of falling apart. To protect herself, Anne had always believed the best in people. She would rather have something be her fault than have to confront someone else.

But Dalton Stewart had deceived her about the one thing in her life that he must have known mattered more to her than anything else—their child. He had manipulated her because he assumed he could get away with it. She despised him suddenly. In his arrogant insensitivity he had shown her just how unimportant she was in his scheme of things.

"Don't blow it all out of proportion," Dalton continued. "Sure, I admit I should have asked you. I'm very sorry now that I didn't. But I was afraid you might say no, because you wouldn't have understood the facts of the situation. Genetics is a complicated science. I told myself how happy you'd be when you gave birth to that perfect child. And I thought that it was far better if you believed the reason for the child's superiority was completely natural—that it all came from you and me. . . . That way, you would always be so proud. . . ."

The receiver, wet from the perspiration of her hand, kept slipping. She clutched it tightly in her fist. "Save your breath, Dalton. I've already called a lawyer and asked him to arrange a legal separation."

"Anne. For godsakes listen to me. Please. Look at how it's all turned out. We've got the greatest little girl in the world. Why should you be upset by that? Why do this to me? And why do this to Genny? It's all working out. Why do you want to ruin everything?"

Anne was unmoved. Her husband didn't know that it had worked out at all. He didn't know what time bombs might lie dormant in Genny's genes. No one did.

"Please, Anne. I love you. I love Genny." Dalton's voice cracked. "I need you, Anne. That's something I'd never have admitted to anyone two years ago. But it's true. You've changed me. Genny's changed me. For the first time in my life I felt happy."

"You only care about yourself, Dalton."

"Promise me you'll think about—"

Anne hung up, cutting Dalton off in mid-sentence.

She sat by the phone for several minutes, trying to regain her composure. She felt tremendous sadness. But she didn't feel any uncertainty. He had betrayed her in the most profound way. It was over with Dalton forever.

Later, Hank Ajemian called. "God, I'm so sorry about what happened. Carol and I are both upset as hell. . . ."

Anne thanked him.

"I didn't know about it, Anne. I swear I didn't. Dalton didn't tell anyone."

"He told the baroness."

"He needed to sell the program to her. Stewart Biotech was facing bankruptcy. Bankruptcy would have been better, to tell you the truth."

"Why?"

"The baroness will end up owning everything. I know how she operates. She'll strip Dalton clean."

Anne asked Ajemian about the Jupiter program. He described the original meetings, and all he could remember about what Goth had said the program would do.

"Goth's dead," Anne said. "How can they even pretend to have any idea of what they're doing? It's dangerous to pursue it. And immoral."

"Maybe you're right."

"Can you do anything to stop it?"

"No chance of that, Anne. Dalton's betting the ranch on this one."

The following afternoon Anne got up her courage and took Genny to see pediatrician Paul Elder. They walked through Central Park from Lexy's apartment to his office and sat in the waiting room for two and a half hours. At seven-thirty his last patient finally left and the doctor appeared, apologizing for the long wait.

"I'm Anne Stewart. This is my daughter, Genevieve."

Elder looked perplexed. "You look familiar, but this little lady doesn't." The doctor bent down and held out his hand toward Anne's daughter. "Hello, Genevieve. How are you?"

Genny held out her tiny hand for the doctor to shake. "Very well, thank you," she piped cheerfully. "You can call me Genny."

"Okay, Genny. You're very grown up, aren't you? How old are you?"

"I was two on New Year's Day."

Elder straightened up, genuinely surprised. "Is that all?"

"I was born with the century," Genny declared, with a proud grin. "That's what Mommy says."

"Well, you certainly don't look like you need a doctor. Are you sick?"

Genny shook her head. "I feel very well, thank you."

The doctor looked up at Genny's mother questioningly.

"I came to see you a little over two and a half years ago," Anne said, suddenly acutely embarrassed. "When I was pregnant. I suppose you don't remember. I wanted you to be Genny's doctor. . . ."

"Oh?"

"You didn't . . ." Anne swallowed her words. She clenched her fists and took a deep breath. This time, she wasn't going to back down. "You wouldn't take us on," she declared in a tight voice. "You told me you didn't have time for me then, or words to that effect. I wouldn't have come back, but something's happened. I'm very sorry to burst in on you like this, but I wanted to make sure that you would see us. Right now, if possible. It's important. I really won't take no for an answer this time. Not at least until you've heard what I have to say. I—"

Dr. Elder rested a hand gently on Anne's shoulder. "Relax," he said. "Of course I'll look at her."

"There's a lot I have to explain first," Anne added, feeling dangerously near tears.

The doctor nodded. He reached for Genny's hand. "We have lots of toys over here in the corner, you know. Would you like to play with them while I talk to your mommy?"

Genny shook her head. "I really don't like your toys very much," she admitted.

"You don't?"

"But I like your doctor things. Can I play with some of your doctor things?"

Elder grinned. "You mean stethoscopes—things like that?"

Genny laughed. "I love stethoscopes! They're my favorite!"

Dr. Elder found Genny a stethoscope, a tongue depressor, a knee mallet, and a few other medical odds and ends and set her up with them at his nurse's desk. The nurse had gone home two hours ago.

Anne sat in a chair next to the doctor's cluttered desk

and spilled out her story in a torrent of words, describing the ZIFT fertilization procedure, the traumatic circumstances of Genny's birth on New Year's Eve, the explosions, the fire, Goth's death, and finally her discovery, just three nights ago, that Goth had done more to Genny than simply correct the gene carrying the fragile X syndrome.

"He used me as a guinea pig to test some kind of new genetic formula," Anne said, twisting her handbag strap nervously between her fingers. "It was something that he had been working on that my husband was going to help him develop."

"But why come to me?"

"Because I remember you said you knew about Goth's work."

"I knew something about him," he admitted. "After medical school I studied genetics. I originally intended to specialize in it."

"Why'd you change your mind?"

"The genetics field was getting too commercial for my taste, for one thing. Private companies were buying up talent and slapping patents on everything. The researchers were losing control to the marketing directors. Genetics today is driven more by the desire for a quick buck, I'm sorry to say, than by science. I guess that accounts for my earlier hostility to you. I apologize. But I don't entirely approve of companies like Stewart Biotech, which I understand your husband owns."

"And you no doubt think I've gotten just what I deserved. But the truth is I had no idea at the time what Goth was going to do. I wasn't told anything. I know it was stupid of me, not to have been more suspicious, but . . ." She paused, struggling to keep her emotions in check. "My God, I'm just so worried about what might happen to Genny—what she might turn out to be. . . ."

"Any cause for worry so far?"

"No. She seems healthy and normal, thank God. Exceptionally precocious, however, if you'll excuse a mother's bragging."

"Has she been sick much?"

"Not even once. She's yet to have a cold, a sore throat,

an ear infection. Anything. And she's been tested for everything imaginable. That was my husband's idea. Now I know why. I brought along her medical records."

Anne pulled a thick folder from her bag and handed it to Elder. He thumbed through it carefully. He looked exactly as unkempt as Anne had remembered him—frayed collar, wrinkled trousers, unruly hair. She found his total lack of physical vanity enormously appealing. It presumed an unselfish spirit—and a mind focused on more important matters.

"It's impressive," he admitted, closing the folder and returning it to her. "No cause for alarm here. And maybe there's no cause for alarm, period."

"I want to believe that, but I don't dare," Anne said.

"Well, it's possible that Goth's genetic tinkering—assuming he did do some—simply didn't accomplish anything. She appears to be unusually bright, but I'd guess she's within the normal range, as such things go. I've met some extraordinarily precocious children. So her high intelligence may be no more than one of nature's random lucky combination of genes, without any credit to Goth at all."

"But she's barely past two. I'm terrified what might show up next week or next month. Or next year."

Elder nodded sympathetically. "I understand. But a tremendous amount of development has already taken place. If there were any gross physical or mental abnormalities, it's likely they'd have manifested themselves by now."

They both turned to the doorway. Genny was standing there, holding her stuffed rabbit in her arms and listening to their conversation. Elder held out a hand. "Come on in, Genny, and let me take a look at you, if that's okay with you."

Genny climbed up on the examination table and Elder gave her a cursory physical examination.

"Will you check Rabbit, too?" she asked, holding up the stuffed animal.

"Sure. Has he been sick, do you think?"

"No, but he fell on his head."

"He did? How did that happen?"

Genny pursed her lips thoughtfully. "Well, I guess I dropped him. I didn't mean to, though."

"Let's take a look at the young fellow."

Genny handed the doctor her stuffed rabbit. Elder made an energetic pretense of examining it, much to Genny's delight.

Anne watched his performance with interest. The doctor won Genny's trust almost immediately.

They were having a very deep conversation about Rabbit. "No concussion from that fall," Elder declared, in a perfectly serious tone. "But that doesn't surprise me. Unlike you and me, he's got a lot of fur, and that helps protect him. You can drop him all you like and it won't bother him at all."

"You're nice," Genny observed. "Especially for a doctor."

"Thank you. You're pretty nice, too. But do you really think doctors aren't nice?"

Genny knitted her brow. "Some of them aren't. Some of them have a bad color, too."

"Bad color?"

Genny sighed. "Well, a *funny* color, anyway. I don't know if it's really bad. You have a nice color."

"I do? What color do I have?"

Genny giggled. Her eyes strayed to the vicinity of Elder's hair and ears. "Don't you even know?"

"Gee, no, I don't."

Genny laughed with delight. "Well, I think it's . . . kinda blue."

"Blue? I see."

"It's a little game she plays," Anne explained. "Don't ask me where she got the idea, but she's quite convinced that everybody has a color."

Genny protested angrily. "They do have colors, Mommy! I'm not making it up. Honest!"

"I'm just trying to explain to Dr. Elder."

Paul Elder stood silently for a moment, contemplating the little girl. He looked to Anne. "Can I ask her a bit more about these colors?"

"I don't mind," Genny interjected. "You can ask me anything you want."

Anne laughed. "There's your answer."

"Okay. How about your mommy? What color is she?"

Genny looked over at her mother with a sassy grin. "Well, she was kinda light blue. But now she's kinda orange, too."

"Where do you see these colors on her?"

Genny drew her hand around her head. "All around here. Can't you see them, too?"

"Nope. I don't see any colors around her head at all."

Anne felt the doctor's eyes on her. He was rather a shy man, she thought, and that made the warmth of his gaze all the more noticeable. She became suddenly aware of her own heartbeat.

Genny was thoughtful. "Well, I thought *doctors* probably could," she announced.

"How about Rabbit? What color is he?"

Genny shook her head emphatically. "Stuffed animals don't have colors, silly."

"No?"

"Only people. And real animals."

"What about you? What's your color?"

Genny chewed on her lower lip, mulling over the question. "I don't have one, either. Well, I think I do, but I think I can't see it because I have to look in the mirror, and the colors don't show up in a mirror, you know. But I bet if I could see myself for real, I could see my color, too. My nanny says I'm white, because I'm too young to have any color, but I don't think she really sees anything. I think she just makes it up. I think I'm the only one who sees them for real. Her color is orange—and yellow, sometimes."

"How about your dad?"

Genny drew in a big breath. "His colors are dark, and sometimes I can't tell what they are. Sometimes he's kinda greenish blue, but then he gets red sometimes, too. Real red—just like the fireplace, when the logs are all burned up and there's only some ... I forget what you call them. . . ."

"Embers?"

"Embers. Daddy looks like embers, sometimes. Especially when he's mad. Or when he's in a hurry. Mommy says he's always in a hurry."

Paul Elder sneaked a look at Anne and smiled. "Don't embarrass your mommy."

"I'm used to it. But I must say she doesn't usually ramble on like this with strangers."

"Dr. Elder's not a stranger, Mommy," Genny insisted.

Elder helped Genny down from the examination table. He handed her his otoscope and she looked into her rabbit's ears with it.

"Auras," Elder murmured, walking back to his desk. "I believe your daughter Genny can see auras."

He saw the expression of alarm on Anne's face and quickly reassured her. "She's not ill. It's not that. But it is unusual."

"What is it? What does it mean?"

"She can see an aura of color around people's heads. It sounds farfetched, I know, but apparently some individuals have this ability. It's rare, but it does exist. My grandmother had it. People made fun of her, so she didn't talk about it in public. But there was no question that she saw some kind of colored margin around most animate objects. I've since read up on the subject a bit. No one's yet come up with an accepted scientific explanation, but it's probable that Genny sees some kind of emitted heat energy that's visible in a portion of the electromagnetic spectrum that most of us are not sensitive enough to perceive. In any case, it's a genuine ability, and it's perfectly harmless." He grinned. "I wish I could see auras. It might help me in my diagnoses."

Anne's earlier anxiety came flooding back. "You think she's psychic?"

"Some psychics do have this ability. But my grandmother wasn't psychic. So, I don't know the answer." Elder squeezed his lower lip thoughtfully between thumb and forefinger. "What surprises me most is that your daughter has this sensitivity at such a young age. That would seem very rare. Fascinating."

Anne asked the obvious question: "Is it Goth's doing?"

Elder didn't deny the possibility. He asked Anne for

Genny's folder and leafed through it again. "This MRI she was given—when was it?"

"A year ago. Just before her first birthday."

"I'm no expert at reading these things, but—would you object if I arranged to give her another one? They're expensive, of course, and she's not ill, but if you really want me to pursue this matter . . ."

"Oh yes, I do. Please. Anything you want to do. I'd be so grateful. The cost won't matter."

"Okay. I'll schedule her for one. Also, I don't see any tests of her general sensory acuteness here. We might just test her eyes and ears—see what they show."

"Whatever you think."

The doctor looked over in Genny's direction. The little girl was busy trying to wrap Rabbit's head in an elastic bandage. "You mind if we do some tests on you, Genny?"

Genny shook her head solemnly. "I don't mind."

Elder looked back at Anne, bending forward in her chair. "Look, this may all be quite fruitless, you realize. I understand your worry. But from the look of things, you've got a perfectly normal child. A superior child, but a normal one."

"That's what my husband said. That's what this program of Goth's is all about. Creating superior children. They plan to start testing it in Europe."

"They?"

Anne explained the business partnership that her husband and the Baroness von Hauser had entered into to develop Jupiter.

Dr. Elder reacted sharply. "I thought the program died with Harold Goth?"

"No. Dalton managed to keep a copy of it."

"What does your husband say? It seems he should be a considerable help here."

"I've left him."

"Because of this?"

"Yes."

"I see. Do you know if he has any data from Goth's work? Goth must have done experiments."

"I don't know."

"What about the program itself? Can we look at it? It's

likely to be the only way we'll be able to determine what Goth actually did to Genny. Short of just watching her grow up."

"It's locked up somewhere. I doubt my husband would allow me to show it to you. He considers it a priceless company secret."

"That's too bad."

"I'll try to get it for you."

Elder looked down at Genny speculatively. "Okay. In the meantime, let's do those tests."

27

"What do you think?" Dalton Stewart asked.

Hank Ajemian tightened his collar around his neck and looked out at the snow-covered mountain ridges that fell away to the north and east. "Nice view."

Dalton Stewart laughed. "That all?"

Ajemian pulled a tissue from his pocket and sneezed into it. "The only thing around here I'd call nice."

The two men were standing on the terrace of a fifty-room mansion, built originally as a vacation retreat for the Romanian Communist despot Nicolae Ceauşescu and his wife, Elena. The mansion, with its surrounding three hundred acres of field and forest on the western slopes of the Transylvanian Alps south of the city of Sibiu, now belonged to the Baroness von Hauser, and it was bustling with activity.

A staff of twenty-five geneticists, doctors, nurses, technicians, and administrators had moved into the echoing stone-and-glass palace and converted it into a laboratory and clinic where this final version of Dr. Harold Goth's Jupiter program was at last to get its initial trials. The first half-dozen of twenty carefully screened local women volunteers had arrived the day before. Their genomes had been obtained and analyzed, their eggs fertilized with their husbands' sperm in vitro, and the zygotes altered genetically according to Jupiter's blueprint. Now they were ready for the ZIFT procedure—the delivery of the altered eggs into their fallopian tubes.

"The middle of nowhere," Ajemian complained, surveying the surrounding vistas of forest and mountain.

"It's perfect," Stewart replied. "When we start bringing

in paying customers, they'll want a lot of privacy. And the Romanians won't give us any trouble."

"Sure. The baroness bought off the whole Romanian government. In the long run, bribery's not a good policy. When they inevitably throw these bums out, she'll have to bribe a whole new bunch, or get thrown out herself."

"You're too cynical, Hank. If the pilot program's a success here, we can always move the operation to another country."

"Sure. And bribe everybody all over again? How many countries will allow it? Not many."

"We only need one."

"There's something else that's been bothering me," Ajemian said, swiping at his nose. "Now that the baroness has a copy of Jupiter in her possession, what's to prevent her cutting us out altogether?"

Stewart cast Ajemian a sharp, disapproving look. "A legally binding contract, for one thing."

"The baroness has a history of getting around legally binding contracts."

Stewart shrugged. "We've gotten around a few ourselves, Hank, if the truth be told."

"They were her goons, New Year's Eve in Coronado," Ajemian said.

"What are you talking about?"

"She was after Jupiter. She sent them to break into Goth's lab and steal the program."

"I've thought of that. But we have no proof. It could have been Yamamoto, Fairchild, Prince Bandar. Even President Despres. Even somebody we don't know."

Ajemian shook his head. "It was the baroness."

"Even if it was, so what?"

"You can't trust her."

"We don't have to trust her," Stewart said. "There's always some risk in any cooperative venture. And in this situation we didn't have any other choice."

"We could have declared bankruptcy."

"That's not a choice. Anyway, the baroness won't try to cut us out. At least not at this stage."

"Why not?"

"She needs my daughter. Until other children are born

under Jupiter and reach the age of three or so, Genny's the only living proof that Jupiter works. The baroness is well aware of that. We have nothing to worry about for several years."

Ajemian sighed. He was exceedingly depressed by the re-entry of the baroness into Dalton Stewart's life. She had saved Biotech from bankruptcy, but the price had been steep. Ajemian was convinced that she would not only steal Jupiter from them but end up taking Stewart Biotech as well.

She seemed to have some kind of hold over Dalton that mystified him. And it wasn't just financial. Was she blackmailing him? He didn't think so. Nobody knew more of Dalton Stewart's dark secrets than Ajemian. He was practically the curator of the collection. If the baroness had tried blackmail, Stewart would certainly have told him.

That left sex.

Ajemian couldn't understand the baroness's appeal. Admittedly, she was attractive, in a severe Teutonic way; but once the real personality behind the façade began to emerge, Ajemian thought, any man in his right mind would run for his life.

But Dalton wasn't exactly in his right mind these days. Ajemian had never seen him in more fragile shape emotionally. Anne's leaving had devastated him. He had retreated deep back into his self-protective shell. Even Ajemian could no longer figure out what he was thinking about. And Dalton's behavior was becoming increasingly reckless and self-destructive.

It was a shame. Dalton had been doing so well. His daughter had opened up his eyes to a whole new way of looking at the world. Suddenly he understood what love was all about. His behavior had improved dramatically. A man who had been emotionally self-centered all his life now knew what it meant to care about someone.

Then the baroness, with one well-placed bombshell at that Long Island dinner party, had destroyed it all.

It was a *damned* shame, Ajemian thought. For the first time in his life, Dalton Stewart allows himself to feel something emotionally—and it blows up in his face.

Of course it was Dalton's own fault. He had been unthinkably insensitive, not telling Anne what Goth was up to with Genny. If he had just explained it to her up front, she probably would have gone along with it. Anne was always eager to be agreeable. But it was too late. The damage appeared to be permanent. Despite his pleas, Anne was unwilling to forgive him. The marriage was over, and the chief beneficiary of the breakup so far appeared to be the baroness.

Stewart was looking at him. "I'm going to stay on here for a while," he said. "I'm going back to Munich with the baroness tomorrow. She's giving me office space, and she's found me an apartment. I want to stay on top of Jupiter. We can't afford to fuck this up a second time."

"What about New York?"

"You're going to have to run things there for me for a while. That okay?"

"Sure. But Biotech's got a lot of problems."

"Between faxes and the phone, you can keep me up to speed."

"How long you plan to stay?"

"Probably until we get the first test group results."

Ajemian's jaw dropped. "Nine months?"

Stewart looked at him steadily. "I'll be back and forth."

The baroness appeared on the terrace, in the company of her creepy personal assistant, Karla.

Where in hell did she find these people? Ajemian wondered. Everybody that worked for her was a little strange. A process of self-selection, Ajemian supposed. She liked to surround herself with weak, dependent types whose unquestioning loyalty she could command. And that weird couple, Katrina and Aldous. What was the story there? He had thought at first that they were her personal servants. Now he was beginning to suspect that they might be her lovers—both of them.

The baroness took Stewart by the arm and led him inside to meet Dr. Laura Garhardt, the head of the resident medical and technical staff. She ignored Ajemian completely, but Karla managed to throw him a nasty over-the-shoulder glance as she followed the baroness and Stewart inside.

The staffing for this new project was a case study of the baroness in action. Every single one of the twenty-five new employees were from the baroness's companies in Europe. Not one was from Biotech. At Ajemian's insistence, Stewart had offered his own slate of candidates, but the baroness had found reasons to object to all of them. Stewart hadn't put up much of an argument; he didn't seem to think it mattered much, at this stage. The whole program was an experiment, he had told Ajemian, and most Biotech employees were understandably leery of it—especially since the work they would be doing was patently illegal in most countries.

So Stewart was perfectly content to let the baroness staff the place entirely with her own people, even though it meant that his influence on the project would be reduced to near zero at the very outset. By the time the place was ready to open for real customers, Dalton Stewart would be watching from the sidelines. And with the baroness's people keeping the books as well, it was a given that she would cheat the living hell out of him.

Ajemian had to do something. He had been racking his brain for months. The woman's public image was so formidable she could get away with anything. She had frequently broken the law in her business dealings—sometimes outrageously—and yet she had never suffered more than an occasional slap on the wrist. Her companies were known to be flagrant polluters, yet not a single Hauser enterprise in Europe had even been fined in the last five years.

Anyone who had the nerve to go against her always seemed to get crushed. Her political power in Germany was so great no one dared touch her. Even the muck-raking left-wing press, a very active force in the new Germany, shied away from her.

Ajemian had been using the Biotech research department to dig up all the dirt on her it could find; but now that she was part of the ownership, he had had to stop. As it was, he lived in dread that she might get wind of how much he had already done. He had removed all the files on her from the department and taken them home. He had erased all traces of the investigation from the computer banks and the backup storage system as well. And he had taken the additional precaution of warning those who had been involved in the research that they would be fired immediately if they ever so much as mentioned it to anyone. Still, he worried.

And what had he uncovered? The most damaging stuff had to do with the right-wing political fringe in Germany. Ajemian had discovered that she was secretly bankrolling the neo-Nazi New Germany party, the ND. Ajemian believed the baroness was also pouring money into similar movements in Eastern Europe, where crime, economic hard times, and political confusion made the right-wing message especially appealing.

If Jupiter proved to be a success, then a lot more money was going to be siphoned off into these causes in the future.

Ajemian took one last look at the view. The Transylvanian Alps. The location was quite appropriate, he thought: the estate of a dead Romanian despot, located in Dracula's own backyard.

What did the baroness really want from Dalton? he wondered. It was hard to believe she was in love with him.

It must be Genny, Ajemian thought. She was the key. Stewart had said as much himself: Genny proved the project worked.

But Anne was clearly determined to get full custody of Genny. And meanwhile, she was doing her best to keep Genny away from Dalton as much as possible. And keeping her away from Dalton meant keeping her away from the baroness.

Ajemian felt a sudden chill at the back of his neck. How far might the baroness go, he wondered, to make sure that she had access to Genny?

28

Lexy helped Anne solve her immediate practical needs. She let her and Genny stay in her large Manhattan apartment as long as Anne wanted, and loaned her the money she needed until the separation papers were finalized.

After a few weeks of adjustment, Anne began to enjoy her new emancipation. By March she had found her own apartment—a five-room floor-through in an old brownstone on West Eleventh Street in Greenwich Village. Genny's nanny, Mrs. Callahan, moved in with them. It was cramped for three people, but Anne loved it.

Lexy began immediately bringing men around to meet Anne. They invariably asked her out, and the results were invariably disappointing, or worse. Anne just wasn't interested in any of them, and she quickly grew tired of fighting them off at the end of the evening.

Her last date—a charming, boyishly handsome, and very rich Italian playboy—was the last straw.

All evening he was the perfect gentleman—a little shallow, but still fun to be with. They had a good time. Anne felt receptive. At her front door, he asked to see her again, and she said yes. Then he asked if he could come up to use the bathroom. Anne showed him the bathroom—off her bedroom at the back of the apartment. When fifteen minutes had passed and he hadn't come out, Anne went back to check on him. But he wasn't in the bathroom. He was lying on her bed with all his clothes off, sporting a big grin and an even bigger erection.

Anne wasn't amused. She scooped his three-thousand-dollar suit and the rest of his clothes off the chair, tossed them out of the apartment, and dialed 911. He was out of the building, half-dressed, seconds before the police arrived.

Anne called Lexy and told her to lay off for a while. She just wasn't interested in romance at the moment.

Her main concern was her daughter.

Dr. Elder promised her all the help with Genny he had time for, but his office was always jammed with patients, and it was all he could do to keep up. His workday began at six in the morning, with hospital rounds, and ended anywhere between seven and ten at night. Part of Sunday seemed to be the only time he took off. Anne felt guilty imposing on him, but she did it anyway. It was part of her new determination to be more assertive.

She also began the study of genetics. She was astonished, and a little discouraged, to discover how much genetics had advanced since she had finished college. Even with her background in the biological sciences, she could make only minimal sense out of the latest books and articles in the field. She realized that to master the subject in any depth was going to require an enormous amount of work.

Once or twice a week she would appear at Dr. Elder's office and make herself helpful doing files, making appointments, and updating charts. Then, at the end of the day, she'd steal a few minutes to discuss Genny and the subject of genetics. Sometimes she'd bring Genny along, and sometimes she'd bring Chinese take-out food and they'd have their discussion over a makeshift dinner. Elder enjoyed these breaks in his busy routine, and Anne felt wonderfully comfortable with him.

Genny's medical history dominated their discussions. The results of the most recent tests were highly unusual. The early testing, done when Genny was an infant, had missed a great deal. The technicians responsible had lacked the imagination to test the girl for anything outside the most obvious medical categories. Even at that, the testers might have been suspicious of their results. Elder had never seen such perfect scores. Genny was a model of robust health in every respect.

The first MRI scan, done when Genny was a year old, might have caught someone's attention, too, but whoever had viewed the results had missed some minor anomalies. Those were now more apparent in the second scan. Genny's brain-wave patterns appeared to be normal, except for one curious thing. The corpus callosum—that thick bundle of nerve-cell strands that connects the right hemisphere of the brain with the left—showed an unusually high degree of neurotransmitter activity. The function of the corpus callosum was still not entirely understood, but it was known to be the main communications link between the two hemispheres. Elder wasn't sure what the test results meant. The neurological specialists he had talked to weren't sure, either, but several had speculated that the girl's brain might be processing a lot more information than a normal brain.

This possibility was reinforced by Genny's scores on the WISC (Weschler Intelligence Scale for Children), which Elder had persuaded a psychologist friend to administer. The psychologist had called Elder immediately after scoring the tests to tell him that Genny was almost off the scale. The test showed an IQ near 200—the highest score he had ever seen.

Elder tested Genny's hearing and vision himself, and the results astounded him. Genny could detect sound waves well below and well above the normal range of the human ear. And her sensitivity was so great that she could detect a mere .02 decibel of sound—equivalent to the sound of a coin dropped on cement from a hundred yards away.

Her vision was equally extraordinary. She could resolve distant objects with acuity approaching that of a hawk; and, even more astonishing, she could see into both the infrared and the ultraviolet ranges of the light spectrum—areas completely invisible to the human eye without the use of special equipment. Elder thought that this probably explained the auras Genny said she saw around people's heads. She could be seeing the individual's body heat, which would register in the infrared range.

Elder had decided to let the remaining three senses— smell, touch, and taste—go untested for the time being. They were more difficult to administer and score, especially with someone so young. And it didn't really matter. He had more than enough to try to comprehend as it was.

The doctor had also measured Genny's physical aptitude, and here he got yet another shock. At twenty-eight months, she possessed the muscular strength and coordination of an eight-year-old boy. He refused to believe these results at first, because her musculature appeared to have the normal tone and firmness for someone her age and size. But he had to accept the evidence of his own eyes. Genny—who weighed thirty pounds—could lift a forty-five-pound weight.

Elder told Anne that he no longer doubted that Genny Stewart's extraordinary abilities were the result of Harold Goth's genetic program. But what completely mystified him was that even accepting a thorough revamping of Genny's genes, these test results were still impossible. It was accepted theory in genetics that you could improve someone's genes only up to the optimum limit found in the human genome. In other words, you could rearrange genetic code so that an individual who would otherwise suffer from defective vision—myopia, for example—would have perfect twenty-twenty sight. But you could not insert code into the genes that would give that person the eyes of a hawk, or the ability to see into areas of the electromagnetic spectrum clearly outside the range of the cones of the human eye, as it had evolved over many thousands of years. Yet Goth had somehow done it.

Elder gave Anne the names of several prominent geneticists who might be able to give more complete help and advice than he could. He also urged her once again to bring him a copy of Goth's Jupiter program. Without an understanding of how that worked, he explained, it was doubtful that anyone would ever be able to understand Genny. And without that knowledge, it was impossible even to guess what might happen to her as she matured.

Anne promised again that she would get the program, although she didn't know how. Dalton had already refused her, and Ajemian told her it was impossible. The few copies that existed were closely guarded.

Genny, meanwhile, continued to produce new surprises. One evening, while rearranging some furniture in her bedroom, Anne had bruised her shin on the sharp steel edge of the bed frame. She sat down on the bed and rolled up her jeans to examine the wound. The spot was swollen and sore and had begun to turn black and blue. Genny wandered in, dragging Rabbit. "What's the matter, Mommy?"

"It's all right, darling. I just bumped my leg."

"Can I make it better?"

Anne laughed and shook her head. "No. It'll be okay."

"But I want to, Mommy. You always make my bumps better."

Anne pointed to the spot on her shin. "Okay, little doctor. It's all yours."

Genny bent close to the bruised area, pressed her little hand against it, and held it there. Anne started. Genny's palm was very warm. She could feel the heat from it spreading through her flesh. The warmth was accompanied by a pulsing, tingling sensation, like a mild electric current. When Genny removed her hand, the tingling sensation lingered. The little girl looked slightly flushed, as if she might have a fever.

"Do you feel all right, darling?"

Genny nodded and smiled.

"How did you make your hand so warm?"

"It's a secret," Genny said in a solemn tone.

"Give us a hint?"

"Well, I don't think I can."

"Have you done it before?"

"Well, just with my dolls, but that was only pretend. I tried to put my hand on Moby Cat where he hurt his leg, but he wouldn't hold still." Moby Cat was an overweight, lumbering, good-natured Maine coon cat Genny had acquired a year ago during a visit with her mother to the ASPCA.

Suddenly Genny announced that she was very sleepy. Anne carried her into her bed. She put her head down on her pillow and fell instantly into a deep sleep.

Anne noticed that the bruised spot on her leg no longer throbbed. An hour later both the swelling and the discoloration had disappeared. There was no tenderness in the area, no trace of the injury whatsoever. Normally she'd have expected to have a visible bruise for a week. She wanted to call Dr. Elder but hesitated; he might think she was getting a little carried away. She called Lexy instead.

"Psychic healing," Lexy announced. "Must be. Fits right in with the auras. Let's face it, your daughter must have psychic powers. Maybe extraordinary psychic powers."

"I don't believe in them," Anne declared.

"No? How do you explain what just happened to you?"

"I can't. But there must be a better explanation than psychic healing."

"More plausible one, you mean?"

"Yes."

Lexy laughed. "Ask your favorite doctor. See what he says."

"I don't dare. He'll laugh at me."

Lexy began researching the subject of psychic phenomena for Anne, and in the weeks that followed they discussed—or argued—the matter frequently. Anne finally brought it up with Paul Elder.

"I don't know," he said. "I don't rule out anything. It could well be that by enhancing the senses genetically Goth may have stumbled across the threshold of the psychic realm. The whole subject of extrasensory perception is an enigma. Genny may give us some new insight into it."

"Do you believe it exists or not?" Anne persisted.

Elder smiled. "You won't let me weasel my way out of anything, will you?"

Anne smiled back. She was beginning to like this man very much. "Don't like to be pinned down, huh?"

"Well, I don't mind being pinned down by you," he confessed.

Anne laughed. Elder flushed with embarrassment at his words.

"Get me a copy of Jupiter," he said, recovering himself. "Then we'll find the answer."

Joe Cooper called the special number and waited for the call back. When it came, he felt a powerful urge not to answer the phone. He was sick of this business. It threatened to go on forever. He hated New York City, and he hated working in a hotel kitchen. He wanted to be reassigned. He sighed and lifted the receiver. The scrambling devices used to make the line secure made Roy's voice on the other end sound disembodied and distant.

"Cooper?"

"Speaking."

"Time to set up a new surveillance."

"Who?"

"Anne Stewart and her daughter."

"Address?"

"A brownstone at 272 West Eleventh Street. She's on the second floor."

"Got it."

"Around the clock."

"I'll need help, then."

"I'll give you two men."

"Visual surveillance only?"

"No. Sound too."

"I'll need at least five men."

Roy was silent for a moment, apparently debating with himself whether the assignment merited such an expenditure of manpower. "Five men, then," he said, finally.

"*Trained* men," Cooper added. "Five *trained* men."

"Of course. Five trained men."

Some time in the spring, Anne began to suspect that people were watching her.

One day she noticed the same man three different times at three different places. First, he was leaning on the rail next to Genny at the polar bear enclosure at the Central Park Zoo; then he was a counter away from her at Bloomingdale's. She spotted him the last time outside a restaurant on Perry Street in Greenwich Village where she and Lexy had gone for dinner. Twice might have been a coincidence, but three times? The next day he was gone.

A few days later, someone else seemed to be following her, but she couldn't be sure. The next several weeks produced similar episodes. No rational pattern emerged. There was never anyone loitering on the street near her building, for example. Mostly it was just this feeling she had of being watched.

Lexy was dubious, but suggested that Dalton might be responsible. With a divorce in the works, his lawyers could have hired private detectives to snoop on her, hoping to prove adultery.

"Why would he bother?"

"Maybe he wants permanent custody of Genny."

The possibility of losing Genny in a divorce settlement had never occurred to Anne. She immediately asked her lawyer to find out what was going on. He called Dalton's lawyers. They swore that they had not hired anyone to tail her. Anne didn't know what to think. If it wasn't Dalton, who could it be?

Or was she just imagining it? Paul Elder thought so.

The evidence remained inconclusive. No one ever approached her or threatened her. There were no strange telephone calls, no anonymous letters in the mail. And most days passed without any hint at all that she might be under surveillance. Other days she could swear there were several people following her.

At first Anne refused to change her routines. The streets of the West Village were generally friendly, nonthreatening places, and she didn't want to give in to whatever invisible force was trying to unnerve her. But finally, to preserve her rapidly disintegrating peace of mind, Anne stopped going out by herself after dark—even to run an errand to the corner convenience store. And she made sure that her daughter was never left alone. She moved Genny into her own bedroom and let Mrs. Callahan have the second bedroom to herself.

The separation agreement allowed Dalton to see Genny on weekends. He usually took her to Long Island; but since he was frequently away on business trips, Genny was so far averaging only a day or two a month at the North Shore estate, and Anne made certain that Mrs. Callahan was with her when she couldn't be.

What else could she do about the situation?

Not much, she decided. Except to be vigilant.

29

"God, I'm nervous," Lexy Tate said, plucking at her blouse with her fingers. "Look at me. I'm sweating. Are you sure we have to do this?"

Anne pressed a finger to her lips and pointed at the cab driver.

Lexy laughed. "Are you kidding? He can't understand a word. It's a city ordinance—no English-speaking cabbies allowed. Look at the name on his license. Ten consonants and no vowels." Lexy bent forward and addressed the driver in a loud voice. "Hey, cabbie. Would you mind sticking your finger in your nose for my friend here?"

The cab driver glanced in his rearview mirror with a big grin. "Okay!" he replied.

"And then put it in your mouth. Okay?"

"Okay!"

Lexy fell back against the seat, giggling uncontrollably.

Anne shook her head in disgust. "You're such a teenager sometimes. I swear to God."

Lexy choked back the rest of her laughter. "I'm just trying to ease the tension. I'm a nervous wreck. I don't know why I agreed to do this. I love thrills, but this is crazy."

Anne was just as nervous, but she was determined to go through with it.

"What if we get caught?" Lexy demanded, for the tenth time.

"We won't get caught."

"Well, just hypothetically. What could we be charged with?"

"I really don't know. Don't think about it."

Lexy shifted nervously on the seat. "Trespassing—if they catch us before we take anything. And breaking and entering. But if they catch us after, it's theft. Grand theft, I think. Or does that just apply to autos? As in grand theft auto? Fuck, I don't know. I've never heard of petty theft. Have you?"

"No. Stop talking about it."

"I guess there isn't any such thing. Anyway, it's not armed robbery, because we're not armed. Burglary—that's what it is. And that's a felony. We could go to jail. Jesus—strip searches ... forced lesbian sex ... badly prepared food. I don't know if I could stand it."

Anne pounded Lexy's knee with her fist. "Lexy, we're not even going to take anything. Now, for godsakes, shut up!"

Lexy slumped back against the seat. "I'm sorry. I babble when I'm nervous. Anyway, I know a hell of a good criminal lawyer. And he owes me."

"There's nothing to worry about," Anne replied in a harsh whisper.

"Are we doing all this for that doctor of yours?"

"We're doing it for Genny."

"Just because that doctor said you should? You trust him that much?"

"He didn't tell me to. It's my own idea."

"Why the hell doesn't *he* go with you?"

"Be sensible."

"You know what? I think you're in love with the guy."

Anne felt her face flush.

"You talk about him all the time—Dr. X says do this, Dr. X says do that. Haven't you noticed?"

"Dr. Elder. Stop pretending you don't know his name."

"How about sexy? Is he good-looking at all?"

Anne gazed out the window at Fifth Avenue. They were just passing Forty-second Street. "Eight more blocks," she said.

Lexy repeated her question.

"Yes. No. I don't know. He's tall and kind of rumpled

and shaggy. And he's great with Genny. They really hit it off."

"How old is he?"

"I don't know."

"You must have some idea. Twenty-two? Seventy-three?"

"Fortyish."

"Single?"

"Yes."

"Probably gay, then."

"He's not gay!"

"How do *you* know?"

"My God, you're a pest tonight!"

Lexy remained silent for several blocks.

"It still puts me in a rage, every time I think about it," Anne burst out. "Using me as a guinea pig, playing games with Genny's life. I can't understand that kind of thinking."

"Dalton was thinking about his favorite subject—money."

"I don't know why I married him. I don't know why I do anything anymore. I wake up now wondering if I really have any idea of what I want out of life. Or even if I know who I am."

"We're all entitled to a mistake or two, Annie. Hell, I've made thousands. God hasn't struck me down yet. Although He may well decide to tonight."

Anne continued on her own line of thought. "I would've forgiven Dalton almost anything before I'd ever have thought of leaving him. Especially since Genny's birth. He really seemed to have changed. But I feel so damned betrayed."

"You deserve much better than Dalton. I've always thought that. We'll find you an available duke or a count somewhere—some dashing European with a country estate outside Paris, a chalet in St. Moritz, and a villa in Juan-les-Pins, so I can visit you year round."

"No more of your dashing anythings. That phony Italian count of yours was the limit."

"You have to give him some points for style. I mean,

suddenly there he is, stark naked on your bed, with a hard-on. Every girl's fantasy."

"It was insulting."

"I'd have jumped right on and screwed his brains out."

"Not my style, I'm afraid. And I'm not the type to have affairs, anyway. I couldn't handle it. Especially now, with Genny."

"What are your plans? To become a piano-playing nun?"

"We're here."

The taxi let them out at the corner of Fifth Avenue and Thirty-fourth Street. It was a chilly spring night. A strong wind gusted down the canyonlike avenue, adding to the discomfort.

"Let's get inside!" Lexy gasped. "I'm freezing."

They hurried down the Avenue to a big office building in the middle of the block and went inside. It was just past one o'clock in the morning, and the guard at the front security desk, a solemn black man in his sixties, looked up in surprise as the two women came bustling in. "You ladies working this late?"

Lexy took charge. "Never on your life," she shot back. "We've been partying. Just stopped by to pick up something *very important* my friend here left on her desk." Lexy gave the guard a big conspiratorial wink.

The security guard shrugged, completely puzzled. "Sign in here," he said, pushing an open ledger across the desk. A cheap ballpoint was attached to the sign-in book by a partly unraveled length of string.

Lexy quickly scribbled "Gertrude Stein" and "Alice B. Toklas" in the column labeled "Name." In the "Company" column she wrote "Macro-peripherals, Inc."; in the "Time In" column, "1:10."

"I'll have to look in your bags," the guard said in a weary voice.

Lexy dropped her thousand-dollar designer pocketbook onto the desk and snapped it open. The guard stirred the contents languidly with a forefinger, then nodded.

"I thought you were just supposed to go through stuff on the way out?" Lexy said.

The man rolled his eyes in bored resignation. "How do I know what you might be taking out if I don't see what you're bringing in?"

Lexy gave him a toothy grin. "Good point, sir."

Anne settled her large leather handbag on the desk and undid the strap. The guard stuck a hand in, felt around, and pulled out a black plastic removable cartridge disk, about the size of a paperback book. "What's this thinga-majig?" he asked.

Anne started to stammer something. Lexy cut in briskly: "It's her homework—what do you think it is?"

"Homework," the guard repeated, turning the RCD over in his hand.

"It's the computer storage disk from her work station. She takes it home every night. Boss's orders."

The guard turned the disk over one more time, then dropped it back into Anne's bag.

"Hey, be careful with that!" Lexy cried. "There's very valuable data on it. If you damaged it, by God . . ."

The guard held up a palm. "Take it easy, ladies."

Anne and Lexy strode swiftly past the security desk to the elevator banks.

"I didn't expect him to pull that cartridge right out of my handbag," Anne said, as the elevator door closed behind them. "I nearly fainted."

"It's just as well. Now he'll expect to see it in your purse when we come back down."

They got off on the thirtieth floor, where the executive offices of Stewart Biotech were located.

The doors on both sides of the elevator banks were locked, but Anne had a key. Dalton had given it to her more than two years ago, so she could meet him there when he was working late. She had used it only once.

Dalton's office was locked as well.

"Now what?" Lexy asked.

"Hank Ajemian keeps an extra key in his desk."

"Suppose his office is locked?"

"It will be. But Hank is always forgetting his keys, so his secretary keeps an extra one in her desk drawer for him."

Anne unlocked Dalton's office with the key from Ajemian's desk and turned on the switch by the door. The room came alive with a muted glow. It was an unusually large space, with Oriental carpeting, antique furnishings, and expensive art hanging on mahogany-paneled walls. The two outside corner walls were glass. Beyond, the New York skyline shimmered in the night, a breathtakingly romantic panorama of bridges, skyscrapers, and street traffic.

"How about this," Lexy purred. "I should have known he'd have the most pretentiously upscale office in the city."

Anne locked the office door behind them and moved behind Dalton's desk. It was an old-fashioned banker's model, its cherry wood polished to a lustrously deep brownish-red sheen. A photograph of Genny, taken by the pool garden when she was a year and a half, sat at one corner, near the telephone console. Anne saw it and felt her anger return. She groped with her fingers along the right inner side of the knee well, found the button, and pushed it.

Across the room, a three-foot-wide hinged section of the bookcase that lined the inner wall swung out silently like a door. Behind it was a small safe, embedded in the thick concrete-and-steel inner core of the building. It was designed to withstand almost any conceivable assault—acid, lock picking, acetylene torch, or high explosives.

Only Dalton Stewart and Hank Ajemian knew the combination to the safe's electronically controlled locking system, but Anne was confident she could figure it out. Dalton was very suspicious about numbers—particularly the number 51371. It represented the date—May 13, 1971—that his father had gone off to prison. He always used it. Every PIN number of every joint account and charge card they had shared had used that same number. Whether he did it out of some kind of masochism, or ritual of revenge or atonement, she didn't know.

Whatever his reasons, she was sure he would have used the same number for the safe's combination, and she was right. As soon as she punched in 51371, the safe door clicked open.

Anne pulled the door back with trembling fingers. If someone should walk in now, there would be no explaining their presence.

The thick steel door swung open easily. Inside, on a series of small shelves, sat stacks of documents—colored folders, contracts, company documents, secret intelligence reports, notebooks, computer printouts, a thick black ledger with several rubber bands wrapped around it, and other odds and ends, including several thousand dollars in cash.

Anne sorted impatiently through the piles several times. Lexy looked over her shoulder. "Find it yet?"

"No."

Lexy sifted through the material in the safe herself. "Jesus, Anne, it's not here."

"It has to be."

"It ought to be pretty easy to see it, then. Who told you it was here?"

Anne slammed the safe door shut. "Hank Ajemian."

"Would he lie to you?"

"No. He even told me the cartridge type and size."

"Did you tell him you were going to try to steal it?"

"*Copy* it. Of course not."

"Then Dalton must have moved it."

They stood looking at each other in the middle of the big office.

"Any idea where else he would put it?" Lexy asked.

Anne shook her head. After all the tension and the effort, the failure to find it made her numb.

She decided to take one more look. She redialed the combination, pulled the door open, removed all the contents, and went through them one at a time, repositioning each item back in its place after she had examined it. The ledger book wrapped with rubber bands was last. She peeled off the bands and opened it.

"Look."

Inside the ledger, neatly tucked into a rectangular recess cut through the middle of the book's pages, was a black plastic RCD. A gummed label on its surface identified it as Jupiter.

"How quaint," Lexy said. "The old Agatha Christie hollowed-out-book trick."

Anne slipped the Jupiter cassette into her purse with the blank one she had brought, and the two of them went out to the rows of secretaries' desks, looking for a computer.

Every desk had one, but none of them was configured to accept this particular kind of RCD.

"Great," Anne said. "We can't copy it."

"What do we do?"

"Take it with us. I'll find a way to copy it, then return it."

Lexy threw up her hands in distress. "Oh my God. You mean we'd have to come back?"

"What else can we do? I've got to have it."

"We can leave the blank one here in its place. Then you don't have to come back."

"Why?"

"They have copies in Munich, or wherever they're doing the actual work on this thing. So they don't need this one at all. It's only a backup. Like the original negative of a movie. They store it and work from dupes. This'll probably sit here for years, untouched."

"I'd rather put the original back."

"Okay. But leave the blank one here, anyway, for the time being. You don't want to have to explain to the guard downstairs why you came in with one RCD and are leaving with two."

"That's true."

Anne substituted the blank RCD for the real one in the hollowed-out space in the ledger book, wrote "Jupiter" on its label, wrapped the rubber bands around it again, tucked it under the pile of documents on the bottom shelf, and locked the safe again.

She slipped the Jupiter RCD into her leather bag, swung the hinged bookshelf back down into position in front of the safe, replaced the office door keys in their proper desks, and hurried out, with Lexy close behind her.

When the elevator doors opened at the ground floor, four armed men in uniform were standing there waiting for them. The patches on their sleeves indicated that they were employees of something called Protectall Security Services.

Anne and Lexy stood in the elevator, paralyzed and speechless. The door started to close again. One of the guards jumped forward and stuck his foot in the way. He waved his pistol at them. "Come on out, girls. Over to that wall over there."

They grabbed the women and led them over to the section of wall at the back end of the elevator bank. One guard, flourishing a two-way radio, ordered them to leave their bags on the floor. They obeyed.

"Now stand facing the wall. Put your hands on the wall."

Anne stole a sideways glance at her friend. Lexy's face looked the way Anne felt—terrified. God, why had she done this? And why had she dragged Lexy into it?

She heard the guards talking. They were trying to decide who should frisk them. They were mumbling, and Anne couldn't make out much of what they were saying.

The night security man who had checked them in suddenly appeared, carrying the sign-in sheet with him.

"These the ones?" someone asked him.

"Yessir. Those're the ones all right." He handed the sheet to the guard with the radio.

"One of you girls Gertrude Stein?"

"That's me, Officer," Anne said, surprised at her own boldness.

"And Alice B. Toklas?"

"She's Alice. What's this all about?"

"There may have been a robbery in the building," he said. "We're going to have to frisk you ladies."

"We're not armed, Officer," Anne said.

"We're gonna have to frisk you anyway."

The guard in charge—the name on his lapel ID was Don Martin—handed his radio to one of the other men. He had decided to reserve the responsibility of the frisk for himself. He walked over to Lexy first and put a hand on her shoulder from behind. "Have to ask you to spread your legs, Alice."

Anne, her hands still planted against the cold marble wall, looked across at Lexy again. Lexy winked back. Martin, a tall, very muscular white male with unkempt blond hair that curled out below his uniform cap, ran his hands quickly up and down Lexy's sides, under her arms, and around her waist. He then bent down and slipped both hands up each leg in turn, stopping a considerate inch or two short of her crotch.

He moved over to Anne. One of his men laughed. "It's a tough job, but somebody's gotta do it, right, boss?"

"Shut up, Darrell."

Martin's frisk of Anne was much more thorough. He slid both hands over her breasts from behind, cupping and squeezing them in his big hands, and then pinching her nipples between his thumb and forefinger. Anne stared at the wall and didn't move. She could smell rum and tobacco on his breath.

Martin knelt down and ran his hand up one leg. Anne closed her eyes and gritted her teeth. Why hadn't she had the sense to wear jeans, like Lexy, instead of a damned skirt?

She felt his hands exploring up along her thigh. It was all she could do to stand still. She could hear the men behind them snickering. Martin ran one hand slowly over her buttocks and began a leisurely stroking of her pubic bone with the other.

She felt his fingers tugging at the crotch of her panties, trying to insinuate themselves inside. She was about to scream when one of the other guards protested that he was taking too much time. Martin reluctantly ended his frisk.

"Look through their handbags, Darrell," he said.

"I did already. Nothing there."

"You check with the night man?"

The night man, standing right there, answered. "Yeah, I looked too. That's what they brought in."

Martin turned to a fifth security guard, just coming off the elevator. "What about the safe, Bill?"

"It was locked."

"Any signs of forced entry?"

"Not that I could see. Nothing missing, I guess."

Martin exhaled loudly, showing his displeasure. "What're you girls doin' here, middle of the night?"

"We just came in to get something from Gertie's desk," Lexy explained in a chirpy voice.

"You work here? In the building?"

"Yes sir. Macro-peripherals, Inc. We both work on software design. You know, for computer programs and related ... computer-assisted peripheral kinds of things."

"Yeah. Well, the alarm went off down in our office for Stewart Biotech, up on the thirtieth floor. You girls know anything about that?"

"No sir," Lexy replied. "Never heard of it."

The guards stood around for a little while longer, talking in low voices. Lexy and Anne remained with their hands against the wall.

"Can we go now?" Anne demanded.

"Yeah. I guess it was a false alarm. But hey, if we need to get in touch with you—"

"Just call Macro-peripherals," Anne snapped.

"Yeah. Okay." Martin eyed Anne up and down with a knowing grin. "Hey, next time I might not let you off so easy."

Lexy picked up their handbags from the floor. "And next time, bozo, we'll report your behavior to Stewart Biotech and to your boss," she said.

Anne grabbed her friend's arm and steered her toward the front exit. "Never mind, Alice. Never mind."

Out on Fifth Avenue, they dashed to the curb to hail a cab. Lexy pulled up her fur collar. "Jesus Christ, I never thought about triggering a remote burglar alarm system. And I thought for sure they'd check out our IDs. That was a close call."

"I'm sorry I got you into this," Anne said.

"Are you kidding? We pulled it off, didn't we? And you were great! Sorry you got molested like that, though. That Martin bastard barely felt me up at all. That really pissed me off."

30

Ambassador Mishima accepted the applause with a bow and a self-deprecating smile. "I welcome you to the glamorous metropolis of Mikasa," he said.

Appreciative laughter rippled through the room. Mikasa was anything but a metropolis. It was an isolated mountain village, a few kilometers inland from the small city of Sapporo, on Japan's northern island of Hokkaido.

His audience, twenty-five men and twenty women, was gathered in a conference room on the second floor of a new building that housed the most modern genetic research facility in the world. Beyond the tightly drawn window blinds of the laboratory building were clusters of cottages and dormitorylike structures and a small pedestrian square with a variety of shops and stores, all spread out in a parklike setting of trees, lawns, and gardens. These buildings had all once been part of the Olympic Village, built to house the athletes at the 1972 Winter Games in Sapporo. Only the laboratory building was new—that and the double rows of high-security cyclone fencing that now enriched the entire village, separating it from the outside world.

The forty-five individuals in the audience had been carefully selected by a special government committee appointed by the prime minister. They were among the very best microbiologists and geneticists in the nation. Together with a staff of several hundred technicians and support personnel, they would live and work in the self-contained isolation of this village for an undetermined length of time. Contact with the outside world would be severely limited and carefully monitored.

All the participants had volunteered for the project—

not just because the pay and the benefits were extraordinary but because serving in the project had been presented to them as a matter of patriotic duty.

There was a third attraction. Although no one yet knew the details of the project, the word was out in Japanese scientific and academic circles that it was to be on the cutting edge of biogenetics. Working on the project would almost guarantee its participants extraordinary professional and academic stature—and a very secure future.

Today, they were to be formally introduced to their work.

Ambassador Mishima coughed gently and began the introduction. He pressed a button on the remote-control unit in his hand, and on a big screen at the front of the room there appeared two black-and-white photographs of an old automobile—a front view and a side view.

"Does anyone know what this is?" he asked.

After a puzzled silence, a young man at the back of the room raised his hand. "It's an American automobile," he said. "A Ford sedan. Nineteen fifty-one, I believe."

Mishima grinned. "Your father must have been in the auto business."

"No. But I was a teenage car nut."

The others laughed and applauded.

"Well, my teenage car nut, your answer was very good, but it was also wrong. The car you see up there on the screen certainly does resemble an American Ford four-door sedan, manufactured in Detroit in 1951. But in fact, this automobile was built in Osaka, Japan, in the year 1952."

Mishima paused to let the surprise sink in, then continued. "Of all the autos ever built in our country, this one is perhaps the most important—because it was assembled in a very unusual manner. In a project sponsored by our government, a dozen American Fords were purchased anonymously in the U.S., imported to Japan, and brought to a small shop outside Osaka. At the shop a trained crew of industrial technicians dismantled the autos piece by piece and examined them exhaustively. Every part was tested, weighed, measured, photographed, and analyzed. When the technicians had learned everything they could,

they put the cars back together again. Then they tore
them apart again, and put them back together again. They
repeated this process over and over, until they knew how
to assemble a Ford sedan in their sleep."

Mishima observed his audience closely as he talked.
The tense, concentrated expressions on their faces told
him that they were trying very hard to anticipate what
possible connection his tale could have to their present
circumstances. He was happy that they were so attentive—and so mystified.

"These men then built their own automobile," he continued. "It was identical to the car they had so thoroughly
studied. Building it was a very difficult task, because in
our country at that time there did not exist the specialized
and sophisticated machine tools and dies necessary to
manufacture such a product. In 1951 we were a long way
from state of the art in any endeavor, but particularly in
automobiles. All our factories had been destroyed by the
bombing. So before these men could make this Ford, they
had first to invent the tools to do it. It took them an entire
year, but they ultimately succeeded. And there, in those
photographs, is the fruit of their labor. It looked like a
Ford, it drove like a Ford, but it was not a Ford. It was
a Japanese copy of a Ford."

Mishima watched the faces. He saw they were beginning to get the point.

"Well, not quite exact," he continued. "The Japanese
Ford got five miles more to the gallon, generated more
horsepower, had better brakes, a smoother shifting mechanism, a more reliable engine, better bumpers, and a more
stable suspension system. The shop in Osaka made only
that one copy. Because, of course, they could not mass-
produce something so obviously stolen from an American
design. No, they did something much better. They took
their experience and went out to design and manufacture
automobiles for Toyota, Honda, Mitsubishi, Subaru, and
Nissan."

His listeners had become very quiet, hanging on every
word. Mishima beamed self-consciously and went on.

"Those of you in this room today are faced with a very
similar challenge. Instead of a Ford sedan to learn from,

you will have the complete computer printouts of three human genomes, obtained from hair samples. One comes from a man, another from a woman, and a third from their young child. In this instance, the child is the 1951 Ford. Your task will be to construct the computer program that will duplicate her genome under the same set of circumstances. Your task is far more difficult than that faced by the men who copied that old Ford. The technologies involved are thousands of times more complex. But in many ways your task is similar. You will be given a product—the girl's genome—to take apart and analyze. And from that analysis, you will work backwards—you will endeavor to reconstruct, by cross-referencing the girl's genome with those of her parents, a copy of the same program that produced those results. It won't be easy. But you have some powerful advantages. You have superior knowledge, superior experience, superior technical skills, and the best computers in the world."

Mishima paused and looked around the room. A woman in front raised her hand.

"Yes."

"Are we to assume that such a program actually exists?"

"Such a program did exist. And the girl is the first and only human being, as far as we know, to have had her germ line altered according to this program's blueprint."

"*Did* exist?"

"Yes. It was developed by Dr. Harold Goth, a Noble laureate, whose name, at least, you are probably familiar with."

Mishima heard some loud groans.

"Dr. Goth died in a fire in his laboratory on the island of El Coronado, in the Caribbean, on New Year's Eve, 1999. We believe that all his records, including this genetic program, were destroyed in the fire. But we're not sure. There is some recent evidence that a copy may have survived. An American and a German company may be collaborating on an effort to field-test it."

"Can't we get a copy?"

"We're trying. But if a copy has indeed survived, it may well be flawed. It may not work at all, for many reasons. And as responsible scientists, you would hardly want to rely on a pirated copy of something as important as this. The whole point of our undertaking here is to reach a deep understanding of how this girl's genome was created, so that we may construct our own working version of Goth's program. And like the copy of the Ford, we will make one that will be better than the original."

An older male on the right side of the room raised a hand. "What results has Goth's program produced in the girl?"

Mishima nodded. "That's an essential question. I cannot answer it accurately now, but we'll do our best to supply you with information as time and the success of our intelligence efforts permit. All I can give you at this point is a general answer. The program has apparently produced a child of markedly superior health and intelligence. That's all we know at the moment."

"Do we know this girl's name? Or anything about her family?"

"For the time being, we consider that irrelevant."

Mishima answered a few more questions, then closed his presentation with a strong dose of chauvinistic appeal:

"You all know, because each of you has been extensively interviewed about joining this project, that our government places the highest priority on the successful outcome of this endeavor. Despite our success in building a peaceful, prosperous, and enlightened society, Japan remains a small island nation in a brutally competitive and increasingly hostile world. The enormous economic boom of the postwar period is well behind us now. We have become a mature, rich, and stable industrial democracy— one of the strongest on earth. But our pre-eminence is by no means assured. In fact, it may be dangerously fragile."

Mishima turned the projector switch on again, and the Ford sedan was replaced by a new slide. It was a chart listing eighteen categories of productivity.

"I thought you might be interested in seeing how the three great industrial nations of the world—Germany, the United States, and Japan—presently stack up against each other in the key areas of national productivity. These figures may surprise you. Germany leads in only one of the eighteen categories: finance, insurance, and real estate. Japan leads in four: chemicals, plastics, and synthetics; cars, planes, and transportation; steel, aluminum, and copper; and electric machinery and electronic equipment. The United States leads in all the rest—thirteen out of the eighteen categories."

There was an awkward silence. Mishima wasn't sure whether it was because his audience was stunned by this revelation or because they considered his patriotic appeal heavy-handed. The last thing in the world Mishima wanted was to be thought of as heavy-handed, but the occasion demanded that he lay it on pretty thick. The government needed these scientific types to understand that this was a national emergency. They had to hit the deck running on this one. One lost day could make a difference.

Mishima turned off the projector, and the chart disappeared from the wall. "For a while we were winners," he said. "But no longer. We coasted on our success through the nineties. Our economic triumphs made us fat and complacent. Now our economy and our standard of living are on the decline. Part of the reason for that decline can be blamed directly on the United States—on its increasingly hostile attitude toward the Japanese people, and on the punitive actions that a series of U.S. administrations has taken—trade barriers, product quotas, tariffs, and all the rest. I need not bore you with the details. Suffice it to say, we are now in a bitter race for our survival as a first-class world power. Since the Communist collapse back in the early nineties, we have witnessed an increasingly belligerent United States doing all it can to sabotage Japan's effort to compete in the world's markets. The psychology of the United States is such that it seems to require an enemy. And now that the Soviet Union is gone, that enemy has become Japan.

"To put it bluntly, we are once again at war with the United States. It's a new kind of war—not the deadly military folly of the past but an economic struggle. The battlefield may seem far more benign and the suffering far less, but the long-term consequences are the same. The loser ends up in the ash bin of history.

"But we are not going to lose. We are a proud and industrious people, capable of rising to a great challenge. Fifty years ago, a previous generation rose from the ruin and despair of a humiliating military defeat to make us one of the richest, most productive societies on earth. We can repeat that miracle again. And this time the task falls to you, the men and women in this room, to lead the way. It will demand commitment and sacrifice, intelligence and hard work. But if you are successful, the reward will be priceless. It is not an exaggeration to say that the re-creation of this genetic program will ensure the Japanese race a place of leadership in the world for many generations to come."

Mishima sensed that his audience was getting restless. It was time to wrap it up.

"The prime minister and the emperor have both asked me to pass on to you their warmest personal appreciation and their deep conviction that once you know the importance of the task before you, you will not let the Japanese people down. I join them wholeheartedly in those sentiments. Now, I thank you very much for your time, and I understand that there will be several more speakers who will answer the many questions I know you must have, and lay out for you in more detail the specifics of the project."

Mishima left the conference hall in a thoughtful mood. He wondered whether this effort was really an example of Japanese foresight and long-term planning, or if it was the beginning of another great folly.

If this genetics project was successful, what would the government do? Cash in on it by franchising it world-wide? This is what the prime minister had told him Japan intended to do. But Mishima didn't believe it. Mishima thought it likely that his country would use the program on itself—initiate a nationwide eugenics program to improve the quality of the Japanese race.

This would be a dangerous course, Mishima thought—a thoughtless plunge into a medical, social, and moral wilderness. No one could predict where such a course might lead the Japanese people, but of one thing he was sure. The rest of the world would never forgive them.

It would probably be better if the project failed.

Unfortunately, his reputation depended on its success.

31

Anne sat crosswise on a chair in the corner of Paul Elder's office, her head resting against the wall and her legs draped over one of the chair's arms. She was reading a thick textbook called *Modern Genetics*. She had been at it for most of the past three hours and had reached only page 15. Still, she hardly minded. She felt quite happy. Indeed, she felt almost blissful, curled up in this cozy, cluttered little office, alternating her attention between the book in her lap and the man hunched over his desk a few feet from her.

Elder suddenly banged the desk with his fist and let out a howl of frustration. "Damn it! I just can't make any sense out of it!"

He was stationed in front of a powerful desktop computer he had borrowed through a friend from a nearby hospital research lab. For the last three hours he had been exploring the copy of Goth's Jupiter program. Anne could see that he was exhausted. It was after eleven P.M., and his day had started at five. He swung his chair around and rubbed his eyes. Anne shut the book and looked at him.

"Something's missing," he said. "But I'll be damned if I can figure out what it is. Either I don't understand the genetics or I don't understand the program—or both. Probably both."

"Please don't try to do any more tonight."

"I'd like to accomplish something."

Elder had explained to her what he was doing each step of the way. He had started out with what he thought was the most straightforward approach. He had obtained from one of his labs several disks with copies of what the lab called "generic" genomes—ones that didn't come from anyone in particular but were useful as test models. He had fed the data from a genome into the program's software as it instructed him to do, and then asked it to alter the genome's DNA code according to its master plan.

"This is the third time I've gotten the same result. I feed the genome data in, the program grinds away on it for a few minutes, then produces a new genome—exactly like the one I just fed it. Somehow I don't think that's what it's supposed to do."

Anne had been thinking about the problem herself. She wanted to make a suggestion but felt intimidated.

Elder was studying her. "What?" he asked.

She looked at him, confused. "What?"

"You wanted to say something. What?"

"Oh, I don't know. Nothing."

He grinned. "Yes you do. Tell me."

"Well, I was just thinking. . . . Maybe you need to feed it two genomes."

"Two genomes."

"Well, after all, it takes two genomes to make a baby—the mother's and the father's. Maybe the program needs the same number."

Elder rubbed his chin and gazed into the middle distance. Anne felt embarrassed; she wished she had kept her mouth shut. Then his eyes lit up. "You're a genius," he said. "And I'm an idiot. You're right. I'm sure you must be. Let's try it."

Elder bent forward, grabbed the stack of disks he had borrowed from the hospital, and sifted through them. He found a male and a female genome, popped the disks into the computer, and fed their data into the program. When it had accepted all the data, a question appeared on the screen:

MALE OR FEMALE (M/F)?

"Look. It's acting differently already. It's asking us whether we want a boy or a girl." Anne came and stood behind the doctor, peering at the screen over his shoulder.

"Let's have a boy," she said. She felt an impulse to rest her hand on the doctor's shoulder, but resisted it.

Elder punched the "M" on the keyboard. A new message appeared:

SELECT PARAMETERS (or strike ENTER for preselected norms).

Elder struck the "Enter" key through a long list of coded parameters that meant little to him. When the list was exhausted, the program followed with these questions:

STORE TO DISK? (Y/N)
PRINT OUT? (Y/N)

Elder punched "Y" for the first, "N" for the second.

TEST TRIAL OR APPLICATION? (T/A)

Elder punched "T."

"Please Wait" flashed on the screen, and Jupiter began working on the data.

"I'm worried about this taking up so much of your time," Anne said.

Elder shrugged. "I don't need much sleep. Even if I did, I couldn't pass this up."

"I was thinking—maybe I could help you."

"You already have."

"No. I mean with your work. Help you around the office. File things, type things. You need a secretary desperately. Carmen's a great nurse, but she spends half her time answering the phone and looking for misplaced records. I could do that. And I could keep your appointments book for you."

Elder seemed alarmed by the idea. "But that's ... I couldn't let you do that."

"Why not? You can't deny you need the help."

"No, but ..."

"And I won't cost you anything."

"No, no. I couldn't let you."

"Yes you could. Look, Doctor, I need *your* help. So let me do something in return."

Elder kept shaking his head. "No, no. I'm sorry. I appreciate your offer, it's very generous, but . . ."

"Will you at least think about it?"

Elder looked relieved. "Okay."

Anne fell silent. She went back to her chair. It was a good idea, she thought. Why did he resist it? It seemed to scare him. She shouldn't have put him on the spot like that. He could have excellent reasons that were none of her business. She knew nothing about his life. What was the matter with her? They had been getting along so well. She hoped she hadn't alienated him.

"Besides," Elder said, pretending to study a manual that was propped open next to the computer, "what would you do with Genny?"

"She has a full-time nanny, paid for by her father, so she'd be perfectly fine at home. But if it was okay with you, I could bring her with me—some of the time, anyway. She'd love it. You know she's very well-behaved. And she'd be so happy to be around some other children."

Anne saw how conflicted he was, but she had the feeling that he wanted her to persuade him. She looked at him pleadingly. "Will you try it? For a week? If you don't think it works after a week, just say so. I won't complain. I promise."

"Okay." Elder let out his breath in a long, ragged sigh. He seemed suddenly disgusted with himself. "Hell, yes," he blurted out. "I'd like you to do it. Having you here helping me would be great. I don't know why I have such a hard time admitting it. I guess I just don't expect anything from anybody."

"Sounds just like me," Anne said.

"Why?"

"That's my life story: don't expect or demand anything from anyone and you'll never be disappointed. I found out it didn't work. I was disappointed all the time."

Elder grinned. It was the warmest smile she had yet seen from him. "I thought you were probably pretty demanding," he said.

"And rich and spoiled?"

"That crossed my mind, too."

"Well, I'm not. I married a man who was rich and spoiled."

"Ah."

"I grew up poor in Vermont."

Elder laughed.

"What's funny about that?"

"Where in Vermont?"

"Near Burlington."

"I grew up in Hartland. Now that's really the sticks."

"You did? My God! I thought you were a native New Yorker. What happened to your accent?"

"I lost it somewhere in medical school, I guess."

"What about family?"

"My folks still live in the house where I grew up. Mom taught grade school, Dad ran a garage. Pretty ordinary people. I go up and see them three or four times a year. I'm their only child. They're pretty proud of me. First doctor in the family."

An urgent beeping from the computer interrupted them. Elder turned to the keyboard and called up Jupiter's results. He printed out the first ten pages of data from each of the two genomes he had fed into the machine, and ten pages from the new genome the program had created, and placed the three sets of fan-fold paper side by side on the floor, to compare their contents. Anne knelt on the carpet beside him.

"Progress," he said, after a short look. "God knows what the program has created, but at least it's different from the two that we fed into it."

Anne gazed at the long accordion folds of paper in complete bafflement. All she could see were endless rows of letters, spelling out nothing. "How can you tell anything from that?"

"I can't. Not yet, anyway. But you can see that the code is different in places." The doctor pointed to a row of letters he had underlined on the same line of the third page of each of the three sets:

ACCTCAGACT<u>GTCTT</u>CACGGTCTAGTCGATCG-ATCG

ACCTCAGACG<u>GAACG</u>CACGGTCTAGTCGATCG-
ATCG

ACCTCAGAC<u>CTCCAA</u>CACGGTCTAGTCGATCG-
ATCG

Anne sat back on her heels. "I see the difference. Is that all there is on all these pages? Just endless rows of A's, C's, T's, and G's?"

"Yup. That's all."

"What can it possibly tell you?"

"Just about everything. It's a complete set of instructions for building a human being."

Anne expressed amazement. "How many pages would there be if you printed out the whole thing?"

Elder scratched his chin. "I don't know. Hundreds, I guess."

"Well, why only four letters?"

"The letters stand for four different nucleotides—adenine, guanine, cytosine, and thymine. They make up the billions of base pairs that form the double strand of the DNA molecule."

Anne frowned. "I should know that, shouldn't I? I mean, I majored in biology, after all. But genetics wasn't emphasized that much. Gregor Mendel and his pea plants is about all I remember."

"Biology has come a long way since you were in college—which couldn't have been very long ago."

Anne flushed. It was the first time Elder had ever made any direct comment about her. Was he being complimentary or condescending? "Is it too late for me to catch up?"

"Of course not. The basic concepts haven't changed. But there's been enormous progress—new discoveries, new terminologies, new techniques. I'm not very current in the field myself. It'd be a full-time job just keeping abreast of it all."

"Will you . . . could you just review some of the basics for me?" It was unlike her to make demands like this on anyone. The impulse surprised her, but she didn't back away from it.

"You might find it tedious."

"No, no. I'm sure I won't."

Elder scratched his chin again. "Well, where to begin? Maybe a quick, simplified overview. Every cell in the human body contains a command center of sorts, a nucleus. You probably remember that from—"

"I don't think blood cells have nuclei," Anne interrupted.

Elder nodded hastily. "That's right. Blood cells don't. But most others do. Anyway, inside each nucleus there are chromosomes—little wormlike clusters of specialized molecules made up of deoxyribonucleic acid, or DNA. We have forty-six of these chromosomes altogether. Everybody's are the same, except males have an X and a Y chromosome, females two X's. These forty-six chromosomes carry all the human genes. And we still haven't found them all. The latest count puts the number at over 150,000. And these genes are not separate entities— they're really just special stretches of DNA code on the chromosomes, each assigned to perform a specific function. No, correct that—each carrying its own set of directions for how to assemble and operate a specific part of the human body. Taken together, the genes make up what we call the human genome. They contain both the blueprint and all the operating instructions for a human being."

Elder picked up the textbook Anne had been reading and found a page showing a diagram of the DNA molecule.

"Each chromosome consists of two extremely long and extremely thin parallel strands of DNA. The strands don't lie straight. Imagine a long rope ladder twisted in a clockwise spiral over and over again until it resembles a tightly knotted bundle of cord, and you'll have a pretty fair picture of what a strand of DNA actually looks like. The rungs of that DNA ladder are formed by these four nucleotides. They bind together in what are called base pairs, two to a rung. But they don't bind in any old fashion. Adenine binds only with thymine, and guanine only with cytosine."

Anne looked directly into Elder's eyes. "Why is that?"
Elder lowered his own gaze. "Hard to say. Probably be-

cause of the way the molecules are shaped. In any case, that's the way it works. So those computer printouts on the floor are some of these long sequences of base pairs. They're coded instructions. A sequence can instruct the cell to manufacture a certain protein, say, needed in the blood, or the brain, or wherever. Let's change the analogy from a ladder to a computer for a moment. As you probably know, all computer language code is built on a simple binary system—long strings of zeros and ones—or yeses and nos, or negatives and positives. When they're put together in a certain order, they instruct a program to do something—to add two numbers together, or to shift one paragraph of type from one place in a manuscript to another place."

"But how can such complicated instructions be composed from just zeros and ones? Or from just combinations of only four letters?"

"What the language gains by being simple, it has to compensate for by being extremely long. A single simple computer instruction can require a sequence of many thousands of ones and zeros. The same applies to our genome. The number of base pairs it takes to initiate a simple chemical reaction is considerable. The number of pairs required to create all our genes is in the neighborhood of three billion."

Warming to his subject, Paul Elder regaled Anne with the processes of cell division, how DNA transfers its instructions via messenger RNA, how cells specialize, how genes were first discovered, how cells replicate themselves, and so on. In his enthusiasm, he shed his fatigue almost magically, becoming more alive and impassioned the longer he talked.

Anne listened with rapt attention. She knew she was being sinfully dishonest, but she couldn't help it. She already knew everything he was telling her, and quite a bit more besides. But she wanted him to talk to her. She was happy just to be close to him, to watch his hands, his eyes, his expressions. As far as she was concerned, he could talk forever about anything at all.

She stuck in another question to keep him going: "Why is it that so little of the genome—these three billion pairs—is actually used to code for specific genes? What's the purpose of all the rest of it—all these millions of pairs that seem to have no function at all?"

A peculiar expression—something between an embarrassed grin and a hurt look—transformed Elder's features. "You know more about this subject than I do, don't you?"

Anne laughed nervously and denied it. She realized that she had given herself away by asking him a question about something he hadn't even described to her. Their eyes met briefly, then veered abruptly away, as if to avoid some kind of emotional collision.

Anne was experiencing the oddest sensations. She didn't feel entirely in control of herself. Impulses she didn't even know she had seemed to be taking over—and she was blindly following them. It was as if some part of her that she didn't know existed had decided to assert itself.

Elder glanced at his watch in shock. "My God. One o'clock in the morning! I've been yakking away like a damned maniac. Why didn't you tell me to stop? You must be ready to drop."

"I loved it. Really, I did."

Elder stood up, took a deep breath, and shoved his hands in his pockets. "Well, anyway," he said, sounding suddenly quite uncertain of himself, "those are some of the basics."

He groped for something else to say. Anne gazed at him with anxious expectancy.

"Well, I'm sorry I went on so long, anyway," he mumbled. "You're too polite."

Anne felt giddy. A sensation of weightlessness took hold of her, as if she were in an elevator that had suddenly begun a rapid descent. Her heart was pounding, her skin prickled, her face burned, and she couldn't catch her breath. "Do you like me at all?" she blurted out.

Elder tried to act as if he hadn't heard the question. A tide of red advanced up from his neck and swept over his cheeks. He opened his mouth, but nothing came out.

"What I mean," Anne continued, in a quavering voice, "is, well, I like you but maybe you don't like me, and that's okay, I certainly understand."

"But of course I do like you," he replied.

"Well, 'like' isn't really what I meant," she stammered. "I mean, what I really mean is—"

Anne bit her lip. She jumped up from the chair, clutching her handbag and shaking her head. "I really must go. My God, I'm sorry. I'm not throwing myself at you. Really I'm not. But you're so ... I never did this...."

She bolted out into his darkened outer office and fumbled with the lock on the door that led out into the building's corridor. Elder followed her, but she got the door open and dashed out into the corridor with the panicked fright of someone fleeing for her life.

"Anne. Wait."

He ran after her out of the building lobby and onto the sidewalk. "Wait. Let me get you a cab, for godsakes!"

She shook her head and set off down the block at a fast trot. She glanced back. He was still following her.

"Anne! It's late. You can't go home by yourself at this hour! Anne!"

Elder followed her for a block, where she hailed a taxi on her own and scrambled in. As the cab pulled away from the curb, she caught one last glimpse of him, standing on the sidewalk.

Back at her apartment, she slammed the door and leaned against it. Her heart was pumping furiously.

Mrs. Callahan appeared from the back bedroom and snapped on the light. "Are you all right, Mrs. Stewart?"

Anne nodded energetically. "Yes—fine!" she gasped. "Sorry if I woke you."

"I heard the door slam," the woman said, eyeing Anne suspiciously. "I was worried. It was so late and you not home yet. Are you sure you're all right?"

"I'm perfectly okay. Please go back to bed."

"Have you been running? You're all out of breath. Did someone chase you?"

"No. I was just getting a little exercise. Please."

Anne finally persuaded Mrs. Callahan that she was all right. The woman returned to bed, muttering to herself.

Anne suffered through a long, sleepless night. At nine o'clock in the morning a package arrived by messenger. It was her RCD copy of the Jupiter program. In the haste of her emotional departure, she had completely forgotten about it.

There was also a note:

Sorry you ran out. Serves me right for being such a bore. Hope you'll forgive me.

Best,
Paul Elder

Anne read the note over and over. She considered calling Lexy and asking her advice, then decided she had suffered enough humiliation for one twenty-four-hour period.

It meant what it said, she decided. No more, no less. He was obliged to return the RCD, so he had thoughtfully included a polite note with it, trying to make her feel a little less embarrassed.

And that's all the note was—polite. No feeling in it at all. Surely the man wasn't so inhibited that he couldn't have responded with a little more affection and warmth if he had wanted to. "Best" indeed. He might as well have said "Sincerely yours."

Anne tore the note up and threw it away. She decided that if he called and said he wanted to see her again, she'd see him again. If he didn't, she wouldn't.

She waited for the call for many days. Every time the telephone rang, her heart lurched.

But the call never came.

Summer and Fall, 2002

32

Dr. Laura Garhardt sat stiffly at attention as Baroness von Hauser thumbed through a thick, leather-bound folder, crammed with several hundred pages of neatly printed test results, including X-rays, sonograms, genome profiles, and medical interviews. The book represented the first comprehensive report on the twenty Romanian women who had volunteered for the pilot genetics program. The report covered the first five months of their pregnancies.

Garhardt and the other doctors on the project had spent a considerable amount of time on the report. They knew from past experience how unforgiving the baroness was of sloppy work or faulty interpretations. At the front of the book was a two-page letter, written by Garhardt and signed by all the researchers and doctors in the project, that summarized the contents of the report. The baroness read the letter carefully several times. The rest of the report—the pages and pages of details—didn't much interest her.

She closed the book and dropped it on her desk. "So," she said, tilting back in her chair and smiling at Garhardt. "Everything is going well."

Garhardt nodded politely. "Yes, Baroness. Exceedingly well."

The baroness studied Garhardt for a few moments, one hand playing idly with a gold pen, first rolling it between her fingers and then tapping it gently against her cheek. "Are all the women following your orders?"

Dr. Garhardt cleared her throat. "Yes. With a few minor exceptions. We've had to remind some of them not to neglect their temperature charts and daily maternity diaries. And several of them have been casual about obeying diet restrictions. I think we have those matters under control, however."

"Yes. You said as much in your covering note. I'm pleased to hear it."

Garhardt said nothing more. She gripped the arms of her chair to keep her hands from betraying her nervousness.

The baroness caressed the pen in her palm. "Do you have any observations—perhaps personal or subjective—that you would like to add that are not in the report itself?"

Dr. Garhardt wrinkled her brow. "No. No, I'm sure everything important is there."

"Any complaints?"

Garhardt caught her breath. If she had had any choice in the matter, she never would have agreed to work for the baroness. But she didn't have a choice. Garhardt's father had been a prominent administrator in the former GDR's criminal-justice system during the days of Erich Honecker's Communist regime. Somehow the baroness had obtained a cache of secret official documents that revealed how her father had been responsible for implementing a Stasi program that coerced judges into sentencing innocent dissidents to long jail terms and placed hundreds of others in mental hospitals. Her father was still alive, living out a peaceful retirement with her mother in a small village in Saxony. If the documents were ever made public, her parents would be destroyed.

The baroness had never overtly threatened to make use of the documents. She didn't have to. It was enough that Laura Garhardt knew that she possessed them. That left it up to Garhardt never to provide the baroness with any temptation to use them.

"No complaints at all, Baroness."

"Is there anything more you want or need? Anything more in terms of supplies or personnel? Is there anything at all the project needs that we have neglected to provide?"

"Not that I know of, Baroness. We are well taken care

of, thanks to the interest and attention you've given the program."

This was not quite true. When the project was first getting under way, Garhardt had insisted that the genetic software, the so-called Jupiter program, should be subjected to rigorous dry runs and other tests before it was tried on any human subjects. The other doctors and researchers were coming around to her point of view when the baroness intervened. Jupiter had already been tested on at least one other woman, she told them, and the results had been excellent. It would be a waste of time if they fiddled around examining something that had already proven itself. They must move ahead with the pilot program as quickly as possible. Reluctantly, Laura Garhardt obeyed.

"I'd like another report in two months," the baroness said. "Of course, if anything unusual comes up, I expect to be informed at once."

"Of course."

"And Doctor, next time don't bind your report in leather. This is not a work of Goethe or Schiller."

"Of course not. I'm sorry, Baroness."

Baroness von Hauser swiveled her chair to one side and focused her attention on the forest of blinking lights on her telephone console. She waved a hand absently toward the door without looking up. "That's all, then."

Dr. Garhardt muttered a barely audible *"Bitte"* and made her exit. In the three years that she had worked for Hauser Industries, she had probably seen the baroness less than a dozen times. And she never had been in her presence for much more than a few minutes. But each time, her fear of the woman took on additional strength. If it had not been for that fear, she would have taken the opportunity the baroness had given her to add a personal observation to the report. But she had not dared. To bring up anything negative, she had learned, was to risk the baroness's displeasure. Better to keep one's mouth shut and stay out of trouble. Better to wait until the next full report was due. With any luck, the next two months would give Garhardt time to decide whether her observation should be made or not.

It was such a very small thing, really—a slight anomaly in one of the blood tests. The hemoglobin profiles were consistently irregular in all twenty-four fetuses. Strange. No visible deformities, though, and nothing abnormal on any of the other tests.

The doctor intended to make a thorough, detailed study of the profiles of the beta and epsilon globin genes from some sample normal pregnancies. But first she would have to locate a quantity of them.

Perhaps in two months the hemoglobin would return to normal. Doctor Garhardt certainly hoped so. She was damned if she wanted to be the one to bring any bad news about Jupiter to the baroness.

33

"Rabbit needs a friend," Genny said. She was tugging her mother in the direction of the stuffed-animal display at the F.A.O. Schwarz toy store on Fifth Avenue.

"I thought Rabbit had quite a few friends. There must be forty stuffed animals back in your bedroom."

Genny shook her head. "I only have thirty-five, Mommy."

Anne laughed. "I forgot you knew how to count that high."

"And he needs a special friend."

"Do you have anyone particular in mind?"

Genny pointed toward an enormous stuffed brown bear. The price tag dangling from one of its paws read $850.

"No," Anne said, very firmly. "He's much too big. There's no room in the apartment for him."

"Please, please, Mommy?"

"And he's much too expensive, as well."

Genny pouted. "I'm going to tell Daddy to buy him, then."

Anne sighed. Her daughter had begun playing Dalton off against her recently. Along with her other precocious habits, she was also beginning to demonstrate a talent for manipulation.

Since the apparent end of her relationship with Dr. Elder, Anne had been spending all her time with her daughter. She had also invested a lot of money in a high-end computer system so that she could continue working on Jupiter on her own. But she hadn't yet mastered the operation of the computer itself. She was still reading the manuals and trying to make sense of it all. She needed help for both the computer and the Jupiter program, but she didn't know where to turn. She wished she could ask Hank Ajemian for advice, but of course that would mean revealing that she had stolen the copy of Jupiter from Dalton's safe.

She began to wish that she had never taken the damned program in the first place. Its very presence in her apartment had become a constant source of worry. It was as if she had stolen a famous piece of jewelry or art. She couldn't mention Jupiter to anyone without risk.

She had called Ajemian anyway, to ask him about the pilot program in Romania. When the babies in the first trial program were born, some useful information might develop that would apply to Genny. And if there were any problems, the geneticists in Romania were far more likely to find them than Anne.

So far, Ajemian had informed her, the mothers were all doing fine.

Genny was tugging at her sleeve.

"Pick out something else," Anne said. "How about that white bunny over there? She's just about Rabbit's size, too. I bet he'd like her."

"How do you know it's a girl, Mommy?"

"Well, I'm not sure. But she looks like one, don't you think?"

Genny shook her head. "I already have three bunnies— Rabbit, White Tail, and Fuzzy. I want that big bear."

"I know what," Anne said brightly. "Why don't we go look at dolls?"

Genny stamped her feet. "I hate dolls."

"You do? How come?"

Genny put her hands on her hips and thought about it. "They aren't real. That's why. They're just pretend."

"You love that big doll that Lexy gave you, don't you?"

"She's not actually a doll, Mommy," Genny corrected. "She's a Raggedy Ann."

Anne looked around the store to see where the dolls were located. Near the entrance she caught sight of a man standing over by the model trains. He was about thirty-five, dressed in a nondescript gray suit and dark tie. She had seen him before. He was following them. She was sure of it.

Anne watched him. He wasn't paying much attention to the trains. He fingered a few of them absently, then glanced in her direction. Their eyes met for an instant. He gave nothing away. He looked past her, as if something on one of the shelves over her head had caught his interest. Then he turned away.

Anne grabbed Genny's hand and pulled her toward the back of the store. She'd wait him out, she decided. Just stay in the store—until it closed, if necessary. Genny wouldn't mind. She could easily spend the entire day there without complaint. If the man was following them, he would be obliged to stay as well. If he wasn't, he would presumably leave. Anne glanced at her watch. Three o'clock. The store closed at six.

Genny was still sulking about the big stuffed bear. She wouldn't let her mother hold her hand. She walked, stiff-legged and grim-faced, from aisle to aisle, refusing to take any interest in anything. "You're the worst mommy in the whole world," she muttered.

Anne kept her eye on the man. At one point he seemed to be leaving. He walked to the entrance, paused, looked out, and then turned around and came back in Anne's direction.

Damn him, Anne thought. How long was she going to have to put up with this? She walked toward the front counter. Perhaps she should report him to the management. But what could she report, really? That she thought he was following her? He hadn't actually done anything. He hadn't spoken to her. He hadn't touched her. They'd think she was loony.

Anne turned away from the front counter and studied the display on some shelves to the left, trying to decide what to do. Maybe it was best just to leave in a hurry—grab Genny, jump in a taxi, and lose him. She walked back down the aisle where she had left her daughter, moping disconsolately by the Lego sets.

Genny wasn't there.

Anne peeked around the corner and down the next

aisle. No Genny. She called out her name in a low voice. No answer.

She glanced down the other two aisles. "Genny, where are you?"

Anne searched hurriedly through the store. Genny wasn't tall enough to be visible over the display shelves, but the man was. She didn't see him anywhere, either.

"Genny!"

Anne ran toward the back of the store, tripping over the foot of a young boy on the way.

She stopped. "Genny!"

No answer.

She dashed to the front of the store. Her mind felt scrambled. "Oh no oh no oh no" rang in her head like an alarm bell. She ran out the front entrance and looked up and down the street. No Genny.

Anne rushed back inside and collared a startled middle-aged saleslady. "My daughter!" she screamed. "She's gone! She's been kidnapped!"

The woman called security. The couple of dozen customers in the store froze in place and looked around them fearfully.

"My daughter!" Anne yelled at them. "She's gone!"

The noise level in the store increased dramatically. Customers and clerks rushed to the front and crowded around the entrance, expecting to catch a glimpse of something—a fleeing car, a police chase.

A security man appeared and asked Anne what had happened.

"He took my daughter!"

"Who did, miss? Did you see anyone?"

"Yes!"

"Try to calm yourself, miss."

Anne couldn't catch her breath to speak. She gasped as if hit in the stomach. She began running aimlessly up and down the aisles, casting her eyes around desperately. "She was right here! A minute ago! That man took her!"

The security man trotted along behind her, trying to keep pace. "What man?"

Anne halted abruptly in front of the stuffed-animal display.

Curled up in the lap of the big stuffed bear, with its paws pulled around her shoulders, was her daughter.

Genny looked up into her mother's still panic-stricken face with a sly, slightly guilty smile. "I was hiding on you," she said.

Paul Elder finished writing in the last patient folder in the pile and pushed the stack to one side. He yawned, rubbed his eyes, and glanced at the clock. Past midnight. He must get to bed. He had early rounds to make at the hospital.

Elder lived nine blocks from his office. He used to enjoy the walk. It gave him a few minutes to relax and get his mind off his work. but during the last few weeks that walk had become a subtle torture. He could think of only one subject: Anne Stewart.

It was extraordinary. He barely knew her, yet he had never missed anyone as intensely as he had missed her ever since the night she had walked out of his office. For the first time in his entirely self-sufficient existence he felt lonely.

He had thought of dozens of plausible reasons to call her. She really did need his help. He had thought of all kinds of advice and suggestions to give her about her daughter. Several times he had actually had the phone in his hand and begun to dial her number.

But so far he had come to his senses in time.

Anne Stewart was not for him. Despite her humble origins, she now enjoyed a luxurious and comfortable existence in a world alien to him. How quickly she would find him and his life boring! Getting involved with her would be crazy and destructive.

And yet . . .

God, how he ached to see her again!

Images of her swam into his mind unbidden. She was the most beautiful creature he had ever set eyes upon. Everything about her—the way she moved and talked and looked at him—held him transfixed. And when they were together their chemistry had seemed so strong.

Yet she had just gone away. Because he had discouraged her. Why hadn't he been warmer, more approachable? Why had he been so damned afraid to follow his own instincts?

No. She'd only break his heart sooner or later. Hell, it felt as if she'd broken it already.

He passed a pay phone. He knew the number by heart. Maybe he should call her, just to talk to her. But it was too late tonight. Tomorrow, then. He'd call her tomorrow for sure.

No, no. That was dumb. He had to just forget about her.

Elder realized that he had arrived at his destination. He walked through the lobby of his apartment building, said goodnight to the doorman, and rang for the elevator. He felt tired, suddenly. He always felt tired, at the end of the day. He worked too hard, he knew. He had to make some changes. Have a little fun. Enjoy life. Not spend so much time alone.

How long would it take? he wondered. To forget about her?

34

"I've spoken to a number of people," the baroness said. She removed her exercise shorts and leotard and stood naked on the bedroom's thick fur rug, glistening with perspiration from her late-night workout. "Very discreetly, of course. The interest is there. We should begin serious planning now."

"A little premature, isn't it?" Dalton Stewart was sitting, fully clothed, on the baroness's king-size bed. He had been napping in a guest room, down the hall, trying to recover from the wine and brandy he had consumed at dinner earlier in the evening, when the baroness had awakened him and invited him into her room. "The babies from the pilot program aren't due for another three months."

The baroness toweled herself off slowly. She was completely unselfconscious in his presence. "And they're all developing perfectly, Dalton. Three months will pass quickly. We should start selecting our first clients now."

"That worries me."

"Everything seems to worry you these days, Dalton. Are you feeling ill?"

"At the moment, yes. From the wine."

"You need more exercise."

Stewart studied the baroness's body as she rubbed the towel energetically across its firm surfaces. Certainly she wasn't one to neglect exercise. She was not precisely his erotic ideal—Stewart preferred his females a bit more lusciously rounded, with fuller breasts. Like Anne.

The baroness arched her legs slightly apart and rubbed the towel briskly against her pubic hair. "We shouldn't wait. We should assume the babies in the test program will be born and develop just as your daughter has developed. We must assume that—otherwise what do we do? Wait for several years to make sure the children are superior? No. We can't wait that long. We have to accept the possibility that someone else may have a copy of Jupiter."

"It's unlikely."

"I don't agree. Goth's assistant sold you a copy, didn't she? Why couldn't she have sold one to someone else?"

Stewart didn't bother to argue the point. She could be right, after all.

"And we must be careful with our own copies," the baroness continued. "At this moment there are four: one in my Munich office, one in your New York office, and two at the Romanian clinic. They must all be copyproof."

"I thought they were."

"Not sufficiently, according to my lab in Munich. They can add a ten-digit access code to the program. If anyone attempts to copy or print from it, or even call it up on the screen, without entering the correct number sequence, it automatically shuts down. The copies in Sibiu and Munich are already encoded that way. That leaves the copy in New York. We must fix it immediately."

"It's locked in a safe in the wall of my office. No one else has access except Ajemian. It's perfectly secure."

"We must code it. That's not an unreasonable request, Dalton. There's no way to copyright Jupiter, after all. It's illegal in most countries. So our only protection is to make sure it doesn't get out of our hands. Karla is in New York now. She could take it to the Munich lab. Would you please instruct Ajemian to give it to her?"

"If you insist."

The baroness wrapped the towel over her breasts and tucked it in under her arms so that it hung from her like a strapless gown. "In the meantime, we must get to work in Romania. We only have a few months to renovate that place."

She headed for the bathroom. She paused at the door and smiled at him. "Don't go away," she said. "I have something important to discuss." She closed the door behind her, and in a few minutes Stewart heard the shower running.

Watching her with the towel had aroused him. Despite his alcohol-induced headache and general lassitude, he thought he could probably perform adequately enough—if she was interested.

If she was interested.

The uncertainty was a novel experience for a man who had indulged himself much of his adult life energetically pursuing and seducing women.

The baroness, he had discovered, was quite different from the women he had known. For one thing, she had an uncanny ability for stealing the initiative—of somehow always being in a position to dictate the terms of their relationship.

He understood now why she was so successful in her business dealings. She was always the most determined, the most organized. She was untiring and perfectly focused. And she always knew exactly what she wanted. This, combined with her willpower and lack of scruples, enabled her to get her way in almost any situation.

She seemed to have no exploitable weaknesses, either. She didn't take drugs, she didn't drink much. She had no family that she cared about, no children, no close friends. And she lived in a fortress environment, protected by alarm systems, bodyguards, and attack dogs.

Gradually—bit by bit, day by day—Stewart found himself sliding into a subordinate relationship with the woman. He was aware that it was happening, yet he felt powerless to do anything about it. And ending their partnership now was out of the question.

He had hoped, in the beginning, to forge some kind of acceptable association with her—if not a completely loving and intimate one, at least an alliance of mutual interest. But that now seemed impossible. She was simply too demanding and difficult a woman, unable to accept any show of affection on his part as anything other than an invitation to tease and manipulate him.

For weeks she would massage his ego, praising him in the presence of others, deferring to him, acting supportive. Then, when he was beginning to feel some comfort in her presence, she would start subtly undermining him by criticizing him or even embarrassing him in public. Nothing about her could ever be taken for granted. She kept him constantly off guard. It was quite maddening.

As for sex, it was to her an itch to be scratched, no more. And the more satisfaction one could get out of the way one scratched, the better—as long as it didn't interfere with one's real life. If he wanted good sex, she explained, then he should learn to experience it her way. He soon found out exactly what she meant.

One night fairly early in their relationship he was awakened from a deep slumber to feel the bed shaking violently under him. The room was in semidarkness. A small lamp was lit on the baroness's dressing table.

He raised his head, alarmed. There was violent movement, other bodies, sharp cries . . . some kind of struggle going on. His first confused thoughts were that the baroness was being attacked by somebody. He twisted around and sat up, ready to fight or flee for his life.

In a few seconds his first impressions dissolved. Fright gave way to astonishment.

Two other people were on the bed—Aldous and Katrina. And both were piled on top of the baroness. Katrina was lying prone with her legs spread wide and her face buried in the baroness's blond hair. Aldous, in turn, was on top of Katrina, grunting like an animal and ramming his penis violently into her from behind. One of Katrina's elbows kept hitting Stewart in the side.

It was too late to feign sleep. He sat there, immobile, trying to decide how to react. Expressions of outrage would probably be laughed at. And retreating from the bed would be cowardly.

The scene changed. The women were now wrapped in a passionate kiss, and Aldous was now pumping away furiously inside the baroness. She was moaning and shuddering with pleasure.

Seeing Stewart awake, Katrina reached a hand across and grabbed his penis. She fished it impatiently through his pajama fly, then squeezed it hard and giggled. She seemed drunk, or high on drugs. In spite of himself,

Stewart felt powerfully aroused. He had had sex with many women, but never in a crowd.

Katrina climbed on top of him. Protestation was pointless. Katrina swiftly straddled his hips and impaled herself on him with a long, shuddering moan.

The baroness reached over and began stroking Katrina's belly. She slipped her hand further down and closed her fingers around the base of Stewart's penis. Katrina increased her movement, pistoning up and down violently. He exploded inside her almost immediately.

Katrina paused, then gently began her pumping motion again. The baroness kept her fingers around him. His penis stayed hard, and within minutes Katrina had him on the verge of coming again. And then her own orgasms began—one after another, at rapid intervals. She shuddered, whimpered, moaned, tossed her head back and forth. Her eyes and jaw shut tight. He could feel her vagina muscles squeezing him powerfully.

The baroness, far more excited now than Stewart had ever seen her, began her own paroxysms. She locked her legs around Aldous, clamped jaw and eyes shut, and launched herself into an extraordinary series of angry convulsions that seemed to last for minutes.

Stewart came again, even more powerfully than the first time. The orgasm seemed to start somewhere in his toes, shoot to the base of his spine and explode through his penis in a scalding eruption that was as painful as it was ecstatic.

Katrina, still in a state of sexual frenzy, rolled off Stewart and returned her attention to the baroness, licking and sucking at her breasts hungrily.

The other three continued their revelry, moaning and squealing and giggling and gasping in various configurations. Stewart, stunned, spent, and vaguely angry, lost interest in the proceedings and retreated to a bed in a room down the hall.

More nights like that first one soon followed. Sometimes only Katrina was present, sometimes only Aldous—whatever suited the baroness's whim. Sometimes they were in costume; sometimes they were in restraints. The baroness loved to wield a whip on both of them.

Conventional sex held little interest for the baroness. Some of what did interest her repelled Stewart—especially her penchant for sadomasochism—but gradually the shock was wearing off, as the baroness repeatedly challenged him to broaden his sexual horizons. Sex became a kind of no-holds-barred competition, a game of sexual chicken. The baroness's kinky tastes kept her constantly out in front of him. She initiated; he reacted, permanently on the defensive.

His sudden immersion in this bacchanalian maelstrom disoriented Stewart. He found himself spending far too much time recovering from some of the sessions, and far too much time thinking about them afterwards. The baroness, by contrast, compartmentalized her life rigorously. Sex was simply not central to the passions that powered her existence.

Stewart suspected that she was laying on all this sex for him at least in part just to probe him for his own weaknesses—to get him ever more deeply hooked and dependent.

By slow degrees the woman was shattering Stewart's complacent assumptions about himself, luring him ever deeper into a pattern of self-destructive behavior.

Katrina had further muddied the situation by developing an attachment to him. She was immature and clinging, and prone to getting herself into trouble. She was also a heavy drug user, and despite the baroness's threats she was unable to give them up. She had been arrested several times; twice Stewart himself had pulled her out of trouble.

Stewart persuaded himself that he was just biding his time. He would tolerate whatever he had to, and eventually things would go his way. Once the Jupiter program was established, the money would start coming in, and he could free himself of his indebtedness to the baroness. He could rebuild and expand his companies and see his empire grow again. And he still clung to the hope that he would eventually persuade Anne to come back to him.

The baroness came out of the shower with a fresh towel wrapped around her. "I was thinking that it might be a good idea if we got married," she said.

Dalton stared at her, dumbstruck.

She smiled teasingly. "Are you against the idea?"

"I don't know. But I certainly assumed you were."

The baroness sat on the edge of the bed and began drying between her toes with the towel. "I've changed my mind."

"Why?"

"Neither of us is suitable for a conventional marriage, of course. You've been divorced twice, and are about to be divorced again. I've never remarried because I knew beforehand that it wouldn't work. But the kind of arrangement that the two of us now have could just as easily be continued in the legal framework of a marriage. And under those circumstances, there would never really be any reason to get divorced."

"Why get married in the first place, then?"

"There are business advantages. For both of us. And that's really how I would view a marriage—strictly as a business contract."

"Anne and I are still a long way from divorced. And there's Genny's welfare to think about."

"Of course. She's the main reason that we should do this," the baroness said. "I can help you get custody."

Stewart brought his eyes up from the baroness's vigorous toweling of her thighs. "How can you do that?"

"Obviously, if you're going to marry again, the court'll look more favorably on you for being able to provide a wholesome family environment for your daughter."

Stewart wondered if the baroness was making a joke.

"And that, combined with an extremely generous financial settlement, should do it. Your wife has no money of her own, after all. She should be grateful for a reasonable arrangement—frequent visiting privileges, that kind of thing."

"The child is much more important to Anne than money."

"Nothing is more important to anyone than money, if there's enough of it. Your wife grew up poor. She doesn't want to be poor again. And she doesn't want her daughter to be, either. She can be persuaded."

"Why do you want me to have custody? You don't like children. And you and Genny certainly didn't hit it off."

"We must have her, that's why. Think it through. So far she's the only proof that the Jupiter program works. Her presence will be wonderfully persuasive. Nobody will be able to resist Jupiter after seeing her. Without her, we run the risk of losing our investment."

Her words hit Stewart like a slap. He felt furious. "You're talking about my daughter as if she was a sales gimmick."

The baroness sat up. "But you must see my point. And you do want custody of the child, don't you?"

"Anne's a very good mother."

"I'm sure she is. And what about you? Do you want to be a good father? Genny cannot live with both of you."

The baroness got up from the bed and disappeared into her dressing room. She reappeared a few minutes later, wearing black silk lingerie. She had combed her blond hair out and anointed herself with a particularly potent perfume. "You can stay, if you like."

No. He needed time to think. "I'm driving back to Munich," he said.

A light rain was falling, and Dalton Stewart drove slowly. All the way down the narrow, twisting turns of Route 16 south from Regensburg through Saal and Abensberg, and on the broad engineered stretches of the E-6 Autobahn from Geisenfeld to Munich, he reflected upon what the baroness had said.

He did want custody of Genny. And Anne would put up a ferocious battle to keep her. So marrying the baroness would probably help him get custody. But then what?

He remembered the rumors about the baroness—the suspect circumstances surrounding the deaths of both her father and her husband.

He stared through the windshield at the deep orange glow cast against the clouded night sky by the lights of Munich, still twenty miles distant.

The baroness didn't want him. It made no sense. She wanted Genny. And marrying him was the only way she could get her. And once she became Genny's stepmother, she'd have no need of Dalton Stewart.

Christ, he thought. He had made a business deal with the Devil.

35

Anne pushed her chair back from the desk. She had made some error, she decided.

She repeated the experiment. She inserted the RCD with her own genome on it into the computer and carefully followed the directions for transferring the date into the database of Goth's program, reading the instructions out loud to herself as she proceeded. Then she repeated the process with Dalton Stewart's genome.

When these steps were complete, she instructed Jupiter to do what Goth had presumably designed it to do—analyze the two genomes and produce the blueprint for a third one that would marry these two, correct any genetic flaws, and add its own mysterious genetic enhancements.

Once the program had done this—and it took a while, because even at the lightning speed with which this computer could crunch data, it had to compare and select among billions of base pair combinations before constructing its new genome—Anne then fed Genny's genome into the database and asked it to compare its freshly created blueprint with Genny's.

Anne had expected the results to show a one-hundred-percent match. The arrangement of all the billions of base pairs along the chromosomes of the two genomes should be identical in sequence. But they weren't. For the second time, they showed a roughly ninety-nine-percent match. And that, in genetics, was not accuracy; it was not even a close miss. It meant that the sequences differed in several million locations. It could just as well be the genome of a chimp or a pig.

She considered the possibilities.

Could some of the genome data itself be flawed? Unlikely. She was sure that both her and Genny's genomes were correct, because she had obtained three genetic samples for each of them, gotten three separate genome readouts from three separate laboratories, and run numerous computer cross-checks on them. She had gotten perfect matches every time.

Dalton's genome had been taken from hair samples collected by Anne from one of Dalton's hairbrushes. Anne had also had multiple tests run on these, and again they had come out identical.

Was the Jupiter program itself flawed?

It was at least internally consistent. It made no mistakes with the material that Anne could cross-check. She had suspected at first that it might be designed to create automatically a different genome from the same two sets each time they were fed into it. That was what nature itself did, after all. Except for identical twins, every new union of sperm and egg from the same man and woman produced a different child, with a slightly different genome.

But the program appeared to be designed to accommodate this. It offered specific instructions that allowed the operator to determine in advance which of a whole range of variables she wished to manipulate and provided her a specific scale of choices to follow. It also allowed the operator to scan any genome fed into it and get back a detailed readout of all these variables.

Anne had done all that. She had loaded into the program the identical choice of variables it had informed her were in Genny's genome, and she had rechecked herself every step of the way. But it didn't matter. Jupiter simply refused to reproduce Genny's genome.

What possibilities were left?

That the hair taken from the brush didn't belong to Dalton Stewart? Or that Dalton wasn't Genny's father? Goth could conceivably have substituted someone else's sperm. For all she knew, he could have used his own.

No, no, no. That was all wrong. Genny's genome had been screened genetically when she was only a few weeks old, and the laboratory results had shown unequivocally that Dalton Stewart was her father.

So it came back to Jupiter. The program was flawed. Yet how could that be?

There was her daughter, Genny—a most extraordinary gifted child. But not just gifted: Genny possessed capacities not known to be in the human gene pool. She appeared to be a unique specimen of Homo sapiens, something never seen before. Where else could these characteristics have come from except from Jupiter?

If the program itself was not at fault, what was left?

Anne could think of only one further possibility: she wasn't using the program properly. Yet if that were so, why did it seem to work at all? Why didn't it just flash a big "ERROR" message at her? Or turn itself off? Anne wished she knew more about computer software.

Anne rebooted the computer, called up the Jupiter program, and looked at the sign-on screen. There was nothing to indicate authorship or anything else. Just the enigmatic direction "LOG ON>."

She hit the Enter key and looked at the next screen. It contained a menu of options. The relevant choice here was item 6: "ENHANCED GENOME CONFIGURATION." She pressed "6" and got a second menu. The relevant item here was number 4: "GENOME PARAMETERS." She pressed "4" and got the long list of genetic variables to choose from. The next direction was "ENTER DATA, FIRST GENOME."

Goth was no doubt a genius, Anne thought, but how had he had time to learn computer programming on top of all the work he was doing in genetics? Programming, especially at this level, was unquestionably a demanding, time-consuming discipline.

She turned the computer off and thought about it. Someone—some programmer somewhere—must have written it for him. She decided to try and find out.

The next morning Anne called a woman she knew from school who worked for Stewart Biotech and, under the pretext of doing some freelance research for someone, asked her for any names that might be in the Biotech files of programmers who specialized in writing software for scientific applications. She got back a dauntingly long list of 145 names. Over a period of days she reached all but three of the names by telephone. They, in turn, gave her other names to call. She eventually talked to over three hundred programmers. None of them had ever worked for Harold Goth.

After three weeks of effort, the task began to seem hopeless. A programmer could be lying to her, fearing that any past association with Goth might be harmful. Or the individual who wrote Jupiter might not have specialized in scientific applications at all. That would open the door to thousands of other possible candidates.

Anne was about to give up altogether when she came across a copy of a genetics textbook in the New York Public Library that Goth had written fifteen years earlier. There were a few paragraphs in the book that dealt with the importance of computer technology in applied genetic research. A footnote at the bottom of the page credited a man named Axel Guttmann of Stanford University for some of the technical information. Goth, she remembered, had once held a teaching post at Stanford.

She called the head of Stanford's biology department, a woman named Margaret Contardi. Axel Guttmann had indeed worked there, Contardi said. She also remembered that he had worked with Goth on some project or other; she couldn't recall what it was. It was a long time ago. Guttmann was a wizard with computer languages, Contardi told her—and particularly good with scientific applications.

"Is Professor Guttmann still at Stanford?"

"Oh, no. He left years ago."

Anne's heart sank. "Do you know where he went?"

"I'm not sure. I think he took a job with the federal government. With the military or some federal agency. I don't recall any more than that."

After dozens of calls to different branches of the federal government, Anne finally located someone at the National Institutes of Health at Bethesda, Maryland, who remembered Guttmann. "He did some classified work for the Department of Energy," a deep male voice replied. "I think he's at IBM now."

Anne called the Poughkeepsie headquarters of IBM. After a wait for the switchboard to route the call to his extension, she found herself talking directly with Axel Guttmann.

Guttmann admitted that he had known Goth. Beyond that, he wouldn't say much. But he was willing to talk to her. He invited her to come to Poughkeepsie—and to bring the Jupiter program with her.

The following Sunday, Anne left Genny in Mrs. Callahan's care and drove up to IBM headquarters in Poughkeepsie, an hour and a half north of Manhattan.

She found Axel Guttmann waiting for her in the nearly deserted main lobby of one of a cluster of buildings that made up the IBM campus. He was big, with a florid face, masses of black hair, flashing dark eyes under eyebrows as thick as brushes, and a big black handlebar mustache over a mouth of big teeth with a great deal of gold inlay. Incongruously, he was dressed in a cheap white shirt, nondescript wrinkled gray trousers, and black shoes. A German-Czech refugee who had emigrated to the United States in 1968, after the Prague Spring, he looked like a Gypsy king whom someone had stuffed into the drab uniform of a computer nerd.

His eyes betrayed a surprising furtiveness. They were constantly moving and shifting, as if he were afraid something unpleasant might be creeping up behind him. Anne wondered if this was a legacy of his years under communism or simply a nervous habit.

He greeted Anne with elaborate continental politeness, obtained a visitor's pass for her, and ushered her down the empty corridors to his office on the second floor, a cramped, windowless space in a state of disarray so chaotic that Anne's first impression was that it had just been burglarized.

Guttmann removed a teetering stack of paper and books from a chair and invited her to sit. He plunked himself down in his own chair, in front of a glowing computer screen. Only the screen was visible. All adjacent surfaces, except for a detached keyboard, were totally buried under paper. Anne wasn't even certain that Guttmann had a desk at all.

"I apologize for the grossly untidy state of affairs," he said, with a self-deprecating grin. "The management threatens to fire me regularly. Of course they won't, because I'm the only living human who knows where everything is in here. And for that same reason, I dare never clean it up, lest I render myself dispensable in the process."

Guttmann's eyes, which had been focused lingeringly on Anne's breasts, finally noticed the thick manila envelope she was carrying. "I see that you're treating the package in your right hand with extreme care. I can only guess that it contains the program you're so eager to have me examine."

Anne handed Guttmann the envelope. "I very much appreciate you taking the trouble."

Guttmann busied himself pushing aside boxes and stacks of manuals to locate a bay for the RCD in the computer tower hidden somewhere under his desk. He found one, finally, and sat back with a sigh of contentment. "This may take a minute," he warned, settling the keyboard comfortably in his lap.

Anne sat silently while Guttmann explored the contents of the Jupiter disk. His fingers flew over the keyboard in a blur of clicks, interspersed with an occasional grunt of impatience.

"It's Goth's baby, all right," he said, not pausing in his keystrokes. Screen after screen of data flickered by.

Suddenly Guttmann banged both fists against his head and uttered a booming shout that made Anne jump. "And it's vintage Axel Guttmann, too!" he exclaimed proudly. "I know my algorithms when I see them."

He swiveled around in his chair. "I wrote it. Most of it, anyway. It took a few months out of my life, I can tell you. I never finished it, though. Goth just disappeared one day. I never saw him again, never heard a word from him. I learned later that Stanford had fired him. And by that time he could probably write program code as well as I could. He was a fast study, that Goth. It's incredibly complicated stuff—so many evaluations to make, so many kinds of criteria. And so much data to crunch. I almost went out of my mind trying to make my humble computer languages perform the kinds of four-dimensional acrobatics that Goth expected. But I did it. I forgot how good I was. But Goth himself—he was crazy, I think. A genius, of course, but obsessed. He must have finished this himself."

Anne explained the genetic trials she had run with Jupiter. "I could never get a match. The program seems to function fine, but the results I get are consistently wrong."

Guttmann laughed. It was a barroom guffaw, as if he had just been told a great dirty joke. "Of course!" he exclaimed. "Goth was a maniac about secrecy. I don't know much about genetics, you understand, but it was clear to me that Harold thought he was on to something big with these new procedures he was developing. He was very arrogant about it. He even made me sign a piece of paper swearing I'd never divulge anything about the nature of the work I'd done for him." Guttmann paused, then continued in a quieter tone. "I never did, either. But now that he's dead, I guess it no longer matters."

Anne was completely puzzled. "What do you mean?"

"Access codes," Guttmann explained. "He always used codes. He drove me up the wall with his goddamned codes."

"But I was able to operate the program. And so were you."

Guttmann patted Anne gently on the knee. The gesture startled her, and she tensed. "Of course . . . of course," he said. "And you got terrible results!"

"Yes, but—"

"Goth used a silent code. It doesn't prohibit access. It does something better. It lets you go right ahead and use the program, in complete ignorance of the fact that your failure to initiate with the correct code renders all your results useless—completely useless!" Guttmann moved his head closer and stared right into her eyes. "A silent code is the best protection," he continued, in a soft voice. "It encourages the would-be intruder into believing he's broken into the program, when in fact he's being hoodwinked. It's as if you cracked a combination safe on the first try, took out the valuables, and found out later they were all fake and sprayed with a lethal poison to boot."

"Then how do you access the program properly?"

Guttmann flashed his gold inlays. "You have to know the access code, of course."

Anne felt the now familiar sense of impending frustration and despair. "But that could be anything, couldn't it?"

Guttmann nodded. "There are millions of possibilities."

"But just now, you searched all through the program, didn't you . . . ?"

"Hah. Yes. Of course. I was studying the program code—the lines of instruction written in computer language. In this case, Language C. Very powerful. It's used a lot in scientific applications."

Anne bit her lip. Guttmann was making her nervous. Despite absolutely no encouragement, he insisted on trying to flirt with her. "I don't know anything about the architecture of computer programs," she replied. "But how could you have looked at all those lines of program without knowing the access code?"

Guttmann produced a self-satisfied little chuckle. "Oh, I do know it. I typed it in at the sign-on. You can hit the Return key at that point, as you've obviously been doing, and get your bogus results, or you can enter the correct code. That's what I did."

Anne laughed. She felt a rush of triumph. Her effort was finally beginning to pay off. "Are you sure it's right?"

Guttmann chuckled again. "Oh yes. Goth always used the same word as his access code. I used to kid him about it, telling him he was defeating his own purpose by being so unimaginative. But it had some special significance to him, it seemed. And I supposed he figured that since I was the only other living human being that knew what the code word was, that it would remain perfectly safe."

Guttmann removed the RCD from his computer and handed it back to Anne. He closed her fingers around it with his other hand. Anne slipped it back in the envelope.

"Well . . . what is it?" she asked.

Guttmann showed his gold teeth again. "First, I have a question for you."

"Yes?"

"How do you come to have this program?"

Anne had thought out in advance what she should say. She hated to lie to anybody; but in this situation, extreme caution was obviously called for. Guttmann didn't seem at all aware of the controversial nature of the program; neither did he appear to know that it had led to Goth's death. So the complete truth was out of the question. "Goth sold it to a company that my husband owns. That was just before he died. Now my husband's trying to figure out exactly what he owns. Since he can't go back to Goth, he's asked me to look into it."

"What does your husband intend to do with it?"

Anne smiled brightly. "Nothing at the moment. He just wants me to help him determine whether or not it has any value."

"Does it?"

"Well, we're not sure, yet."

Axel Guttmann poured on more questions, and Anne had trouble trying to fabricate persuasive answers. His sudden curiosity alarmed her. She couldn't tell if he was genuinely suspicious of her or just trying to keep her there.

He finally ran out of questions. It was Sunday, the place was empty, and Guttmann just sat there, staring at her, his eyes appraising her body with a rude frankness.

"So will you tell me the code word?" she asked.

"I'm not sure," he replied.

"Oh? Why?"

"I think I might need a little persuasion."

Oh God, Anne thought. "If you're thinking of some financial consideration," she said, "I'm sure we could arrange something—"

"I'm not," Guttmann interrupted. He wet his lips with his tongue.

"No? Then what . . . ?"

"I was thinking of a more personal consideration. A little exchange, you might say. I give you what you want, and you give me what I want. . . ." He let his sentence trail off suggestively.

You creepy bastard, she thought. It was clearly time to leave. Anne got quickly to her feet and held out her hand.

"Well, thank you for your time," she said in a cold voice. "If you change your mind about money ..."

Guttmann remained in his chair. He grabbed her hand and grinned at her. "I'm not going to change my mind."

She tried to pull her hand back, but his grip tightened. He yanked her toward him. She lost her balance and fell forward onto his lap. He locked his arms around her waist and neck and pressed his mouth against her lips. His tongue slithered against her teeth, trying to pry them apart. A hand squeezed her breasts, and she felt his penis bulging against her thigh.

Guttmann was strong and determined. Screaming out in a deserted office building would be a waste of breath. She opened her mouth to allow Guttmann's probing tongue partway in, then bit down hard. He fell back—shocked, astonished. He groaned, then clapped a hand over his mouth. Blood oozed between his fingers. She pulled free of his lap and started to run. He caught her and spun her around. She brought one foot up swiftly. The toe of her sneaker met the middle of his groin with a solid thud. He gasped, staggered, and doubled over.

He didn't seem inclined to pursue his attack, but Anne didn't wait around to find out. She tucked the envelope with the RCD under her arm and fled from the building. She ran to her car in the parking lot, got in, slammed and locked the door, and sat there, trembling violently from the fear and anger boiling in her blood.

When she felt calm enough to drive, she started the car and headed slowly back for Manhattan.

She was happy she had fended him off so decisively. But the encounter depressed her.

Giving into Guttmann's demands was out of the question. But how else was she ever going to get the access code from him?

36

It was an exclusive gathering. The baroness had chosen the twenty couples from an initial list of two hundred. Each couple was being charged the equivalent in German marks of half a million dollars to be the first to participate in the program. They had all been interviewed several times, and their medical, social, and financial histories taken down in detail.

They were all rich and well connected. Five couples were from Germany, five from France, four from England, two from Italy, and one each from Spain, Austria, Sweden, and Switzerland. The youngest woman in the group was twenty-four; the oldest, thirty-five. Three of the husbands were titled nobility; two of them were billionaires.

Dalton Stewart had played no part in their selections. Nor had he sought any. He was content to let the baroness stick her neck out for this first round of customers. If Jupiter worked as advertised, he expected to initiate the second round with a group of Americans.

The baroness had been careful to understate Jupiter's promise. The couples had been told that they could expect mentally and physically superior offspring, and that was all. They were at Schloss Vogel for a series of informal talks on the procedures they were to undergo the following week at the clinic in Romania.

As the guests arrived, they were shown to their bedrooms—large, spacious suites on the upper floors of the castle. Later, the baroness conducted them on a tour through the 250-year-old building's seemingly endless spaces: the huge Hall of Knights, with its display of medieval armor and weaponry; the baroque chapel, with its enormous stone arches; the grand salons; the two-story-high dining hall with its tapestries and balconies; the tower rooms; the ramparts; the arsenal; the keep.

The dungeon, located at the bottom of a long circular stone staircase several levels below ground, was especially popular. The guests inspected the various medieval instruments of torture with avid curiosity.

The center of attention was something called the "little maiden," a modified version of the infamous iron maiden. The iron maiden was a giant iron box about the dimensions of a large coffin stood on end, with a hinged door on the front. The insides of the back and the door were studded with hundreds of long, sharp iron spikes, so that when a victim was put inside and the lidlike door screwed closed, the spikes would pierce his flesh from head to toe in hundreds of places. The little maiden differed in that her spikes were considerably shorter. It was possible, unless one was very fat, to stand up in it with the door closed without a single point touching one's skin. The little maiden was considered a more effective torture because of the exquisite mental duress it inflicted on its victim. Some were able to hold out for hours before finally collapsing against the spikes. Amid a great deal of giggling and laughter, several of the guests got inside and had the door closed on them.

But Schloss Vogel's biggest attraction was its ingenious network of secret passageways. The baroness passed out flashlights and took the guests through the main one—a three-level passage twenty inches wide inside the interior walls of the main section of the castle. One entered the passage through a hidden doorway in a basement closet, climbed a long flight of extremely narrow steps to the second floor, then walked along a kind of gallery past a row of small wooden doors that gave access to a row of bedroom suites on the castle's south side. The doors were cleverly hidden in the wood paneling in the bedrooms, and each one contained a small peephole.

The gallery then took a ninety-degree turn and continued inside the inner wall on the western side of the building. At the end of this first gallery another narrow flight of stairs led up to a similar gallery on the floor above.

The main part of Schloss Vogel had been built by Baron Hugo von Ullricht in 1752. He included the passageways so that he could spy on his guests. Legend had it that several rivals met with mysterious deaths during overnight visits to the Schloss. The castle was added onto by subsequent members of the family, and the custom of building in secret passages continued. A later Baron von Ullricht was said to use them to visit the bedrooms of various mistresses without raising a scandal. The last Baron von Ullricht, who occupied Schloss Vogel until 1923, was reputed to be in the habit of spying on his guests as a sexual diversion. In 1923, the baron's wife was murdered in her bedroom under circumstances that strongly suggested that the baron was responsible. Many believed that during his voyeuristic rounds he had caught her in bed with another man. The police failed to bring charges against him, but the murder ruined him socially. He sold the castle to the von Hausers and moved to South America.

The baroness had spent a fortune restoring the estate. She had also spent a fortune on security. A high wall encompassed the entire thousand acres, and it was electronically monitored around the clock. No one could ever get over the wall or through any of the three gates without his presence being detected immediately. Not that anyone would want to. A couple of dozen Dobermans and Alsatians—all trained attack dogs—were turned loose to roam the property every night. Anyone caught on the castle grounds after dark was in trouble.

With these guests the baroness wasn't taking any risks. The dogs would be kept securely locked out of sight in their kennels for the weekend. A security force of twenty men had been brought up from the Hauser plant in Regensburg to fill in for the dogs.

After the tour, the baroness hosted a get-acquainted cocktail party.

Most of the public rooms in Schloss Vogel, with their huge fireplaces, deep stone window casements, and high walls of stone or dark wood, were predictably gloomy and medieval in feeling. For this first formal gathering, the baroness had picked one of the brighter chambers at the end of the south hall. She had had all the heavy wood furniture, stuffed animal heads, and coats-of-arms removed and the space redecorated in light colors, with overstuffed casual sofas and chairs, bright pillows, throw rugs, end tables, floor lamps, and wall tapestries depicting pleasant pastoral scenes. Huge vases of flowers lightened the darker corners, and large mirrors reflected and magnified the light, giving the otherwise somber hall a cautiously festive atmosphere. Drinks and canapés were served by an attentive group of waiters.

Dr. Laura Garhardt and three other members of the team of obstetricians and geneticists who were to perform the work were present to explain procedures and answer questions. The baroness knew that a success with this initial group was critical. They could be counted on to spread the word quickly among their friends. For the same reason, failure could be disastrous.

The baroness, looking spectacular in a floor-length red gown, welcomed the group with a calculated dose of flattery. She congratulated them on being chosen for this historic event, and praised them for the pioneering role they were about to embark upon, and the enormous contribution their sacrifice was going to make to the noble cause of science. She detailed the weekend's events, and then introduced Dalton Stewart.

He added a few welcoming remarks of his own, including a brief and very sanitized description of how this remarkable genetic program had come to be developed. It was still somewhat experimental, he warned, and of course it remained highly secret. But he reassured them that so far their results had been extraordinary.

"Just how extraordinary I'll now demonstrate," Stewart said. He glanced expectantly to his right, where one of the waiters had uncovered a large TV screen. All eyes in the room turned to follow his gaze. The screen flickered to life, and the guests saw a beautiful little girl playing the piano in a large, sunny room.

"This is Genevieve," Stewart began. "She'll be three years old on January first. She was the first child conceived under this program. And I am very proud to tell you that she also happens to be my daughter. . . ."

He spoke slowly, giving the baroness time to translate his remarks into German and French.

"This scene was shot at our home in Long Island," Stewart continued. "Genny, as we call her, has never had any piano lessons. She plays entirely by ear. If she hears a song once, she can reproduce the melody perfectly. Of course, her hands aren't yet large enough for her to reach all the keys, so her chord accompaniment is necessarily limited."

After a few minutes of piano, the camcorder cut to a new scene, showing Genny reciting by memory in a child's singsong tones a passage from Shakespeare's *The Merchant of Venice*. The third scene showed Genny being handed a children's book by her nanny, Mrs. Callahan.

"You've never seen this book before, have you, Genny?"

Genny looked the book over. "No, ma'am, I have not," she responded in a very adult and authoritative tone. The guests chuckled appreciatively.

"Then turn to page five and read what it says there, please," Mrs. Callahan said.

Genny turned to page five, studied it with a concentrated expression, then began reading the words out loud: " 'Isn't it funny how a bear loves honey. Buzz, buzz, buzz, I wonder why he does.' Hey," she added. "It rhymes!"

The guests laughed. Stewart saw the amazed delight on their faces.

He continued his narration through several more taped scenes. One showed Genny climbing through a jungle gym and swinging on a trapeze bar. It was immediately apparent that her speed, grace, and agility far surpassed what would be expected from a child of three.

Genny's mother was conspicuously absent from the video. Stewart had recorded all the scenes at his Lattingtown estate during one of the weekends Genny was in his custody.

Stewart made a few closing remarks about Genny's high IQ and robust health, and the probability, based on the genetic enhancements of the program, that she would live to be a hundred or more. He apologized for not being able to have his daughter there with him in the flesh, but promised that they might well meet her in the near future. No mention was made of Genny's heightened sensory acuity. Stewart himself remained unaware of it.

Following the video presentation, the guests were ushered into a lavish banquet in the castle's enormous dining hall. Despite their worldly sophistication, they were all quite astounded by what they had seen and heard. The dinner table buzzed with enthusiastic talk about Genny Stewart, the program, and their own imminent participation in it.

The guests inundated the baroness, Dr. Garhardt, and Dalton Stewart with questions and praise for several hours, and went off to bed, finally, sated and weary, but excited.

Later, Dalton Stewart found the baroness in her upstairs study. "I'm going back to Munich tonight," he said.

The baroness had changed into a melon-colored peignoir and done up her hair. She was reclining on a small chaise and studying what looked like a financial report of some kind. She looked up at him. Her light blue eyes seemed to examine him with unusual intensity. It was a look he had seen before: concealed anger. "It's late," she said. "You should stay."

Stewart shook his head.

She picked up a black plastic RCD from the end table beside her and handed it to him. "We finally received your copy of Jupiter from New York. I have it right here."

Stewart took it and looked at it, confused. "Did they encode it already?"

"It's blank."

"What do you mean?"

"There's nothing on it. No Jupiter program. It's blank."

"Somebody sent the wrong cartridge, then."

"No. This was the only one in the safe in your office. That's what I was told."

"That can't be. Did you speak to Hank Ajemian?"

"No. I'd like you to."

"I will."

"Because I believe he has stolen it."

"Nonsense."

"Does anyone else have access to your safe?"

"No," Stewart replied, raising his voice. "But if Ajemian were going to steal it, he'd have made a copy, for chrissakes, not sent you a blank. He's not stupid."

The baroness stared at him. Obviously she didn't believe him. She waited a few beats and answered him in a soft voice: "All I know is that your copy is now missing."

"I'll talk to him. There must be a simple explanation."

"I hope so. You realize this could ruin everything."

"I'll talk to Ajemian tonight."

Stewart left the baroness and drove back to Munich. By the time he reached his apartment, it was two-thirty A.M. It would be eight-thirty P.M. in New York. He dialed Ajemian's home number.

He answered after eight rings.

"It's Dalton. We've got a problem."

"I could have guessed." Ajemian sounded depressed.

"The RCD you sent to Munich—the baroness says it's blank."

"That's not possible."

"Did you check it?"

"No, but no one else can get into the safe."

"Is it possible it was already blank when I put it in the safe?"

"I don't think so."

"Well, the baroness thinks you stole it."

"That figures. She's been dying to nail me on something."

"What else could she think?"

"Maybe she's lying. Did you check the RCD yourself?"

"No."

Stewart pressed a hand against his forehead. He had a sharp headache. "I don't know what the hell to think, Hank. I was hoping maybe it was a mix-up. That you took the cartridge out to make a copy before sending it over here, and then you just sent the wrong RCD."

"I did copy it—just to protect us. But I'm positive I sent over the one that was in the safe."

"Did you check the copy you made?"

"No. But I will, as soon as I get into the office."

"Couldn't you have switched them by mistake?"

"No. And if the one in the safe was blank, then my copy will be too."

"Will you check it?"

"I said I would."

"Let me know right away."

"A blank RCD's not your only problem," Ajemian said. "Unless we can renegotiate a better repayment schedule out of her than the one you agreed to, Biotech is going to default."

"I'll take it up with her."

"Do more than that. Get us better terms."

"I'll do what I can. Just find that RCD, Hank."

There was an awkward silence. Finally Ajemian spoke. "Get out of there, Dalton, for chrissakes. Before it's too late. Cut your losses."

"Just find that goddamn missing cartridge!"

Stewart dropped the telephone receiver back onto its cradle and sank down onto a sofa. He felt an overwhelming fatigue. He propped his elbows on his knees and rested his head in his hands. If Ajemian couldn't find the copy, then all copies of Jupiter would now be in the baroness's hands.

He was damned if he was going to let her cut him out of Jupiter. He had to do something. Thank God at least he still had Genny.

37

Anne surveyed the narrow, cramped apartment room she had converted into a study. There was a desk with a computer and a printer on it, a small table stacked high with manuals, RCD cartridges, and journals, and two bookshelves so crammed with books that it was physically impossible to wedge one more in, vertically or horizontally.

She had been working here on her own for months, trying to unravel the mysteries of the Jupiter program. The effort had given her an immediate sense of purpose, and had helped keep her from brooding about her failed marriage and from worrying about the future.

Now, thanks to Axel Guttmann and a one-word access code he refused to divulge, her effort seemed at an end. For the past three days she had wrung her hands in anger and frustration, trying to come up with some plausible way she might still get Guttmann to give her that one crucial word.

She had asked Lexy for help, but Lexy's advice always came back to the same thing—give Guttmann what he wanted. For a while she had seriously considered it. But even if she could overcome her loathing long enough to submit to him, she had to reckon with the possibility that he might try to string her along indefinitely, or even mislead her with phony code words. And there was always the possibility that he might be dangerous as well as loathsome.

The only other approach was to try to guess what the code word might be.

She had tried the obvious words, like "Jupiter," "Goth," "Genome," "Nobel," and "DNA," hoping for a lucky break. Each attempt was tedious and time-consuming, since it required testing each new word by feeding her genome and Dalton's genome into the database all over again and seeing if she got a result that matched Genny's genome. She knew the effort was futile. There were just too many possibilities. The word could be the name of someone Goth knew. It could be a nonsense word. It could be anything. She could spend years trying to find it.

But she couldn't let it alone, either. Each day, she'd come back to the computer and try a few more, hoping for a miracle.

She reread all Goth's published works, underlining words he seemed to use often, making lists of names and subjects and places and anything else that potentially interested him, looking for some pattern that might at least let her narrow her search.

After days of fruitless effort, she was taken by a new inspiration. She remembered having seen a copy of a book with a title something like *The Complete Guide to Sherlock Holmes* in Goth's laboratory at the hospital in El Coronado. It was the only book she ever saw in his vicinity that related to anything other than the subject of genetics, and it had surprised her. He had also said something about being a fan of Sir Arthur Conan Doyle's. Maybe he had picked his code word from one of Conan Doyle's stories. It was a thin reed of hope, but it was better than nothing.

Anne went to the public library and checked through everything available by or about Arthur Conan Doyle. There was quite a list. She took home half a dozen books, including *The Complete Sherlock Holmes,* and started reading them.

Anne had never read anything by Conan Doyle, and her only acquaintance with Sherlock Holmes came from snatches from old Basil Rathbone movies she had seen her mother watching on television a long time ago.

After reading a few of the stories, she began to see how Goth might have identified with Holmes. They were both puzzle solvers of sorts, and they were both loners—maverick geniuses who had little patience for society's conventions.

She thumbed through several guides, reading short summaries of the many tales involving the great detective and his friend Watson. She was sure she was on to something.

Several days and two hundred potential code words later, her optimism faded. She might have narrowed the search, but she had not narrowed it enough. There were still too many possibilities.

She skimmed through Goth's writings again. They were all about genetics. And they were all written in a dense, turgid style, using language even scholars in the field would have found daunting.

Anne tried another hundred words, but the right one continued to elude her. She shut the door to the study and didn't go back inside for a week. She spent the entire seven days with her daughter, who had begun to feel neglected.

When the week had passed, she opened the door to the study again, not sure what she intended to do. She glanced around the disordered mess of books and papers. Immediately that familiar sensation of frustration and futility began to overwhelm her. She backed out of the room, shut the door again, and walked down the hallway toward her bedroom.

She stopped suddenly. She walked back to the study door, opened it, and peered inside.

The book had caught her eye before but had failed to register its message on her consciousness. Now it did.

It was jammed sideways on top of the tightly packed row of books on the top shelf of the bookcase nearest her desk. Its title was *The Double Helix*. Written thirty-four years earlier, it described the discovery of the shape of the DNA molecule and opened the door to the eventual breaking of the DNA code itself. It was a classic in the scientific literature. Anne had read it in college.

There were two authors. One of them was an Englishman named Francis Crick. The other was an American—a scientific maverick not unlike Goth. Goth had cited him frequently in his own writings. His name was James Watson.

She felt a slight tingling.

Watson.

The same last name as Sherlock Holmes's erstwhile companion, Dr. John Watson.

The same initials, too. One had been a medical doctor, the other a scientist. Goth had been both. It could just possibly be, she thought. Simple, obvious. Probably too obvious. And hadn't she already tried the word "Watson"? She couldn't remember.

Anne turned on the computer and waited for Jupiter to boot up. She balled her hands into nervous fists. She had been disappointed so many times before.

At the prompt Anne typed "WATSON" and hit Return. "Please let this be right," she whispered. "Please."

Nothing unusual happened. The program displayed the identical prompts as it had always displayed. She caught her breath. Maybe nothing different was supposed to happen.

She worked her way through Jupiter's long list of options, fed her genome into the database, and repeated the process with Dalton's genome. When the program finally began printing out its new genome, she was afraid to look at it. She pressed her hands against her eyes and took several deep breaths. She uncovered her eyes, finally, and stared at the printout. This time Jupiter had answered with an exact duplicate of Genny's genome.

She felt breathless. She had just reproduced the identical blueprint that Harold Goth had used to alter the genetic code of the fertilized egg he had implanted in her womb almost four years ago.

Anne went out to the kitchen refrigerator. It was one o'clock in the morning and she suddenly realized she was ravenously hungry. She opened a bottle of Pinot Grigio and consumed half of it, along with a leftover bean salad that Mrs. Callahan had made, a turkey drumstick, a small carton of yogurt, and a wedge of Camembert.

She went to bed that night in a kind of giddy, astonished euphoria, as if she had just won the Nobel Prize and couldn't quite believe it.

The excitement of her accomplishment died the next morning. Despite her discovery of the access code, she realized she still had no understanding at all of how Jupiter achieved its results.

And trying to improve that understanding quickly became as formidable a task as finding the code word itself had been. She spent more weeks analyzing the genetic script of Genny's genome. She tried to determine which genes Jupiter had copied whole from one parent, which ones were the result of recombination (a mixture of both parents' genes), and which, if any, Jupiter had created on its own.

When Anne wasn't bent over her computer, she was buried behind growing stacks of textbooks and scientific journals. She checked so many volumes out of the medical library at Columbia University that one of the librarians complained about it.

She begged and borrowed sample genomes—normally prohibitively expensive items—from wherever she could. Some came from some of her old biology professors in college and others from people she had worked with at the Vermont laboratory now owned by her husband's parent company, Biotech.

With these extra male and female "parent" genomes she used Jupiter to create several dozen new "son" and "daughter" genomes. With these additional genetic blueprints she could make comparisons and begin to isolate patterns in Jupiter's manipulation of gene structures.

Two problems threatened to derail her from the start. First was the tremendous complexity of the subject itself. She frequently felt on the verge of losing her intellectual grasp of it. Her feelings about Goth and genetics in general underwent constant shifts: one day she would be frustrated and confused beyond endurance; another day she would be overcome with awe and admiration at the magnificence of it all. She would marvel at how anything as complex and as elegantly designed as life could ever have come into existence. The more one knew about genetics, she thought, the more necessary it became to believe in God. Chance and evolution alone could not possibly account for such a dazzlingly intricate cascade of miracles.

The second problem was the absolutely staggering

amount of data involved. Along the spiral ladders of DNA that made up each human genome there were those three billion individual base pairs of nucleotides. About two billion of them served no known function. The remaining one billion made up the individual genes that determined the sex, shape, size, color, personality, intelligence, and every other aspect of each individual of the animal species Homo sapiens.

Some of the genes were quite simple and straightforward in the functions they performed. The roles of others were either still hotly debated or unknown. Some genes were quite small, containing only a few thousand base pairs. Others were enormous agglutinations several hundred thousand base pairs in length. And the alteration of a single base—the change of the sequence ATTC to AGTC in a certain location in the overall sequence, for example—could completely alter the functioning of the entire gene, even shut it down altogether. The knowledge of what precise alterations in which genes caused what changes in the function of the genes was the basis of the whole science of genetic engineering. Hundreds of thousands of experiments had been conducted, hundreds of thousand of papers had been written to this end, and still so much remained unknown.

Without the high-speed computer and sophisticated software that could catalogue, analyze, sort, cross-reference, and manipulate tremendous amounts of data in milliseconds, Anne would not even have been able to begin her quest to understand Jupiter. But even with the help of this advanced equipment, the mysteries of Goth's program—how he had been able to extract from the human genome the kinds of extraordinary functions she saw in operation in her daughter every day—continued to elude her.

Anne felt reasonably certain that Jupiter must call for some unusual alterations of some genes somewhere, but so far she had been unable to find even one. A special genetics screening program, a copy of which she had borrowed from the lab she once worked for in Burlington, had combed repeatedly through the sequences of Genny's genes and failed to find any marked alterations in the arrangements of the base pairs. It had also failed to find any in the other Jupiter-created genomes.

Every one of the gene sequences analyzed—and the screening program had analyzed over a hundred thousand—came out as either a duplicate of one of the parent genes or a combination of both, and all were well within the accepted parameters of the patterns of genetic inheritance. It was maddening. Anne couldn't extract even a hint as to how Genny could possess such extraordinary faculties.

Genny's eyesight, for example. Anne knew from the tests Paul Elder had administered that her daughter could see across a broader band of the light spectrum than normal. Yet none of the genes that controlled Genny's eyesight showed any abnormalities. In fact they were exactly the same as Anne's, base pair for base pair. Logically, then, Genny's eyesight should be within the normal range, the same as Anne's. But it wasn't.

No unusual sequences of base pairs—or evidence of any additional sequences—appeared on the genes responsible for the functioning of Genny's other senses, either.

Anne considered one last possible solution to the mystery. She had read that widely separated and apparently unrelated genes, sometimes even located on separate chromosomes, frequently worked in collaboration. So it was plausible that Genny's extraordinary capacities were the result of new and unknown combinations of genes working together.

Checking this theory out quickly proved to be a practical nightmare. Every one of Genny's 150,000-plus genes had to be compared against a series of genetic models that covered the known human genetic range. After a month of exhausting labor, Anne managed to process only ten thousand of Genny's genes. The results: zero. She had uncovered irregularities in coding, but that was normal; human DNA was enormously repetitive and redundant. But in the crucial areas of protein coding and control sequences, nothing unusual or suspicious had turned up.

At the rate she was progressing, she realized, it would

take at least two years to analyze the entire genome. There must be a better way.

Lexy dropped in frequently, and occasionally they went out for lunch or dinner. But Anne was always impatient to get back to work.

"You're turning this into an obsession," Lexy told her.

"I have to know."

"Why? What good will it do you?"

"Genny's not even three years old yet. Her development's only beginning. Something could go wrong. I've got to be prepared for it if it does."

"Give yourself a break. You're getting dark purple circles under your eyes. You look like your mascara slipped."

"I don't use mascara."

"And you're losing weight."

"Nothing wrong with that."

"Listen, Annie. You've lost at least fifteen pounds in the last three months. Your ribs are beginning to show. Make the damned thing public. Go to the press. Lay it out. Tell them about Genny. Tell them what happened. They'll eat it up. Or go to the NIH. Get the government involved. Let the scientists who're supposed to know what they're doing slave away on it for a while."

"I'm doing fine by myself. And going public would be crazy. I have to protect Genny. And I want to stop Jupiter, not promote it. It's immoral to manipulate the design of human beings like this. Not to mention dangerous."

"You've told me that a thousand times. I'm beginning to believe it. But how does what you're doing prevent Dalton and that kraut Valkyrie Baroness Brünnhilde von Mauser from developing it?"

Anne smiled.

"Is that supposed to be a gloating expression?"

"Jupiter won't work the way they're using it." She revealed to Lexy her discovery of the silent access code.

Lexy shrugged. "How do you know somebody at Biotech or Hauser hasn't figured that out already?"

"I seriously doubt they could."

"Well, let's celebrate, then. You need some serious air

and refreshment. There's a new Italian restaurant on Bank Street. Let's go try it."

Anne looked wistfully at her computer screen, its rows of glowing amber letters beckoning to her. "I'm really not that hungry, Lexy."

"Damn it, do I have to force-feed you? Come on!"

38

Anne made the breakthrough by accident. Blurry-eyed and groggy one evening after staring at the computer monitor for hours, she suddenly realized that she could no longer understand the information on the screen in front of her.

She typed out "HELP." She did it as a desperate joke—as a protest at the ordeal Jupiter was putting her through. Even though her knowledge of the field of genetics had vastly increased from what it had been only months before, it was mostly still so new to her that she frequently found it necessary to stop what she was doing and consult some reference or other in order to refresh her memory about a process or a term. The job was made all the more time-consuming and discouraging by the fact that Jupiter had no manual to explain how it worked. Considering the size and sophistication of the program, it was something of an accomplishment that she had learned how to operate it at all. But she constantly wondered if there might not be other things it could do for her, if only she knew how to ask.

Jupiter had a main menu, but all it did was list, in the vaguest language, the program's primary functions. Within each of these functions there were no help menus at all. Goth—and Guttmann—had designed the program for Goth's use; so explanations were apparently not considered necessary.

So she just typed "HELP" and punched the Enter key.

The screen abruptly changed. The rows of data were swept away and replaced by a single query:

"AREA?"

Anne stared dumbly at the word, not sure what to do

next. It had taken her request for help seriously. Why? What had she been doing before she had typed "HELP"?

She remembered that she had been copying data from a genome reference book that listed all the known genes, their functions, and their locations on the chromosomes.

She had decided that instead of plowing through the entire genome, she would concentrate on the genes related to the senses. This was the area in which Genny was most obviously different.

Anne had started with eyesight. Using the reference book, she had painstakingly typed into Jupiter's database the tags and locations of all genes known to be associated with eyesight, so that Jupiter could locate them in Genny's genome and call them up on the screen for her.

She had entered them all, but now she couldn't remember how many there were supposed to be. The reference book would tell her as soon as she located the right page, but instead she decided to ask Jupiter. She typed out "How many genes?" and hit the Enter key.

Jupiter responded immediately: "FOR WHAT FUNCTION?"

My God, she thought. She had stumbled upon a whole new interface. Jupiter was now really talking to her.

"Eyesight," she typed.

"THERE ARE 42 GENES IN THE ALI SIGHT CLUSTER. ENUMERATE?"

Anne shook her head. That was clearly wrong. She repeated the question and got the same reply. She picked up her reference manual again and found in a glossary that the actual number of genes involved with human eyesight was thirty-six. A difference of six—not very close at all.

She put down the book and stared for a long time at the message on the screen: "THERE ARE 42 GENES IN THE ALI SIGHT CLUSTER. ENUMERATE?"

Then it occurred to her. She felt that same electric tingling sensation she had felt the day she stumbled onto the code word "Watson."

She typed "YES."

Jupiter immediately threw up on the screen specific chromosome locations for forty-two genes: 13q46, 13q49, 13q56, 13q57, 13q58, 20q34, 20q37, and so on. Anne printed them out and then checked their locations off against the list in the reference manual. When she was finished she was left with the six genes unaccounted for in the reference. They were located at Xq12, Xq14, Xq24, 4q350, 4q370, and 4q371.

Anne tried the same exercise with hearing, taste, touch, and smell. In each area Jupiter offered up a list that exceeded the reference guide's list by anywhere from six to ten genes.

When she had identified all the sensory genes not accounted for in the reference book, she took a closer look at one of them. She asked Jupiter for a display of Xq12—one of the six unlisted sight genes—located on quadrant 46 of chromosome 13.

Jupiter promptly displayed Xq12. It was twelve kilobases long—a medium-size gene. Its function, according to Jupiter, was to code for the production of a protein that would enhance the light-gathering abilities of the cones of the eyes. Anne printed out the entire sequence of Xq12 and compared it with other genome printouts. What was immediately apparent was that the gene was located in an area where no genes were known to exist. The same was true of the five other extra sight genes. They were all to be found in sections of filler, or "junk," DNA—long stretches of nucleotide sequences of unknown purpose. Goth seemingly had achieved his results not by altering existing genes but by creating new ones.

But how could he have created them? No one, not even a genetics genius like Goth, could have possessed the knowledge required to fashion an entirely new gene, let alone several whole new sets of them. The state of genetic engineering fell far short of such a capability. Only God, or the process of natural selection, acting over millennia, could accomplish such miracles—and then only by a prolonged process of trial and error involving vast numbers of a species.

But the genes were obviously there.

Anne glanced over at her desk clock. Did it really say two A.M.? It seemed that she had just seen Genny to bed a few minutes ago. She had been parked in front of the computer the entire day. Her back ached. Her head was spinning and her eyes burned. And she was famished.

She turned off the computer, got up, stretched, and went into the kitchen. The insides of the refrigerator looked like an alien landscape. Almost everything in it had been put there by either Mrs. Callahan or Lexy.

She found a slice of quiche and a nearly empty bottle of seltzer water near the back of the top shelf. She heated the quiche in the microwave and ate it while standing over the sink. The seltzer was completely flat, but she gulped it down.

In bed, she couldn't sleep. She dozed off briefly at around three-thirty and had a dream in which she met Dr. Goth in a laboratory somewhere. He appeared as a well-decayed corpse, able to move and talk. She wanted to ask him questions about the Jupiter program, but he just grinned at her. His bare skull was visible through the rotting flesh of his face. His eyes seemed to float in sockets of bone, and there were no lips or gums around his teeth. He was wearing what looked like an animal skin around his bony frame. In one hand he brandished a large bone. He looked like a relic from the Stone Age. He lunged at her suddenly, swinging the bone at her head.

Anne sat up, trembling. She pressed her face into her hands and rocked gently back and forth, waiting for the remnants of the nightmare to evaporate. After a few minutes she slipped out from under the covers and went over to check on Genny. The child had kicked her blanket off and was lying sideways across her bed. Anne straightened her out and covered her again.

She sat on her bed, fully awake now.

Jupiter would give her no peace. She went back to the study and turned the computer back on.

As soon as the program booted up, Anne asked it to call up one of those extra sight genes—the one located at Xq12. Next she directed Jupiter to highlight the sequences that began and ended the gene. Jupiter obliged. Anne studied the sequences, then checked them against several reference sources. They were precisely what they should be—promoter sequences that carried the coded instructions necessary to turn a gene on and off.

Anne printed out the entire sequence of the gene and then asked Jupiter to call up her own genome and tell her how many sight genes it contained. Jupiter answered thirty-six. She repeated the process with Dalton's genome and several others she had at hand. In all of them Jupiter found only thirty-six sight genes.

Anne then printed out the area of her own chromosome 13 that corresponded to the location of the sight gene at Xq12 on Genny's genome. She did the same with Dalton's chromosome 13. She aligned the three printouts on her desk and studied them. She expected to find the whole twelve-kilobase-long sequence that formed Genny's extra gene entirely missing from the other two printouts. But that's not what she discovered at all. To her astonishment, all three of the printouts showed identical sequencing, with one small but crucial difference: the stretches of twelve kilobases on her genome and Dalton's genome were not bracketed by promoter sequences. Their genomes contained the same gene as Genny's, but theirs was inactive. Turned off. Shut down, like engines whose ignition systems had been removed.

The gene at Xq12 in Genny's genome was therefore not a new gene at all. It was an old gene—one that had been abandoned, probably tens of thousands of years ago. It was a vestige from mankind's prehistoric past. The human genome had long been assumed to carry chunks of its heredity in the long stretches of inactive DNA, but no one had yet made a thorough study of it. Science had had its hands full the last two decades just trying to determine the functions of the genome's active genes.

Anne repeated the same exercise with the other five extra sight genes in Genny's genome and got the same results.

So Goth's great secret was not that he had invented anything new but that he had discovered something lost. He had salvaged old genes from mankind's past—genes that evolution, for one reason or another, had seen fit to abandon—and switched them back on again, using standard, well-understood DNA control sequences. And by so doing, he had created Genevieve Stewart, a new human with extraordinary capabilities.

Anne recalled the bone Goth had wielded in her dream. He had collected prehistoric fossil remains—had left boxes of them behind at his old laboratory in Coronado. He must have extracted DNA fragments from them. That was probably where he had discovered these genes.

So Genny was not a new kind of human so much as she was a return to a kind of human who must have existed a long time ago. She was a kind of throwback—yet a throwback markedly superior to the present model.

During mankind's evolution the genes responsible for these superior abilities had been shut down. Why? Had their survival value been lost?

It was no doubt true that senses as keen as Genny's were hardly necessary in today's world. They were perhaps even a handicap, overloading the mind with more information than it could usefully process. But superior strength? Health? Intelligence? They had enormous survival value. Why had they declined? Was mankind somehow gradually weakening its own gene pool?

And what other vestigial genes might Goth have reactivated?

Anne asked Jupiter for a total gene count of Genny's genome. Jupiter gave the number as 150,826. She called for the totals in her genome and Dalton's. The numbers came back the same for both: 150,022. That meant Genny was carrying 804 extra active genes. Her additional sensory genes totaled only 54. That left 750 unaccounted for. How many of those could be devoted to enhancing intelligence, health, and strength? Certainly not all.

Anne thought about Genny's remarkable healing ability. And her seeing auras. They no doubt accounted for some of the extra genes as well. But could they account for so many?

What else was there hidden in Genny that hadn't yet surfaced? It frightened her to contemplate the possibilities.

Anne yawned so hard her jawbone cracked. She felt a profound fatigue. The implications of her discovery would take months to sort out and digest. Meanwhile, she wanted to sleep for a week.

The telephone rang. She looked at the little clock by the computer. Just six A.M. She fumbled for the receiver. She felt so weak, so crushed by the weight of her fatigue, it was all she could do to bring the receiver to her ear.

"H'lo."

"It's Hank Ajemian, Anne. Sorry to call so early."

"S'okay." No point in telling him she hadn't really been to bed yet. "How are you?"

"I thought I'd better call you."

"Something wrong?"

"Everything's wrong. The baroness is taking over. She's got control of Jupiter. In another month or so she'll probably have control of Biotech as well."

"It doesn't really upset me very much, Hank."

Anne could hear a snuffle at the other end of the phone. "They're accusing me of stealing a copy of Jupiter."

"I don't follow you."

"Remember I told you we keep a copy of Goth's program in Dalton's office safe? The baroness demanded it be sent to Munich to be copy-protected. She was just angling to get control of all the copies. I sent it, but before I let it go, I made another copy, just to protect Dalton."

Anne felt suddenly short of breath.

"When they got their copy, they found it was blank. Empty. Nothing on it. I couldn't believe it. I thought they were lying. Then I got the copy I had made from it and put it in the computer. It was blank too. The only possible explanation was that someone had stolen the real copy from the safe and substituted a blank. But Dalton and I are the only ones with access to the safe. Dalton had no reason to take it, so naturally the baroness is convinced it was me. But it wasn't. I don't know what the hell to do. I think somehow she's framed me, but I can't figure out how. Nobody could get into that safe. Even if they knew its location and the right combination, they'd still trip a burglar alarm. Nothing had been touched. I think that somehow the blank must have been switched for the real one before we even put it in the safe the first time. But how the hell can I prove it?"

Anne struggled with her conscience. She was too sleepy to think straight. But she knew she couldn't let him take the blame for something she had done. "I took the copy, Hank."

There was a prolonged silence at the other end of the line. When Ajemian finally answered, he sounded more hurt than alarmed. "Christ, Anne. I wish you'd've told me. How did it happen?"

Anne sighed. Poor Ajemian. Caught in the middle. She had great affection for him, but he still worked for Dalton, still looked out for Dalton's interests. She couldn't be completely open with him. Reluctantly, she described how she and Lexy had broken into Dalton's office and replaced the Jupiter RCD with a blank one.

Hank's gravelly voice became louder, sharper. "Anne. Listen. Just let me come over and make a copy. You can keep the one you have. I won't tell him you took it. Just let me copy it. I'll make two copies—send one to Munich, put the other away for Dalton. I'll tell him there was a mixup. It'll get me off the hook."

Anne smiled. "Okay, Hank."

"Thank God. . . . Anne, you're an angel. I'm so sorry you got mixed up in this."

"I know."

"How's Genny?"

"Wonderful. As ever. More surprises every day."

"How are you doing?"

"I've been working on Jupiter."

"Working on it?" Ajemian's tone was disbelieving.

"I've discovered a lot."

A few beats of silence. "You have? Like what?"

"Jupiter has an access code. It won't work without it."

"You sure of that?"

"Quite sure."

"The geneticists in Romania must know that."

"I don't think they do."

"Do you know the right code?"

"Yes."

"How did you find it out?"

Anne didn't reply.

"Anne. How the hell do you know this? Who told you?"

"No one told me. I worked it out by myself."

"Are you going to tell Dalton?"

"I wasn't planning to. You can tell him if you want."

"You're kidding. He won't believe it for a second."

Anne laughed. "Well, just tell him I told you." She could picture how Dalton would take the news—how incredulous and angry he would be. Sweet revenge.

"Then he'll know you have a copy of Jupiter. And he'll assume I gave it to you."

"Tell him the truth. Tell him I stole it."

She heard Ajemian sigh.

"Well, tell him whatever you like. I really don't care. You know my feelings. I don't think anybody should have Jupiter. I don't want anybody else to be used as a guinea pig the way I was. And especially I don't want anybody using it just to make money."

"I don't know what to say, Anne."

"When are those Romanian babies due?" she asked.

"About a month . . . maybe less. Are you positive it'll go wrong?"

"I'm pretty sure."

"What'll happen?"

"I don't know. But the babies probably won't be normal."

"If I could tell Dalton something about Goth's code and how it works, he might believe me. You don't have to tell me everything, Anne. Just give me some plausible details."

"No," Anne said, her voice firm. "I can't. I'm sorry."

"But you know how Dalton is. You've got to give me some plausible evidence. He won't believe for a minute that you could possibly know anything about Jupiter."

"You're right, Hank. He probably won't. We'll let him learn the hard way."

"You have to realize how desperate he is. He's depending completely on Jupiter to save him. He doesn't have anything else. If he thinks you hold the key, he'll do what he has to to get it from you."

"I'm not afraid of Dalton, Hank."

She could hear a long, drawn-out sigh of resignation on the other end of the line. "Okay. I'll warn him. And I'll tell him you told me."

Anne sensed Ajemian's despair. She didn't share it. "Things will work out, Hank."

"I don't see how, Anne. Jesus, I really don't see how."
Ajemian hung up.

Anne turned off the computer and the desk lamp and
went to the window. She opened the drapes and looked
out. The first glimmers of dawn had settled a dim red
glow on the tops of the roofs across the street. Below, the
rows of neatly fenced backyards were still sunk in a pale,
ghostly gray. No one was abroad. The back windows of
the brownstones across the way on Perry Street were all
dark.

Except for one. On the top floor of the building directly
opposite hers a shade on one window was raised partway
up and the room inside was illuminated by a bright light.
She had thought the apartment behind that window to be
unoccupied.

She could see three men. They were standing around,
talking casually, as if taking a break from their work. One
was dark-haired and muscular, another red-headed and
slight. The third man, older and taller than the other two,
had a peculiar-looking long face, with big ears and close-
set eyes. His hair was snow white and his skin dark black.
She thought that she had seen him somewhere once before, a long time ago.

Mounted on tripods and clearly visible just inside the
window were two large pairs of binoculars. Their lenses
were pointed directly at her. One pair appeared to have a
camera attached to its back end. On a third tripod just behind the binoculars was what looked like a small TV satellite dish. That was also pointed directly at her.

PART III

HOMO SAPIENS REX

Winter, 2003

39

The call came in the middle of the night. Dr. Laura Garhardt groped in the dark for the telephone receiver and tried to clear the sleep from her throat. "Yes?"

"Doctor. It's Franz Hartmann, at the clinic."

"Yes, Franz."

"One of our women in the pilot program was just brought in, about fifteen minutes ago."

"Who?"

"Nadja Georgiescu."

Garhardt sensed the anxiety in Hartmann's voice. "What's the matter?"

"She . . . We delivered her baby."

"So soon?"

"It was stillborn."

Dr. Garhardt pressed a hand over her eyes. "What was wrong?"

Hartmann didn't answer immediately. Garhardt repeated the question.

"We don't know," he said. "You'd better come down."

Garhardt threw on some clothes and hurried through the long, deserted corridors of the palace. Rather than wait for an elevator, she ran down the four flights of stairs and across the building's main lobby to the wing in which they had installed the clinic. Hartmann met her at the door to the delivery area. The tall young doctor's face was grim.

"How is she?" Garhardt asked.

"Nadja? She's all right. We gave her a tranquilizer and put her to bed." Hartmann ushered Dr. Garhardt into a small laboratory down the hall from the OR and the delivery rooms.

"Over here," Hartmann said, pointing toward the counter along the far wall. A bundled-up white cotton blanket lay on the black Formica surface. Large areas of it were covered with a mysterious dark brown stain.

Hartmann pulled the cloth aside to reveal the dead infant. Garhardt uttered an involuntary gasp, closed her eyes, then opened them and stared at the nine-pound baby boy lying inert and lifeless on its back, its eyes closed, its head turned to the side. One arm was stretched out, the fingers extended from its tiny hand, as if it had reached out to clutch at something during its last moments. Garhardt gently pushed the arm down against its side.

"I drew a blood sample," Hartmann said. He tilted his head in the direction of the lab bench across the room, where two technicians, also just roused from sleep, were beginning work preparing the sample for tests.

Garhardt just nodded. The infant looked entirely normal.

Except for the color of its skin. It was a dark shade of blue. Garhardt had a terrible premonition. She touched a patch of the chocolate-brown stain on the blanket. "Is this its blood?" she asked.

Hartmann nodded.

"Hemoglobin M," she muttered.

Hartmann didn't reply. He was watching her nervously, waiting for her to tell him what she wanted him to do.

"Take a mucus sample for DNA testing," Garhardt said. "I need chromosome 11. Isolate and sequence the beta globin and the epsilon globin genes. As soon as possible."

"Okay."

"And get all the other women in the program in here immediately. Start calling them right now. I want blood and tissue samples taken from all the fetuses this morning. Run the same tests on the globin genes. Get the whole staff up. We need the results today. And keep the women here."

Hartmann went off to find the list of phone numbers for the other twenty-three women. He shouted at somebody to wake the second ambulance crew.

Garhardt took one last look at the inert form of the infant on the lab bench and then gently pulled the cotton blanket over it and went to her office to wait for the results of the testing.

The hours passed with a glacial slowness. Garhardt drank cup after cup of black coffee and alternately paced her office and stood by her windows, staring out at the snow-covered peaks of the Carpathian Mountains to the north. She filled a hypodermic syringe with a powerful tranquilizer and injected it into her forearm. It failed to still the panicky tumult boiling in her chest.

All during the early hours of the morning the pregnant Romanian women were brought in, undressed, and put to bed. Long needles probed into their uteruses and through the amniotic sacs to extract a few drops of blood and a few cells of tissue from the still-living embryos inside. The blood and tissue samples were swiftly processed and analyzed.

It was late at night before the results were complete. They confirmed Garhardt's worst fears. The fetuses of all twenty-four of the women in the test program had the same problem—an error in the genetic coding of the epsilon globin genes, causing them to produce a defective hemoglobin called hemoglobin M.

This same error sometimes occurred in natural circumstances, usually on a beta globin gene. Those who suffered from it had blue skin and blood the color of chocolate. Ordinarily they survived, because the mutation appeared in only one of the two copies of chromosome 11 that everyone was born with. But the tests of the twenty-four fetuses in Doctor Garhardt's program all showed the identical flaw occurring on both copies of chromosome 11. The coding error was incredibly minute—one incorrect nucleotide sequence out of three billion. And it was absolutely fatal. Every single one of the fetuses would either be stillborn or die shortly after birth. Nothing could save them. They were the victims of a design flaw.

If she had been allowed the time and expense to subject Jupiter's blueprints to the kinds of preliminary screening tests she had requested, all this might have been avoided, she thought.

Might have been avoided.

She would have checked Jupiter's beta globin sequences for the kind of coding error that would produce hemoglobin M, but she might well have overlooked epsilon entirely. The epsilon globin gene functioned only during the first few weeks of an infant's existence. Then it shut down entirely, leaving the task of hemoglobin production to the other globin genes, primarily beta.

The error was not an accident, Garhardt realized. The odds of forty-eight parents having identical flaws in the epsilon globin genes of their germ cells were so astronomically great as to be beyond the realm of the possible. The error was obviously in the Jupiter program itself. She satisfied herself on this point by running Jupiter through a new computer trial, using a male and a female genome whose globin genes were known to be normal. From them, Jupiter produced a new genome with the same fatal error in the epsilon globin genes of both chromosome copies.

Sabotage, she thought.

But who had done it? Some disgruntled scientist here in the labs? Or had someone inserted the error earlier, in the original hard-disk copy of the program, before Garhardt—or even the baroness—had come into possession of it? Some employee of Stewart Biotech, in New York, perhaps?

What other possibilities remained? Dr. Harold Goth might have made the mistake himself a long time ago, when he first encoded the program to a computer disk. But there was the Stewart daughter, Genevieve. She had not suffered from hemoglobin M, or, if her tests were to be believed, any other disorder.

Could the Stewart child be a fraud? Garhardt had never actually seen her or tested her herself.

Speculation was useless. It didn't matter anymore. It was the baroness's reaction that would matter. A preventable mistake had been allowed to occur. The test program had been utterly destroyed and the future of the entire project thrown into doubt.

The baroness would hold Garhardt responsible. And the baroness was a vindictive woman.

Garhardt had told the entire staff, except for those monitoring the pregnant women in the clinic, to get a good night's sleep. She would telephone the baroness and relay her instructions to them the first thing in the morning.

It was now almost midnight, and she had not yet placed that call. She could not bring herself to do it.

She sat at her desk through the night, thinking. Around two o'clock she had an idea. She could order C-sections immediately for the remaining twenty-three women. If the infants could be transfused daily for several weeks, until their beta globin genes kicked in to replace the defective epsilons, they might be saved. Some of them might be saved, anyway. Some would still probably be born dead, before transfusions could even begin. Maybe all of them would be born dead.

And what was the point? The mistake in Jupiter could be corrected and a second pilot program begun, but for Garhardt herself it was too late. The damage was done. It could not be hidden.

At four o'clock in the morning, groggy from lack of sleep and the heavy doses of tranquilizer she had been injecting, Laura Garhardt decided that she had had enough . . . more than she could bear.

She mixed a lethal amount of tranquilizer in the hypodermic syringe, twisted a tube around her forearm to get a good bulge in a vein, and injected the drug into her bloodstream.

In a matter of minutes the small office around her grew dim and muffled and began to fade from her sight. She folded her arms on her desk and laid her head on top of them. She felt dreamy—then weightless, serene. She drifted into a deep sleep. From sleep she slipped into a coma.

Dr. Hartmann found her dead at her desk at eight A.M.

40

Dalton Stewart opened his eyes but didn't move. It was still dark in the room. For a few seconds he thought he was in his bedroom on Long Island.

He stared up into the dark. His head felt swollen and sore, and he could hear the blood pulsing in his ears. He was in the middle of the worst hangover he could remember.

He felt confused as well. He squinted at the bedside clock. It was just past seven in the morning, and he was still in Munich.

He remembered waking up some time in the middle of the night. He had a vague recollection that he had talked with Ajemian. Ajemian had told him something about Anne. He couldn't remember what it was. Maybe he had dreamed it. He pressed his palms against his eyes to shut out the painful daylight. No. It had been something important.

Stewart rose gingerly from his bed and stumbled into the small room next door that he used as an office.

There was a message on the machine. He pressed the Play button, then heard Ajemian's voice:

"Sorry to call in the middle of the night, Dalton, but this is urgent. Please call me back as soon as you get this message. You can reach me at—"

Stewart was shocked to hear his own voice, raw and groggy with drink, suddenly interrupt:

"What the hell you want?"

"Sorry, Dalton. I know it's late—"

"What the hell you want?"

"Are you drunk?"

"Probably."

"I located our missing copy of Jupiter. Anne had it."

Stewart heard himself mumble an indistinct curse. "You give it to her?"

"No, I didn't. She took it herself."

"Not possible."

"Let me tell you what happened. She broke into your safe and took it. She left a blank in its place."

"This a goddamn dream, or what?"

"It happened, Dalton. And she wanted me to tell you."

"Who did?"

"Anne did. Dalton, are you listening to me? She told me Jupiter won't work the way you're using it."

"How the fuck she know?"

"She's been working on it."

"Bullshit. I've got to sleep, Hank."

"She says without the right access code—"

The conversation ended. The answering machine beeped three times and then rewound the tape.

He listened to the taped message again and then dialed Ajemian's home number in Croton-on-Hudson, New York. Ajemian answered immediately.

Stewart apologized for the previous conversation. "I was drunk. I thought I was having a bad dream. What the hell's going on?"

"Anne says Jupiter won't work."

"Yeah. I already know that."

"You do?"

"The Romanian mothers started giving birth yesterday. All stillborn. Every damned fetus. Something wrong with their blood. And the doctor there, Laura Garhardt, killed herself. The baroness is in a tearing rage. She's convinced it's sabotage. Anyway, the program's a total washout."

"I'm sorry."

Stewart sat down on the edge of the desk. "Yeah, I know. You warned me. What else did Anne tell you?"

Ajemian described their conversation in detail. Stewart sat rubbing his aching forehead with his fingers, trying to organize his thoughts. "You've got to get that copy of Jupiter back from her," he said finally. "And the access code."

"Not me, Dalton. This is your business."

"You're right there in New York, for chrissakes. And she'll listen to you."

"She's already listened to me. I asked her for the code. She refused. She doesn't want anyone using Jupiter. She believes it's dangerous."

Stewart felt a surge of fury. "She's calling the shots all of a sudden?"

"She hasn't forgiven you for what you did."

Stewart rubbed the back of his neck. The hangover fed his anger. "If she knows something about Jupiter that I don't, she's going to have to tell me what it is."

"Don't do anything you'll regret."

Stewart didn't reply.

"And you've got to get the baroness to give us some debt relief," Ajemian said. "Our payments are eating up all our profits. We'll never get Biotech turned around unless she gives us a better repayment schedule."

Stewart looked out the window. A light, misty rain was falling. "Now's not the best time to negotiate with her. She's chewing on the carpets."

"Well, that's the situation. It's up to you."

Stewart didn't want to wrestle with anything as mentally tiresome as rescheduling Biotech's debt, or anything to remind him of the precarious condition of his business empire. "I'll talk to you about this later," he said.

"There won't be a later, Dalton. I'm quitting."

"Don't talk nonsense."

"We're fighting each other, and it's getting worse every day. The situation here at Biotech's impossible. The baroness wants to keep the company on the ropes, and you're not here fighting for it. I don't know what the hell you *are* doing. But it's not like it used to be between us. I owe you a lot, Dalton, but I can't continue in these circumstances. I'm getting out now, before things fall apart completely."

Stewart didn't have the energy to argue with him. "I'll talk to you later."

He cradled the phone slowly. He pressed his fists against his eyes. Ajemian was an alarmist. He knew the situation was bad, but things were not going to fall apart. He was not going to let them. Never. He'd be damned in Hell before he'd repeat his father's disgrace. He was going to turn things around. Starting today. Starting right now.

He found some painkiller in the bathroom medicine chest, swallowed it, and forced himself through a long, very hot shower. By the time he had shaved and dressed himself, it was eight-thirty A.M.

He stopped off at a restaurant a block away and took his time eating breakfast. After two cups of coffee, his head still pounded, but with a diminished ferocity.

He returned to his apartment, called the Hauser company receptionist, told her he wouldn't be in today, and then asked her to put him through to the baroness. The baroness was not in.

Stewart reached her at Schloss Vogel.

She was still in a fury from the failure at the Romanian clinic. She told Stewart that she was firing the entire staff.

"What good will that do?"

"What good? They were incompetent idiots!"

"They were the best people you could find," Stewart reminded her. He relished the opportunity to rub it in.

"It was Garhardt's fault," the baroness fumed. "The woman was against the project from the beginning. She may have sabotaged it."

"You have any evidence?"

"She was in charge. She had the final approval of all the genome sequences. Either she purposely tampered with them or failed to discover that someone else had tampered with them—"

Stewart cut her off. "Let me tell you the real reason the project failed. Because of you. You insisted on rushing the project, and this was the result. Jupiter will function properly only if fed the right access code. This was Goth's way of protecting the program from theft."

"How do you come to tell me this now?"

"Because I just found out."

"How is that?"

"I'll explain it later. First, I have a proposition to make. I expect to have the correct access code shortly. When I have it, we'll set up a new pilot program. But this time, *I* intend to run it. And I intend to staff the project exclusively with my people."

"And are you going to pay for it, too, Dalton?"

"No. You are."

"How do you intend to make that happen?"

"Because you're intelligent enough to see it's the only thing to do. We both need the program to succeed. I'm now offering you the only chance left to rescue the project. But it'll have to be on my terms this time, not yours."

The baroness laughed derisively. "And how do you expect me to accept such nonsense. Access codes—*mein Gott*! Dalton, you've gone quite mad."

"Those are the terms. If you don't like them, I'll develop Jupiter on my own."

"So you kept a copy. You've been planning this all along."

"No, that's not right. But Ajemian did find our copy."

"Where?"

"It's not relevant. I'm going ahead on this. With your backing or without it."

"How? Who'll loan you the money?"

"Take my word for it, Baroness. I can get it."

"Bring me proof that Jupiter will work your way, and I'll accept your terms."

"I thought you might."

Stewart hung up before the baroness had time to say anything further. For the first time that day he began to feel some optimism. Jupiter still mattered to her. That was good. Because he was going to do to her exactly what she had been trying to do to him—screw her out of the deal completely.

And if the baroness tried to get around his terms, that'd be okay, too. He'd cannibalize Stewart Biotech. He'd sell off enough pieces of it to finance a couple of years of development. And the hell with the rest of the company—

there wasn't much left, anyway. He'd break it up and let the baroness and the banks fight over the scraps.

He called the airport and booked a flight to New York City.

41

The men across the way were still watching her. During the day they kept the window shade pulled three-quarters of the way down. Anne could see nothing through the open space between the shade and the bottom sill, but she knew that in the darkness on the other side those huge binoculars and that dish antenna—presumably a listening device—were trained on her. At night the shade was often all the way up, and the room dark.

She had decided they must be Dalton's doing—no doubt with the baroness's encouragement. She wondered how long they had been at it. Days? Weeks? What could they have found out? Could they have seen her use the Watson access code?

Her computer monitor faced away from the window, so they could not have read anything off the screen. Print-outs were another matter. She had often left them on the top of the small bookcase under the study window, and she had frequently dumped piles of books and papers on the chair beside it. Both areas would be easily visible to those binoculars. Had she exposed anything of value? The more she thought about it, the more frightened it made her.

She did have one advantage: they didn't know she knew they were watching her. She continued to open the drapes at the same time every morning and close them when she retired at night.

She gathered together all the important material relating to Jupiter, removed the Jupiter RCD from the computer, and packaged everything in a cardboard box. She put the box in a shopping bag and took the material to a bank on Fourteenth Street and locked it in a safety deposit box. Knowing that someone might be following her, she took the bag and the now empty cardboard box back with her to her apartment. In the study, she turned on the computer, called up her word-processing program, and created a document with the title "JUPITER INSTRUCTIONS" in boldface across the top. On the page below, she made up an elaborate series of steps that one supposedly had to take in order to make the program work. When she was finished, she looked at it and decided that it wouldn't fool anybody.

She finally hit upon something more subtle. She wrote what appeared to be a letter addressed to her from a fictitious professor of genetics at MIT. In the letter he referred to his past working relationship with the late Dr. Goth and explained that in order to make the Jupiter program function, it was necessary to initiate it with a password. That password was "Minerva."

She printed the letter out and read it through a few times. There was still a problem: the letter wasn't typed on departmental letterhead. Maybe her fictitious professor wouldn't have used it, but it looked suspicious; and one telephone call to MIT would confirm that he didn't exist.

Two problems, one solution. Anne slapped the letter down sideways on the top of the bookcase, then quickly placed a book across the top of the sheet, concealing the date, the address, and the missing MIT departmental letterhead. Just to make sure they got a good photograph, she turned on her gooseneck desk lamp and directed the light toward the top of the bookcase. She left the room that way and went into the kitchen and had lunch with Genny and Mrs. Callahan.

After lunch Anne returned to the study with Genny. She looked at the letter lying on the top of the bookcase. Surely the men in the window across the way had photographed it by now. She dropped another book directly on top of the letter and turned off the lamp.

"Will you read me something, Mommy?"

"I will."

Anne read to Genny for about an hour. Actually Genny did most of the reading. She had been able to spell out words since she was two, but in just the last six months her reading ability had developed enormously. She could sound out almost any word in, say, *The New York Times,* and she knew the meanings of ninety percent of them. Of course, many subjects still baffled her, because she couldn't place them in a meaningful context.

But she was learning fast. She already knew who the President was, and she could recite from memory all the states and their capitals, and a mass of other data she had absorbed from an almanac Mrs. Callahan had given her. But at the moment she was entranced by Nancy Drew mysteries, which were much more fun than the *Times.*

"Why are you worried, Mommy?"

Anne shrugged and smiled. "I'm not worried."

Genny laughed. "Yes, you are too worried. I can tell."

Anne embraced her. "How can you tell?"

"I don't know how. But I can."

"Will you be able to explain it to me someday?"

"I hope so, Mommy."

"Anyway, you're right. I am a little worried."

"You should go see Auntie Lexy, then. She always cheers you up."

"Well, as a matter of fact, Lexy and I are going to have dinner together. So when Mrs. Callahan comes back with you from the puppet show this afternoon, I'll be out."

"Can we get a video?"

"Okay. But just one."

"Can I wait up for you?"

"You better not. You've been up past ten every night this week."

"But I don't need all that sleep."

"You certainly *do* need all that sleep."

"No I don't. Really. I wake up at night sometimes and stay awake for a long time."

"You do? And what do you do during all that time?"

"I like to listen to sounds in the street. I like to listen to people. I can hear them talking. And I can smell a lot of different things. Strange, funny things. It's fun."

"You really should be sleeping. It's not good for you to stay awake at night."

Genny scratched her cheek thoughtfully. "I have something to show you, Mommy," she said finally.

"Yes?"

"You promise you won't be angry?"

Anne narrowed her eyes, mystified. Genny had never made such a request before. "I can't promise. But I'll try."

Genny thought about this for a moment, then nodded. "Okay. Follow me." The little girl led her mother to the apartment's front door.

"It's about Bomber," she said, pointing to the door. "He's out in the hall."

Bomber was the upstairs neighbor's pet schnauzer. He was a minor nuisance in the building, frequently running loose in the hallways and barking at all hours. Twice he had chased Moby Cat, and once caught him and roughed him up. Genny disliked the dog intensely.

"Loose again?"

Genny nodded, but she had a peculiar look on her face. "Go see him," she said.

Anne opened the door and looked up and down the hall. No sign of the dog.

"He's downstairs, Mommy."

Genny followed her mother down the stairs to the small vestibule just inside the brownstone's outside door. She pointed to the floor. The dog was lying there, on its side, quite still, its eyes shut.

Anne bent down and gently patted the dog's neck. It was immediately apparent that the animal was dead.

Anne rushed upstairs to inform Bomber's owner, a middle-aged woman named Mrs. Berkin, whom Anne had met only once. She spent the next forty-five minutes consoling the distraught woman. Eventually she helped the woman carry the dog upstairs and called a veterinarian for advice on disposing of the animal.

Once back in her own apartment, Anne asked Genny how she knew that something had happened to Bomber.

"He was bad," Genny said. "He tried to hurt Moby Cat again."

"I know that, darling. But do you know what happened to Bomber? Did you see anyone do anything to the dog? Or feed him anything?"

Genny shook her head. She wore an unmistakable look

of guilt. Anne was perplexed. "You asked me not to be mad at you. Why should I be mad at you?"

"It was me, Mommy."

"You?"

"Bomber was bad, Mommy. He tried to bite me, too."

Anne's puzzlement grew. "What do you mean? What did you do?"

"I just . . . squeezed him."

"Squeezed him? How?"

Genny put her little hands around her mother's neck to show her. "I did it real hard. Until he stopped moving. It didn't take long at all. He was bad, Mommy. You know he was bad. I didn't want to tell Mrs. Berkin, but he was a very bad dog."

Anne knelt down and pulled Genny close to her. Tears welled up. *Dear God, dear God.*

"I'm sorry, Mommy. Don't cry. Bomber was bad."

Anne hugged her hard. My precious child, my precious child.

She felt engulfed by fear. Thoughts about all those atavistic genes in Genny's genome swam through her mind. What was she going to say when people found out that her daughter was an experiment in human genetic engineering?

And what was she going to do if something like this happened again?

That evening Lexy and Anne had dinner at a restaurant off Seventh Avenue. Anne poured out the whole story about Genny and Bomber.

Lexy made light of it. "I don't believe it for a minute. Genny wouldn't do anything as monstrous as that. Strangling someone's pet schnauzer? Come on! The child has an overactive imagination. I know she didn't like the animal. She probably saw the dog dead and fantasized that she had killed it. I'll bet the downstairs neighbor fed the beast a poison hamburger. Things like that happen all the time. And the dog was a miserable little cur, anyway. Forget it."

"But Genny's very strong physically. She *could* have done it."

"But for godsakes, you'd have heard something, like the dog yowling."

"Oh, God, Lexy, I want to believe you."

"Then believe me. And have another glass of wine."

Lexy was far more interested in the men staked out in the apartment facing Anne's study. She asked a thousand questions, then rendered her verdict: "I told you. It's Dalton. He hired them. He's trying to catch you in flagrante delicto, so he can get a better divorce settlement. And win custody of Genny."

"I'm not sure he even wants custody."

"Of course he does. Remember, she's the only proof that Jupiter works. Knowing Dalton, he'd probably parade her around Europe with a tin cup. Anything to make a buck. And speaking of flagrante delicto, how about giving that Dr. What's-His-Name a call? You desperately need a little romance in your life."

"I wish you wouldn't keep bringing him up. I want to forget him."

"You want to forget you made a fool of yourself, that's all."

"That too."

Between them they drank a bottle and a half of wine, and by the time Anne got back to her apartment on West Eleventh she felt a little foggy, but much less anxious than earlier in the evening.

Mrs. Callahan came out to greet her.

"Oh, Mrs. Callahan, you didn't have to stay up."

"It's okay, Mrs. Stewart. I took a nap earlier."

"Did Genny get to bed at a reasonable hour?"

Mrs. Callahan stared at her with a confused expression.

"What's the matter?" Anne asked.

"Well, Genny's been gone since seven."

"Gone? Where's she gone?"

"Well, Mr. Stewart picked her up."

"What?"

"He said it was all arranged."

Anne's euphoria evaporated. "Where did he take her?"

"Long Island, I suppose."

"Why didn't you go with her?"

"He told me that you'd agreed it wasn't necessary."

Anne grabbed the phone and dialed the house in Lattingtown. The phone rang ten times before someone finally picked it up. It was the housekeeper, Mrs. Corley.

"It's Anne Stewart, Mrs. Corley. Is my husband there?"

"No, he's not," she snapped. Since Anne had walked out on Dalton and was no longer the head of the household, Mrs. Corley saw no reason to be civil to her.

"Where is he, do you know?"

"I have no idea."

"I'm looking for my daughter, Mrs. Corley. Is she there?"

"No."

"Where is she?"

"I have no idea."

"This is serious, Mrs. Corley. Dalton's taken my daughter without my permission. I'm about to call the police and report it."

"I wouldn't bother, Mrs. Stewart. They left on a plane for Germany hours ago."

Anne hung up. "The bastard!"

Mrs. Callahan was standing by the phone, wringing her hands in anguish. "I'm sorry, Mrs. Stewart. I thought it was arranged. He said it was all arranged. I didn't—"

"It's not your fault, Mrs. Callahan. Go on to bed."

"But I'm very upset. . . ."

"Go on to bed. I'll talk to Dalton in the morning and we'll straighten it out."

Mrs. Callahan went off to her room, sobbing quietly to herself. Anne sat at the kitchen table, drinking coffee and trying to decide what to do. Dalton had obviously planned this carefully. It would have taken him time to get Genny a passport, for one thing. In the back of her mind, behind the jumble of emotions she was feeling, a stark terror loomed. What if he meant to keep Genny? How was she going to be able to get her back?

By three A.M. Anne felt exhausted. She went into her bedroom and lay down. After a while she drifted into a troubled sleep.

At six A.M. the phone rang. Anne groped for the receiver.

"I'm in Munich," Dalton told her. "I have Genny here with me."

"Why are you doing this?"

"I want you back, too."

"You have some way of showing it. Why did you take her?"

"You know damn well why."

"I don't know damn well why. But I'm coming to get her."

"Good. Be on the seven P.M. flight from JFK to Munich tonight. And bring the copy of Jupiter you stole from me with you. And the access code that goes with it. Otherwise you don't get Genny back. We'll meet you at the airport."

Anne started to reply, but Dalton had already hung up.

42

Dalton Stewart and his daughter emerged from his Munich apartment early in the morning. While he locked the door, she ran ahead to summon the elevator. When the doors opened, she jumped on ahead of her father.

"Which button, Daddy?"

"K-1."

Genny scanned the rows of buttons, found the one labeled K-1, and pressed it. "Is that the underground garage?"

"That's right."

"Is Mommy going to stay with us?"

"I don't think so. You and Mommy will be going back to New York. Probably tomorrow."

Genny's eyes watched the flashing numbers on the panel above the door as they descended the ten floors toward the garage subbasement. "Do you love me as much as Mommy does?"

Stewart felt his throat constrict. "Oh, yes. Even more."

"Mommy said no one could love me more than she does."

"Well, I guess we're tied, then. Because no one could love you more than I do, either."

"Don't you miss Mommy?"

"Yes," he muttered. He did.

"I miss Mommy already," Genny declared.

"We'll see her soon."

Genny looked thoughtful for a moment. "I'm glad both you and Mommy love me, but I wish you still loved each other, too."

"I wish we did, too, honey."

"Do you think you will again sometime?"

"Maybe. I hope so."

The fact that he was using his daughter as a pawn in a power struggle with Anne and the baroness did not make him feel good about himself. He knew it would probably end forever any chance of reconciling with Anne, but he was backed into a corner. This was his only way out. If it worked, everything would become possible again. And he'd prove to his daughter just how much he really did love her. There would be no end of what he would do for her. He'd fulfill her grandest dreams, her most extravagant ambitions.

The elevator stopped and the doors rattled open.

Genny slipped her hand inside her father's and skipped along beside him toward his car, a gray BMW parked near the back. "Do you love someone else now, instead of Mommy?"

Her father laughed. Genny had peppered him with hundreds of questions ever since he had picked her up in New York. She would ask three or four or a dozen completely trivial questions and then suddenly spring a zinger on him when he least expected it. "No," he said in a stern voice, hoping to scare off any further inquiry along this line.

Genny was not deterred. "Mommy told me you loved the baroness."

He started to say that she was just a business associate, but under the circumstances it sounded ridiculous. "No. I don't love the baroness at all."

Genny craned her head up to look directly into her father's face. "Well, I don't even *like* her at all," she declared in an emphatic tone.

"No? Why not?"

"She's bad, that's why."

They arrived at the car. Stewart unlocked the door on the driver's side. Genny was right. His relationship with the woman was a simple case of mutual exploitation. He had lusted after the woman sexually, but what he had really wanted was her money and her connections. The baroness in turn had wanted his empire, Stewart Biotech, to give her a foothold in the United States market. And of course both of them had wanted Jupiter. A couple of predatory animals, that's what they were, each circling the other and snarling over who was going to get the spoils of the hunt.

"Mommy has a friend, too. And I like him a lot."

"Who's that?"

"Dr. Elder."

"Oh." Stewart had never heard of him.

"She doesn't see him anymore," Genny said. "I wish she would, though. He taught me lots of neat doctor things. He showed me how to use a stethoscope."

Stewart wasn't listening. He was thinking how Anne still held the key to everything. Literally. God, he hoped she did. The nightmare possibility that he was risking so much on the assumption that Anne knew for certain what she was talking about frightened him. But if she did—if the access code really worked—then that was all that he needed.

And Anne would have to cooperate if she wanted Genny back. But he hoped, he prayed, he could persuade her to give him Jupiter and the code willingly.

Genny squeezed past him and crawled across the driver's seat to the passenger side. Stewart heard someone calling. He looked around. About six cars away, a tall, thin man with a black mustache was motioning at him and shouting *"Bitte!"* in a loud voice.

Stewart hesitated. The man's attitude annoyed him. Only in Germany would somebody shout at you to demand your help. "I don't speak German," Stewart shouted back.

"You English?" the man asked.

"American."

"Good. You can help me. I dropped my key. I can't bend over to pick it up. My back is very injured, *ja*?"

Stewart cursed under his breath. He ducked down to look at Genny, squirming around playfully on the leather seat to warm it up.

He felt like a heel not offering to help the man, but there was something suspicious about him. He was too young to have a bad back—and too young to be driving a new, top-of-the-line Mercedes. The hell with him.

He started to get into the car. No sooner had he lifted

his foot than he felt a powerful blow land against the back of his skull. It hit with such force that he toppled forward and smashed his head against the car's roof. Another blow landed behind his ear. He sagged backwards, unconscious.

A man caught him under the arms, dragged him away from the car, and dropped him on the garage's concrete floor. He fished in Stewart's jacket pocket for a wallet, found one, and opened it. He grabbed the handful of bills inside and then threw the wallet onto the floor.

Two other men—the thin one who had called out to Stewart, and a short, thickset man who had been crouched down out of sight—came running over from the Mercedes and closed in quickly on the front doors of the BMW.

Genny reacted instantly. She fell across the driver's seat, pulled the door shut, and reached for the button that would lock all four doors automatically. The thin one, approaching the driver's side, saw what she was trying to do and managed to get the door open a split second before Genny could hit the lever. He yanked the door wide and grabbed her arm.

Genny twisted away from him and scrambled into the backseat. His partner opened the passenger-side front door and leaned in. "Watch the back door!" the other one yelled.

Genny had the back door open and was squeezing out. The heavy one threw his weight against it, to force Genny back inside. The thin one opened the other back door and reached across the seat to grab her. Genny shoved harder against the door. The heavy one tried to hold it but lost ground. The bottom edge struck him in the shin and he lost his balance.

His partner grabbed Genny's ankle and pulled her back across the rear seat. Genny turned on him and rained a flurry of lightning punches to his face. He let go of the ankle to ward off the blows. In that fraction of a second, Genny jumped out and dashed across the garage.

They came after her, both yelling at the third man for help.

He looked up, annoyed. He had explicit instructions to

kill Stewart, and he had been keenly anticipating slamming his blackjack repeatedly against his head.

But the girl was running straight for him, and running incredibly fast. She was not to be hurt, but under the circumstances a quick, hard crack on her skull was clearly going to be necessary. When she was almost on top of him, he whipped the blackjack around violently, aiming for the side of her head.

He missed completely.

Her head plowed into his groin and sent him flying. The concrete floor crashed against his back. He rolled over, gasping for air.

Genny could not find her way out of the garage. The elevator car had gone back up, and she couldn't find any stairs. As a last resort, she tried to escape up the exit ramp, but the thin man and the thickset one cut her off and grabbed her, one on each side. She shook one off, then bit the other's hand. He bellowed, but held on long enough for his partner to get a grip on her arm again. She kicked and thrashed with all her might, whipping her thirty-five-pound body back and forth, trying to throw them off balance. It was all they could do to hold on, but hold on they did.

The third man caught up to them and began slashing at her wildly with the blackjack. She dodged several blows and managed to kick him twice in the legs, but finally he locked an arm around her neck long enough to smash the blackjack against her head. With the third blow, she collapsed into unconsciousness.

They carried her to their Mercedes, threw her in the back, and drove out of the garage, one of the men on either side of her. They tied her arms together behind her, locked her little ankles in handcuffs, and stuffed a gag in her mouth. They weren't taking any more chances.

Anne Stewart's plane touched down at the Munich airport at ten A.M., an hour behind schedule. Anne hurried through customs and out into the arrivals area. There was no sign of Dalton.

She waited for a few minutes, then called his office number at Hauser Industries. The woman who answered told her that he had left word that he wasn't coming in to-day, that was all. Did she care to leave a message? Yes, Anne said. If he called in, tell him she was waiting for him at the airport.

For the next half-hour Anne paced the terminal, fighting down the anxiety in her stomach. Why wasn't he here?

Suddenly she heard herself being paged, in English, over the public address system. "Will Mrs. Anne Stewart please report to the information desk on the mezzanine level?"

Anne hurried up a flight of steps to the mezzanine and looked around for the information desk. She spotted it off to the right and started toward it.

It was a small, circular counter, occupied by a young blonde in a blue uniform. Two men were standing next to her. They appeared to be waiting for somebody. One had his elbow on the counter top. He was dark and muscular, with sunken eyes, a sharp, protruding Adam's apple, and a muscle in one cheek that twitched constantly. Anne had seen him somewhere before. She ducked quickly out of sight.

Where had she seen him? . . . The night of her dinner for the baroness on Long Island. She had gone out to the kitchen to talk to Amelia. She'd seen him there, sitting at the kitchen table with the baroness's chauffeur. He was a bodyguard.

Were they looking for her? She decided she had better find out. She retreated back down to the ground level, changed some American money for German marks, and found a public phone. She redialed the Hauser Industries number in Munich. The same woman answered.

"This is Mrs. Stewart again. I'm still waiting for my husband. In the meantime, could you please put me through to Baroness von Hauser?"

"I'm afraid she's not here, either, Mrs. Stewart."

"Could you tell me where she is?"

"Schloss Vogel. I'll give you the number."

Anne dialed the new number and was eventually put through to the baroness.

"Frau Stewart?"

"Yes."

"You've received my message?" The baroness was trying hard to sound friendly.

"No," Anne said.

"But you are at the airport, *ja*?"

"If you have a message for me, please give it to me now."

Hesitation at the other end. A muffled scratching noise gave Anne the impression that the baroness had cupped her hand over the phone for a few seconds to talk to someone else. "I sent two men to pick you up," the baroness said. "They are at the airport now, looking for you. They'll bring you to Schloss Vogel."

"I'm not going to Schloss Vogel."

"Of course you are," the baroness replied, her voice unnaturally cheerful. "There's nowhere else for you to go."

"Why? What happened to Dalton?"

"I'm afraid he's had a little accident," the baroness said, in a very matter-of-fact tone.

Anne clutched the receiver against her neck, too stunned to speak. She took a deep breath to compose herself. "My daughter. Where is she? Do you know?"

"Oh, we have your daughter here with us. And she's fine."

"How did she—?"

"She's just fine," the baroness repeated soothingly. "She's anxious to see you, of course."

"Please bring her to the airport. As soon as you can."

"That's not possible."

"Why not?"

"You know very well why not, Frau Stewart. I need something from you first."

"What are you talking about?"

The baroness laughed. "You really must come to your senses, Frau Stewart."

"I have the copy of Jupiter with me. If that's what you want, you can have it. That's all I have to give you. Now you must return my daughter immediately."

"I want more than that. I want all the information in your possession—all of it. Including, of course, the correct access code. I've invested a great amount of effort and money developing Jupiter. I'm entitled to this information."

"You've kidnapped my daughter."

"Sooner or later we'll discover our mistakes anyway, but you can save us a great amount of time."

"I'll go to the police, then."

The baroness's voice turned threatening. "Listen to me, Frau Stewart. You're being very stupid. My men will bring you up here and we will negotiate and reach an agreement. You and your daughter can be on a flight back to America by this evening."

Going to the castle was out of the question. Anne didn't even know for certain that the woman had Genny in her possession. "There's nothing to negotiate," Anne answered. "I'll tell you everything I know. I'll give you the damned access code. I'll give you everything. Just please bring Genny to the airport."

"I don't intend to come to the airport. You must come here."

"First I want to speak to my daughter, to know if she's all right."

"You cannot."

"Please, if you really have her, just bring her to the airport. I'll give you everything I have. Please! Why can't you do that?"

The baroness raised her voice to a shout. "There is no other way. Do you understand me? If you want to see your daughter alive again, I'd advise you to get up here as quickly as possible!"

Paul Elder arrived at his office at seven-thirty A.M. to find Carmen, his nurse, in tears.

The place had been burglarized. The waiting room and the examination room were only slightly out of order. But his small office, disorganized in the best of times, was an unrecognizable shambles. Every drawer had been pulled open, every shelf emptied. The floor was ankle-deep in paper, books, and medical samples.

The place had been broken into before. Elder heaved a

giant sigh. "Report it to the police, Carmen. I'll start cleaning up."

By eight-thirty a semblance of order had been restored, and Elder started seeing his patients.

The police arrived an hour later. They asked Elder what had been taken. He thought about it, looked around his office, and then decided that nothing he could think of was missing. The police went away.

At nine that evening, as Elder was preparing to lock up, he discovered what was missing: the RCD cartridge in the computer he had borrowed and not yet returned. Two spare cartridges were missing as well. The significance of the theft dawned on him immediately. Somebody was looking for Jupiter. He no longer had it, of course. He had returned it to Anne some time ago.

If there was ever an excuse to call her, this was it. He grabbed the phone and dialed her number. No answer.

He kept trying the number until eleven o'clock. He knew Anne employed a live-in nanny. Why didn't she answer? Where was everybody?

Elder took a cab to Anne's Village address. Her name was still on a mailbox. He rang the bell. No answer.

He rang the superintendent's bell.

After a delay, the super appeared at the door. Yes, she still lived here, but she was away. No, he didn't know where she had gone, and it was none of anyone's business, anyway.

The super started to close the door.

"Wait. Tell me—was her apartment burglarized recently?"

The super gave him a strange look. "You police?"

"I'm a friend. I was a friend. . . ."

"Last night. The bastards made a mess, too. There was another lady staying there—maid or nanny or something. She moved right out. Scared the poor woman half to death."

43

Stewart let the stranger help him up. He spoke only German, so Stewart couldn't understand him, but the gist of his questions were obvious. What had happened? Did he need help? Did he want an ambulance or a doctor? Stewart kept shaking his head. He picked up his wallet, lying a few feet from him on the garage floor, and checked its contents. The cash was missing, nothing else.

The man helped him to the elevator. Stewart thanked him and insisted he was all right.

Back in his apartment, Stewart examined himself. He had two swollen bruises on the back of his head. But aside from the pain, he felt normal—no memory or vision problems. He swallowed some painkillers, then took a cold shower.

There was a Mauser automatic hidden under some socks in the bottom drawer of his bedroom dresser. He dug it out, filled the clip from a box of bullets next to it, and slid it into place in the grip. He had acquired the pistol two months ago, on the Romanian black market. He had never owned a pistol before, and he had never fired this one. He wasn't even sure why he had bought it.

Stewart suddenly missed his chauffeur and bodyguard, Gil Trabert, who was on an extended vacation in the States. He could have used him today.

He put on a lined trench coat and stuffed the pistol in the inside breast pocket. It caused the coat to bulge noticeably. He stuck the box of bullets into a side pocket and went back down to the garage.

Several minutes later Stewart was out on the autobahn, heading north, toward Regensburg. He pushed the accelerator to the floor, and the BMW screamed down the sparsely traveled highway at 125 miles an hour.

Genny grew tired of crying. She was still frightened and unhappy, but crying didn't make her feel any better. It only made her eyes sore and her head throb.

She felt the bump over her ear. It was hot, swollen, and tender. She looked at her knees. She had skinned them against the concrete floor of the garage when the men had dragged her to their car. She pressed her hands against them and concentrated on generating some healing power. The effort exhausted her after only a few minutes. And the knees still felt the same.

She wondered what had happened to Daddy. Why hadn't he come to get her? She hoped he wasn't hurt.

If there hadn't been three of them in that garage, she thought, she could have gotten away. Anyway, she was proud of how well she had fought them off, even if they did finally catch her.

But now that they knew how strong she was, they were treating her with extreme caution. As soon as she had come to, some woman had injected her with a powerful tranquilizer that made her feel very weak and sleepy. Two men had then carried her up into the room, removed her handcuffs, locked the door, and left her.

The effects of the drug were finally wearing off, but Genny worried that the woman would come back and inject her again.

She walked over to the room's one small window and looked out. The ground seemed a long way down. Even if she could squeeze out the window, it was much too far to jump. Beyond the fields around the castle, she could see only forest. No other houses anywhere; just very steep hills and deep woods.

How would Mommy or Daddy ever find her here?

She heard the faint, intermittent hum of highway traffic far away. She picked up other sounds—the scurry and cries of animals and insects, the chirping of a bird, the distant barking of a dog, the subdued clank of a cowbell. Several times she caught the shrill voices of children playing.

The weather was sunny, but a chill March wind was gusting. There were still patches of unmelted snow in the forest's most shaded spots.

If she could reach the forest, she thought, she could probably hide there until she could find somebody's house. But it would be awfully cold at night, and they had taken her coat. And there was a high fence around the whole place.

She could see big dogs roaming the grounds below. She didn't like dogs much anyway, and these looked especially mean. How was she ever going to get out of this place?

She thought of her mother again, and tears welled in her eyes and ran down her cheeks. Mommy had told her that if anything ever happened to her she should try to be brave. She must have meant a time just like this. Genny sniffled and brushed her tears away.

If they were going to harm her, they would probably already have done it, she guessed. So they must be keeping her here until her mother comes to get her. But why was it taking her so long? She must have landed at the airport hours ago. Maybe she doesn't know where this castle is, Genny worried. It was probably very hard to find.

Genny went into the bathroom and filled a glass with water. She brought the glass out and sat down on the bed with it. She wished she had some books to read, or at least some pictures to look at. They hadn't left anything in the room at all.

She remembered several books of hers that had castles in them. Some of them looked a lot like this one. *Cinderella* was one. *Rumpelstiltskin* was another. And there was one about a girl that was locked up in a castle, just like her. What was her name? Rapunzel. That was it. She had long blond hair that she could roll all the way down the side of the castle tower until it reached the ground. Genny tugged at her own golden locks. They barely reached her shoulders.

In another book she remembered—maybe it was *Babar the Elephant*—there was a door right in the floor. When Babar opened it he found a secret passage that led right out of the castle. Genny studied the bare wood floor around her. There were definitely no trap doors in it.

She was hungry. She hoped they didn't forget to bring her some food. It'd be much harder to be brave if she didn't have anything to eat.

Hours passed and no one came. Genny skipped around the room and jumped up and down on the bed for exercise. She loved to jump on beds, but her mother was always telling her to stop. This time there was no one to tell her anything, so she jumped to her heart's content. Then she sat on the bed and sang all the songs that she knew and told herself some stories, pretending that it was her mother reading them to her.

She frequently went over to look out the window. The driveway was on the other side of the castle, so when her mother came up the drive she wouldn't be able to see her. But she thought she might be able to smell her scent as soon as she came inside.

She could detect scent traces of the baroness and the men who had brought her here. There were many other odors, but they belonged to people she had never seen.

As the hours passed, Genny found it getting harder and harder to be brave. If her mommy didn't get here pretty soon, she decided, she was going to have to cry.

The first consular assistant, P. Kenneth Thorpe III, steepled his eyebrows together in an expression of mild discomfort. He was young, plump, and fair-skinned, and he took himself very seriously. "That's quite a story, Mrs. Stewart," he said. "You'll have to admit."

Anne was sitting in the small hard-backed chair facing Thorpe's highly polished antique desk. "Is that all you can say?"

Assistant Consul Thorpe leaned back in his chair and wiggled his gold pen nervously between his thumb and forefinger. His pale blue eyes glanced around the room, as if he wished there were someone else present he could talk to, instead of Anne. "What do you expect me to say?"

Anne could barely conceal her fury. "That you're going

to do everything possible to find my daughter. And that you're going to start doing it right now."

The assistant consul sighed, rode his chair back up to a level position, and glanced down at the notes he had taken.

"Are you aware, Mrs. Stewart, that the Baroness von Hauser happens to be one of Munich's—indeed, one of Germany's—most prominent citizens?"

"She has my daughter!" Anne shouted. "I don't care how damned prominent she is. She's kidnapped her!"

Thorpe cleared his throat. "Yes. So you've told me. I might point out to you as well that the baroness is also extremely wealthy. She really has no conceivable reason to kidnap anyone."

"I've explained to you what she wants. She wants information from me in return for my daughter."

"Why don't you just give her this information, then?"

"I offered to. But she refused."

"But why would she do that?"

Anne clenched her fists. "I've told you. She's trying to develop and exploit a genetic formula that originally belonged to my husband. The formula was used on my daughter. . . . Look, this is hopeless. You won't believe anything I tell you. I want to talk to someone else."

Thorpe arched an eyebrow in disapproval. He didn't appreciate this attempt to go over his head. "There is no one else here in a position to help you, Mrs. Stewart."

"Then call the police!" Anne cried. "If they go up there they'll find my daughter!"

Thorpe glanced anxiously toward the door, apparently afraid that Anne's yelling might be overheard. "The police have to have a very plausible reason for doing such a thing, Mrs. Stewart," he replied. "Search warrants are required in Germany, too, you know. Just like the United States. And for good reason. As you can imagine, Baroness von Hauser would not be very pleased to have her premises searched unless there was a very well-established reason for doing so."

Anne stood up. "You won't do anything?"

Thorpe motioned to her to sit down. She remained standing.

"I can see that you're upset," he said in a placating tone. "And that's understandable, of course—if what you say is true. But Mrs. Stewart, you must be patient. Of course I'll do all I can. As soon as we can get a confirmation of your alleged missing husband, we'll take matters from there. We'll investigate. We'll contact the appropriate authorities. If your daughter is truly missing, then I'm sure she'll show up soon. It seems to me highly likely that she's still with her father. If she doesn't show up soon, we'll urge upon the appropriate authorities that they redouble their efforts. In the meantime, you really need not worry unduly. Munich is a very safe city. There's not anywhere near the crime here that you'd find in New York or Chicago or Los Angeles. Far from it. The Germans are a very law-abiding people—"

"And you're a jerk, Mr. Thorpe," Anne cut in angrily. "A stuffy, conceited little jerk. If anything happens to my daughter, I'll hold you personally responsible."

"Now really, Mrs. Stewart. I can see that you're very upset, but—"

Anne stormed out, slamming the ten-foot-high oak door to his office so hard it shook the paintings on the wall and rattled the tray stacked with empty coffee cups and saucers sitting on his secretary's desk.

Out on the street once more, Anne glanced around her, not really seeing anything. She felt panicked and helpless. What was she going to do?

Dalton Stewart raced northward in the BMW, his mind churning. He tried to order his thoughts calmly, rationally. He had to get Genny back. Nothing else mattered.

He looked down the highway. A big trailer truck had moved out into the passing lane and pulled abreast of the car in front of it. Now it was moving along beside the car. At 125 mph, Stewart was rapidly closing in on the truck. He slowed and flashed the high beams of his headlights several times, to no avail. He slowed further and hit the horn with his fist. The truck, now only a few hundred feet in front of him, still refused to move out of the left lane. It continued to stay precisely abreast of the sedan in the right lane. Stewart looked at the speedometer: his speed had fallen to about 85 mph.

Stewart swung in to the right lane and flashed at the automobile, a black Audi. The Audi also ignored him. He swung back into the left lane and looked in the rearview mirror. Another truck—also a semi—was coming up in the right lane. A third truck moved out from behind that one to pass it.

In a few seconds the two trucks behind him had closed the gap. The one in the right lane was now traveling alongside him. The other one was directly in back of him, practically riding on his tail.

The truck behind kept closing in. All he could see in his rearview mirror was the massive steel grille of the vehicle's radiator. He accelerated until he was a car length from the back bumper of the truck ahead of him. The truck behind closed right in on him, moving up just inches from his bumper. The rear end of the truck in front was now hanging right over his hood. On his right, the third truck presented a solid wall of white corrugated steel. Four huge tires on the twin rear axles were rolling furiously along the roadway three or four feet from the side of his car. On his left, the median divider pitched down sharply and then up again at an even steeper angle, to meet the lanes on the other side.

The truck behind nudged his tail. The BMW bounded forward and bounced against the front truck's bumper.

Stewart's hands squeezed the steering wheel. His foot was frozen in place on the gas pedal. There was no room to maneuver. Even the slightest change in speed would bring disaster.

But if he did nothing, they'd crush him.

"Hello? Alexandra Tate?"

"Yes."

"I'm sorry to bother you. My name is Paul Elder. I understand that you're a close friend of Anne Stewart's."

"Yes, I am."

"Well, this is a little embarrassing, I'm afraid—"

"Oh, don't *worry*. I *love* to hear embarrassing stuff."

"Well, I'm worried about Anne. I have no right to be worried about her, but I am. . . ."

Bored and anxious, Genny prowled around the small bedroom and bath that made up her prison. She found an old-fashioned men's razor on top of the medicine chest in the bathroom. It had been there a long time, and the blade had rusted away.

Genny pushed the bed a couple of feet to the side and crouched down beside it. The ancient floor showed signs of dry rot. Near the wall, one of the bed's iron legs had, over time, worn a substantial depression in one of the boards. Using the flat corner of the razor to saw away part of the edge of the board, Genny was able to get underneath with her fingers and pry up a six-inch-long fragment of one plank. It immediately disintegrated into dusty, flaking pieces.

Genny had expected that as soon as the floor plank had come loose, she would be able to look right down to the floor below. She was disappointed to discover that beneath that board was another one.

She jammed the handle end of the razor down into the wood of the subfloor. It was punky and soft. Soon she was able to punch the handle completely through.

For half an hour she worked furiously, pulling up more pieces of rotted floor planking until she had removed a ragged, roughly rectangular section about a foot wide and a foot and a half long. That left the subfloor. The entire surface that she had exposed felt rotted and soft, but the wood was thicker than the floor planks, and she couldn't get her finger around the edges to pry up on them.

She stood up and jumped on the spot. It sagged, but nothing gave way. She jumped half a dozen times, but the subfloor held.

She stopped and listened. She was afraid someone might have heard her jumping. After a few minutes, she decided that no one was coming to investigate.

She moved the bed so that one side of it lined up with the edge of the rectangle of exposed subflooring, then climbed up on the mattress. She focused on the spot, twenty inches below her feet, took a big breath, and jumped.

Both heels struck the spot together. The wood gave way with a splintering crack, and Genny disappeared through the floor.

44

Anne spent most of the afternoon at a Munich police station.

At first everyone appeared eager to help. But there was a language problem. The only individual who spoke English was a middle-aged desk sergeant. He ushered her into his cubicle of an office, ordered her some coffee, and listened attentively, staring alternately at her face and the front of her blouse, as she poured out her story.

When she finished, she discovered that the man's understanding of what she had just told him was hopelessly garbled. He seemed to think that her husband and the Baroness von Hauser had run off together and taken Genny with them in some kind of transatlantic custody battle. Anne tried repeatedly to explain, but the sergeant, whose name was Ottmar Klempe, just couldn't seem to get it straight. And he was becoming angry and impatient with her, because he thought she was questioning his ability to understand English.

When he began to perceive that she was accusing the Baroness von Hauser of kidnapping her child, he wagged an admonishing finger at her. He leaned forward across his narrow metal desk and addressed her in an ominous tone. "Der Baroness iss fery powerful. Fery, fery powerful. You should not say about her such sings."

Anne walked out of Klempe's cubbyhole and returned to the front desk. She demanded to see the chief of the Munich Police Department, or whoever was in overall authority.

Heidi, the young woman at the front desk, was no longer eager to help. She was annoyed that Anne couldn't speak German. She also didn't like her persistence. She demanded to see Anne's passport again, and this time she held on to it.

Klempe, meanwhile, had emerged from his cubicle and was regaling everyone behind the waist-high, glass-topped barricade that separated the department's working area from the public lobby with his version of Anne's story. Several employees began making loud comments; others stared at her. Anne understood very little, but it was obvious that they were discussing the merits of her charges.

She sat on one of the red-and-blue plastic chairs arranged along the wall, determined to stay until someone agreed to do something. Ten minutes later, Klempe, in an almost comically officious tone, relayed the news to her that the chief would indeed see her, but she might have to wait. He was very busy.

She said she'd wait.

The attention of the station switched away from her as completely as if she had walked out the door. She was a problem, and someone higher up had just taken her off their hands.

Anne sat on the hard red plastic chair for over an hour, watching the riffraff of the Munich streets—prostitutes, pimps, pushers, and an occasional drunk-and-disorderly—parade past her on the way to an arraignment or a lockup. Lawyers and family and friends of the arrested filled the chairs around her, smoking and talking in voices amplified by the tile walls around them.

The frustration of not being able to communicate added greatly to Anne's panic. She feared that she would just go berserk and start screaming at people if the chief didn't send for her soon.

At five P.M. a woman in civilian clothes came to the gate in the barrier and called out Anne's name. Anne jumped up and ran over, tears of relief in her eyes.

"I'm sorry to keep you waiting so long," the woman said in almost accentless English. "The chief has been very busy. My name is Marthe, by the way."

Anne shook the woman's hand. "I'm so glad you speak English. I've felt so lost and alone ever since this happened."

"I understand very well. I'm sorry." She escorted Anne down along a corridor to the back of the building, and then into an elevator. She pressed the button for the top floor.

"Does the chief—what is his name?"

"Werner Schmidt. Chief Werner Schmidt."

"Does Chief Schmidt speak English?"

"Yes, he does. Better even than me."

"Thank God for that."

From the elevator bank on the top floor, Marthe ushered Anne down another long corridor. This one had plush carpeting, and the noise level was far quieter than below.

Marthe showed her into the chief's office and settled her in a seat next to a big, dark wooden desk. There she waited another ten minutes before Chief Schmidt appeared. He was a tall man with dark hair, a walrus mustache, and a distinct no-nonsense air about him.

Anne's passport was on his desk. He picked it up, glanced at it, then handed it to her.

"I am sorry for the long wait, Mrs. Stewart. Please tell me your problem." His voice was neither hostile nor friendly. It was neutral, withholding judgment.

"I arrived here this morning from New York. I was supposed to meet my husband, Dalton Stewart, at the airport. He has an office here in Munich. My daughter was supposed to be with him. He never showed up. I was paged at the airport by Baroness von Hauser. I assume you know who she is?"

Schmidt nodded. He had an elbow up on his desk and was cradling his head delicately in his hand—thumb under chin, forefinger against cheek—giving her his full attention.

"She told me that she had my daughter. How she got her I don't know. She wants information from me. I agreed to give it to her if she'd bring my daughter to me, but she insists I go to her place—a castle somewhere in the country. I've never seen it. I'm afraid to do that. I don't trust the woman. I'm at the end of my rope to know what to do—"

Schmidt interrupted. "Do you know what has become of your husband?"

"No. The baroness said he was in an accident. Do you know?"

Schmidt shook his head no. "Do you have the information the baroness wanted?"

"Yes." Anne removed the black plastic RCD from her handbag and handed it to Schmidt. She explained what it contained.

Schmidt turned the cartridge over in his hand, then gave it back. He didn't seem especially interested in it.

"Mrs. Stewart," he said in a low voice. "Before you came in, I took it upon myself to telephone the baroness, so that I would be better prepared to talk to you. Would you like to hear what she told me?"

Anne met the chief's dispassionate gaze with a look of surprise. "Of course."

"Very well." Schmidt pulled a small notebook from his pocket, opened it, glanced at a page, and looked up at Anne. "She did indeed admit to me that she has your daughter—Genny, is that her name?—yes. She has Genny with her. She explained to me that the girl was brought to her estate—Schloss Vogel—by her father, yesterday. He left Schloss Vogel this morning to pick you up at the airport and bring you back to the estate. When it was apparent that he had not arrived to pick you up, the baroness called the airport and had you paged. When you called her, she told you that Genny was safe with her, but that she didn't know what had become of your husband. She offered to send someone to the airport to pick you up, but you refused. Instead you insisted that she bring a large sum of money to the airport before you would give her this computer cartridge. The cartridge, as she explained it to me, is the property of a joint venture between her and your husband. You're now separated from your husband?"

"Yes, but—"

"The baroness told me that you stole this cartridge from your husband's office in New York, because you knew it was valuable, and wished to force your estranged husband and the baroness to pay a ransom for its return.

She said your motive for this was twofold: first, to get
money, of course; second, to get revenge on both her and
your husband. The baroness and Mr. Stewart are to be
married, as I understand it, pending his divorce from you.
And she did also warn me that you might claim that she
was kidnapping your daughter. If you want your daughter,
she informed me, all you have to do is go to Schloss
Vogel, give the baroness the cartridge, and pick up your
child."

The chief tucked the notebook back in his suit pocket
and smiled patronizingly at Anne. "Now, doesn't it sound
to you, Mrs. Stewart, that what the baroness told me is
probably the truth?"

Anne just stared at the man. She could no longer summon the kind of outraged anger she had unleashed against
the official at the American embassy. She felt truly alone
and abandoned.

For an instant Stewart was tempted to do nothing, to accept the fate offered him. Let the damned murder run its
course. Solve all his problems. Foot steady on the gas
pedal, holding the speed at 85 mph; hand steady on the
wheel, straight ahead. Do nothing, and let it all come to
an end in the next few seconds.

But he had to get his daughter back.

The thought of Genny made him want to weep. He was
so proud of that child. So intensely proud. And he had
never really been proud of anything before.

Genny was valuable beyond all the money in the world.
She was a new kind of human. Homo sapiens rex—
smarter, stronger, and healthier than anything the world
had ever seen. No one yet knew her potential. But what
was truly important was that she was his child, his only
child. He'd get her back. Whatever he had to do, he'd get
her back. Nothing would stop him.

He sensed the roadway curving slightly to the right.
The back end of the truck in front was no longer parallel
to his windshield, but bending slightly, opening a few
more inches of room on his left side.

It had to be now, before they were through the turn.

He cranked the wheel sharply left.

The BMW lurched out of its three-walled moving prison with a high-pitched squeal of tires and plunged down the bank of the median divider.

Stewart straightened the steering wheel instantly and began applying the brakes. The surface was rough grass, and the car bucked furiously as it shot diagonally down toward a concrete drainage ditch at the bottom of the divider.

The left front tire slammed into the ditch. The car swerved, throwing the back left tire into the ditch as well.

Trapped in the concrete channel, the BMW continued forward, tilted over at a forty-five-degree angle. The car's undercarriage scraped along the near edge of the ditch with a shower of sparks and a shriek of tearing metal.

Directly ahead the ditch terminated in a concrete catch basin. Stewart clutched the wheel and hit the brake pedal with all his strength. The pedal slammed against the floorboard with no resistance. The brake lines were severed.

Stewart yanked the emergency brake. The BMW's momentum slowed. Stewart pulled harder. The emergency brake line parted and the handle, its purchase lost, flew backwards in his hand.

Stewart jammed the shift lever into first gear. The car's momentum slowed further, but not enough to stop short of the catch basin. The left front edge of the bumper hit the concrete first and crushed against the left front tire. The bottom of the radiator struck next, and the car's front end, designed to give way under high impact, collapsed back against the reinforced frame of the passenger compartment.

Amidst the buckling and rending of metal and a rain of thousands of pellets of safety glass, the BMW came at last to a halt, tilted steeply on its left side.

The safety bag deployed, slapping back hard against Stewart's face and chest, and then deflated. Black smoke billowed from the accordioned remains of the engine compartment.

Stewart was shaken up but conscious. He pulled on the door handle. The catch released, but the door wouldn't open; it was wedged against the concrete side of the⁻

drainage ditch. He pressed the button to open the window, but the window didn't move. He tried the other windows. None worked.

He grabbed the hand hold over the passenger-side door and pulled himself across the front seat. He braced his feet against the driver's side door and pulled on the passenger side door latch. The latch clicked open. He pushed the door outward, but it was tilted up at such a sharp angle it refused to stay open. He braced one foot on the side of the driver's headrest and pushed himself about a foot closer to the passenger door, but he still couldn't hold the door open and climb out at the same time.

Stewart could now smell gasoline mixed with the acidic, choking stench of the black smoke.

Genny pulled herself up to her hands and knees and looked around. She had landed on her feet and then fallen forward and banged her head and the heels of her palms. She felt dazed, but after she stood up her head cleared and she knew she wasn't badly hurt.

It was quite dark. What light there was seemed to come from far above. She looked up and saw the small hole in the floor she had fallen through. It was far out of her reach.

Gradually her eyes adjusted to the dim light. She turned around, trying to determine where she was. There were walls on either side of her. They were so close that she could touch them with her elbows.

She was in a narrow passageway. The floor was wood and the walls were stone. Down one way it was pitch-black, but in the opposite direction she could detect a faint amount of light. She decided to go that way. Keeping one hand on the wall to guide her, she started off, placing each foot carefully ahead of her, inches at a time. The old plank flooring creaked, and her feet crunched on occasional pieces of stone and cement that had fallen from the walls over the years.

The air in the passageway was stale and chilly; it irritated her lungs when she inhaled. Thick cobwebs brushed against her face. She stuck her free hand out in front of her to ward them off. Layer after layer of intricate olfactory sensations swarmed through her nostrils, forming a complex tapestry of ancient smells, from the pungent bittersweet of decomposing wood and insect and rodent remains to the dusty, astringent sting of the masonry. It reminded her of the musty, dirt-floored cellar under the old stable at the house on Long Island.

The light became a little brighter. She could see a dimly glowing area in the distance. She increased her pace, taking full steps.

The dim light was coming from a tiny hole in the wall, too high up for Genny to look through. She put her hand against the wall, then braced her feet against the opposite wall and walked her way up the stone until she could put her eye to the opening. She saw part of a bedroom. There was a double bed with a canopy over it, and a big, round, windowed alcove with melon-colored drapes. A polished antique desk and chair were positioned on a small oriental rug in the center of the alcove. The floor, decorated in an elaborate parquet design, gleamed warmly in the late-afternoon sunlight. Clothes were thrown on the bed, along with some funny-looking black and red underwear.

Genny listened for sounds. No one seemed to be in the room. She put her nose to the peephole and sniffed. Cigarette smoke. It was from a different kind of cigarette—not the kind the people from home usually smoked. She could also smell several kinds of soaps, colognes, bath oils, and shampoos. And some kind of alcoholic drink. She could catch subtle traces of a woman's odor. Not the baroness's, though—Genny would recognize her smell immediately.

Genny dropped back to the floor, then reached up and probed the edge of the hole with her fingers. She felt a round metal plate on a pivot that could be swung down to cover the opening. She moved it back and forth a couple of times, then left it as she had found it. The part of the wall around the hole seemed to be wood.

Genny continued down the passage. Six feet further along she ran smack into a wall. When she had recovered from her surprise, she felt around with her hands and feet and discovered that the passage continued to the left. It was utterly black. Even with her extraordinary eyesight, she could see nothing. She moved her hands carefully along the wall surface. The stones were rough and irregular, and she had to proceed slowly. She listened for sounds. Someone was walking along the other side of the wall on her left. She heard a door open and close nearby.

Her fingers made contact with more wood. She reached up and felt another small metal disk like the first one. She slid it back and forth but saw no light. There was probably a room on the other side here too, she decided, but something must be blocking the view. A door opened and closed somewhere nearby, and she could hear, further away, the soft murmur of women's voices, talking in German.

There must be a door somewhere, she thought, because she could smell the odors left by people who had been in the passageway recently. If only she had a flashlight.

Genny yawned. It was her nap time. She was also thirsty and had to go to the potty. She thought she should probably turn around and go back to her room. Later, she could explore further. Then she remembered the hole she had fallen through. It was so high up. How was she ever going to climb back through it?

Genny pressed her hands against the walls and moved forward cautiously. She heard a muffled scurrying close by, then some high-pitched squeaks. Mice. She wished she could see them. There must be a lot of them around, because she could smell their urine everywhere, as well as the peculiarly delicate musty scent of their fur.

Genny felt a slight current of air moving against her face. Where was it coming from? she wondered.

She took another step forward and fell through the dark.

45

Dalton Stewart crouched with his feet braced against the driver's-side door, and pushed up against the passenger-side door with his head and both hands. The smoke was choking him and his eyes were swimming. He pushed until he was standing erect, his head and shoulders out the doorway, still bearing the weight of the door. He brought one foot up onto the passenger-side headrest, then heaved himself up again.

He finally crawled out, bearing the weight of the door all the way. He flung his feet free and rolled onto the ground, letting the door slam closed again.

He coughed and rubbed his burning eyes. The smell of gasoline made his nose sting. The gas tank under the rear trunk had ripped open and fuel was pouring out of it, flowing down the concrete ditch toward the smoking engine compartment.

Stewart staggered to his feet, patted the breast pocket of his trench coat, felt the pistol, and started climbing back up the grass bank toward the roadway.

He reached the shoulder of the highway and turned around just in time to see the BMW engulfed in flames. He felt both dazed and exhilarated: nothing like a narrow escape to make one feel lucky.

Stewart brushed himself off, waited for a break in the traffic, then crossed the roadway to the right side and started walking. Cars had slowed to watch the fire, and someone pulled over to offer him a ride almost immediately. He was an old man driving a beat-up Opel Kadet. He spoke almost no English, and Stewart was grateful for that.

Stewart managed to communicate to him that he

wanted to go to Regensburg. The old man muttered some
objections. Stewart got the impression that he thought he
should get off at the next exit and report the accident.
Stewart insisted on Regensburg. The old man ignored
him. He took the next exit off the autobahn and deposited
Stewart squarely in front of the police station in the tiny
village of Geisenfeld.

Stewart stood on the sidewalk until the old man's Opel
had disappeared around the corner, and then went in
search of a car rental agency. There was none in the town.
Stewart ended up paying an exorbitant price with a credit
card to "rent" a very used Volkswagen sedan from the
owner of an auto repair shop.

Stewart drove north to Neustadt and Abensberg on
Route 300 as fast as the narrow, winding road would permit, then took Route 16 to Regensburg. He wondered if
the men in the trucks were still looking for him. He knew
it was unlikely they would spot him in this car; but every
time he encountered a large semi on the highway, he felt
his chest tighten.

In Regensburg, he wound through the narrow medieval
streets of the city center and turned into the Haidplatz, the
town's oldest square. He parked the VW across the
square from the entrance of one of Regensburg's more
notorious clubs, a raffish hole-in-the-wall establishment
called the Tischgespräch—German for "table talk."

It was the middle of the afternoon. Some time in the
next seven or eight hours Katrina would pay her nightly
visit to the club. The club's manager dealt drugs on the
side, and Katrina was one of his regular customers. She'd
stay awhile, have a drink, buy some heroin, shoot up in
the ladies' room, and then go back to the castle. Stewart
knew her routine because he had accompanied her on
several occasions. He had even tried the heroin.

He sat back to wait for her.

Genny sat up and felt around carefully in the dark. She
had tumbled down a steep, narrow flight of stairs. Her
head hurt, and so did one of her arms. Fortunately, the
steps and the floor she ended up on were made of wood,
not stone. She guessed she was okay.

She crouched forward, feeling the way with her hands, and began to explore the passage on this level. Barely three steps from the stairs she felt the way blocked by a solid wall. She felt around, but there was no question that it was a dead end.

She groped her way back to the stairs and stood there, listening. She could still hear the squeaking of mice. And the smell of people was much stronger here than on the floor above.

She worked her way around behind the stairs and discovered that the passage extended back in that direction. Feeling her way cautiously, she walked the full length of it. It was exactly like the floor above—a narrow passage that went around a ninety-degree corner. After she had advanced about twenty feet past the corner, she got down on her hands and knees and crawled. Her bare knees felt very sore.

Her hand soon felt the top edge of another wooden stairway. She turned around and backed carefully down the steps. When she finally reached the bottom, she noticed that the atmosphere was quite different. It was damper and warmer, and the odors of laundry soap mixed with those of wood shavings, paint, and fuel oil.

A few feet from the stairs she saw what looked like four faint lines of light in the shape of a rectangle. She stretched a hand out and felt wood. A door. Along one side her fingers encountered three small hinges. On the other side she found the door's handle. She pressed down on it and felt a little click as the latch slipped free. She pushed tentatively. The door moved with a squeak. She pushed a little more. The door opened further but made an even sharper squeak. She peeked around the edge.

The door opened into a small closet. She pushed the door open further, moving it as slowly as she possibly could to minimize the squeak. When it was about a quarter open, she slipped out. The opposite wall of the closet contained another door. She opened it and peeked cautiously around the corner.

A long, low stone passageway rambled along under a spaghettilike mass of pipes, conduits, and wires suspended from a series of heavy archways. Bare bulbs hung down every thirty feet or so, their low wattage casting dim, pale yellow pools of light onto the rugged stone. She heard the hum of a furnace nearby, and low voices. The people smells down here were strong and salty.

Genny tiptoed down the corridor, keeping close to the wall. She saw an open doorway on her left and stuck her head around. Inside was a low-ceilinged chamber that had been converted into a laundry room. On one wall were several washing machines and dryers, and shelves stacked with linens. At a big table in the center, a stocky, gray-haired woman in a blue uniform dress was ironing something. Next to her another woman was folding sheets and towels.

Genny retreated back to her closet, then explored another arched passageway on the other side, peeking quickly in the open doorways as she raced along. She saw a dark, dirty room with a furnace in it, another filled with big pumps and tanks, and a third that was a kind of repair shop. She darted in and looked around. Lights were on over a workbench, and her nose told her that someone had been there as recently as a few minutes ago. The floor was cluttered with sections of metal plates. Someone was repairing a suit of armor.

Genny glanced over the tools on the workbench. The height of the bench's surface just barely allowed her to see over it on her tiptoes. To her delight she discovered a flashlight. She grabbed it and slid the switch forward. It worked.

Next to a metal vise she spied a package of cigarettes and a small box of matches. She grabbed the matches and tucked them up inside the cotton sleeve of her blouse.

An old sword was clamped in the vise. She twisted the vise's handle a couple of turns and pulled the sword out. It was about three feet long and surprisingly heavy. Her spirits soared. Now, she thought, let someone try to catch her. . . .

From the shop Genny wandered past a large area stacked with firewood for the castle's many fireplaces. She smelled fresh air. There must be a door to the outside, she thought, to bring the wood in. She started looking for it, then heard steps coming from the other direction.

She ran back into the repair shop and ducked under the workbench. The steps came closer. From under the bench she could see green trousers and brown work boots by the doorway. They paused, then came into the shop and moved toward the workbench.

She clutched the sword resolutely in her little hands and squeezed as far into the corner as she could and waited, heart pounding. The green trousers took something down from a shelf over the bench, then turned out the light and left.

When she was sure the way was clear, Genny hurried back to the secret passageway behind the closet, lugging the cumbersome sword along with her. Once inside, she turned on the flashlight and scampered up the steps.

With the light, she was able to see what had eluded her in the dark. There were many little peepholes in the walls, all of them covered with sliding metal discs—and all of them too far over her head for her to look through. Around each peephole, she now could see, were small wooden doors as well, each one cut flush into the stone. She tugged tentatively at one, but it appeared to be locked from the other side.

Genny climbed the second flight of stairs and found the spot where she had fallen through. She shined the flashlight up at it. It looked very high. There were wooden beams overhead that bisected the passageway at regular intervals, but they were at least eight feet beyond her reach.

She had to get back through that hole somehow. The walls of the passageway were of rough stone and so close together that she thought she might be able to climb right up them by putting a foot on each side.

She braced her hands against the walls, placed her sneaker in a little foothold on the right side, then brought her left foot up and wedged it in another little depression between the stones on the other wall. It was awkward, but if she was careful and took her time, she thought, she could probably make it. She jumped back down.

The flashlight was a problem. She needed it to find

footholds and handholds as she climbed, but she also needed her hands free. She tried holding it in her mouth, but it was too big.

There was no choice but to try to hold the flashlight in one hand. It reduced her ability to brace herself against the wall, but she still thought she could manage it.

The sword was another matter. There simply was no way she could carry it up with her. Reluctantly, she left it on the floor of the passageway.

The first few feet up went easily enough, but she couldn't train the flashlight down enough to find good toeholds in the stone. She had to feel her way with her feet, and that made the climb slow and strenuous. Each upward placement of hand and foot got harder and harder. The stone scraped at her wounded knees and made them bloody again. The muscles in her legs began to tremble from the exertion, and her energy started to fade. Eight feet up, part of the wall crumbled loose under her left foot and she slipped partway down. She adjusted quickly and found new toeholds before she fell. She gasped, caught her breath, and looked up. Not much further. She gathered her courage and willpower and started up again, inching along from handhold to toehold.

Genny's head finally emerged through the hole. She quickly threw her arms out across the floor to take her weight. She let go of her flashlight, then pushed down against the floor until she had raised her knees through the hole.

She kicked one leg out, then the other, then rolled onto the floor, panting for breath. When she felt strong enough to get up, she pulled the bed over the hole, hid the flashlight and the small box of matches under the mattress, and went into the bathroom to wash up and use the potty.

Anne left the Munich police station in a state of shocked disbelief. She was trembling from head to foot. There was nothing left for her to do but confront the baroness by herself. She was afraid to do it; the woman terrified her. But she'd do whatever she had to do to get Genny back. The certain knowledge that she was in the right armed her with some small courage.

She took a taxi back out to the airport, picked up her luggage, and rented a car.

She asked an English-speaking woman at the rental counter if she could provide directions to an estate called Schloss Vogel, somewhere outside the city of Regensburg, and someone there knew precisely where the castle was located.

The woman marked the spot on a road map and handed it to Anne with a smile. "They said you can't miss it. It has four big turrets on the corners, and it stands on very high ground back off this road. But . . ." The woman paused.

Anne waited. "But what?"

"Well, they said you won't be able to get very close to it. The owner doesn't like visitors. There are big fences, and dogs to keep people away."

Anne thanked the woman and tucked the map into her handbag. "No problem. I have a standing invitation from the owner."

The drive took Anne a little over an hour.

By the time she saw the castle, looming to the east over the winding mountain road just north of the village of Regenstauf, she became worried that the baroness might not accept the code word "Watson" as genuine. Anne had already tried one deception, after all—feeding the phony word "Minerva" to the men spying on her apartment. Whose men were they, anyway? Dalton's? The Baroness's? In any case, she had to convince the woman that this time she was giving her the real thing.

As well as the Jupiter RCD, she had brought with her copies of three genomes—Dalton's, Genny's, and her own. With them, and the use of a computer, she could feed Dalton's genome and her genome into the program, run it, and produce an exact copy of Genny's genome. But would the baroness accept it?

The driveway leading to the castle was hard to miss. It was blocked by a mammoth gate of wrought iron bars and a big sign: EINTRITT VERBOTEN.

Anne drove the car up to the gate. TV cameras were mounted on each of the stone pillars framing the gate. A harsh, scratchy voice, amplified by a speaker hidden somewhere around the gate, challenged her: *"Was wünschen Sie?"*

Anne swallowed. "It's Anne Stewart," she replied in a loud, firm voice. "I'm here to see the baroness."

"Warten Sie einen Augenblick, bitte."

Anne shook her head. "I don't speak German."

There was no answer. She repeated her request several times but got no reply. Minutes passed. Suddenly the baroness's voice reverberated through the air. Her tone was cold. "Anne Stewart?"

"Yes."

"Have you brought the necessary items?"

"Yes. I must see my daughter first."

There was a brief pause, then the baroness's voice again:

"Very well. Drive up to the main entrance. Do not get out of the car until the doorman opens your door for you. If you do, the dogs will come after you."

The gate rolled open, and Anne drove through. The bottom part of the drive wandered through a heavy forest of evergreens. After several hairpin turns, the forest gave way to a wide apron of fields and vineyards, and then a series of lawns and formal gardens that sloped down and away from the castle.

Gigantic and forbidding, Schloss Vogel dominated the landscape. The central part of it rose over the high gray-black walls of cut stone that formed its base like a squat, four-cornered tower. The narrow windows, deeply recessed in the thick stone, looked like gun embrasures, and the big, round turrets on each corner reminded Anne of prison watchtowers.

Then the dogs appeared—at least a dozen. They bounded rapidly through the gardens, ran out onto the driveway and fell into place behind the car. Anne glanced nervously in her rearview mirror. They were following her like a pack of hounds on a trace. But these weren't foxhounds; they were Dobermans and Alsatians.

There was something distinctly eerie about their behavior. They trotted silently along behind the car, as if they were politely escorting it up to the castle. Not one of them barked once. Yet their silence only magnified their menace.

The drive circled under a large entrance portico at the front of the castle. Anne drove underneath and braked to a stop. Iron portcullises dropped down over both ends of the portico, shutting the dogs out and Anne in.

A doorman with a trim mustache came around toward her door. Anne grabbed her bag from the passenger seat and let him help her out.

"Guten Tag," he said, with a solemn frown.

Anne nodded curtly, hugging the bag to her side.

A second doorman rushed ahead to open the castle's big double door for her. As soon as she was inside, the first doorman grabbed her around the throat from behind and twisted her arm up behind her back. The other one yanked her handbag away from her.

They marched her through several grand salons, past a gigantic staircase, through the enormous Hall of Knights, all the way to a service elevator somewhere in the back of the building. They took her up two flights, then down a long hallway. They knocked on a door. Anne tried to suppress her anxiety and compose herself.

A thickset woman with blond hair braided and coiled around her head opened the door and let them in. It was a bedroom. No one else was present.

The man holding her let her go; the other one gave her handbag to the woman.

"Welcome," the woman said, without a trace of irony. "My name is Karla. I am the baroness's personal assistant. The baroness cannot see you now. She asked me to relay these instructions to you, which she said you would understand. On that desk by the window you will find a legal-sized notepad and some pens. The baroness wishes you to write down for her all the relevant information you have."

Anne shook her head. "I want to see my daughter," she demanded. "Right now."

A look of distress spread across Karla's face. "The baroness has given me very explicit instructions," she warned. "When you have provided the information she requires, you'll be allowed to see your daughter."

Her arms folded defiantly across her chest, Anne faced the woman. "I'll do nothing until I see my daughter. Tell the baroness that, please."

Karla ignored Anne's words. "I will leave you here to write out the necessary information," she said. "When you are finished, you may knock on the door. Hans and Wolfgang will both be on the other side, in the hallway. They will call me and I will take the material to the baroness immediately."

"Didn't you hear me? I'll do absolutely nothing until I see my daughter!"

The assistant hesitated. She stared at Anne angrily. She hadn't expected any resistance. "Frau Stewart," she replied, in a low, conspiratorial tone. "Your daughter is perfectly fine. I promise you. She is upstairs, waiting for you. Please hurry and give the baroness the information she needs and I will take you to her."

The woman turned and hurried from the room, taking Anne's handbag with her. The two men followed her out. Anne watched the door slam and listened to the key rattle in the lock.

The hours passed. No sign of Katrina. Maybe she didn't patronize the Tischgespräch anymore. She was so mercurial and impulsive that almost anything could have happened in the last couple of weeks to alter her routine.

But Stewart was counting on her still needing her daily fix. He doubted that she had kicked her drug habit. So unless she had had a falling out with the manager, she'd show up. He would just have to be patient.

After the sun set it grew cold. Stewart started the car every half-hour to let the heater warm up the interior.

The idle waiting left his mind in danger of wandering into treacherous terrain. He forced himself not to think beyond the minute. His plan would succeed, like all plans, one step at a time. If he started ruminating about either the past or the future, he knew he could come unraveled fast.

At 9:30 Katrina's red Mercedes convertible coupe roared into sight, tires squealing. She circled the square twice. Finding no parking place, she pulled up into the no-parking zone in front of the club's entrance.

Stewart watched her get out and go into the club. She was wearing one of her ankle-length fur coats. Her unsteady gait suggested that she was probably drunk. Stewart climbed out of the VW and hurried across the square to Katrina's car. The convertible top was up, but, typically, she hadn't bothered to lock the doors. He pulled the driver's seat forward, squeezed his tall frame into the cramped rear, and slammed the door. He crouched down as low as he could manage behind the front seats, reached into his trench coat's breast pocket, and fished out the Mauser pistol.

Ten minutes later Katrina came sailing out of the door of the club. The sides of her unbuttoned fur coat flapped back, revealing black mesh stockings, a short skirt, and a see-through blouse. She opened the door and sank into the driver's seat with a loud whimpering sigh.

Stewart rose up behind her.

Katrina jerked around and shrieked. When she recognized who it was, she laughed. "Dalton! *Liebchen!* What are you doing?"

She was drunk. And now full of heroin as well.

"Take me back to the castle with you."

"Of course, *Liebchen.* Did your car break down?"

"The baroness has my daughter," he said in an even voice.

"But—"

"I'm going to get her back. I need your help."

"Why?"

"Let's go. Right now."

"It's too early. I was going to visit a girlfriend."

"Drive us back to the castle."

Katrina whined. "Let's go have some drinks first. I've been so bored all day. And Aldous has been a bastard. And I feel like fucking, *Liebchen.* We can do it at my girlfriend's. She wouldn't mind—"

"Now. Let's go."

"But *Liebchen*—"

"Now, goddamnit. Let's go." Stewart brought the pistol up into view and pressed the muzzle against her neck.

Katrina began to cry. "Please take the gun away, *Liebchen*."

"Start the fucking car."

The twelve-mile drive to Schloss Vogel was mostly a silent one, with Stewart crouched behind Katrina, holding the pistol to the back of her neck, and Katrina whimpering sporadically. Twice she nearly went off the road.

When the gate came into view, Stewart gave her his instructions. Once through the gate, she was to drive up to the portico, stop the car, and hand him the keys. They would go in together, with him holding the pistol on her. She was going to have to be his hostage, he explained. He was going to hold the pistol at her neck until the baroness turned Genny over to him.

He had planned for Katrina to drive him and his daughter back into Regensburg, but she was too unstable to risk it. Instead he'd let Katrina drive them down into the village, put Katrina out on the street, and drive Genny to Regensburg himself. There they could transfer to his rented VW and drive back to Munich.

"But the baroness knows you won't shoot me," Katrina protested.

"You'll have to persuade her that I will."

"*Liebchen,* please. I can't do it. I don't feel well."

"You'll feel a hell of a lot worse if you don't. Let's go."

An electronic device at the gate identified Katrina's car and the gate rolled open. She threw the car into first gear and roared through, throwing up a shower of white pea stones behind the wheels.

"The baroness will be so furious," Katrina sobbed. The driveway turned sharply, and Katrina steered the car drunkenly onto the narrow dirt shoulder and almost into the ditch. Stewart grabbed the wheel with his free hand and pulled the car back onto the drive.

"She won't care if you shoot me or not," Katrina blubbered. "She won't believe you. She'll tell you to go ahead and shoot me."

Stewart didn't bother to reply. The drive sloped upward across an open lawn and then leveled out as it neared the portico. Suddenly the castle's outside spotlights blazed on. There were several dozen of them, mounted on the portico, on the castle turrets, and along the high walls of the keep. They bathed a large area of the lawn and driveway in bright light.

Katrina tromped on the brakes and the Mercedes skidded to a halt fifty feet short of the portico. She dropped her head down against the steering wheel. "I can't do it, *Liebchen*. The baroness will be so furious!"

Stewart jabbed the pistol barrel behind Katrina's ear. "Start the car!"

Katrina shook her head.

Stewart heard something slap lightly against the door. He glanced out. Two Dobermans had come up alongside. They pressed their muzzles against the bottom of the window.

Suddenly Katrina yanked the keys from the ignition and opened the door. Stewart grabbed for her coat collar but came away with a fistful of fur. She rolled out, scrambled clumsily to her feet, and bolted for the portico. One of the Dobermans lunged at her, sank his teeth into the trailing edge of her coat, and pulled her down. Katrina screamed with terror.

Stewart climbed over the seat and groped frantically for the door handle. He found it and slammed the door shut, grazing the snoot of the second Doberman in the process.

46

Anne sat in the room for several hours. She wrote nothing on the pad of legal paper provided for her. She wondered how long they would wait. Was she being stupid?

Repeatedly she was tempted to concoct a page of phony information, if only to get to see her daughter, but she hesitated. In the long run it might prove a bad idea.

But she felt that if she didn't do something soon, she would collapse from the mental strain. The baroness had tremendous advantages in the situation. All Anne had was a few bits of information the baroness was determined to have. As soon as she gave those away, she would be completely at the woman's mercy.

She paced the room, trying to decide what to do.

Footsteps and voices erupted in the hall outside.

The door opened. The baroness's two thuggish bodyguards, Hans and Wolfgang, looked in. Then Karla stepped into the room. Behind her was the baroness.

Anne had not seen her since the night of the dinner party on Long Island many months ago—the night the baroness had informed her that she had been used as a guinea pig by Harold Goth. The night she had moved out on Dalton Stewart.

The woman looked older than Anne had remembered her. And haggard. There were heavy circles under her eyes, and the once barely noticeable wrinkles at the corners of her mouth and eyes had deepened.

Anne remained standing by the window.

"You have written out the information, *ja*?" the baroness said.

Karla went over to the desk and looked at the legal pad.

"Gar nichts," she murmured in a shocked whisper. Nothing at all.

The baroness strode heavily across the room and slapped Anne across the face with great force, snapping her head to the side. Anne gasped and brought a hand up to her cheek.

"You are a stupid, stubborn woman, Frau Stewart! If you want to see your daughter I would suggest you get busy immediately. Do you understand me?"

Anne stared at her without speaking.

The baroness called out in a loud voice for Hans and Wolfgang. They came quickly into the room. The baroness spoke to them in a rapid monotone. Anne saw Karla's face become quite pale.

The two men seized Anne by the arms and dragged her down four flights of stairs to the dungeon in the subbasement. She didn't resist. They pulled open the door to the little maiden, positioned her inside, closed the door, and screwed it tight.

Anne stood inside the device, more astonished than frightened. How could the woman do something like this? What did she hope to accomplish? Was she crazy?

At first Anne didn't know what was supposed to happen to her. She could feel the pointed spikes in front and in back of her; but as long as she stood exactly in the middle, nothing touched her. She looked up. There were four small airholes in the top, about six inches above her head. Except for the tiny amount of light visible through those holes, she stood in complete darkness.

After a few minutes the nature of the ordeal she faced began to dawn on her. The iron box was about two feet in width and depth and six feet in height. She could not sit, kneel, or lie down. And the spikes prevented her from moving more than a few inches in any direction. All she could do was stand in one place. For the first hour or so, this would not seem like much of a punishment; but after three or four, the need to sit or kneel would become overwhelming. Her knees would tire and buckle, or she would faint. Then the real torture would begin.

She wondered how long the baroness dared to leave her there.

* * *

Five minutes after Genny climbed back up through the hole in the floor and repositioned the bed over it, some food was brought to her. Two men stood in the doorway holding rubber truncheons while a third carried in a covered tray, put it on the table by the window, and hurried out.

Genny pulled the cover off eagerly to view her meal. Along with a glass of milk and a slice of black bread, there was a dish with a greasy fat sausage on it, a pile of limp, smelly cabbage, and another pile of cooked, sliced potatoes in an oily dressing. Genny consumed it all.

As soon as she had finished the meal, fatigue overcame her. She lay down on the bed and fell immediately asleep.

She awoke several hours later refreshed but still hungry. She hoped the next meal would taste better. Maybe they'd include a dessert. She loved desserts best of all. Mommy would never let her eat very many, though— only on special occasions. And she would never ever let her eat any candy. It was about the only thing about Mommy she didn't like. Except for that, she loved Mommy more than anyone in the world. She promised herself that she would never be mean to her or refuse to do anything she asked her to do—ever again. She would never eat another dessert in her whole life if Mommy didn't want her to.

Genny stiffened.

The faintest trace of a familiar odor—barely a few molecules of it—tickled her nose. Excited, she rushed to the door and pressed her nose against the narrow crack between the bottom of the door and the floor. Her nostrils were overwhelmed by the scents of floor wax, stain, and various chemicals. She got up and walked back to the bed and sat on the edge. She couldn't pick up the scent anymore.

But a few minutes later she smelled it again. She crawled under the bed and put her face over the hole in the floor. It was coming up from the secret passageway. It was very faint, but there was no mistake what it was.

Mommy was here, somewhere inside the castle!

Genny got up on the bed and jumped up and down, shrieking for joy. Mommy was here!

She ran excitedly back and forth between the window and the door, over and over and over again. Finally, exhausted and out of breath, she sat back down on the bed. Why was it taking her so long?

An hour passed, and Mommy didn't come. Finally she heard footsteps coming toward her door. Her heart started pounding so hard she thought it was going to fly out of her chest.

The door opened and she ran toward it.

The same three men had come back again. But Mommy was not with them. They left her a dinner tray, picked up the lunch tray, and departed.

After a few minutes Genny went over to look at what was under the cover. Some kind of goulash with noodles and more cabbage. No dessert. She ate the slice of bread, drank the glass of milk, and then started to cry.

They weren't going to let her mother come get her. She had to do something about it, right away.

Genny pulled the flashlight out from under the mattress and then pulled the down quilt off the bed. She pushed the bed aside and stuffed the quilt through the hole in the floor. Before she dropped it, she held a corner and let it fall out as far as it would go. When it was hanging straight down, she released it. It fell in a nice pile directly under the hole. She then grabbed the pillow from the bed and stuffed that through the hole as well. It landed on top of the quilt.

Now all she had to do was drop herself down on top of them. Then she was going to find Mommy, and she and Mommy were going to get out of this awful place.

With her hands and teeth she ripped the mattress apart and made a big pile of the stuffing over by the window. She threw the mattress ticking over the loose down and feathers, then maneuvered the table across the floor until she had it centered over the pile. For good measure, she ripped the curtains from the window and dumped those on top of the table, along with the towels from the bathroom.

She was about to throw the sheets onto the pile as well

when another idea occurred to her. She ripped a narrow strip from one end of a sheet, threaded it through the metal loop on the base of the flashlight, knotted it, and draped it around her neck.

Genny fetched the box of matches she had taken from the basement repair shop, then cranked the casement window open as far as it would turn. A chilly breeze blew into the room. She struck one of the matches against the side of the box and held the flame against the ticking. It went out. She tried three more. The fourth one worked. The ticking smoldered for a few seconds and then caught. A dense cloud of smoke began to darken the room.

Genny pulled the bed back into place over the hole. The longer it took them to find it, the better, she decided. She crawled under the bed, swung around, and stuck her legs down into the hole. She turned on the flashlight and braced herself on the edge with both hands. She took one last look at the smoking pile of mattress ticking. The mattress cover had caught, and orange flames were spreading rapidly across its surface and licking at the underside of the table.

Genny eased herself down until she was entirely through the hole, clinging to the edge of the floor by her fingers. Then she let go.

Half a dozen dogs milled around Katrina, snapping and growling. Repeatedly she tried to get to her feet, but each time the dogs pulled her back down. Her screams continued, but they were losing volume.

Stewart could not understand why no one had come out to rescue her. He slid the safety catch on the pistol and pressed the button to roll the window down the inch or two he needed to stick the barrel out.

Nothing happened. Katrina had taken the key. Without the ignition on, he couldn't open the windows. He looked down. One dog remained by the door, baring his teeth at him.

Stewart took a chance and opened the door a crack. The Doberman immediately pressed his muzzle through and twisted his head sideways, trying to widen the crack.

Stewart placed the pistol against the dog's head and pulled the trigger.

The explosion rocked the car and filled the interior with the acrid stink of gunpowder. The dog was gone. Stewart's head rang.

He opened the door further and tried to aim at the dogs mauling Katrina. At this range he couldn't shoot without risking hitting her. He fired two shots over their heads anyway, hoping to panic them into a retreat. The dogs jumped at the noise, then continued their attack.

Her screams had subsided to a choked, sobbing wail. Stewart couldn't stand it. He got out of the car and ran over to her. He dropped to his knees and quickly shot two of the dogs at point-blank range. He aimed at a third, but another dog clamped his jaws on Stewart's right arm and pulled it down.

Stewart transferred the pistol to his left hand and shot the dog in the chest. More dogs came toward him. Katrina rose to her hands and knees and tried to crawl away. Her fur coat, except for a sleeve and part of the back, had been ripped off. A low gurgling moan escaped her mouth; then she was silent. One of the dogs seized the back of her neck between its jaws and pinned her down on the grass. Stewart shot the dog in the head from behind. The animal yelped and collapsed.

Katrina didn't get up.

Stewart ran back to the car. He jammed his fist against the horn and held it there. He could see people at many of the windows, but still no one would come out.

Two more dogs ran over to Katrina's inert form. Stewart opened the car door and fired at them. Neither bullet hit, but both animals bounded off, yipping loudly.

He counted the dead dogs. At least five. He could see five or six more lurking in the shadows behind the portico, uncertain as to their duty.

He jumped back out of the car and ran over and knelt down by Katrina. She was unconscious but still breathing. The flesh of her face and neck showed puncture wounds and long gashes. Blood was oozing out of her from a dozen places.

Stewart picked up a large shred of the fur coat and felt

in its pocket for the key to the car. Four of the dogs came out from the shadows of the portico and moved toward him. Instead of lunging at him like the others, they were showing a little caution—and some cleverness as well. They spread out, like a hunting party, and began creeping toward him, ears back and bellies low to the ground, from four widely separated directions. He saw a fifth dog emerge at a trot from behind the portico and circle around behind the car.

Stewart grabbed two other pieces of the coat from the driveway, looking for the second pocket. He found it, but the key was not in that one, either. It must have fallen out.

He stood up, walked a few paces toward one of the advancing dogs, stopped, took careful aim, and pulled the trigger.

Instead of the explosion of a departing bullet, all he heard was the dull metallic click of the firing pin striking an empty chamber.

Genny landed feetfirst on the pillow, then rolled over onto her side. She stood up, completely unhurt, pulled the flashlight from her neck, and shined it around the floor. The sword was where she had left it. She picked it up and started down the passageway.

She covered the length of the upper level as fast as her little legs would carry her, stopping a few seconds to hold her nose against each door, hoping to catch a trace of her mother's scent.

She reached the end of the passage and ran down the narrow stairs to the next level below. Whatever thin traces of her mother's presence remained in the air, they were being rapidly overwhelmed by other, newer scents. The sounds of running feet seemed to reverberate everywhere through the ceilings, walls, and floor. And she could hear loud voices now, coming from different parts of the castle. They've found the fire, she thought.

On the lower floor, she stopped to hoist herself up the wall and look through one of the peepholes. Lights were on. She could see the backs of women at one of the windows, watching something outside. Mommy was not among them.

Genny reached the steps leading to the basement and stopped. Someone was coming up. She could hear heavy footsteps and see the fleeting shaft of a flashlight beam. She fled back up the stairs to the upper floor and retreated across the top level all the way to the corner. There she stopped.

The ceiling of the passageway beyond the corner was on fire. It had already burned through the floor above and was eating its way rapidly along the ancient, dust-dry timbers and planks. While she watched, a chunk of burning wood fell on the pillow and quilt she had thrown down through the hole. The bedding burst quickly into flame.

Genny ran back down the stairs to the floor below. At the corner she switched off her flashlight and listened. The man who had come up from the basement was advancing slowly along the passageway, sweeping the dark with the beam of his flashlight. Genny ducked her head back just before the light caught her.

She was trapped, now, between this man and the fire in the passage above. She knelt down, turned out the flashlight, gripped the sword firmly with both hands, and waited for him.

Anne tried to keep her spirits up with anger, but she could feel her strength rapidly ebbing. She shifted from one foot to the other and tried to pretend that she was going for a walk, but so close were the pointed tips of the spikes that even that minimal amount of movement brought them sharp against her flesh.

She tried using the pain by pressing her knees against the tips so that the sting of their points could stimulate her fatigued muscles. But that tactic was no longer working. Her legs were beginning to burn from the stress.

She found that if she put her arms down straight at her sides and moved them slightly back until she could wrap each hand around a spike at about mid-thigh level, she could temporarily take some of the weight off her feet.

But it was only a matter of a little more time before her legs would refuse to hold her upright.

Stewart turned and ran for the car, then stopped. One of the Alsatians had planted itself directly in front of the opened door. The dog's eyes were fixed on him. Its lips were drawn back, exposing its long rows of incisors in a mock grin. A guttural snarl issued from its throat.

The other dogs were patiently encircling him. He felt mesmerized, watching them. They spread out and approached him obliquely, trotting back and forth in a zig-zag pattern to narrow the gaps between them so he could not slip through.

He knelt down, one eye on the dogs, and ejected the empty clip from the pistol's grip. He laid the pistol and clip on the ground while he fumbled for the box of extra bullets in his pocket. His kneeling emboldened the dogs. They approached at a trot. He tore the box open, snatched up a handful of bullets, and started forcing them into the clip. Several spilled to the ground. He couldn't see what he was doing. He managed to get three in the clip. The dogs were getting too close.

He pulled off his coat, grabbed the pistol and the clip, and ran. The lawn sloped directly to the vineyards and the trees beyond. If he could make it to the trees, he could climb up out of their reach.

He ran as he had not run since he was a little boy— with the full-out abandon of despair. He strained to force his limbs to move faster than they had ever moved. The rush of energy bore him, weightless, over the ground.

He knew the dogs were right behind him, but he couldn't hear them. His ears were filled with the sound of his feet hitting the earth and the noise of his heart pounding under his ribs. The trees, faintly illuminated by the castle's spotlights, looked a long way off. He tried to jam the clip into the pistol on the run, but couldn't manage it.

The lawn darkened beneath his feet and came to an end. He was in the vineyard now, rushing between rows of vines. The trees at last were getting close.

A sudden tug at his sleeve. The clip slipped from his

hand and fell. He tried to increase his pace. His lungs sucked in the air in loud, gasping gulps.

He thought of a fox hunt long ago in Leesburg, Virginia; the owner of a pharmaceuticals company had a big horse farm there. He remembered the fox zigzagging across the field, a reddish blur in the morning light, the hounds of death baying on its tail.

Teeth snapped at his left hand. He felt a momentary sting and then nothing. Two were running abreast of him now. He could hear them slapping against the branches of the vines on each side of him along the narrow path. He threw the pistol at one and heard the weapon thud into the soft vineyard soil.

The dogs were closing in, snapping hungrily at his heels, his arms. He wanted to slow down before his lungs burst, but the trees were still so far away.

A heavy weight crashed against his back. A momentary sensation of a warm breath on his neck, of claws digging into his shoulders. Jaws captured a pants leg. He tried to shake them off and keep straight on for the trees, but the sudden tug threw him off stride.

He pitched forward, between the rows of vines, and the dogs crowded over him, whimpering in their eagerness. He could smell them, hear them, see them, feel them. They were at his neck, his chest, his arms, his legs.

He flailed and screamed. He felt the weight and pressure of the bites, the warm release of his blood.

His heart hammered mightily. His senses felt so sharp. He glimpsed the stars in the sky brighter and bigger than he had ever seen them. And behind the spots of light around the castle walls he saw a bright red fire burning.

He remembered fireworks on the Fourth of July when he was a boy—how the vivid noise and color, building to a crescendo, had once stirred his soul—God, so long ago.

His last thoughts were of his daughter, Genny. His heart filled with a bitter sorrow. He would never know now what would become of her. His heir, his flesh and blood, and he had failed her, just as his father had failed him.

Genny could still hear someone in the passageway. A flashlight beam shined down the narrow passage and splashed against the wall right next to her. Once, she heard him come almost to the corner, then turn back.

A long time seemed to pass. People were running and shouting all through the castle. Genny could hear the fire crackling above her. The air in the passageway was getting hot.

She expected to hear fire sirens and fire engines coming up the driveway, but none did.

She began to feel afraid. She had to find Mommy. She peeked around the corner. It was dark. The man had gone. She stood up, turned on the flashlight, and started back along the passageway. She reached the far end and was about to start down the steps to the cellar when she heard him coming back up. He was shouting in German. Someone was with him. Genny caught a whiff of the baroness's perfume. Then she heard her voice.

She turned and headed back around the corner. The sword fell from her hands and clanked on the passage floor. She scooped it up and continued.

At the stairs to the upper floor she paused. She didn't want to go back up. The fire was getting loud and hot. Smoke was billowing down the stairs.

She trained the flashlight on one of the big crossbeams over her head. If she could get up there, they might not see her. She let her flashlight hang from her neck on its ribbon of torn sheeting and tried to decide what to do about the sword. She couldn't carry it, because she needed all her fingers free to climb the wall.

The man and the baroness were getting closer. Genny could smell the peculiar odor of the drug that the woman had injected in her earlier. The baroness must be bringing it to inject her again.

Genny slipped the ribbon of sheet off over her neck, twisted it around the hilt of the sword, then draped the whole affair back over her neck, positioning it so the flashlight hung down in front and the sword down in back. The weight of the sword immediately pulled the ribbon up tight against her throat, but that was just as well, since it brought the flashlight into a better position for her to see.

She braced hands and feet against the walls and started

up. She managed the first few feet quickly, keeping herself in place by dint of sheer strength; then she couldn't find a toehold. She slid a foot up repeatedly, groping in the dim light for some slight depression in the stone surface.

A piece of the wall under one foot crumbled away beneath her, and she fell. The sword twisted around and wedged itself between the walls, nearly choking her on the ribbon as she fell past it. The ribbon tore loose and the flashlight bounced against the wall, hit the floor, and went out. The sword followed, clanking down in the dark, narrowly missing her leg.

Genny felt around frantically for the flashlight, found it, but couldn't get it to come back on again. The baroness and the man were very close. They had stopped talking. They must have heard her fall.

No time to find the sword. She braced her hands and feet against the walls again and started up. This time she found footholds all the way.

A red glow from the fire above filtered down the stairs through a swirling haze of smoke at one end of the passage. In the other direction, the beams from the two flashlights played along the walls.

Genny stopped. She could see the crossbeam now. She was just about level with it, but it was well to one side and out of her reach.

Both of them came around the corner and passed directly under her. The baroness was holding something that looked like a pistol.

They hesitated when they reached the stairs. Then the baroness squeezed past the man and started up. From the top she shouted something in an alarmed voice. The man turned and retreated back along the passage. The baroness came quickly down the steps and hurried to catch up to him.

Genny felt her foot slip. She pressed it harder against the stone. The baroness saw the sword and stopped directly underneath her. After a moment's hesitation she kicked it to one side.

The rock under Genny's foot came loose and crashed to the floor.

The baroness whirled around. She pointed the flashlight upward and caught Genny in its beam. Genny let herself drop. The moment she hit the floor she recovered her balance and ran toward the stairs. The smoke and heat coming down from above were too strong for her to go any further.

The baroness hurried toward her, pointing the pistol and talking soothingly. Genny felt something sting her left shoulder. She slapped against the spot reflexively and felt the shaft of a tiny dart. She jerked it out quickly and threw it to the floor.

The baroness stood in the passage, ten feet away, shining the beam in Genny's eyes and waiting.

Genny put her head down and lunged forward. She struck the baroness in the legs and knocked her off balance, but as she tried to squeeze past her in the narrow space, the baroness smashed the butt of her tranquilizer pistol on her head and knocked her down. Before Genny could recover, the baroness delivered a hard kick directly against her chin. The little girl howled with pain and rolled over onto her stomach. She took two more blows against the back of her head.

Before the baroness could land a third, Genny scrambled to her hands and knees and crawled back toward the stairs. The tranquilizer dart, despite the speed with which she had removed it, was making her groggy.

She reached the bottom of the stairs and stopped. She looked behind her. The baroness had put down her flashlight and was kneeling on the floor, reloading the tranquilizer gun.

Genny came running back. In the dim light she could make out the silhouette of the jagged piece of rock that had fallen from the wall. She knelt and grabbed it. It was about the size of a softball. She threw it as hard as she could. It struck the baroness in the face.

The woman fell sideways. Her shoulder hit the wall and spun her around. She threw her arms up, then toppled backward onto the floor. Her foot kicked the flashlight and sent it rolling along the passage.

Genny snatched up the flashlight and then jumped over the baroness and grabbed the sword, lying near the wall a few feet away. The baroness was on her back. Her eyes were open. She appeared conscious but dazed. Genny set the flashlight on the floor, wrapped both hands tightly around the sword's handle, and drove the fat blade through the baroness's stomach. The tip struck her almost precisely at her navel. It ripped easily through cotton blouse and silk slip, through flesh and stomach walls, and came to rest firmly wedged against the inner surface of the spinal column.

The baroness groaned. Her hands came up, felt the blade of the sword impaling her, then dropped back. She cried out in a hoarse, quavering voice. Her eyes fluttered closed, then opened. She found the strength to grab the blade of the sword again. She pulled at it with one convulsive effort, and the sword came free, clattering on the stone. The baroness raised herself on her elbows. Blood bubbled from her stomach. She screamed again, louder. She gasped for breath, then screamed again.

Genny picked up the flashlight and ran as fast as she could. She reached the long steps to the basement and hurried down them. At the small closet she paused and listened. She could still hear the baroness, far above her. Her scream had lost power; it sounded like a sorrowful moan. Genny aimed the light in both directions down the basement corridor. No one was in sight. All the lights were out.

She ran through the basement until she found steps up to the ground floor. It was dark there as well. People were milling around, shouting. Stray beams from other flashlights crisscrossed the floors and walls. Everyone seemed intent on getting out. Genny saw light beyond the windows. The whole outdoors flickered in an orange glow from the castle's burning roof and upper stories.

Genny wandered through the pandemonium, not knowing what to do. Traces of her mother's scent were impossible to isolate. Smoke was overpowering everything. She clambered up the main staircase and ran through the halls, looking in every room.

She picked up the scent again. She followed it to a bedroom down the end of a long corridor. The door was open, and the scent was strong, but Mommy was no longer in the room. She must have gotten out with everybody else, Genny decided.

She raced back downstairs and made her way to the front entrance. People were crowded under the portico, crying and shouting at each other. No one paid any attention to her. She wondered why they stayed there and didn't go out onto the lawns. She squeezed through, trying to discern her mother's scent from the confusion of odors around her. She couldn't find it.

She saw why no one was leaving the portico. Both exits were barred by the huge portcullises. Out on the lawn men with tranquilizer guns were shooting at the dogs.

Someone shouted something. The others cheered. The portcullis gates on both sides of the portico started clanking upward, and everyone surged out onto the driveway and the lawns.

Genny looked at every face. Her mother was not among them.

Dozens of fire trucks, police cars, and ambulances came racing up the driveway, their sirens wailing mournfully in the night air.

Genny ran back inside. She hurried through the echoing dark rooms on the ground floor, swinging the flashlight from side to side. She screamed "Mommy!" over and over again at the top of her voice.

No one answered.

Ladders went up the side of the building. Bright emergency lights came on. Firemen were coming in with lights, masks, tanks, axes, and hoses. One saw Genny and ran toward her. *"Auskommen, Mädchen! Auskommen!"* he yelled.

Genny switched her flashlight off and ran around a corner into the dark before he could catch her. Other firemen joined the chase. Eventually they cornered her in a pantry off the main dining room, grabbed her, and dragged her outside. She kicked and screamed. "Mommy! Mommy! Find my mommy!"

Out on the portico she slipped free and ran out onto the lawn. Satisfied that she was out of harm's way, the firemen turned their attention elsewhere.

The moment they were out of sight, Genny slipped back inside.

There was still the basement, she realized. It took her a while to find the stairs again.

She rushed down and ran through the warren of subterranean chambers, calling out for her mother in a tear-choked voice.

Then she caught the scent. "Mommy!" she screamed. "Mommy!"

She had to force herself to slow down and follow the scent. She sniffled repeatedly to clear her nose. She felt very tired, very groggy.

The scent trace took her along a low, narrow passage to a set of old stone steps. She ran down them as fast as she could. At the bottom the scent was stronger. She called out again but got no answer.

The scent was strongest by a big iron chest at the back of a low-ceilinged chamber full of strange, unfamiliar objects. "Mommy! Are you in there?"

No answer.

Genny shined the flashlight over the front and saw the two screw-latches. She twisted the bottom one open. The top one she couldn't reach. She looked around. No chairs. Nothing to stand on. She ran all the way back up the steps and through the basement until she found a wooden crate. She lugged it down to the dungeon, propped it in front of the Little Maiden, and attacked the top screw-latch. It required considerable strength to turn it. She finally worked it free. She jumped down and yanked on the door. Her little body was soaked in perspiration. The door came open at last.

Her mother stumbled forward half a step and fell on top of her.

Genny rolled her over. There was blood on her clothes. "Mommy! Are you all right?"

"Can't walk," she whispered. "Go get help."

"I can't! They don't understand me. They won't let me come back."

"Stay with me, then, darling."

"But Mommy, we have to get out! The castle's on fire. Can't you crawl? I'll help you."

Anne tried to crawl, but her knees, swollen from the hours of standing and punctured by the maiden's spikes, were too stiff to move. She asked Genny again to go find help.

Genny grabbed her under the arms and dragged her across the dungeon floor to the bottom of the stone stairs. A stream of foul black water was now running down the steps. It quickly soaked Anne's clothes.

Tears started down Anne's face. Once again she told Genny to go get help. But Genny just shook her head. She put the flashlight in her mother's hand, got up on the first step behind her, locked her arms around under her, and dragged her up the step.

Step by step, inch by inch, she pulled her mother up. Water, pumped by the firemen onto the castle's walls and washed through the burning, centuries-old timbers, ran down the steps in a torrent now, its foul stink blending with the acrid stench of the smoke.

Genny slipped on the stone and the water carried them down half a dozen steps before she could gain a secure foothold again. Anne tried to help, but she simply couldn't move her legs.

Genny began to feel dizzy and weak. She sat down behind her mother and rested for a few minutes.

Then she redoubled her effort. And this time, after an eternity of tugging and pulling, sitting and resting, tugging and pulling, she succeeded in reaching the top step.

She dragged her mother off to the side to get her out of the path of the water, and again sat down to recoup her strength. The tranquilizer seemed to be hitting her harder now that she had expended so much adrenaline.

Despite the long struggle up the steps, they were only as far as the basement floor. Water was gushing down from hundreds of places in the ceiling. A tremendous crash overhead shook everything around them. Part of the castle had collapsed inward. They couldn't go upstairs.

Genny remembered the fresh air she had smelled near the area with the fireplace wood. Gathering herself for one last exertion, she took hold of her mother again and dragged her backwards through the maze of cellar passages until she found the place where the wood was stored.

A short distance beyond was the door. It was barred by a big hardwood plank resting in iron brackets. Genny lifted the plank off and yanked the door open. Outside there were more stone steps. A gust of smoky air swirled in.

Straining for a few last dregs of strength, Genny tried to pull her mother through the bulkhead doorway and up the cellar steps. They were so close to freedom now, so close to safety; but the child had already exerted herself beyond even her incredible powers. She had nothing left.

She sat with her arms wrapped around her mother from behind, and rested her shoulder and head against the side of the bulkhead and closed her eyes. "I'm sorry, Mommy," she whimpered.

Near dawn the firemen found them, unconscious at the bottom of the bulkhead steps. The blaze had at last been extinguished. The castle's interior had been completely gutted by the fire, but the exterior walls still stood.

A rescue crew moved them quickly by ambulance to a hospital in Regensburg.

Summer, 2003

47

Anne held up a hand to shield her face from the sun. She was sitting on the deck of Lexy's summer house on the Maine coast. It was a warm, clear day in late August, and the waters of the bay were unusually blue and serene. A couple of fishing boats were visible on the horizon, and a big, two-masted schooner was tacking out of the harbor against a lazy wind.

Anne was near the end of a long convalescence. Only a few small scars were visible on her knees and her shoulders as evidence of her ordeal at Schloss Vogel. Emotionally, she was still fragile, but each day she felt stronger.

"I really don't want to write a book about it," she said.

"You'll make a fortune," Lexy insisted.

"I can't write, for one thing. For another, I don't want the world to know. For Genny's sake. She's got to grow up with this."

Lexy refilled their wineglasses. "We'll get you a collaborator. That's the way books get written these days. And you can just leave out whatever you don't want the world to know. If you don't write it, someone else will. And then you'll have no control over the material."

"Who else could tell the story?"

"Hank Ajemian, for one."

"Hank doesn't ever want to think about it again."

Lexy grinned. "That leaves me," she said, jabbing a thumb at her chest.

Anne laughed. "I suppose you'll want a part in the movie version, too."

"And why not? You don't dare tell me I don't deserve it. After delivering that superbaby of yours on the dark earth beside a burning building in the Caribbean on New Year's Eve? After helping you steal the Jupiter file from Dalton's office safe?"

"And I'll be forever grateful."

"By the way . . . are there any copies of Jupiter left anywhere?"

"I don't know. But it doesn't matter. No one has the access code except me."

"What about that guy at IBM?"

"Axel Guttmann. Yes, that's true. He has it."

Lexy tapped a fingertip against her wineglass and looked knowingly at Anne. "Did you keep a copy of Jupiter? Tell me the truth."

Anne didn't reply.

"I thought so. What're you going to do with it?"

"I'm going to go back to school first, get a doctorate. Then I'll think about it. It should be studied. But it's so dangerous, I don't know who I could ever trust with it."

"Don't trust anyone. And don't study it. Deep-six the damned thing. It's cursed. Think about yourself. Write a book. Become a celebrity. Have some kicks."

"I'd rather be a scientist."

Lexy yawned. "You could be both. But you're probably right. Being a celebrity is awfully tacky these days, anyway."

"What's Genny doing?"

"Getting something to eat, as usual. That child of yours has the appetite of a starving elephant. I swear she must consume ten thousand calories a day."

"She has a fast metabolism."

"Part of her Jupiter profile?"

"Probably. God, Lexy, I worry all the time what'll become of her. Her playmates already know she's different."

Lexy laughed. "I'd worry more about her playmates, if I were you. Thank God she has your modest, agreeable disposition. Otherwise I'd be afraid of her myself."

A car turned off the road and came slowly up the driveway on the other side of the house. Lexy leaned out of her beach chair and looked around. "Oh, listen. I've asked someone over for dinner. That's him. He wants very much to meet you. I hope you don't mind."

Anne groaned. "What is this one? A rich, divorced Maine lobster fisherman?"

"I guarantee you'll be crazy about this guy," Lexy said. "He's great company and he's dying—and I mean absolutely dying—to hear your story."

Anne heaved a sigh. She slipped her terry-cloth robe on over her bathing suit, then pulled her sun hat down over her face. "I'm not even presentable."

Lexy snickered. "Don't go anywhere. I'll fix him a drink and bring him out."

Ten minutes later Lexy appeared with the male friend in tow. She was giggling like a prankish schoolgirl. Anne pushed up the brim of her sun hat to get a look. She saw street shoes and then an exceptionally wrinkled wash-and-wear summer suit. The man wearing them had dark hair. He was very tall, with a sensitive face and pleasant eyes. He looked embarrassed.

"Anne, I'd like you to meet Dr. Paul Elder. . . . You may remember him from a previous lifetime."

Their eyes met. Both started to say something at the same time, and then stopped. Their faces turned red.

Lexy shook her head in wonderment. "Boy, I can see we've got a couple of real party animals here." She turned back toward the house and bawled out at the top of her voice: "Genny! Come on out here and say hello to your future stepfather!"

Ambassador Mishima beamed. The soft flesh of his face was suffused with a luminous glow, as if lit by some internal power source.

He had a right to be proud, of course. This was his project as much as anyone's. He had pushed for it, and continued to push for it—at great personal risk to his reputation—when others were long past giving up.

"How many babies?" he asked, looking through the glass walls of the center's big new maternity suite, built specifically for this occasion.

"Forty," Yamamoto answered.

"And all healthy?"

"Five died. The rest are healthy."

"We'll have to wait for tests, of course," Mishima said, more or less rhetorically.

"Yes."

"But this is very promising. Wouldn't you agree?"

Yamamoto nodded. "Very promising. The genomes all conform to the results—exactly as projected."

Mishima scratched his cheek thoughtfully. "We should begin varying the sequences of the new genes with the next batch. Let's not rest on our laurels. Let's find out how far these new genes can be pushed. Or perhaps I should say these new *old* genes."

Yamamoto nodded.

"There is no new thing under the sun," Mishima said, with a broad grin. "Ecclesiastes."

"I'm sorry?"

"The Christian Bible."

"Oh."

"I want the whole team honored," Mishima said.

"That'd be fitting."

"It's been a strain on them. Particularly all these months of secrecy. And they are heroes—authentic heroes. The country owes them a great debt."

"But the project must remain secret."

Mishima sighed. "Unfortunately. I just hope I live long enough to see the Americans' reaction when we finally spring it on them."

"Not to mention the rest of the world."

The ambassador's expression grew somber. "Of course. That too."

Genny picked up a stone from the beach and looked back up at the deck of the cottage where her mother, Paul Elder, and Lexy Tate were sitting. "Watch this one, Paul!" she shouted.

"Okay. I'm watching," he said.

"That's the last one, Genny," Anne warned.

Lexy looked at Elder with a sly grin. "So you're already 'Paul' now."

Elder shrugged. "I don't want her to call me 'Doctor.' "

Genny whirled around like a shot-putter and hurled the stone far out over the water.

"Very impressive!" Elder cried. "You'll make the big leagues easy with an arm like that."

"Don't give her any ideas," Anne said. "She's become a real show-off lately."

"She's just trying to impress 'Paul,' " Lexy said.

"Just what I need," Anne answered. "Competition from my three-year, eight-month-old daughter."

Genny picked up another rock and threw it out over the water. She looked back. Paul wasn't watching anymore. She sighed and wandered down the beach. She was happy that her mother and Paul were together again. She hoped he really would become her new daddy. He was a lot of fun. And she could learn all about being a doctor from him. *If* she was going to be a doctor. Right now she wasn't sure; there were a lot of things she wanted to do.

She found a big white stone half-buried in the sand and pulled it out. Another one for her collection. She tossed it up in the air and caught it. It felt nice—smooth and heavy.

She looked back down the beach toward Lexy's cottage. She wanted to go back and ask Paul to come and play with her out on the beach, but Lexy had told her that it was important for her to let Mommy and Paul spend time together alone. She didn't see what was so important about it, but she promised Lexy she would.

Genny wandered further down the beach and then turned onto a sandy path that ran back to the town road. There were a lot of bushes here, but she could still catch glimpses of Paul and her mommy on the porch. Their heads were very close together.

A white car was parked further up the path. People used the path to get to the beach, and it wasn't nice for someone to block it like this.

She had seen the same car there yesterday, and the day before. The same two men in the front. One of them was looking at Lexy's house with a pair of binoculars.

She picked up a few more stones, cradled them in her arms, then ducked into the bushes and worked her way through the undergrowth until she was abreast of the car. She put her rocks down in a pile in front of her, collected a few more from the ground nearby, and crouched down to study the men.

One man had a thin, pale face, with big ears and small eyes. His head was completely bald. The other man had white hair and ebony black skin. Their auras looked scary; they were flickering and jumpy, constantly changing colors.

Genny didn't know who they were, but she didn't have to. She understood that they were bad, and that was enough.

She picked up a rock, stood up, gauged the distance, and let it fly. It struck the binoculars and knocked them out of the man's hand.

Genny threw another stone. It sailed through the open driver's-side window and hit the bald-headed man right in the forehead. The other man quickly wound up the window.

She threw two more. The first smashed against the side-view mirror; the second hit the rolled-up window and shattered it.

The engine started and the car backed up. Genny grabbed her biggest stone, the white one, and hurled it as hard as she could. It shattered the windshield.

The car roared in reverse up the path, swerved crazily out onto the town road, braked with a loud squeal, slammed into first with a gnashing of gear teeth, and accelerated off down the road in a screech of peeling rubber.

Genny stood watching, hands planted on her hips.

If they came back tomorrow, she decided, she'd really get them good.